THE PEARL OF PENANG

CLARE FLYNN

Storm

Copyright © Clare Flynn, 2019, 2023

The moral right of the author has been asserted.

Ebook ISBN: 978-1-80508-451-0
Paperback ISBN: 978-1-80508-432-7

Previously published in 2019 by Cranbrook Press.

Cover design: Debbie Clement
Cover images: Alamy, Shutterstock

Published by Storm Publishing.
For further information, visit:
www.stormpublishing.co

ALSO BY CLARE FLYNN

ONE

When the letter from Douglas Barrington arrived, Evie Fraser was at breakfast. Instead of eating, she was thumbing through the situations vacant pages of *The Lady* magazine. It was a weekly ritual that Mrs Shipley-Thomas, her elderly employer, had long since given up complaining about. After nine years working as a paid companion, Evie would have loved to break free and try something different. But every time she identified a position that might be promising, she weighed it against her current one and found it wanting or insufficiently different to justify the upheaval and the inevitable distress of her employer. Mrs Shipley-Thomas was all too aware of Evie's frustrations, but had grown complacent, believing her companion would never do anything about them.

A letter addressed to Evie was a rare occurrence. Mrs Shipley-Thomas looked up from shuffling through her own correspondence and frowned. 'This one's for you, my dear. It looks rather interesting. All the way from Malaya. Judging by the number of times it's been forwarded, it's a wonder it got here at all.' She tapped the envelope with a fingernail.

'I don't know anyone in Malaya.' Evie put down her teacup.

'It seems you do, my dear. Perhaps it's a long-lost admirer trying to track you down. Not that it's any of my business.' The old lady snorted, evidently amused at the improbability of her paid companion having such a thing as a gentleman friend.

Evie reached to take the missive, feeling a little frisson of excitement, then braced herself for disappointment. Nothing in her life ever justified a sense of anticipation. She turned the envelope over in her hands. It had been forwarded from her former home to her family's solicitors and thence to here.

Unfolding the thin paper, she flattened out the crease. It was written using a typewriter and its sender must have positioned the paper in the carriage at an angle so the words were sloping slightly from left to right, probably unintentionally. The keys had been hit so hard that in places the letters had pierced the paper. It indicated haste and a lack of care, probably executed by someone unaccustomed to typing. The date was about seven weeks earlier. She glanced at the bottom of the page first and saw it was from her mother's cousin, Douglas Barrington.

Penang
February 15th 1939

Dear Evelyn,

News of the death of your father has finally reached me here. Please accept my belated condolences. I also understand your mother is now living in America and that you are unattached. I will come straight to the point. Following the death of my wife, Felicity, I am in need of support and companionship and it occurred to me that our interests may coincide. If you are willing, I am prepared to make you an offer of marriage. I regret that the distance involved and my business commitments here in Malaya prevent my journeying to England to ask you in person.

If this offer is acceptable to you, I will make arrangements for your passage to Penang. My friend, Arthur Leighton, the District Officer here, will be in England on home leave with his wife Veronica, returning in late June and they have offered to accompany you on the voyage. I look forward to hearing your response. If I have misunderstood your circumstances, please accept my apologies.

Yours sincerely

Douglas Barrington

'Oh my goodness!' Evie dropped the letter, then picked it up and read it again. 'How extraordinary!'

'Don't keep me in suspense, dear girl. Spill the beans.'

'It's a proposal of marriage.'

'By letter? Gracious! These modern men. Who on earth is it from?'

'You'd better read it.' Evie held out the piece of paper.

'I don't have my glasses. Just give me the gist.'

'It's from my mother's cousin. He's asked me to travel to Malaya and marry him.'

'Heavens above. Your mother's cousin? He must be far too old for you.' She picked up the sugar tongs and dropped a lump into her tea.

'Actually, he's younger than Mummy. About twelve years older than me.'

'And have you met this ill-mannered man?'

'Just once. At his wedding. I was only fifteen. He danced with me.' She closed her eyes, summoning up the memory. What she didn't say was that it had been the most thrilling thing that had ever happened to her. He had been the most handsome man she'd ever seen. Thinking about it now made her feel giddy with the romance of that moment.

'At his wedding?' Mrs Shipley-Thomas looked horrified.

'His wife has since died.'

'When?'

'He doesn't say.'

'And based on one dance with you many moons ago he's decided you'll make him a suitable spouse?' She gave a little snort. 'You must have made a big impression.'

'I'm surprised he remembers me at all. He appears to have made the offer on the assumption that I'm on the shelf and desperate.'

'Well you are, aren't you?' Mrs Shipley-Thomas gave another little snort. 'How old are you now, Evelyn? Thirty?'

'Twenty-seven.'

'I think that qualifies you as an old maid.'

Evie pushed back her chair, sending her tea sloshing into the saucer.

'Do be careful, dear. You really are the clumsiest girl. Where are you going now?'

'To write my reply.'

'Good show. Waste no time in sending him packing.'

'I mean to say yes.'

'What?' Mrs Shipley-Thomas's face contorted with shock.

'I intend to accept his proposal. You're quite right. I *am* desperate to avoid becoming an old maid. And I can think of nothing more exciting than going to live in a faraway place and marry a handsome man.'

'You're not serious. You can't possibly do that. I was only teasing you about being an old maid. I didn't mean it. Don't be hasty. At least give it some thought. Malaya is a long way away.' She gripped the edge of the table, the blood draining from her face. 'Besides – what will become of me?'

'You've plenty of time to find another paid companion. I won't be leaving until the end of June. Mr Barrington has to make the travel arrangements.' Evie picked up her copy of *The*

Lady and handed it across the table. 'There are plenty of promising candidates advertising their services in here.'

Heart hammering, she left the room, her dignity only slightly impacted by tripping and stumbling on the rug.

Safely in her bedroom, Evie leaned against the closed door, waiting for her pulse to stop racing and her chest heaving. What had she done? It wasn't too late to go back downstairs and tell Mrs Shipley-Thomas she'd had second thoughts. Her employer would be relieved and Evie could remain in her safe cosy world where nothing out of the ordinary ever happened. A short business-like letter to Douglas Barrington and the episode would be forgotten and her life could go on as before.

She moved over to her desk and took up a piece of writing paper and her fountain pen.

Dear Douglas

Thank you for your kind thoughts regarding the loss of my father. His death was a great shock but I have had nearly nine years to adjust to life without him and my mother.

Thank you also for your offer of marriage. I regret I am unable to accept

Evie struggled to come up with an acceptable basis to refuse her cousin's proposal. She could hardly write *because I am scared stiff,* yet in truth that was the only reason for her reticence.

The death of her father, his decision to take his own life rather than face the consequences when he was caught up in a financial scandal, had knocked Evie for six. Even now, years later, she missed him and despite what he had done, grieved for him and felt abandoned. When her mother had wasted no time after his death before joining her long-term lover in the United States, Evie's world contracted further. While she and her mother had always had a strained and distant relationship, finding herself completely alone had not been easy. Her dreams of marrying, or of pursuing her education, were shattered.

Becoming a lady's companion had been based on necessity not inclination.

Hands propped under her chin, she tried to think it through. It was foolish to let annoyance at Mrs Shipley-Thomas's insensitivity push her into a decision with lifelong consequences. Something so momentous required a more measured and rational approach. She must set aside her emotions and let her head rule her. Taking another piece of paper, she drew a line down the centre and headed one column *Reasons to Accept* and the other, *Reasons to Refuse*, and began to fill in the spaces beneath.

The arguments for refusing consisted of:

I barely know him

I have no idea what living in Malaya would be like

He's much older than me

His letter was blunt with no hint of romance

Once I go I may not be able to come back

It's a huge risk

After a few minutes she crossed out the third item. Twelve years wasn't that much of an age gap and hardly a reason in itself not to marry Douglas Barrington. She drew a circle around the last item, as that was the crux of the matter – the other points were all different aspects of risk.

Turning to the empty first column she wrote:

Dancing with Douglas Barrington was one of the most exciting and memorable moments of my life

I've always wanted something interesting to happen to me

I hate living here

I'm bored with working for Mrs ST

Mrs ST doesn't appreciate me

If I don't do this I'll spend the rest of my life wondering what might have happened

This is probably my last and only chance for love, marriage and a family

Douglas is the most handsome man I've ever met.

She read the list again and thought it sounded very childish and superficial. She crossed out the last point. On reflection the most salient point was the one about spending the rest of her life wondering 'what if?'. She drew a circle round that. In the end it all boiled down to whether she wanted to grasp hold of life or cower timorously and carry on with her humdrum existence.

She dipped her pen in the inkwell and filled it. Taking a new sheet of paper, she crafted her reply to Douglas Barrington.

A telegram arrived from Douglas Barrington two weeks later, advising Evie that his friend, Arthur Leighton would be in touch about travel arrangements. Mrs Shipley-Thomas pleaded with Evie to stay, offering her first a bigger bedroom with a view over the garden, then when that failed, a substantial pay rise. Evie was determined to resist such blandishments, telling herself that if her employer valued her so highly she should have offered them before there was the threat of her leaving. When the pleading became anger and resentful silences, Evie knew she had made the right choice. Mrs Shipley-Thomas was governed entirely by self-interest and clearly didn't give a fig about Evie's welfare and future. After all, why should she? As the weeks passed, Evie's fears diminished and her excitement grew. She couldn't wait to get on the ship and wave goodbye to dreary England and her dreary life.

As soon as a suitable replacement was found within the pages of *The Lady*, Mrs Shipley-Thomas told Evie she would pay her wages until the agreed leaving date, but she would like her to go now, as Miss Prendergast, the new companion, was willing to start immediately. Relieved to be free of what had become an oppressive atmosphere, Evie took a room in a boarding house in a cheap and unfashionable area of London while she waited for the date she was due to sail.

Mr Leighton had been in touch by letter to suggest Evie meet his wife for lunch, in order that Veronica might impart some advice about life in Malaya and what Evie needed to pack for the journey.

The women arranged to meet in the restaurant in Marshall and Snelgrove. Anxious to make a good impression, Evie wore her best suit, even though it was too warm that day for wool and it was a little dated. In her haste, she got on the Tube in the wrong direction and had travelled four stops before she realised her mistake. Late for the appointment, she had to miss her planned visit to the powder room to repair her lipstick and check that her slip wasn't showing. As a result she was hot and dishevelled when she rushed into the restaurant, before remembering that she had no idea what Veronica Leighton looked like.

Standing on the threshold, Evie looked about, trying to decide which of the unaccompanied women might be the wife of a senior civil servant. She approached a matronly woman in her late forties, but it wasn't her. About to enquire of a harassed mother with a baby – Mrs Leighton may well have a child – she felt a tap on her shoulder and almost jumped out of her skin.

'Miss Fraser?'

Spinning round, she nearly crashed into the speaker, who took a step backwards. 'Steady on!' the woman said curtly.

'So sorry. You're Mrs Leighton?'

Slender and willowy, Mrs Leighton had the grace and figure of a ballet dancer. Her dark glossy hair was swept back into a tight chignon. Big almond-shaped eyes were highlighted with kohl and mascara, and her pale skin had a translucent glow that belied the fact she lived in a hot climate. Her mouth was a tight Cupid's bow, glossy with the brightest, reddest lipstick Evie had ever seen. She was dressed in a deep green silk costume that looked as if it came from Paris, set off by a pearl necklace that left no doubt as to its authenticity. Automatically, Evie put up a hand to cover her own cultured pearls, then dropped it. There was no point. She knew she must appear cheap and shabby next to this exotic and expensively-dressed goddess.

Mrs Leighton looked Evie up and down critically – Evie detected a slight curl of the lip. Perspiration beaded on Evie's forehead. Damn the silly choice of a woollen suit when it was early summer.

'I'm frightfully sorry I'm late. I got on the wrong underground line.'

Mrs Leighton's eyebrows lifted. 'Always better to take a cab, darling,' she drawled. 'The underground's so grubby.'

Evie felt shabby and awkward. In contrast, Mrs Leighton was like a rare butterfly.

With the slightest inclination of her carefully coiffed head, Mrs Leighton summoned the head waiter to show them to their table. It was a corner one with a good view of the room, yet a distance away from the mêlée. 'Thank you, Robert,' she said, breathily, conveying in her intimate tone that she was a familiar and much-valued guest.

Once they were seated, Evie said, 'You're a regular here, Mrs Leighton?'

'What makes you think that?'

'You seem to know the waiter.'

Mrs Leighton gave a little laugh. 'I make it my business to behave as though every waiter is my dear friend. That way one gets the best table and the best service.'

'But you knew his name.'

'Only because I asked him. Really, darling, don't you do the same?'

'To be honest I never eat in restaurants.'

Mrs Leighton made no verbal response, but Evie sensed

disdain mixed with amusement. She squirmed inside, her palms clammy. This was going to be an ordeal.

They made their choices from the menu – for Evie, lamb cutlets, for her companion, a salad. No wonder she was so svelte.

Veronica Leighton leaned forward, her gaze fierce. 'How long have you known Dougie?'

Evie stammered. 'He's my mother's only cousin. So I suppose all my life.'

'That's not what I meant. How *well* do you know him?'

Blood rushed to Evie's cheeks. 'Not well at all.' She hesitated then, unable to dissimulate under the gaze of Mrs Leighton, added, 'We've actually only met once. At his wedding. Years ago.' About to add that they had danced together, she stopped herself in time.

'Poor dear Felicity. Dougie was devoted to her. He was utterly devastated when she died. We all were.'

Evie fidgeted with her napkin. 'I remember she was very beautiful.'

'As an angel. Graceful,' she said pointedly. 'And a wonderful person too. So full of life. Always smiling and laughing. Such fun. Everyone adored Felicity.'

'How did she die?'

'You don't know?' Mrs Leighton frowned as Evie shook her head. 'Malaria. Three years ago. Tragic. So terribly, terribly sad.'

The waiter brought their food, but Mrs Leighton barely paused. Her salad lay untouched as she continued to speak. Evie tucked guiltily into her cutlets but pushed the potatoes aside.

'Of course, none of us expected Dougie to marry again. We're all utterly mystified.' Her piercing eyes fixed on Evie and she gave a little shake of her head, which conveyed that the mystery was even greater now that she'd actually met the intended bride. Evie wanted to get up and run out of the room but she made herself sit it out.

Mrs Leighton answered her own question. 'I imagine it's because he needs a son. The one thing dear Felicity didn't give him. Just little Jasmine. And he can't possibly hand his inheritance on to her.'

'Jasmine? He has a daughter?' Evie put down her knife and fork, appetite gone.

'Gracious! You don't know Dougie at all, do you? Jasmine is seven years old and is living in a convent on the mainland.'

'The mainland?'

The tutting was barely disguised. 'Penang is an island. Haven't you even looked at a map, Miss Fraser?'

Evie, mortified, couldn't manage another mouthful. Mrs Leighton made her feel like a naughty schoolgirl – one lacking in any sophistication and by implication clearly an unsuitable spouse for Douglas Barrington. Her face must be red and blotchy and she wished she'd had time to stop at the powder room.

Drawing air deep into her lungs she let it out slowly. 'Mrs Leighton,' she said at last. 'As you will have gathered, I know next to nothing of Douglas Barrington and his current circumstances. After my father died, my mother went to live in America and I'm afraid I lost track of family matters.'

Mrs Leighton pushed her untouched salad away and motioned for the waiter to remove it. 'So, what on earth possessed you to accept a marriage proposal from a man you hardly know?'

'If you don't mind me saying, Mrs Leighton, I'd prefer not to answer that. Your husband suggested that you might be willing to offer me some advice about living in Malaya. What kind of clothing I need to bring. That sort of thing. If you're not prepared to do that, I will pay the bill and bid you goodbye. I have a lot to do before we sail.'

Leaning back in her chair, Mrs Leighton nodded. 'So you *can* stand up for yourself. That's good. You'll need to with Dougie. I was worried you were going to be a doormat. Believe me, he'll try to make you one.' She glanced around the room and caught the eye of their waiter. 'Why don't I order us each a "Gin and It"? We can have a good chat and then look at clothes together. Cotton and linen. Just day dresses – you can buy silk over there and get your evening gowns made up. There's a fabulous little Indian chappie who can run up a gown in an afternoon. I'll introduce you. He can copy a design straight out of *Vogue*. For daywear keeping cool is the thing. It's hot as blazes in Penang. All year round. You can probably get rid of most of your wardrobe as it's far too steamy for things like that.' She gestured dismissively at Evie's wool suit.

Clapping her hands together she said, 'How does that sound? Oh, and shall we dispense with the formalities? Call me Veronica.' Her mouth formed a smile that her eyes didn't echo.

At least the full-on attack had stopped, but Evie had already decided that Mrs Veronica Leighton was a first-class bitch.

Half an hour later, having written a list dictated by Mrs Leighton of essential items to bring with her to Penang, Evie had had enough advice and was determined it wasn't going to extend to choosing her new wardrobe. Quite apart from being bossed around, the kind of clothes Mrs Leighton had in mind would be beyond her limited budget. Pleading a headache, she made her escape and took the much-maligned underground to High Street Kensington and bought herself a couple of cheap cotton frocks and some new underwear in Barkers. She could get more clothes made when she got to Malaya. Her existing wardrobe was unsuitable for a hot climate. At the suggestion of the landlady of her boarding house, she took her winter clothing to a nearby church, for distribution to the poor. Her limited funds were now almost exhausted. She'd need to stretch the pennies until the sailing date in a week's time.

That night, as she lay in bed, struggling to sleep, she wondered whether she'd made a terrible mistake in agreeing to marry Douglas Barrington. One thing she had not included on her decision-making list was the question of why Douglas had made such an offer in the first place. It now seemed reckless of him – and even more reckless of her in accepting.

Why on earth had he asked her to marry him? And why hadn't he mentioned he had a daughter? Would the little girl be living with them after they were married? Was he really only marrying her to father a son? Why choose her? He barely knew her.

Veronica's words kept repeating in her head. How could Evie ever expect to replace the beautiful Felicity? She'd been crazy to think she might. And hadn't Veronica said that all Douglas's friends were amazed at his decision – and all of them had adored Felicity?

Tossing and turning on the lumpy mattress, she thought back to the wedding of twelve years ago. The bride had been breathtakingly beautiful and a perfect match for her dashing groom. While Douglas Barrington had indeed danced with the teenage Evie, he'd also danced with almost every woman present that day. She was deluded to imagine that he had retained the memory of her over the years. But she couldn't help hoping that he had, that he might even one day come to care for her. Then reality struck again. How could she, a woman more at home on a hockey pitch than a dance floor, ever hope to win the love and affection of such a man?

A week later, Evie stood on the quayside looking around, trying to spot the Leightons among the crowd thronging the water-front. She couldn't board the ship yet as Mr Leighton was to meet her and hand over her ticket. Most of the people on the dock appeared to be friends and relatives there to wave off passengers. She began to panic.

'Yoo hoo! Evelyn!' The call came from above.

Looking up, Evie saw Veronica Leighton leaning over the guard rail on one of the upper decks of the ship, waving a silk scarf as though she were a French revolutionary leading the mob into battle.

A man appeared beside Evie, his hand extended in greeting. 'You must be Evelyn. I'm Arthur Leighton. Pleased to meet you.'

Evie had to hide her surprise at Veronica's husband. Her assumption had been that scary Veronica would be married to a handsome lounge lizard. But instead of a suave and elegant roué, Arthur Leighton looked more like a schoolmaster: dishevelled, with a thick mop of sandy hair that flopped over his brow until he brushed it away with his fingers. He appeared to be younger than his wife, but Evie had never been good at guessing people's ages. With one finger he pushed up his spectacles from where they had slipped down his nose, and grinned at her with a wide and genuine smile. Arthur Leighton reminded her of a Labrador puppy and Evie knew at once she was going to like him.

TWO

Evie took to life on board as though born to it. Blessed with a gentle passage through the Bay of Biscay and safely into the Mediterranean, her good humour was aided by the absence of Veronica, who remained confined in her cabin. Even the gentlest of swells evidently made her nauseous.

After they passed the Straits of Gibraltar, Veronica emerged on deck briefly, only to retreat again, pale-faced and gaunt. Her hair lacked its previous lustre and her eyes were devoid of make-up.

In contrast, Evie loved the rise and fall of the ship and experienced no nausea. On dry land she was liable to trip over the slightest obstacle but at sea she coped well with the need to brace herself and find her balance.

When the ship reached Port Said, Evie felt the thrill of the Orient in the chaos of bumboats surrounding the ship. The gully-gully men and souvenir sellers clamoured to make deals, selling everything from trinkets and fruit, to slippers and camel-leather bags. In between the traders, young boys dived into the waters to retrieve coins flung to them by passengers.

The ship bunkered here – taking on board coal to fuel the

next leg of the voyage. Even this operation seemed exotic, as Evie watched small, wiry, Tamil coolies scamper up and down, carrying heavy baskets of coal on their heads.

Port Said was an opportunity to go ashore to shop at Simon Arzt – the emporium where East met West. Passengers disembarked to restock their tropical clothing, including the pith helmets that were *de rigeur* throughout the British Empire. It meant Veronica put in another brief appearance – like many *habitueés* she had stored some of her lightweight clothes there, and intended to replace them in storage with the furs and heavier clothing she had needed for the British winter and spring.

By the time they entered the Suez Canal, Evie was wishing the voyage could go on forever, partly because of her growing trepidation about how Douglas would receive her in Penang. She was terrified he would regret his hasty offer of marriage – perhaps even withdraw it and send her back to England with her tail between her legs. The prospect of becoming stepmother to a little girl was also daunting. Having no siblings and no friends or relatives with young children, Evie had little or no knowledge of what it took to bring up a child – and her own experience with a cold and distant mother was a poor preparation.

Traversing the Suez Canal gave her another insight into the increasing foreignness of the world beyond Gibraltar. It was peculiar to be sitting on the deck, under a sunshade, as the ship sailed through the middle of the desert. Egyptian traders with camels and donkeys, men in small boats, villages with flat-roofed concrete dwellings like children's building blocks, minarets, palm trees, and everywhere the pale yellow sand of the desert.

Since Port Said, Arthur Leighton had been occupied for

most of the day with a heavy burden of paperwork, and by night he often dined in their cabin with his wife. Evie walked the deck with him in the late afternoon and now and again joined him for a pre-dinner cocktail. She took her own dinner in the wood-panelled dining room, where she was seated with an elderly couple travelling to India to visit their son and daughter-in-law, and a missionary and his wife, headed for Burma. Occasionally, if Veronica was sleeping, they were joined by Arthur, who proved to be an excellent dinner companion, helping the conversation flow – presumably a skill essential to his profession.

While they strolled together on the promenade deck, Arthur told her something about his life and asked about hers. There was no sign of the judgmental attitude his wife had demonstrated – Arthur took a friendly interest in Evie and gave no indication that he found her life mundane or worthy of pity. She was unaccustomed to spending time with members of the opposite sex – Mrs Shipley-Thomas had rarely received guests and when she did they were other women. But Evie felt comfortable and relaxed in Arthur Leighton's company and they enjoyed easy and amicable conversations.

One afternoon, while leaning against the rails at the stern of the ship, watching the ship's wake, she found herself telling Arthur about what had happened to her father. 'I had no idea that Daddy had done anything wrong. He worked for a bank and they claimed he was diverting client funds into his own account.'

'You believe he was wrongly accused?'

'I did at first. It was too painful to think him capable of such wrongdoing. But the evidence was incontrovertible.'

'I'm sorry, Evie. That must have been tough on you.' His eyes were full of concern.

'It was awful coming to terms with the fact that my father was a thief. Even though he probably didn't see it that way himself. I expect he thought making a few false entries on a ledger was a less heinous crime than committing a burglary.' She shrugged ruefully. 'A gentleman's crime. His death was the final proof for me that he was guilty.' She looked out to sea. 'He left a note confirming his wrongdoing. Said he'd been overcome by greed. But I think it was more about fear that he was going to lose my mother.'

Arthur looked at her with a quizzical expression.

'Mummy was romantically involved with an American man, Walter Winchgate. He's stinking rich. Something to do with oil. When Daddy found out she was having an affair, he must have thought he couldn't win her back unless he could offer her the same kind of life that Winchgate could.' She shook her head. 'My mother is a materialistic woman. Very self-centred. Money is everything to her. Family is nothing.' She gave Arthur a rueful smile. 'When Daddy died in disgrace and there was no money left, she married Wingate.'

'But what about you?'

'Mummy never had much time for me. We're very different. A clash of personalities. Since she went to America we've barely been in touch. I write occasionally; she sends cards for my birthday and Christmas.'

Arthur said nothing, but kept his eyes on Evie's face.

'In the letter he left for us, Daddy said he'd only wanted to do the best for her. He apologised for bringing shame on the family name and on Mummy and me.' She sighed. 'But I'd rather have lived with the shame than have him die. I miss him terribly.'

'How very sad. He took his own life?'

'Blew out his brains with a pistol he'd kept from the war.'

'Good God. That's dreadful. You didn't...'

'No. I didn't walk in and find his body or anything ghastly like that. He would never have put us through that. When he

discovered the police had been called, he did it in his office at
the bank.'

Arthur placed his hand for a brief moment on her arm and
squeezed it gently. 'When did all this happen, Evie?'

'Nine years ago. Mummy went off to join Walter Winchgate a few months later, once the funeral was over and it was
clear there was no money in the estate.'

Arthur looked aghast. 'She just abandoned you? You must
have been so young.'

'Eighteen. She did ask if I wanted to go with her to America, but it was a half-hearted suggestion and she seemed relieved
when I said I didn't. I saw an advertisement for a position as a
lady's companion in Hampshire, applied and got the job.'

'It must have been lonely.' His eyes were full of concern.

Evie had told him more than she'd intended. Embarrassed,
she turned her head away. More than anything, she hated to be
pitied. Tears stung her eyes but she blinked them away and said,
smiling, 'Not at all. It was good to have a solid reliable job. And
Mrs Shipley-Thomas wasn't such a bad old stick.'

'But friends? Family?'

Evie shrugged. 'I was kept busy. I do a lot of reading and
walking. I was happy enough. There's some lovely countryside
in Hampshire.' She glanced at him and could see he wasn't
convinced. 'Enough about me. What about you?'

He shrugged. 'Not a lot to tell. Veronica and I were married
ten years ago. I was working in Africa at the time. We moved to
the Straits Settlements soon after. First in Selangor, and for the
last seven years in Penang.'

'You met in Africa?'

'Yes. Nairobi in Kenya. Veronica grew up there.' He looked
at his watch. 'It's time I went. I promised to bring her a cup of
mint tea to calm her stomach.'

'She's still feeling queasy?'

'Veronica hates to be at the mercy of anything outside her

control.' He stopped abruptly and nudged his spectacles up his nose, giving Evie the impression he too had said more than he intended.

A couple of days later, Evie was walking back to her cabin after a game of bridge. She wasn't keen on card playing but Mrs Shipley-Thomas had sometimes coerced her into joining a rubber if she was short of a player, and here on the ship it was a way to kill time.

As she was about to pass the Leightons' cabin, she realised the door was open and, hearing voices, she slowed down. She hadn't intended to eavesdrop but once she'd heard a few words, she halted and pressed herself against the wall, unable to move forward or retreat.

'Honestly, Arthur, you know as well as I do that Dougie is going to bitterly regret sending that drunken letter. It may have seemed hilariously funny at the time but it's well and truly backfired. The woman's obviously desperate to get married and was never going to get another offer. He must be reeling from the shock that she accepted.' She gave a little tinkling laugh. 'The girl's so awkward. She can't move without sending things flying, or tripping over her own feet. Really, darling, you have to agree, Dougie's made a colossal mistake.'

Without waiting to hear Arthur's reply, Evie ran back down the corridor, shaking with anger, tears burning her eyes.

From that point onwards, she avoided the Leightons. On such a large ship it wasn't difficult, provided she remained alert. By the time they were passing through the Red Sea, Veronica had emerged from her self-imposed purdah, seemingly fully recovered, and was often to be seen sipping cocktails in the bar – usually surrounded by men – or reclining gracefully in swimwear in a deck chair to show her long lithe figure to best advantage, but never venturing into the pool.

As for Arthur, Evie knew he usually worked in the ship's library or the Smoking Room, so took care to avoid those areas. Instead of strolling on the promenade deck where she was bound to bump into him, she took to climbing up and down the companionways to get her daily exercise. The rest of the time she sat in a secluded corner on one of the quiet back decks, or hid out in the Ladies Only salon, where Arthur couldn't enter and Veronica never would. At dinner, instead of joining her table, Evie took her meals in her cabin.

A heavy misery had swamped her, weighing her down and making her wish she'd never set out on this foolhardy mission. She watched the dawn break as they reached the end of the Red Sea, the ship close to the coast where the bright orange rising sun burned behind the dark outline of rocks. The flaming brilliance faded to pale pinks and purples, beneath what promised later to be a blue cloudless sky. The huge ball of the sun rose up above the horizon, a blazing orb of fire emerging from behind hills. Minutes later, the colour had drained from the sky and the ship had moved past the coastline, into the empty churning waters of the Gulf of Aden, under a burning, now white, sun. Evie sighed. Such beauty. Sights she had never dreamt she would witness. Yet instead of exulting in the experience, all she felt was an empty numbness.

Late one afternoon, sitting on the aft boat deck as the ship made its stately progress across the Arabian Sea towards Bombay, a shadow fell across the book she was reading.

'There you are, Evie.' Arthur Leighton squinted at her, the sun in his eyes. 'Have you been avoiding me? I haven't clapped eyes on you for days. Were you unwell? I asked your steward but he said you were out and about. I've been searching the ship for you.' His eyes looked concerned and not a little hurt.

Embarrassed, Evie said, 'I was a bit under the weather. I didn't think I'd make very cheerful company so I've been keeping out of the way for a while.'

'May I?' He gestured towards the deck chair next to hers, then sat, sideways on, so he could see her. 'Are you sure you're all right?'

Evie pursed her lips, then saw his face had such a kind and concerned expression that, before she could stop herself, she'd blurted out the truth. 'Actually, I've had a bit of a wobble. Realised I've been a frightful chump in agreeing to come to Malaya and marry Douglas when I don't really know him. I expect he made his offer without thinking through the implications and by now he'll be wondering how to get out of it.' She pleated the fabric of her dress through restless fingers. 'I was wondering if I ought to get off the ship when we reach Bombay. Only I've no money to pay the passage home. What do you think I should do?'

Arthur frowned and shook his head. 'Has Veronica been filling your head with nonsense? Sometimes she speaks out of turn. She seems to find it amusing, but it can be bloody hurtful.' He looked uncharacteristically annoyed.

Blushing, Evie said, 'No. I've not spoken to her in days. It's just that the whole idea seems such a crazy enterprise that I can't think why I ever agreed to it.' She smoothed the creases out of her dress then gathered the fabric up again, rippling it nervously through her fingers. 'My life had become so dull and predictable and I didn't want to spend the rest of my days reading aloud to Mrs Shipley-Thomas and, after her, a succession of old ladies, while life passes me by.'

She looked up at him, afraid he would think her foolish, but his face showed only attention and concern.

'When Douglas Barrington's letter arrived it was as if my prayers had been answered. It was an opportunity to start again, to see something of the world, to embark on an adventure, to do something unpredictable and spontaneous for the first time in years. It was the only way I could see to get out of my rut.'

'I understand.' Arthur nodded. 'That all makes perfect sense. So, what's made you change your mind?'

She hesitated then said, 'If I'm honest I suppose I'm worried about what people will think. That they'll say I'm a desperate spinster who's grasped her only chance to hook a husband.' She gave a dry laugh. 'And they'd be right.'

When Arthur said nothing, she stumbled on. 'But more than that I'm worried that Mr Barrington – I mean Douglas – it seems odd to call him that when I barely know him. That he must surely be having second thoughts himself. I can't imagine what would possess a man like him – successful, comfortably off, handsome – to ask someone like me to marry him when he must have the pick of the field. There. You have it.' She bit her lip and waited for him to reply.

He reached out and took her hand, holding it in his for a just a brief moment. 'I don't know what you mean when you say someone like you. I happen to think Doug is a very fortunate man that you're willing to become his wife. It shows you have pluck, Evie. You're a brave girl. Fearless, in fact. Not many people would do what you're doing and that's to be admired. And you're kind, intelligent, independent, interesting. All in all, you're a very attractive woman and if you ask me, Doug is a very lucky chap.'

Evie felt a rush of gratitude mingled with disbelief. Was he just trying to be nice? Did he mean it? Would he later laugh about what he'd said with Veronica? 'Thank you,' she said, deciding to accept the compliment graciously. 'That makes me feel better. I hope you don't think I was fishing for compliments?'

'You don't need to fish for them, Evie. You deserve them.' His mouth formed a smile but his eyes looked sad. 'You do however need to go into this crazy enterprise, as you call it, with eyes wide open. Penang is a beautiful place. Quite magical. But Malaya's not an easy country to live in if you're not born to it.

The climate in the Straits is hot and humid all year round and it can take a long time to adjust. Some people never do. Felicity certainly didn't.'

Evie looked at him, shocked.

'She struggled from the moment she arrived and never settled. It was a constant source of tension between the two of them. Maybe I shouldn't be telling you this, but I think you've a right to know.' He reached into his pocket and pulled out a packet of cigarettes and offered her one. It was the only time she'd seen him smoke. She shook her head.

'When Felicity married Doug she thought she'd signed up to a life in the Home Counties. Two years later Doug's bachelor uncle died, leaving him the rubber estate on Penang island. He was determined to take it on. He hated his job in the City and the thought of owning land and making a living from it appealed. Like you, he wanted adventure.' Arthur lit his cigarette and drew on it slowly. 'Felicity took some persuading. She didn't want to leave her friends and family, and was nervous about moving overseas. She was expecting Jasmine at the time which can't have helped. But Doug can be very persuasive. He swept her up in his enthusiasm and they went off.'

Evie was rapt with attention, waiting as Arthur took a second slow draw on his cigarette before stubbing it out. 'Trying to give the blessed things up,' he said. 'From the moment they arrived it was a disaster. Felicity hated Penang. She felt isolated on the rubber estate, so Doug bought a house in George Town for her to use when she wanted. But she disliked that even more. There may have been more for her to do in town but the humidity can be suffocating in the lowlands. She had a very difficult time with Jasmine's birth and was in poor health from then on. She appeared to lose all her zest for life.'

None of this squared with the eulogy to Felicity that Veronica had given. She'd described her as a human dynamo, not a wilting flower.

Arthur swung his legs round and leaned back into the deckchair so Evie could no longer see his face. 'Veronica and I were posted to Penang around the same time the Barringtons arrived. As we're similar ages, naturally we became friends. It was sad to watch as Felicity faded away. She was always ill. One thing after another. Coping with a baby was too much for her so she left the care of Jasmine to a servant and grew more and more listless. It was as though she had no interest in anything or anyone. Almost as if she were willing herself to die. An extraordinary business. She contracted malaria and had no strength to fight it. Doug sent the child away to be cared for by the nuns and threw himself into running the business, so we rarely saw him in town any more. Jasmine was just three or four.'

'How awful for the poor child to lose her mother so young – and to be separated from her father.'

He nodded. 'I think Doug would like her to be at home. I know that's one of his reasons for wanting to re-marry. And from everything you've told me, Evie, I think he's made a wise choice in you. I'm not saying you'll find life there easy, but you're made of stronger stuff than Felicity was.'

Evie stretched her mouth into a smile. 'You've cheered me up, Arthur. Thank you. I don't know how it will be, but rest assured I'll give it my best effort.'

He got to his feet. 'That's the spirit.' Giving her a mock salute, he added, 'See you at dinner tonight?'

'I'll be there.'

When he'd gone, Evie hugged her knees, experiencing a new burst of energy. She wouldn't let Veronica get under her skin again. Hadn't Arthur himself said she enjoyed making trouble? Not for the first time she wondered how they'd come to be together. They were the most unlikely of couples. But people did say opposites attract.

.   .   .

With her first sight of Penang, Evie was entranced. The island was covered with jungle and the coastline was rocky. As the ship sailed between the mainland on the port side and the island, the dense jungle gave way to breathtakingly beautiful sandy beaches. Then there was George Town, with its elegant colonial buildings. How had Arthur described it? The Pearl of the Orient. All around the strait there was shipping, from Peninsular and Oriental passenger liners, numerous cargo vessels and tramp steamers, ferries, junks and sampans.

After they docked in Penang, at Swettenham Pier, Evie said goodbye to the Leightons, who were travelling on to Singapore. They assured her they would be in George Town in a couple of weeks, after Arthur's post-leave briefing session at his Singapore headquarters.

'I'd rather come straight back to Penang, but Arthur needs me,' Veronica told Evie. 'He hates to travel without me.' She put a hand proprietorially on his arm. 'My darling boy won't let me out of his sight. And he's hopeless without me to organise him.'

Evie found this hard to believe. As a senior civil servant with extensive responsibilities, it seemed unlikely he'd have attained and retained such a position if he were disorganised. Arthur made no comment but his face showed his embarrassment.

The couple's relationship mystified Evie. Arthur seemed too ordinary to be married to an exotic and beautiful creature like Veronica. There was nothing sleek and polished about him, with his tousled hair, constantly slipping spectacles, too-baggy trousers and frequently ink-stained fingers. Veronica, when in his company, was always on her best behaviour. When they were together, she touched him constantly – a hand on his arm, a palm brushed against his cheek, her arm slipped through his – demonstrating possession, and making clear to the world that they were a couple. Yet, on board, she spent much of her time in the bar, flirting with any available men. Evie had often viewed her from a distance, watching her preen, perform and soak up the admiration of her coterie of admirers as they jostled to buy her next drink. Veronica was a man-magnet. If she entered an empty room, within moments it was packed. Women, on the other hand, tended to give her a wide berth. Evie was glad to see the back of her, even if it was only for a matter of days. Having Veronica around while she was getting to know Douglas would have sapped her confidence.

As she prepared to go ashore, Evie's nerves returned. Thanks to her conversation with Arthur, this time it was not due to self-doubt but nervous excitement. In a matter of days she would be married. At least she presumed she would. Other than the telegram to confirm the Leightons' contact details in London and the departure date of the ship, she'd heard nothing more from Douglas. Would he expect her to call him Doug – or even Dougie as Veronica Leighton did? Was he as excited about what was happening as she was? Would he be as handsome as she remembered?

While Arthur Leighton seemed to believe her forthcoming marriage would be a successful and lasting one, it was none-theless a marriage driven by convenience. Douglas Barrington needed a wife to keep his house, bring up his child and, hope-fully, provide him with more children. While maybe in time he might grow to love her, it was too much to expect that he would feel that from the start.

Evie, however, was certain she would love him at once. How could she not? Over the years, the memory of that waltz together had never faded. It was a moment frozen in time. The feel of his hand in the small of her back, the warm touch of his smooth fingers, the way he had led her so that she hadn't felt at all clumsy, but light and graceful. Even though it had been the occasion of his marriage to the beautiful Felicity and Evie had known he was merely playing the part expected of him, she had treasured the way he had made her feel. That dance had

marked her transition from childhood and her hope for the
possibilities ahead of her. Maybe it was a foolish fantasy – a
little girl's dream of a handsome prince – but this dream was
coming true.

She would do her utmost to be a good wife to Douglas, to
make him happy, to give him cause to love her. She would be
different from Felicity. Life in Malaya might prove a challenge
but she was determined to adapt to it. Hot weather wasn't going
to get her down. And anyway, people did acclimatise eventually
– the Leightons certainly had. But she reminded herself they'd
lived in Africa beforehand, so they would have been used to the
heat.

As she stood at last on the dockside, Evie's heart jumped in
her chest and she struggled to breathe. Douglas Barrington
wasn't there to meet her. A Malayan man moved towards her
purposefully. She swallowed her disappointment and forced a
smile. He introduced himself as Benny and told her he was
Douglas's *syce* in George Town.

'I look after motor car and house of Mister Ballington when
he in George Town. Not much time. He not here today, *Mem*.
He busy. In Singapore. Come. Bags in car.'

Evie was crushed. After the long sea voyage, and building
herself up for meeting Douglas at last, it was all for nothing. She
was stung. Since he was travelling down to Singapore, why
hadn't he suggested she stay on board and meet him there?
Common courtesy dictated that, when she'd come so far and
risked so much. For him to have been unwilling to spare the
time to greet her in person was a humiliation. Her resolve to be
a supportive and compliant partner evaporated. Digging her
fingernails into her palms, she struggled to prevent her emotions
showing on her face, and followed a smiling Benny to the
waiting car.

Once inside the vehicle, which thankfully had been parked
in the shade, Evie leaned back and took a couple of deep

breaths, while Benny loaded her modest amount of luggage into the boot. Calm down, she told herself. Maybe Douglas has good reason not to be here. Some kind of crisis? Perhaps he's as nervous as I am. Don't get off on the wrong foot. Don't spoil things by being moody.

Grateful for a breeze through the open car window, she wiped her face with a handkerchief. It was so hot and humid that the perspiration was running down her brow, the salt stinging her eyes. She'd never been so hot in her life. Veronica had been right – the heat was bestial.

She leaned forward to speak to Benny. 'Is it always this hot?'

'Yes, *Mem*. We say here there is three season. Hot, Hotter and Hottest.' He looked over his shoulder and beamed at her.

'Which one is it now?'

'Only Hot.' He made a little giggling sound.

She leaned back against the burning leather, her poplin dress already damp and clammy.

'Use fan, *Mem*. In back of seat.'

She found a finely carved wooden fan in the pouch of the seat and taking it out waved it vigorously in front of her face. How was she going to bear it if every day was like this?

She gazed through the open window, curious about what would be her permanent home. George Town was charming, with its classical Georgian buildings dating back to the days of the East India Company, and its Chinese shop-houses with stores at street level and balconied dwellings above. There were also newer, grander houses, many set in large grounds looking onto the sea. Arthur had told her wealthy Chinese traders had settled here, as well as the colonial Dutch and French before the British had seen them off. Today it was a mixture of races and nationalities – native Malays, immigrant Chinese and Indians, British and other European nations. The island was a centre for the production of silks and spices as well as the rubber for which Malaya was renowned throughout the world.

On first impressions, the island captivated Evie. The land rose to high uplands in the centre with sandy beaches, fringed with palms, around its perimeter. If it weren't for this ghastly clammy heat, she might even go so far as describing it as a glimpse of paradise. Arthur had been right when he'd said it was magical.

They turned onto a narrow road which took them away from the seafront. The houses here were smaller town houses, mixed in among Chinese-style villas. Pulling up outside an ugly box-like building, more fitting the Home Counties than the Orient, Benny said, 'Here we are. Dis it.' She tried not to be disappointed that it was not a pretty Georgian house or a large mansion in its own expansive grounds. Don't rush to judgement, she told herself.

Inside the house, the rooms were dim behind shuttered windows, but thankfully cooler than out in the full sun. It was larger than it appeared from outside. In the centre of the ground floor was an open area of double height, the upper floor landing overlooking it on three sides, so that it formed a kind of internal balcony, defined by open lattice working, with narrow supporting columns. A ceiling fan whirred above her head.

The other members of the household were lined up waiting to greet her. Benny first introduced a woman – evidently the housekeeper – as 'Aunty' Mimi. A tiny Chinese woman, thin and fragile in appearance, Aunty Mimi had short black hair, streaked with grey and was elderly but evidently still agile. Another Chinese, a smiling toothless man, was introduced as 'Cookie'. Evie guessed they were married to each other, but was afraid to ask and no one enlightened her. Finally, there was a young Malay man, who was introduced merely as The Boy and evidently considered unworthy of the dignity of a name.

Benny said, 'Only Aunty Mimi and me speak English. You soon learn speak Malay, *Mem*. Also two *kebuns* to work in garden.'

Overwhelmed, the prospect of ever speaking even basic Malay felt beyond Evie. She was exhausted. Perhaps once she'd freshened up and had a sleep, things would be less daunting.

Aunty Mimi led Evie upstairs into another darkened room. Opening one shutter she showed her a large rear garden, where the sunlight was filtered by a collection of tall trees. Evie could hear the tinkling of water but couldn't see its source. Around an expansive lawn was a vibrant display of colourful flowers that lifted her spirits a little.

A large low bed stood in the centre of the room, draped with mosquito nets. Something else to get used to. There was a ceiling fan above the bed, but it was motionless. Aunty Mimi pointed to the bathroom beyond, where, as well as a 'thunder box' raised up on a shallow platform like a throne, there was a bath tub and a separate shower area, with a tall Shanghai jar, filled with water to flush the toilet and dip into for cold showers. Fresh towels were laid out on a wooden table beside a dish of soap. Someone had placed a hibiscus flower on top of the towels. Smiling at this touch, Evie noticed a huge centipede scuttling across the floor and shuddered.

The woman placed her palms together and bowed solemnly over her hands, then turned to leave.

'Wait a moment! When do you expect Mr Barrington to come home?'

Aunty Mimi shook her head. '*Tuan* not come here many time. He live in other place.'

'Do you know when I will go to this other place?'

The old lady with the smallest movement of her head indicated it was a question she couldn't answer. 'Benny bring up bags. When you ready I make tea.' With that, she left the room.

Torn between the need for a cup of tea, a good sleep – and possibly a good cry – Evie chose to have a shower first. She stepped out of her damp cotton frock, rolled down her stockings – she certainly wasn't going to be wearing stockings again, unless she absolutely had to – and peeled off her soaking wet underwear. Pouring the cool water over her hot skin was a shock, but also a blessed relief, and the soap was scented with what she thought was jasmine. When she'd finished her ablutions, she returned to the bedroom, noticing her suitcase and holdall had been placed on top of the wardrobe and, while she'd been taking her shower, someone, presumably Aunty Mimi, had unpacked her clothes and put them away.

Her spirits low, she went downstairs, hoping a cup of tea might revive them. So far everything was telling her she had made a terrible mistake.

THREE

It was three days before Douglas Barrington turned up.

Evie passed the time exploring the streets of George Town in the early mornings, before it became too hot to venture out. Even in the cooler part of the day, it was stifling, and she had failed to understand how much the humidity affected the body. Penang was like living in a Turkish bath with no reprieve. As she gradually began to acclimatise, she took increasing pleasure in the novelty of being on this sub-tropical island, with its crowded streets, colourful fruits and spices and exotic smells. It was impossible not to be intoxicated by the sweet fragrance of hibiscus, frangipani, sandalwood and ylang-ylang, the whiff of salt from the sea mingling with the smell of fish, the heady scent of incense which caught the back of her throat as she walked past the many small temples, the aroma of nutmeg and cardamom and the unspeakably foul stench of durian fruit. Passing the Chinese shop houses, the smell of food cooking pervaded the air, as meat was stirred into smoking hot coconut oil or mingled with sesame and soy. She marvelled at how the cooks were able to stand beside steaming vats of noodles and rice, rapidly stirring the food in their woks, in this oppressive heat.

In the afternoons, Evie sat in the relative cool of the garden reading a book. Even under the shade of the tall hardwood trees, it was hot. There was little or no breeze to cool her, and the air hung heavy and damp, wrapping her in a suffocating blanket. No wonder Felicity Barrington had hated the climate.

She supposed she ought to write to her mother and fill her in on her new location and circumstances, but decided to put it off until she had something concrete to report. She could hardly tell her she'd travelled all the way to Malaya to get married, only to find her husband-to-be had yet to put in an appearance. As to how Mrs Barbara Winchgate would react to her daughter marrying her cousin, she couldn't imagine. Douglas's age fell between the two of theirs, and neither mother nor daughter had known him well. No. It was better to wait until the deed was done. There was something appealing about the prospect of, for once in her life, astonishing her mother.

Late on the third afternoon, as Evie sipped iced water and tried to concentrate on the collection of poetry she was reading, she sensed a presence in the garden. She put down her book and looked up. A sleek black dog with a white flash on his head ran across the sun-dappled lawn and came over to sniff her. Evie reached a hand out to pat him. 'Well, hello there, fellow, what's your name?' As her hand moved to stroke the dog's head, he curled back his lips, bared his teeth and growled at her.

'Here, Badger.'

Evie looked up to see a man standing hands on hips, studying her. The late afternoon sun was behind him and the light too strong for her to see more than his shadowed outline but she knew at once it was Douglas Barrington. The dog trotted over to him obediently and lay down at his feet.

'He doesn't like strangers. He's a working dog. Better keep

your distance until he gets used to you.' His voice was deep and sonorous.

Blinking, Evie jumped to her feet and moved towards him. As she got closer, she realised he was frowning, looking at her as if trying to work something out. The years had greyed his wavy brown hair at the temples, his skin was a dark mahogany with spidery white lines radiating from his eyes, between his brows and round his mouth and nose, where wrinkles had blocked the reach of the sun. He was wearing the white man's uniform – knee-length khaki shorts and a short-sleeved shirt. Despite the signs of age, he was still a handsome man, and she felt a ripple running deep inside her.

'You're Evelyn?' He gave his head a little sideways shake as if he'd just woken up. 'You seem different from how I remembered you.' He was still looking her up and down.

Stomach churning, throat dry, Evie moved towards him. She'd hoped for a different kind of welcome. They were, after all, distant cousins. Why not an embrace? A warm and friendly hug, even a peck on the cheek. Instead, Barrington proffered his hand, shook hers briefly, and jerked his head in the direction of the open French window. 'Benny's mixing some sharpeners.' He turned and walked back inside the house, his dog at his heels. Evie followed them inside, her heart sinking.

'I'm having a *stengah*, but I know most ladies prefer *pahits*.'

She looked at him blankly.

'*Stengah* is whisky and soda and *pahit* is gin and bitters – pink gin.'

She didn't really want a drink at all, but told herself it would steady her nerves. 'Thank you. Gin please.'

Douglas sprawled in one of the heavy teak chairs and polished off his whisky and soda in a few gulps, as if it were water. He held out the empty glass for Benny to replenish. Evie took a small sip of her gin, grateful for the sharpness of the alcohol opening her parched throat.

'Did you have urgent business in Singapore?' she asked.

'What do you mean?' He took another gulp of his drink, avoiding her gaze.

'I... er... I had thought... that you'd be here in George Town when I arrived.' The sound of her own voice was thin, barely a whisper. Get a grip of yourself, Evie.

'I've a business to run. It's a full-time job.' He pulled a pipe from the pocket of his shorts, tamped the tobacco down and lit it. Puffing on it, he stroked the dog which lay stretched out at his feet.

The tension in the room was palpable. The ceiling fan whirred slowly above them, the clock ticked loudly and the dog's breathing was soft but audible. Evie could feel her heart hammering inside her chest. What was going on? She was certain he'd been surprised when he'd seen her. Shocked even.

Then it hit her. He'd thought she was someone else. That afternoon of his wedding he'd danced with several of the young women present. Had he mixed her up with a different girl? Someone more beautiful? Someone more interesting?

Douglas continued to puff on his pipe and drink his scotch, now at a more respectable pace. He was behaving as if she were invisible. She wished she was – she'd have liked to float away and disappear forever. The utter humiliation of it.

As though endowed with a sixth sense, Benny appeared and refilled his employer's glass. Evie had barely touched hers.

Douglas looked up from his *stengah* and studied her. 'I wasn't sure you'd show up,' he said at last. 'Thought you might get cold feet at the last minute and not get on the ship.' He closed his eyes momentarily. 'I'll say one thing for you, Evelyn Fraser, you're a brave woman.' He gave a dry laugh. 'Or possibly a foolhardy one.'

She said nothing, conscious that he was watching her. But at least he was speaking.

'It must have taken courage to agree to throw your lot in

with a man you barely know. I take my hat off to you.' He turned his attention back to the whisky in his hand, swirling it around so the ice chinked. 'But now that you're here, do you still intend to go ahead with the plan?'

'What do you mean?'

'If you want to back out I'll understand. No hard feelings. I can sort out a passage back to Blighty for you. Now that you've experienced something of the Straits and realise what you'd be letting yourself in for.'

A shiver ran over Evie's skin, despite the heat of the early evening.

He was trying to back out. He didn't want to go through with the marriage. Indignant, she decided she wasn't going to let him off the hook so easily. Not after she'd travelled all this way, given up her home and a perfectly good job, built up her hopes and readied herself for a new future. The gall of the man was breathtaking. She'd come here to marry him and she was jolly well going to do it.

'I've seen very little of Penang so far, but it is a beautiful place. Yes, the heat and humidity have been a shock but I'm sure I'll get used to it eventually. Even after a few days it's already a bit easier.'

He looked at her. His eyes were an intense blue. When he frowned, as he was doing now, they narrowed and his face took on an aspect that bordered on cruel. Cold, hard, almost ruthless. It didn't stop her being attracted to him though. She told herself she was as bad as the heroines in Mrs Shipley-Thomas's romance novels, but couldn't help wondering what it would be like to be kissed passionately by such a man. To be desired by him. Would she ever find out?

'My late wife found the climate here unbearable. Most Brits do. Especially the women. Maybe you're made of sterner stuff.' His expression implied his doubt about that.

'I hope so. I'll try to adapt.'

He gave a little snort of disbelief. 'Perhaps.'

Dispirited, she wanted to run away. To rush through those French doors, out into the garden and from there into the street. To get away from the rejection. But she stayed where she was, clutching the glass of gin in which the ice had melted.

They fell into a silence that was far from companionable. To break the tension, Evie spoke again. 'The Leightons told me you have a daughter, Jasmine. Will she be living with us? After the wedding, I mean.'

It sounded presumptuous to refer to their marriage when he had only just offered to arrange her return home, but Evie was both confused and angry. Did he want to wait, to see how they got on before making the commitment to marriage? Yet he had made a clear offer – surely he didn't expect to back out now. Having come this far she wasn't going to let him wriggle out of it.

Evie realised she wanted to stay, in spite of Douglas's coldness and his evident lack of any feeling for her. She was attracted to him and would move heaven and earth to make him feel something for her. It might take years, it might not happen at all, but she'd do her damnedest to make him care for her, or at least to win his respect and possibly some affection. Anything was better than the dead-end she was stuck in back in England. The future was what she would make of it. She would have to be brave. Her only chance was to speak up.

Suppressing her wounded pride, she pressed on. 'Will I meet Jasmine soon?' she asked, hoping he wouldn't notice the tremor in her voice.

'My daughter is in a convent school. She's settled down well. I don't want her education adversely affected. She's gone through a lot, losing her mother so young. The last thing she needs is constant change and disruption.'

'But I thought you wanted to have her at home? I got the impression from the Leightons that–'

'The Leightons don't know everything. Even if they might think they do.' He put his pipe down.

The third whisky was dangerously close to being finished. Douglas Barrington clearly had a great tolerance for alcohol. Evie remembered the words she'd overheard Veronica saying, about him writing the letter while the worse for drink. Maybe there was truth in that? Maybe his proposal had been a joke he hadn't expected to result in an acceptance.

Taking a deep breath, Evie clasped her hands together and leaned forward. 'I think we need to get a few things straight. You made me an offer of marriage and I accepted. Your proposal was unusual, but that was part of its appeal. My circumstances have been straitened since the death of my father. I have no qualifications. I have no money.' She was conscious that she was talking at a rapid speed but wanted to get it all out before she lost her nerve. 'Living in the countryside as a companion to an elderly lady, my horizons were narrow, and my opportunities to meet people extremely limited. Marrying you opens a door to something different in my life.'

Evie took another gulp of air. 'We barely know each other, but I promise you, I will do my utmost not to disappoint you as a wife. Now that we've met again, if you want to back out of this arrangement, that's your prerogative, but if not, I'm ready to throw in my lot with yours.' She took a large gulp of her drink.

He raised his eyebrows. 'Quite a speech.' He got up and walked over to the French windows and stood looking through the mosquito screen.

It had turned dark outside and Evie could smell the cloying scent of flowers. Douglas stood there for several minutes with his back towards her, gazing into the starlit garden.

Just as she was about to break the tension, he turned back to face her, and said, 'Forgive me for putting it this way, but as far as I'm concerned, this is a business transaction. You appear to be a strong and healthy woman and you certainly have plenty of

courage, so yes, my offer still stands. For my part, I will provide
you with a home, a generous allowance, anything material you
need. For your part, I will expect you to run this household and,
assuming my daughter takes to you, there's no reason why she
shouldn't live here under your care.' He looked away. 'The offer
is made in the expectation that eventually you will bear my children. I am the last of the Barringtons and I want to pass on the
family name and the rubber business to my sons.

Evie blushed, but relief ran through her. 'When will we be
married?'

'Whenever you want. In the next few days if you wish.' He
sounded as if he were discussing a trip to the bank, not the
arrangements for a life-changing ceremony. 'But I don't want a
fuss. Not a big affair. I haven't the time. I did the big wedding
thing when I married Felicity. I don't want to go through all that
again.'

Swallowing her disappointment at his dismissive and
unsentimental approach to matrimony, Evie nodded. It wasn't
as if she wanted a big fancy wedding herself. After all, apart
from the Leightons and the servants, she knew no one in
Malaya. There were no friends and family to invite – she had
none. Her mother's absence wouldn't be a cause to mourn.

Forcing a smile, she said, 'It's a deal!' and held her hand out
for him to shake.

That evening, after her conversation with Douglas Barrington,
Evie dined alone. As soon as they had concluded their deal, he
went off to meet someone at a place he referred to as The Club,
making it clear the invitation didn't extend to her. As he left,
Badger going with him, he called back over his shoulder. 'Oh,
and call me Doug. Everyone else does.' The irritable tone indicated it was less an invitation than an order. 'No one's called me
Douglas since my mother died.'

Was this what Evie could expect – lonely dinners alone? It wasn't her idea of marital bliss. Even suppers with Mrs Shipley-Thomas seemed a more appealing alternative. And she didn't like the idea of calling him by a name that everybody else used. She was jolly well going to stick with Douglas.

Over a mostly silent breakfast the following morning, Douglas announced he was going to the mainland and would be back that evening.

'May I come with you?'

'No. Not a good idea. I'm going to the convent to bring Jasmine home. Better that I do it alone so I can explain what's happening. I don't want her upset. She'll need a bit of time to get used to the idea of you being around. If she takes to you, she can stay, otherwise I'll take her back after a few days.' He finished his tea, got up from the table and left, his dog padding along behind him. He had made no eye contact with her during the entire exchange.

Evie wanted to cry with frustration. He was so closed-up, so cold, so unfeeling. The way he talked of his own daughter, of returning her to the nuns if she didn't settle – as if she were an unwanted library book. He seemed to lack even the slightest capacity for empathy, for any appreciation of how difficult this was for her – let alone how Jasmine might feel. Pushing away the surge of self-pity welling inside her, she decided she needed to distract herself. Since Douglas had made it clear that he expected her to run the household, she might as well start there. She would ask Aunty Mimi to show her round the entire house and explain everything involved in its running.

This plan was more straightforward in its intent than its realisation. Aunty Mimi was occupied in the kitchen, ironing while Cookie was preparing vegetables, and her puzzled expression and monosyllabic responses signalled that she was less than impressed by Evie's desire to understand the workings of the household. Retiring from the kitchen abashed, Evie concluded that perhaps her initiative had been premature. Aunty Mimi could well be unaware of her impending marriage to the head of the house. Better to wait until the deed was done and any ambiguity removed. Meanwhile, she could easily explore the rest of the house on her own.

She began downstairs. There was only one room she hadn't yet seen. She eased open the door to find that it was a study. Dominated by a lacquered wood desk inlaid with mother of pearl, it was a beautiful room. A rich brocaded upright chair stood in front of the desk, a *chaise longue,* piled with linen cushions, was in front of the window, and one wall was lined with bookshelves that reached almost to the ceiling. Evie ran her fingers along the spines of the books as she read the titles. Among others, she found a full collection of Dickens, Hardy, the Brontes, Robert Louis Stevenson, George Eliot, Walter Scott, some more recent books including several Agatha Christies and a few by Somerset Maugham, as well as English translations of Victor Hugo, Tolstoy and Chekhov. Better than the fare she'd had to read to Mrs Shipley-Thomas. There was enough to keep her occupied for years. Judging by the condition of the spines and the pristine dust jackets, no one had yet got around to reading them.

On the opposite wall was a decorative Chinese lacquered cabinet containing a collection of fine china that looked hand-painted, and an array of ornaments and curios carved in jade, ebony and ivory.

Moving over to the desk, on top of which was a small stack of notepaper and envelopes, she imagined Douglas sitting here penning his proposal to her – then remembered it had been typed.

Like the drawing room, the study gave onto the garden. Evie looked forward to sitting in this exquisite room in the rainy season, curled up on the *chaise longue*, devouring a book.

Suppressing the feeling that she shouldn't be wandering

around the house like this, she went upstairs. Didn't she have a right to explore? This was her home – at least when in George Town. There was of course also the rubber plantation, where she imagined they would spend most of their time after they were married. She wondered if Douglas would take her there straight after the wedding.

Her own bedroom was one of three on one side of the landing – she found another near identical guest room at the far end, looking out onto the street. In between was a smaller, sparsely furnished box room with a single bed, probably intended originally to house the servant of a guest.

She turned her attention to the doors on the opposite side of the landing. The first opened into a room with a single bed and shelves which contained a collection of china dolls and neatly arrayed toys. Jasmine's room. Despite the prettiness of the soft furnishings, it had a sad, neglected air about it as though it was rarely used. Evie got the distinct feeling that while it had been designed to appeal to a little girl, Jasmine herself had made little or no impression on it – perhaps as she was rarely here. The dolls on the shelves looked unloved and barely touched. A rocking horse in front of the window was in the pristine condition it must have been in when it was delivered – perhaps a Christmas or birthday gift. Everything was too orderly – a child's room from an illustrated magazine, rather than one inhabited by a real child. She straightened a rag doll that had been sitting on the only chair and had flopped over onto its side, then left the room, closing the door behind her. She had found no clue as to what kind of girl Jasmine was, or what her interests were. Hoping that before long this bedroom would be occupied, she imagined herself sitting here reading a bedtime story to the little girl who one day might come to think of her as her mother.

The room next door was a bathroom, the wall tiles decorated with motifs of shells, sailing boats and starfish.

Hesitating a moment outside the last door, Evie told herself not to be an idiot, and opened it. The master bedroom was larger than the other rooms, and had a dual aspect. She paused for a moment on the threshold, taking in its simple beauty. A white shuttered French window gave onto a balcony overlooking the garden, furnished with a table and two rattan chairs. A perfect place for taking breakfast or drinking tea.

She moved over to the bed. It was vast, draped with mosquito netting and covered with an embroidered ivory silk bedspread. The stitching was hand-done: an intricate display of leaves and flowers with a peacock as centrepiece. Caressing the coverlet with her fingers, she smoothed the soft silk under the flat of her palm and felt the raised thread of the embroidery work.

She struggled to imagine herself lying here in this bed with Douglas Barrington beside her. She had no idea what to expect when that finally happened. Of course she knew the facts of life, but the sex act was something other people did. Evie didn't want to think it was something she would soon have to participate in herself. The prospect was alarming. The thought of Douglas and herself, naked under these sheets, sent a shiver of longing through her, tempered by fear.

How utterly her life had changed. Just a few months ago she had barely heard of Malaya and the idea of living here and being married with a ready-made family would have seemed bizarre. She told herself that once the wedding had happened and they were finally man and wife, everything would be fine. If only Douglas shared that hope. His behaviour so far made it seem a forlorn one.

She tried to work out which side of the bed he slept on, but the lacquered wood night stands that stood guard were devoid of any evidence, each bearing only a table lamp. The room contained no sign of Douglas's presence. It felt like a hotel room, readied for the next guest.

Noticing a pair of doors, she pushed one open and found

herself in a dressing room. This room told a different story. The mirrored table was piled with a collection of feminine pots and potions, in coloured glass jars. A Mason Pearson hairbrush lay on its back, several long blonde hairs caught woven into the bristles. Evie picked up a china perfume atomiser, puffed a light spray onto her neck. It was fresh, sweet – perhaps a note of gardenia. After the impersonality of the rest of the house, it was a surprise to find these unexpected remnants of Felicity's life here. It was as if the former Mrs Barrington had merely stepped out of the room for a while.

Evie drifted towards a line of lacquered doors and opened one. Douglas appeared to have done nothing to remove Felicity's effects from the house. Inside the wardrobe a rich rainbow of silks, taffeta and satins hung from tightly packed rails. Evie reached out and touched one of the dresses. The fabric was like gossamer between her fingers. Examining the discreet label hand-sewn inside, she saw it was a Fortuny. Unable to resist, she slipped it off the hanger and held it up to herself, moving in front of the cheval mirror in the bedroom. Of course, the gown was far too small for her – Felicity must have been four or five inches shorter and more slender than Evie, but the colour – the palest jade – was perfect for Evie. Holding it with one hand against her shoulder and the other to her waist, she imagined wearing a dress like this while dancing under a starry sky with her husband-to-be. She swayed gently from side to side, eyes closed, the delicate silk under her hands, the strains of a waltz in her head.

'Why you in here? This private. Your room on other side.'

Evie spun round, almost jumping out of her skin with fright. A stony-faced Aunty Mimi stood, fists on hips in the doorway. But to Evie's absolute horror, standing just behind her was Veronica Leighton.

Blood flooded into Evie's face and her skin burned with embarrassment. Her shaming was total. She'd not felt as humiliated since she was four and had wet her knickers at nursery school.

There was a moment's silence, as Evie longed to wind the clock back, then Aunty Mimi rushed into the room, snatched the gown from her hands and took it back into the dressing room.

As Evie stammered, searching for something to say, Veronica Leighton, leaned against the doorpost and drawled, 'You look like you need a stiff gin, darling. Why don't I get Benny to mix us some?' At the top of the stairs she called back to Evie. 'And remind me to introduce you to that chap I mentioned so he can run you up a few frocks of your own.' Pausing before she went down, she added pointedly, 'In the right size, of course.'

Aunty Mimi emerged from the closet, gave Evie an angry look and headed for the door.

'Aunty Mimi, I'm sorry. Please don't mention this to Mr Barrington.'

Her humiliation was complete. Apologising to the servants. She'd be a laughing stock if Veronica heard that.

Wishing herself safely back in Hampshire, Evie struggled to rescue the situation. 'I was just... you see... Mr Barrington... I... we...' Should she tell Aunty Mimi she was soon to be married to Douglas? Of course she couldn't. It wasn't her place to do it and it might only make matters worse. Better to retire wounded and try to recover later once she was established as the new mistress of the house. Meanwhile, she must swallow her pride and pray that the housekeeper would say nothing to Douglas.

Aunty Mimi scowled and said, 'I no tell Mister. I keep secret. You not come in here again. Is private. Not your room.' She wagged her finger in the air as if scolding a small child.

Relief flooded through Evie and she fled downstairs to the next ordeal – facing Veronica.

Mrs Leighton was in the drawing room, standing in front of

the open French window, looking out onto the garden. She turned round and handed Evie a glass of gin and tonic, ice chinking.

'Thank you, but isn't it awfully early in the day to be drinking?'

'You're as bad as Arthur.' Her laugh was false. 'Anyway you look as if you *need* one. That's always a good time to drink. Gin's positively medicinal, darling.'

Evie took a tentative sip and felt inclined to agree. She sank onto the sofa. The alcohol went straight to her head, immediately easing her embarrassment. Veronica, with a graceful bending of the knees, lowered herself into a seat opposite, her long slim legs to one side. She sniffed the air. 'Naughty girl! You're wearing Felicity's scent as well. Better make sure you shower it off before Dougie gets back. You don't want to upset him.' She shook her head solemnly and Evie felt herself blushing again.

Deciding a change of subject was needed urgently, Evie said, 'I didn't think you and Arthur would be in Penang so soon.'

'The darling boy did so much preparatory work on the voyage out that he was in his boss's good books and was able to get away earlier than expected.'

'Was it some kind of project?'

Veronica snorted. 'Good grief. How would I know? Or care?' She took another sip of gin. 'I've no idea what Arthur does. Government business is all terribly tedious. Anyway, we travelled up on the train yesterday and this morning ran into Dougie on the quayside at Butterworth, heading the other way. He said he was off to fetch the brat home, so I thought I'd scoot over here and find out how you're getting on and how you feel about it.'

'Don't you like Jasmine? Is she really a brat?'

'All children are brats. Even pretty little things like Jasmine. If it were me I'd leave her with the nuns. Or even better, send her back to England to boarding school. Best thing for her. And for you.' She pushed a cigarette into a long ivory holder, lit it, drew and exhaled a cloud of smoke that spiralled up towards the dormant ceiling fan. Having taken an initial puff, Veronica let her cigarette burn away, using the holder instead to make extravagant gestures as if she were conducting an orchestra.

'I'm hoping that Jasmine and I will get along and that she will stay here with us. It must have been very unsettling for the poor child to lose her mother when she was so young.'

'So you and Dougie haven't got cold feet and called the whole thing off?' Veronica leaned forward, her elbows on her knees. She reminded Evie of a beautiful bird of prey, waiting for the moment to strike.

'Of course we haven't.' Evie knew she sounded snappy, but Veronica was clearly baiting her.

'Well, well. That's a surprise. I had a bet with Arthur that once you'd spent twenty-four hours here you'd be on the next ship back to England.'

'You and Arthur had a bet?'

Veronica laughed her tinkling laugh. 'Well I made the bet. He didn't actually comment. You know Artie – he's like the Sphinx. But do tell, Evie. What was it like when you and Dougie met again?' She gave her a knowing look. 'Did celestial choirs sing?'

Evie felt herself starting to perspire again, a damp clammy feeling in her armpits and under her breasts. Veronica's slender body appeared to be immune to the heat. It was anger and embarrassment that was helping to raise Evie's body temperature. Veronica seemed to know – or sense – that all was less than perfect between her and Douglas. Perhaps he had even confessed to her that he'd mistaken Evie for another guest at his wedding.

She told herself not to be cowed by the woman. 'Everything went very well.' She smoothed a crease from her skirt.

'Come on, darling. You have to tell me more than that. Was it romantic? Passionate?' She looked at Evie pointedly. 'Businesslike? Or maybe even... awkward?'

Evie's skin prickled and she shifted in her seat. Veronica was watching her like a hawk. 'I'd prefer to keep what happens between Douglas and me private.'

Veronica laughed. 'Of course. I can see you're being coy. Never mind. I'll save your blushes. Dougie will spill the beans when I next see him – I'm very good at squirrelling all the dirt out of him.' She fixed her gaze on Evie again. 'But don't worry, darling, I won't say a word about your little dressing up session today. Your secret's safe with me.'

Before Evie could reply, the woman drained the contents of her glass, and jumped lightly to her feet. 'Must rush. So many calls to make. But I had to make you my first, dear girl. Don't get up!' With that, she swept out of the room and the house.

Evie sat fuming, so incensed she couldn't finish her 'medicinal' gin. Leaving it on a side table she went into the garden and paced up and down in the shade of the tall casuarina trees. When the heat of the day and her own anger got too much for her, she went inside and ran upstairs to her bedroom to wash away all traces of Felicity's perfume. Afterwards, she switched on the ceiling fan and threw herself down on the bed.

She had no idea how long she'd been asleep when Aunty Mimi came in to wake her.

'*Tuan* and Jasmee waiting you. *Tuan* say you come downstairs. Dinner nearly ready.'

Heart thumping at the next ordeal awaiting her, Evie followed the Malayan woman down the stairs and into the drawing room.

Jasmine Barrington was a tiny figure, dwarfed by the chair she was sitting in so that her legs dangled in front of her, unable to reach the floor. Her blonde hair was pulled back into plaits, each tied with a brown silk ribbon. She was wearing what was evidently school uniform: a yellow gingham dress with white ankle socks and bar shoes. Her face was pale with a cluster of freckles around her nose. Wide blue eyes dipped to the floor, after a furtive glance at Evie, giving the impression the little girl didn't want to be here.

Evie bent down in front of the child, her hand extended for a formal handshake. 'You must be Miss Jasmine Barrington. I'm very pleased to meet you. My name is–'

Before she could introduce herself, Douglas interrupted. 'This is Miss Fraser, Jasmine. She's going to be staying here with us.' No mention of the upcoming wedding. Addressing Evie he added, 'I'll see you both later. I'm dining at The Club tonight.' Without waiting for a response he went out of the room, leaving Evie stunned.

She looked at the little girl. 'It looks like it's just you and me this evening, Jasmine. Shall we go and see if Aunty Mimi has the supper ready?'

FOUR

Evie and Douglas Barrington were married the following week. The ceremony, such as it was, was conducted in the old Anglican church, St George's. The only guests at the service were the Leightons, who acted as witnesses, and Benny, who drove the car.

Jasmine was not included in the wedding party. She was left behind in the care of Aunty Mimi – Douglas had brushed off Evie's request that she be present at the service, saying that he knew what was best for his daughter. Evie wasn't even sure he had told the child what was happening. Her own overtures towards Jasmine had proved fruitless – all attempts to get her to talk were met with silence and the sucking of a thumb.

Glad that she had splashed out on one good frock before leaving London, Evie wore a navy and white linen dress, teaming the outfit with her old but serviceable pearls, a hand-me-down from her grandmother.

The ceremony was a rushed affair, and Evie felt deflated rather than exhilarated as they were declared man and wife in front of the empty church. The groom did not kiss the bride.

To her dismay, as soon as the ceremony was concluded, Mrs

Leighton announced that she had arranged a surprise party for the couple. Douglas appeared furious.

'You didn't expect to get away without a little reception, did you, dear boy?' Veronica said. 'That's not fair to darling Evie. Anyway, it's all arranged. Champagne on ice. Just a tiny little celebration.'

She faced Evie. 'We can't wait to give you a real welcome and everyone's dying to meet you and make their congratulations.' Leaning forward to air-kiss her, she enveloped Evie in a cloud of Shalimar.

Douglas said nothing. He closed his eyes, like a man who'd just been told he had a terminal illness. In the car on the way to the Penang Club his expression remained angry and he maintained his silence.

The Penang Club was a large tiled-roof Victorian building, surrounded by trees with shorter palm trees in front of its porticoed entrance. To Evie's astonishment and Douglas's evident fury, as soon as they entered the building a gathering of around forty people were waiting for them. 'Surprise!' The guests were all assembled in the central entrance hall which was dominated by portraits of Queen Victoria and George V and a collection of intimidating oil paintings of past club presidents.

A beaming Veronica clapped her hands together. 'Everyone's been dying to meet you, Evie. The old devil can't keep you hidden forever. They all want to get to see the blushing bride.' She put a hand on Douglas's sleeve. 'Surely you didn't expect it to be just us four? We can't possibly let wedding bells go unmarked.'

Arthur looked embarrassed. This was clearly entirely Veronica's doing.

Evie discovered later that, special occasions aside, women were barred from the Club other than to dine in the Grill Room, so Veronica had clearly gone to much effort to get around this sanction. When they entered, champagne was chilling in buckets and waiters moved around between the guests offering canapés. The sound of increasingly well-oiled voices was deafening and Evie felt awkward and uncomfortable. After a while, most of the men drifted away to the men's bar, leaving the women, gathered in small groups, talking intently and noisily. Evie realised she had no idea where Douglas was. They had been separated almost as soon as they entered the throng. After being introduced to her, the other women appeared to lose all interest in her and soon began to talk shop with each other.

Exhausted, and stressed from so many introductions to people whose names she would never remember, Evie ached to leave. Like a butterfly pinned to a specimen tray, she was being passed around for inspection and approval. If she had hoped to be welcomed warmly and enthusiastically into their inner circle, she was to be disappointed. The ladies appeared to operate as a clique, slow to accept outsiders or newcomers. Her nerves raw and her head throbbing from too much champagne and a vain effort to remember names, she escaped to the ladies' powder room.

Once inside a cubicle, she told herself to calm down. These people would eventually accept her and possibly even become her friends. It was only natural that at the beginning they would be cautious about her and she would feel like an outsider. She remembered her first term at boarding school and how different it was from what followed. Girls who had cold-shouldered her had become firm friends and alliances inevitably changed as time went on. That was what she needed to do. Give it time.

As she sat in a stall, treasuring this quiet moment away from the intimidating throng, she heard the door to the Powder Room open and two or three people came in.

'You're not serious, Vronnie!' The speaker had a drawling tone that made her sound bored.

'I told you. I'm absolutely certain. He mistook her for another woman. It has to be that. He's been propping up the bar ever since he got here, getting absolutely sozzled.' Veronica's voice was unmistakable. 'Dougie would never have chosen to get hitched to someone like her. Remember they'd only ever met once and that was years ago. He obviously muddled her up with someone else.'

A third voice chipped in. 'You can't seriously be suggesting he went ahead and married her knowing she was the wrong woman?'

'Once she'd trekked all the way to Malaya he could hardly send her back again, could he? Parcel her up to return to sender!'

Evie winced as she listened to the ripples of laughter but Veronica wasn't done. 'Besides, Dougie only cares about what will happen to his damned rubber estates. As long as she can give him a couple of brats why should he be bothered? What's that expression? You don't look at the mantelpiece when you're poking the fire.'

More gales of laughter. 'Really, Vronnie. You are the giddy limit!'

Evie was humiliated. She could hear the sound of handbags opening and closing and a tap running. The women seemed to be repairing their makeup. No one had gone near the cubicles.

The woman with the drawling voice spoke again. 'The girl does seem gawky. Not fat exactly, but very big-boned. Not at all like Felicity who was such a delicate, pretty little thing.'

Veronica's voice cut through the air again. 'But Felicity didn't cope well with being here, did she? Dougie's not daft. He probably decided that it was better this time to pick someone made of sturdier stuff. Evie definitely has child-bearing hips and appears to have the constitution of an ox.'

'The body of one too.' Gales of laughter followed.

'You two are awful. Her face is actually quite attractive – she has great big eyes and lovely skin. And her hair's a lovely colour.'

Veronica snorted. 'Her skin will be like leather after a few months here. She spent hours sitting out on deck on the ship out here. I'd be amazed if Dougie can manage to get it up for her.'

Evie was shaking with anger. What should she do? Stay hidden and hope they hadn't noticed that one of the cubicles was occupied? Or brave it out and shame them? On a sudden impulse, and unable to stand the sniggering, she flushed the lavatory and pushed the door open. She had nothing to be ashamed of. Better to face down the three witches than cower in a corner herself.

Veronica was sitting on a chintz-covered armchair, her cigarette holder in one hand. Her eyebrows rose a fraction as she registered Evie's presence but she made no other sign of acknowledgement. The drawling woman, a redhead, whom Evie remembered was called Dolly something, was perched on top of the dressing-table unit that ran along one wall, her legs swinging like a pendulum. The third woman, who'd been introduced as Flora Davenport, a petite blonde with narrow cat-like eyes and a tiny mouth, was standing in front of the mirrors, applying lipstick.

Evie could hear their collective intake of breath. Saying nothing, she moved over to the basins and washed her hands, taking her time and relishing the embarrassed silence. Out of the corner of her eye, she saw Dolly slither down from her perch while Flora appeared frozen in front of the mirror, the application of her lipstick forgotten.

From her corner seat, Veronica was the first to speak. 'As I was just saying, Evie, you must come and join us in our next tennis game. Rowena's ankle won't be mended for some time yet so you could make up our four for doubles. You do play don't you?' Her tone conveyed the impression that she thought it unlikely.

Evie had been captain of the school tennis team and was a frequent winner of house and school tournaments. 'Tennis isn't my cup of tea,' she lied. Without a backward glance she left the room.

Avoiding the gathering in what was designated the Small Drawing Room, Evie slipped through an open full-length window into the garden. Apart from a few people playing croquet on the lawns at the side of the building, there was no one outside in the grounds of the club. Brimming with hurt pride and suppressed rage, she settled herself on a wooden bench under a palm tree.

She must be the laughing stock of the club and probably half of George Town. It was obvious that in this narrow expatriate society, rumour and gossip spread like sparks in a tinder pile. Were the women right about her? Was she so unappealing that her new husband would probably have to shut his eyes and think of England in order to fulfil his marital obligations? Even here, alone and unobserved, her face still burned and her eyes stung with tears she was determined not to shed.

If only she could walk out and go back to the house. But she hadn't a clue how to get there. She had lost her bearings during the five-minute motorcar trip from St George's. The cruel words of Veronica and her cronies whirled around her brain, a constant repetition like a phonograph with its needle stuck in the groove. They thought her an unattractive woman whose husband had only married her because he couldn't be bothered to 'send her back' like an unwanted parcel. Their words cut her to the quick – particularly because she recognised some truth in them. Cruel, but possibly accurate. How could she have even entertained the possibility that one day Douglas Barrington might come to care for her? How could she even have any feelings for him herself if this was how he thought of her? She couldn't possibly love a man who was physically repelled by her. Why hadn't she overheard their poisonous chatter a day or so sooner, when there had still been a possibility of calling off the wedding? Evie slumped forward, her head in her hands and her heart despairing. The person she missed most right now was her father and, not for the first time, she cursed him for what he'd done to destroy the family, her future and her sense of self.

'So tell me why the bride is lurking alone in the shrubbery?'

Evie nearly jumped out of her skin.

Arthur Leighton gestured towards the bench. 'Do you mind if I join you? You look as though you could do with cheering up.'

His kindly tone of voice was too much for her and she felt the tears spring up. She pulled out her handkerchief and blew her nose. 'I'm sorry. I'm feeling a bit low.' She looked up at him, and tried to force a smile to her face. 'Just wedding jitters.'

'I think it's a bit more than that isn't it, Evie?'

'What do you mean?'

'I happened to hear Veronica and her pals talking. Soon after you apparently overheard them yourself. Knowing that little coven of–' He hesitated. 'Well, I can imagine they were doling out some less than complimentary comments.' He placed one hand on her arm. 'I'm sorry you were subjected to it. Don't listen to them, Evie. They're like that about everyone – even each other. Speaking ill of people is a sport to them – but it's completely meaningless.'

'It's very hurtful actually.'

'I've no idea what you heard them saying but whatever it was it wasn't true. They make up for their own inadequacies by tearing others apart. You're just the latest in a long line. I'm ashamed that my wife is one of the culprits, and I've long since given up trying to understand why.'

Evie wanted to say that Veronica was not just a culprit, she was the ringleader. But she realised Arthur must be only too aware of that.

He sat with his hands on his knees and she felt calmed and

comforted by his proximity. He had nice hands. There was something solid and dependable about Arthur. Straightforward – what you saw and heard was what he meant – no double talking.

'Do you think I'll ever fit in here?' Before he could answer she added, 'But I'm not sure I even want to.'

'I wouldn't blame you if you didn't. I often feel that way myself. I sometimes think I'm only accepted because they all feel they have to keep on the right side of me.' He brushed an insect off his trouser leg. 'And as they're all terrified of my formidable wife that's another reason they want to keep me onside.' He gave a hollow laugh.

Evie wanted to ask him how he had come to be married to Veronica when they were so very different, but despite his warmth and his being the only person in Penang that she felt comfortable with, she hesitated to broach the topic. Instead she asked him about Douglas.

'You and Douglas are awfully different and yet you're his best friend.'

'Doug doesn't really do friendship. I suppose, if I'm being generous, I'm the person he trusts most – but if I'm being honest, I'd say it was more that I'm the person he dislikes least.'

She looked up at him, puzzled. 'Are you saying my husband isn't a very nice person?'

His mouth twitched at the corners. 'I'm merely saying that he's a hard man to get to know. He's very much a loner. Doesn't open up to anyone.' With a dry laugh he added, 'Mind you, none of us men are very hot on revealing what we think or feel. One thing a public school education provides is an unsurpassed ability to suppress one's emotions.'

'You don't seem at all like that.'

'That's probably because I didn't go to public school. I'm a grammar school boy. It made it damned hard to rise even to the far from heady levels I have achieved in the civil service. I'm not one of *them*.'

'And is Douglas?'

'No. He's different altogether. He went to Eton but he doesn't behave like the rest of them. He's very much his own man. Doug prefers his own company. He's passionate about rubber and everything to do with his estate. Shows up at the club on the rare occasions he's in town but the rest of the time we never see him.'

'Is that why Felicity preferred living in George Town? Did she like the club and everything that comes with it?'

'Felicity hated Penang. Full stop. She wanted to be back in England. There was no way that Doug would ever agree to moving back there. She found the rubber estate isolated and missed her old social life and her family. When he wouldn't sell up and move back to England she felt he'd let her down.' He leaned back, stretching his long legs. 'According to Veronica, Doug had promised Felicity when he persuaded her to move out here that it would only be for a few months, a year at most, until he could find a buyer for the place. But he fell in love with the rubber business, with the countryside, with Malaya, with being a planter. That's why they got the house in George Town – he thought if she was here in town it would give her some companionship and interests, but all Felicity wanted was to be back home.'

'Golly. Life must have been very difficult for them.'

Arthur shrugged. 'You could say that.'

They lapsed into silence. After a few minutes he leaned forward. 'Evie, I may be speaking out of turn but you're so different from Felicity and I'm sure you will adapt well to life here. You don't strike me as the kind of woman who wants to spend her time playing bridge, gossiping and hanging round the tennis club. But you have to be aware that living on a rubber estate can be very lonely.'

'I'm used to being on my own,' she said brightly. 'As long as I have books to read I can keep myself occupied. And there'll be a house to run, Jasmine to care for and maybe, God willing, in time some children of my own.'

He looked away, then nodded. 'Doug is very much a free spirit. You'll need to be patient. He's not the easiest of men to get along with. And...'

'And what?'

'Nothing. I'm sure it will all be fine.'

Evie glanced at her wristwatch. It was already almost six. She jumped up. 'Aunty Mimi is preparing dinner for seven o'clock. Any chance of you rousing Douglas from the bar? I'm not allowed in there.'

Arthur's lips stretched into a tight line. 'I'll do my best. Wait here. No need for you to face the rabble again tonight.' He went into the building.

Evie could still hear the buzz of conversation and laughter, but now there were also the strains of jazz music coming from a gramophone somewhere inside. Light spilled out from the tall open windows onto the darkening lawns.

Arthur emerged after a few minutes. 'I'm sorry, Evie. Doug says he's going to be a while. He wants you to take the car back with Benny and he'll see you at the house later.' His face was solemn and he looked as mortified as she felt.

It was like a punch in the stomach. Evie slumped back onto the wooden bench and looked up at Arthur. 'Is he really going to leave me alone while he stands at a bar and drinks himself insensible? Does he expect me to go home and have dinner alone yet again? On my wedding day.' She could barely get the words out, she was so choked with emotion.

'I'm so sorry. It's unforgivable, but it's how Doug is. You need to give him time.'

'Time for what? I've barely shared more than a few sentences with him. He drank his way through half a bottle of scotch on the first night, before walking out on me to come here. Since then he's failed to show up for dinner at all. What have I done? Why did I ever agree to go through with this?'

Arthur said nothing but she could see his fists were clenched so tightly his knuckles were white.

'I thought at least today of all days he'd deign to break bread with me. After we stood there side-by-side and made those vows.' At last she could hold back no longer and began to cry. Tears of anger, frustration, loneliness and fear.

'I don't know what to say, Evie. He's behaving like an absolute cad. I can only think that he's afraid.'

'Afraid?' She could hear the pitch of her voice rising. 'Afraid of what?'

'You, I expect. Strange as that may seem. He's been through a lot with Felicity dying. Maybe he's anxious about spending time alone with you. He's not a sociable man. He's used to his own company.'

Evie wiped her eyes but more tears were coming. Her lace-edged handkerchief was already sodden.

'Come on. Let's get you in the car. Benny's parked at the front.' He handed her his own handkerchief. 'Dry your eyes. I'm going to head back to the bar when you've gone. I'm going to try and talk some sense into the man. Don't worry, Evie. I'm sure things will soon settle down. Just give it time.'

FIVE

Jasmine had already eaten and gone to bed when Evie sat down to her solitary dinner. She shuffled the food around her plate unable to eat. Afterwards, too angry even to read a book, she retired early to bed in the guest room as usual.

Under the flimsy sheet and shrouded by the mosquito nets, she struggled to sleep. She longed for oblivion – a few hours where she could escape into dreams, hopefully ones unpopulated by Douglas Barrington. She didn't want to think about him, about this godforsaken country or the loathsome people at the club. The dreams she craved were of the English countryside, of leafy lanes dappled with sunshine, cows and sheep grazing in green fields, the sound of woodpeckers, the pealing of bells for the Sunday service. Not this infernal heat and not the horrible events of this, her wedding day.

But sleep evaded her. Evie lay awake, rolling from one side to the other, sheets damp with her perspiration, mind racing. Her heart hammered in her chest and her nerves were so raw that her skin felt tight and her pulse throbbed at her temples. All the time she saw Douglas Barrington's face. Her husband's face. The face of the man who had stood beside her repeating the marriage vows, before abandoning her in search of comfort from a bottle, rather than from her.

She punched the pillow. Why, why, why had she ever agreed to go through with this horrible loveless marriage? It couldn't even be described as a marriage of convenience when it clearly was anything but convenient to the groom. What had Douglas hoped to gain from it? If he wanted children, standing around in a bar pouring whisky down his throat was hardly the way to conceive them. Was she so horrible, so unappealing that he couldn't even bear to be in her company on their wedding day? How did he think all those mean-minded people at the Penang Club would react to knowing he was getting drunk while his new bride was alone at home? She had never been so utterly humiliated in her entire life. Surely he too would be the subject of inevitable gossip.

Arthur Leighton, when he'd returned from the bar, had looked embarrassed on her behalf. Those kind eyes had been full of pity for her and she didn't want his pity. No. She didn't want it at all.

She'd pack her bags and tomorrow morning make enquiries as to the next ship back to England. Arthur could arrange it all for her and Douglas would have to pay for it. She knew Arthur would help her. He was the only person she trusted. Maybe she had nothing and no one to go back to in England, but anything, any job, no matter how humble, would be preferable to the torturous situation here. She wouldn't even need to go through the shame of a divorce. The marriage was unconsummated and could surely be annulled. But she would think about all that later. Besides, it didn't even matter: she had no intention of ever marrying again.

Deciding to start packing immediately, she clambered out of bed and went over to the wardrobe. Her suitcases, which had been stacked on top, had disappeared. The packing would have to wait until tomorrow. As she went back to bed, she tripped

and stubbed her toe, slumping to her knees on the polished
wood floor. Nothing was going her way. Powerless, robbed of all
agency, even over her own belongings.

At some point, she must have crawled back into bed and
drifted off to sleep. The next thing she was aware of was
someone silhouetted against the muslin drapery of the open
windows. Douglas was here in her bedroom.

How the hell did he have the nerve to come in here unin-
vited after what had happened? Feeling angry but vulnerable,
she pulled herself up into a sitting position. He moved towards
her and sat down at the foot of the bed. In the pale moonlight
she could see that his hair was wet. She drew her knees up to
her chest but said nothing.

'I'm sorry, Evelyn. I behaved badly. You don't need to tell
me. I've already had Arthur Leighton reading me the riot act.'

She remained silent.

He spoke again. 'Only, I didn't want a fuss. No party. I told
Veronica that. But the bloody woman's a law unto her self. And
I told you too. Didn't I? I said I didn't want a big do.'

'So it's my fault, is it?'

'Well you could have told her you didn't want to go to the
damned club.'

'She's your friend. I barely know the woman. It wasn't my
place to interfere and anyway I thought you'd agreed. I didn't
know all those dreadful people would be there. She said it
would be just the four of us.' Indignation was mounting. How
had what started out as an apology from him turned into an
accusation of her? 'I've never felt so humiliated and embarrassed in my entire life. I can't stand your horrible club. I can't
stand Veronica Leighton and I can't stand you.'

To her horror he started to laugh. 'That's a relief. I thought
it was just me.'

Ignoring his amusement, she said, 'Look, I think we both
need to acknowledge this was a crazy idea. We should never

have gone ahead with it. I'll pack my things tomorrow morning and ask Arthur if he'll help me sort out a passage back to England.' She swallowed. 'I'm sure you'll be as relieved as I to see me go but I expect you to pay the travel expenses. It's the least you can do.' She could feel herself shaking with relief – she'd managed to stand up for herself.

He made a little snorting noise. 'I really have screwed up, haven't I? Arthur told me I had. He told me I didn't deserve you. He seems to have a bit of a crush on you himself. Singing your praises he was.'

Evie didn't know what to say. She needed to keep on track and get things sorted once and for all. 'We're both intelligent enough to acknowledge that this whole thing was a foolish gamble. It's a pity we didn't realise that this morning. But we can arrange for an annulment once I'm back in England.' She swallowed again, nervous, but determined. 'I'll see my solicitor as soon as I reach London. I will of course expect you to pay any costs involved.'

'No.'

'You won't pay the costs? It's the least you should do after what I've gone through.'

'No. I don't want to annul the marriage. I don't want you to leave. I'm sorry we got off to a bad start but that's not a reason to give up before we've even given it a go.'

'You must have drunk more than I thought. You're clearly still intoxicated.'

'I'm sober as a judge.' He held a hand out in front of her. 'Look. Steady as a rock.'

'I can't imagine how that's possible. You must be immune to alcohol.'

'It probably has something to do with the fact that I've been for a swim in the sea to sober up.'

'What?'

'Arthur insisted. He poured black coffee down me then

drove to the beach and we went swimming. Always the best way to clear your head.'

Evie found herself imagining him running down the beach in the moonlight, plunging naked into the sea, and tried to force the image from her mind. She mustn't allow herself to weaken.

'Will you give me another chance, Evelyn? We got off on the wrong foot but maybe we can make it work. Surely it's worth a try?'

Stunned by his change in behaviour, she stared at him in the half-light. His hair was still damp. She wanted to stretch a hand out and touch him but she was paralysed, uncertain, wrong-footed, dismayed. Eventually she said, 'I don't trust you. I don't trust you at all. Mrs Shipley-Thomas was right. You are a rude, ill-mannered man with no courtesy or consideration.'

'Who on earth is Mrs Shipley-Thomas?'

'Never mind. You have treated me in an appalling way and should be thoroughly ashamed of yourself. I too am ashamed for letting you put me in this situation.' She filled her lungs and expelled the air quickly. 'This is quite literally the most horrible thing that's happened to me since my father died. Go away and let me go to sleep.'

Douglas was still sitting at the end of the bed. Evie waited for him to get up and leave the room, but he didn't move. They both sat motionless and silent for more than a minute At first she thought he'd fallen asleep sitting upright.

Suddenly he got up and moved around to the other side of the bed. He sat down on the edge, closer to where she was.

'Here's the situation as I see it. This morning we were both prepared to go into this marriage with our eyes open. We were both prepared to take the risk. Then Veronica Leighton comes along and throws a party, knowing bloody well it is the last thing on earth I want. According to Arthur you got caught up in her little coven of bitches and heard some things you didn't want to hear and which were almost certainly all untrue. This kind of thing is exactly why I didn't want a wedding party. If I could kill that woman I'd happily do it. I tolerate her only because Arthur, who is the only truly decent person I know, is lumbered with her. Since neither you nor I has any time for the woman, why are we letting her ruin our marriage before it's even started?'

'Veronica Leighton is not the reason I'm leaving. You are.'

'Fair enough. And I've apologised. But she is the reason I behaved the way I did today.'

Evie's patience was wearing thin. 'For heaven's sake. She threw a party you didn't want to go to. That's no reason to dump me among a bunch of strangers then send me home alone. That's no reason for you not being able to stand the sight of me enough to have dinner on a single occasion since I've been in this godforsaken country.'

He sighed. 'You're right. When you put it like that. I'm sorry, Evelyn. I've behaved badly to you.'

She couldn't help snapping back at him. 'And call me Evie. No one's called me Evelyn since my mother.'

Recognising the accusation he'd made himself the evening they'd met, he smiled. It broke the tension and she found herself smiling too. He reached a hand out and touched her arm, taking her hand in his. 'Give me a chance, Evie. Forgive me. I'll try to make things right between us.'

Evie was uncertain. Still bruised from what had happened, she wasn't ready to trust Douglas.

'I don't know. When we talked that first night I thought we'd got things straight but it seems we hadn't. I can't cope with a marriage where my husband won't even eat with me.'

He shook his head. 'What more can I say? I'm sorry. I'm not great company. I don't like small talk.' He sighed. 'Look. I'm going to be as straight as I can. I married for love the first time. Maybe this time round if it's on a more practical footing we may just make a go of it. I can't love you, Evie. But I can be civil to you. I'm not a great conversationalist but if you don't mind long silences I'll sit down and have dinner with you whenever I'm here in George Town. I don't–'

'What do you mean whenever you're in George Town?'

'I'm a planter. That's where I'll be most of the time.'

'But I'll be there too.'

'No.'

She shook her head, mystified. 'What are you talking about?'

'You'll live here. You and Jasmine. Not at the estate.'

'Why not?'

'It's a rough and ready place. A place of work. It's not comfortable. You wouldn't like it.'

'I should be the judge of that. I'm very adaptable. Luxurious surroundings aren't important to me. Besides we can make it more comfortable. I can help make it a home.'

He raised both hands, palms towards her. 'No. That's not up for discussion. I don't want either you or Jasmine there. Far better that you stay here. I promise I'll come to George Town at least once every two weeks – I have business to deal with here anyway. And Jasmine needs to be at school. I've decided she's not going back to the nuns. She can stay with you and go to school here in Penang. It will do her good to spend time with you. She needs a woman to care for her.' He paused, before adding, 'She needs a mother.'

'Jasmine won't even speak to me.'

'She will. Once she gets used to you. That will happen sooner if I'm not around.'

'But–'

'No buts. That's the deal, Evie.'

She felt numb. What should she do? It was a strange kind of marriage if they were to spend most of their time apart. And he was such a cold person. So indifferent to her feelings. Yet returning to England would be an admission of failure. There was nothing there for her to go back to. And maybe, given time, Douglas might start to feel differently about her. Once they knew each other better. He might even become fond of her if she made herself useful to him – indispensable. And in particular if she could give him the son he wanted.

'But when you wrote to me you said you wanted a companion.'

'I do. I need you to care for Jasmine and be here when I return. From time to time I have to entertain people to dinner – agents, buyers and inspectors. I'm also expected to turn up for various functions – local Chinese and Malayans as well as expats. I loathe that kind of thing and stick out like a sore thumb as a single man. Having a wife makes it all easier.'

Evie would probably loathe that kind of thing too – especially if it was anything like her experience at the club today. She swallowed and said, 'All right. I'll give it a go. But on the condition that if you behave again the way you did today I intend to leave immediately and go home to England. And that includes if you fail to keep your promise to stay in George Town in this house every couple of weeks.' She paused. 'And when you're here you'll take your meals with me.'

After a little flicker of hesitation in his eyes, he said, 'Agreed.'

There was another long silence as if both of them were weighing up what should happen next. Evie, nervous, but anxious to seal their agreement, pulled back the bedsheet. 'Since it's still our wedding night, you'd better come in.'

Douglas undressed quickly and complied. They lay side by side on their backs for a few moments. Evie was tense, uncertain what to do. Then he placed a hand on her stomach over the thin muslin of her nightgown. She shivered.

For a woman of her age, Evie lacked experience in matters of the heart. While young men had occasionally caught her eye, with none had it got so far as an invitation to dance, let alone courtship and kisses. She hesitated to blame the scandal around her father for the ruination of her prospects, but it was undeniable that it had changed the course of her own life. At what should have been the time to embark on romantic adventures, she'd been interred on the outskirts of a small Hampshire village, with an old lady. On the occasions when she ventured out to exchange library books or shop for personal essentials, any potential candidates would have been busy at work. If Mrs Shipley-Thomas had ever felt guilty about her companion's isolation she gave no indication. So, apart from the odd cheeky wink from the butcher's delivery boy, she'd had few encounters with men, and none of her age or class.

Her knowledge of sexual matters was not informed by experience but gleaned – probably with questionable accuracy – from other girls at her boarding school and embellished by the novels she'd read aloud to her employer. These lacked anatomical details and involved much sighing, swooning and burning lips. Right now, none of these things were happening to her, or evidently to Douglas. She'd no idea if her lips would be on fire when in contact with his, as he showed no sign of kissing her. His eyes were tightly closed and his mouth set in a hard line. When his hand moved from her stomach to her breasts she experienced an involuntary shiver of pleasure. The hand moved down beneath her nightgown, rucking it up around her waist.

'Open your legs,' he said.

Trembling, she did as he asked. His hand moved up her thigh until he was touching her up there, where she'd never been touched by anyone, except experimentally and guiltily herself. As his fingers explored her, she started to think this might actually turn out to be enjoyable – until he lifted his body over hers, guided himself into position and without warning thrust inside her.

It was like being torn apart. She suppressed a cry and prayed it would be over quickly. Douglas's eyes were still closed, his forehead creased in concentration, her breath rasping as he moved inside her while she lay motionless beneath him. She tried to think of something else, to listen to the sound of cicadas, to breathe in the scent of gardenias through the open window. Just as the pain began to recede, he grunted, the thrusting stopped, and he rolled off her. She felt something warm and sticky running between her legs.

'You all right?' he asked in a tone that implied little interest in her response.

'Yes,' she said, relieved it was over.

'It'll be easier next time. The first time is hard for a woman.'

He slid off the bed and moved across the darkened bedroom to the door. 'Goodnight,' he said, leaving her to weep silent tears into her pillow. After a few minutes, she got up and went into the bathroom to wash him away.

Next morning, daylight showed her the blood-stained evidence of the loss of her virginity. Evie burned with embarrassment at the thought of Aunty Mimi changing the sheets and knowing what they'd done. She felt exposed, invaded, defiled. Facing Doug over breakfast would be an ordeal. But better to get it over with.

In the dining room there was only Jasmine at the table.

'Where's your daddy?'

The little girl said nothing, just stared solemnly at Evie with big round eyes.

'*Tuan* go to lubber estate.'

Evie jumped in fright as the voice came from behind her. She'd never get used to Aunty Mimi's approach. One moment she wasn't there, then she'd materialise from nowhere, a tiny spectral presence, her footsteps making no sound.

'Oh,' said Evie, unsure whether she was disappointed or relieved at her husband's absence, then deciding she was annoyed. Why did he do this? Disappearing like that without telling her? Didn't she deserve the common courtesy of him informing her of his whereabouts? It was intolerable. She was his wife. After what he'd done to her last night that was incontrovertible.

Forcing a smile to her face for the little girl's benefit, she said, 'Why don't we do something nice today, you and I?'

Aunty Mimi answered for the little girl. 'Jasmine go school. Benny waiting in moto car.'

Of course the child would have to go to school, but Evie didn't even know where the school was – presumably somewhere here in George Town as Jasmine was no longer to board with the nuns on the mainland.

'I'll come with you in the car today, Jasmine. I'd like to see your new school and meet your teacher.'

The child remained mute, staring at Evie as though still unsure who she was or why she was here.

'*Mem* no need go. Benny take Jasmine.' Aunty Mimi moved towards Jasmine and took the girl by the hand. 'School expecting her. *Tuan* he allainge it.'

'Thank you, but I intend to go all the same. At least today. I want to meet Jasmine's teacher and find out where the school is.' Her heart was thumping. Why did the woman intimidate her so much? If Evie didn't assert herself now, at the beginning, it would be too late.

Aunty Mimi scowled, but raised no further objection.

SIX

Evie climbed into the motor car behind Benny. Jasmine sat beside her, maintaining a wide gap so that she was closer to the door than to Evie, sitting back in the seat, her skinny legs stretched in front of her. The child remained silent, pressing herself into her corner like a frightened little mouse.

The streets of George Town were crowded with bicycles and rickshaws and Benny seized any opportunity to blast the horn.

Evie racked her brain, searching for something to say to Jasmine that might coax a response from her. Putting a hand lightly on the girl's arm she said, 'I expect you're feeling quite nervous, aren't you, going to a new school for the first time.'

The little girl turned her head and fixed her eyes on Evie.

Determined to follow through this minor breakthrough, Evie went on, 'I remember when I was a little girl, I was so terrified the first time I went to school, I wet my knickers.'

Jasmine's eyes grew bigger and a little giggle escaped from her. At last, a reaction.

'But once I got to school I realised there was no need to be afraid.'

'Why?'

Only one word, but Evie felt a thrill of triumph.

'Because I soon discovered everyone else was scared too.' She ventured a smile. 'And I wasn't the only one who wet her knickers.'

Jasmine snorted in disgust. 'I won't wet my knickers. Only babies do that.'

'Of course you won't. You're far too grown up.' Keen to keep this tentative conversation flowing, she added, 'But even grown-ups can get scared sometimes.'

'Do you get scared?'

'A bit.'

'What of?'

'Oh, lots of things. Coming to live here in a new country. Meeting new people. Being so far away from home and everyone I know.'

'Where's your mummy and daddy?'

Evie bit her lip. 'My mummy lives far away in America and Daddy's in heaven.'

'That's where Mummy is. She went to live there with the angels when I was a baby. Maybe she knows your daddy.'

'I'm sure she does.'

The little girl's face was solemn. 'I suppose you'll go and live there too, won't you? And Daddy. I'll be all on my own with just Aunty Mimi and Benny and Cookie.'

In the driver's mirror Evie could see that Benny was smil-ing. She felt a rush of affection for the child that took her by surprise. 'No, Jasmine, I have no intention of going to live in heaven. At least not until I'm very, very old, and that's a long time away. And your daddy. He's not going to leave you.'

'So, why did my mummy go? Didn't she like me?'

Evie laid her hand gently on the seven-year-old's arm. 'I'm sure your mummy loved you very much.'

'Why didn't she take me with her to heaven?'

'Your mummy only went to heaven because she got sick. You're not going to get sick. Your mummy would want you to have a long and happy life, until one day in many, many years when you're a very old lady you'll meet her again when *you* go to heaven.'

'How old?'

'Very, very old. Maybe eighty or ninety.'

'Or a hundred?'

Evie smiled. 'Yes, probably a hundred.'

'My mummy used to cry all the time. She didn't want to play with me. She was mean.' Jasmine's lips were trembling and her eyes threatened tears.

Pulling the little girl against her chest, Evie said, 'I promise I won't be like that. I'd love to play with you and I promise not to be mean.' She hesitated, circumspection battling with honesty, then decided honesty should prevail. 'My mummy was often mean to me too, so I know how horrid that is. And I don't have any friends here in Penang, so I'd be really pleased if you'd be my friend.'

Jasmine considered for a moment, before saying, 'But I don't want to call you mummy.'

'Then why don't you call me Aunty Evie?' She held out her hand.

The child put out her own small one and they shook. As they sealed their new friendship, the car glided to a stop in front of a large white building surrounded by palm trees. Benny walked round and opened the door. Evie got out, offering her hand to help Jasmine. 'Come on,' she said, 'Let's go and see what this place is like. Please wait for me, Benny. I'm going to talk to Jasmine's teacher.'

Jasmine's new teacher was a smiling redhead with a freckled face and warm eyes. She bent her knees and squatted in front of the little girl. 'Pleased to meet you, Jasmine. I'm Miss Helston.' Standing up, she addressed Evie. 'And pleased to meet you too, Mrs Barrington.' They shook hands, then the teacher called to a girl around Jasmine's age. 'Penny, this is your new classmate, Jasmine. Please take her and show her the playground. Don't forget to introduce her to the other children before Assembly.' Penny took Jasmine's hand and the two small girls slipped away. Miss Helston sighed. 'Children are so accepting of each other at that age. Don't worry about your little girl, she's in good hands here. Do you have a few minutes?'

'As long as you need. That's why I'm here.'

The woman looked relieved. 'I'm so glad you came. Mr Barrington told the head that Jasmine would be brought here by your *syce*, but I so much prefer to meet the parents. Let's sit down over here in the shade. I have about fifteen minutes before I'm expected at Assembly.' She gestured towards a wooden bench under a jacaranda tree. 'Please tell me about Jasmine. I understand she's been boarding at the convent in Butterworth?' Her face was puzzled.

Evie felt herself starting to blush. It was embarrassing explaining her circumstances. 'Jasmine's mother died some years ago. Her father thought she'd do better being cared for by the nuns. He's a rubber planter and his work is very demanding of his time.'

Miss Helston was listening intently. 'Yes, I know Mr Barrington.'

'He and I have only just married.' She hesitated, the blush intensifying. 'Yesterday in fact.'

'Oh, my goodness. How terrific! Congratulations.' Miss Helston's smile was generous and genuine. 'I'd no idea.'

'I've only been in Penang a couple of weeks so I'm still feeling my way. And I'm afraid I know little of Jasmine. She's frightfully shy and I'm trying to gain her trust.'

'Poor mite! Don't worry.' The young woman seemed to sense Evie's discomfort. 'She'll be fine. Children at the school often come and go as their parents get posted elsewhere. Some are only here for a while before they're packed off to board back in Britain or up in the Cameron Hills. Have you recently arrived from England yourself?'

Evie nodded. 'My first time out of the country. Well, apart from France.'

'It must be a bit of a culture shock. I'm British too, of course. Here since I was a small child and I've never been back. My father works for the Hong Kong Shanghai bank. Maybe one day I'll get a chance to see England again.' She laughed. 'But enough about me. Let's talk about Jasmine.'

Evie flushed. 'I'm sorry but there's nothing else I can add.' Deciding to tell the truth she said, 'To be honest, Miss Helston, just now in the car is the first time I've managed to get so much as a word out of her. I imagine her mother's death was difficult for her and... well, she's unsure about me and my relationship with her father.' Jasmine was not the only one unsure about that.

'Understandable. Don't you worry. She'll soon come out of her shell. It's a very friendly school.' She twisted round to face Evie fully. 'Look, why don't you come to tea one day at our house? I can tell you about Penang and let you know how Jasmine's settling in. How about next week? Thursday at four?' She told her the address.

'That would be lovely. The *syce* can drop me off after he's picked Jasmine up.'

'Bring her too. One of the other girls in her class lives next door to us. They can play together while we chat.'

'That sounds wonderful.'

'See you on Thursday.' Miss Helston hurried away into the school building.

As Evie walked back to the waiting car a weight lifted from her shoulders. A friendly face. A warm person. A similar age to her. So different from those witches at the club. She sent up a silent prayer that maybe she had found a friend.

. . .

Returning to the house, Evie found Veronica Leighton waiting for her. Wearing beige linen 'pyjama' trousers, her silk blouse emphasised her small frame and the fashionable lack of breasts. As always in encounters with Veronica, Evie immediately felt ungainly in her faded cotton frock, and oversized with her ample bosom. To her irritation her guest behaved as the hostess, summoning Aunty Mimi to bring them lime juices with soda in the garden. Evie smarted, but decided to rein back her annoyance until she knew what Veronica wanted.

Expecting some kind of excuse or apology for the sniping gossip she'd overheard in the ladies' powder room, Evie should have realised by now that wasn't Veronica's style. Indeed it was hard to imagine her ever asking forgiveness of anyone for anything.

Mrs Leighton draped herself over one of the large wicker garden chairs, took out a fan and gave a long sigh. 'It's always so damned clammy compared to Africa. I'll never get used to it. One needs to change clothes at least four or five times a day. Such a bore.'

Evie said nothing, waiting to find out why Veronica was here.

'The old crow in there said you'd taken the child to school this morning.' She gestured towards the house. 'What on earth possessed you?' She took a silver case from her handbag, snapped it open, removed a cigarette from under the retaining bar, screwed it into her lacquer holder but didn't light it.

'I wanted to be with Jasmine on her first day. It's daunting starting a new school.'

Veronica's expression was disbelief. 'She's a child, Evie. That's what they do. Go to school. You shouldn't be doing anything so tedious as that. It's what the servants are for.'

'But I'm Jasmine's step-mother—'

'Exactly! You're not even her own mother.' She leaned forward. 'My advice, darling – don't try too hard. You don't want to seem desperate. Kids sense these things and take advantage. God! Children are so boring. Much better to keep the girl at arm's length. When she's older and ready to enter society it might actually become more interesting. You know, helping her choose clothes. Dishing out the advice.' She paused. 'But I am Jasmine's godmother, so I'm probably better placed to do all that.' Her mouth formed a smile that could only be intended to patronise.

Evie was saved from delivering a response by the arrival of Aunty Mimi bearing a tray. Once the drinks were served, Evie asked, 'What brings you here this morning? You must have lots more interesting things to do.'

Veronica acknowledged the evident sarcasm with a half smile. 'I wanted to see how you're doing, darling. Check you're all right. You left early last night. And old Dougie was a few sheets in the wind. Arthur had to take him for a swim to sober him up.'

Evie sipped her coffee, holding back from a reply.

Undaunted, Veronica pressed on. 'Aunty Mimi tells me he headed back to the estate before dawn this morning.' Her eyes widened in feigned concern as she stretched a hand out and touched Evie's arm lightly. 'I do hope everything's all right between you?'

'Perfectly fine.' She tried to inject an airy nonchalance into her voice. 'Why would it not be?'

Veronica pursed her lips. 'It's not exactly the way one expects the groom to behave on his wedding night. You must be dreadfully disappointed.' She leaned back in her chair. 'Or... perhaps... you and he have come to an arrangement? How do I put it delicately... *un mariage de convenance*. The French are so good at this kind of thing – they have a term for everything in matters of the heart – or possibly in your case – of the head.'

'I've no idea what you're implying, but as I've told you once before, what happens between me and my husband is our affair only.' Evie realised her voice sounded prim, tight, high-pitched. She took a big gulp of air and dug her fingernails into her palms.

'No need to get all stroppy, darling. I only wanted you to know that I'm here to help – if things get too much you can confide in me. Arthur and I are Dougie's oldest friends out here. We understand all his... his foibles.'

'I don't need any help, thank you. Is there anything else I can do for you?' She could feel her heart thumping as she said it. Anger was making her brave.

Veronica looked affronted. 'I brought you the details of my little Indian tailor chappie, Mr Ramanathan.' She handed her a card. 'As I said, I only want to help you settle in. I realise how strange everything must seem here after England.'

Evie muttered a thank you and accepted the card. It would be so satisfying to confront Veronica about what she'd overheard in the powder room, but she decided to hold back. What was the point? The woman must know she'd heard everything. What difference would telling her make? Clearly Veronica had no intention of apologising or attempting to put a different slant on the conversation. But there was no different slant possible. Those words could never be taken back and Evie realised she was grateful – if there had ever been a risk of her trusting Veronica Leighton it would never happen now.

'Anyway, darling, one other thing. I almost forgot the main reason for my calling today. I'm here to invite you to play croquet next Thursday afternoon. It will give you a chance to meet some of the girls properly. It'll be such fun.'

'I can't. I'm already doing something on Thursday.'

Veronica's surprise was evident. 'Oh do tell!'

'I'm having tea with Jasmine's teacher. She invited me this morning.'

'Well cancel. We can find an excuse.'

'I don't want to cancel. I like Miss Helston.'

'Miss Helston? No, no, no!' Veronica shook her head in an exaggerated manner. 'N.O.O.U! Noou!' Her lips formed a small circle as she formed the long drawn out sound. Seeing Evie's puzzlement, she added. 'Not One Of Us.'

Evie resisted the temptation to reply that was what she liked about the teacher.

'She's a nobody. Inconsequential. Her father's just a bank clerk. Not very clubbable.' She patted Evie's arm in that irritating patronising manner she had. 'No background. No breeding. And the mother! She has a North Country accent – imagine! Lived here for years and never managed to lose it. Frightful people. No, darling you must make an excuse. You don't want to get wrapped up with Miss Helston – at least not outside the school premises – and certainly not accepting an invitation to tea!'

'Thank you for the advice, Veronica, but I intend to ignore it. I liked Miss Helston enormously when we met. I think we'll have a lot in common and I'm sure we'll get on famously.' She paused, relishing the look of horror on Veronica's face, then said, 'She's someone I feel I can trust. Not the kind to gossip behind people's backs.' Shaking as she said it, she felt a huge wave of relief. 'If there's nothing else I can do for you, I need to get on.' She rose. 'Thank you again for recommending Mr Ramanathan. I'll be sure to pay him a visit some time.'

SEVEN

Jasmine began talking to Evie after that first trip to school. She appeared to have settled in well and was eager to tell Evie about what they'd done in class each day, and proud to show off her drawings. Each afternoon, Evie made sure she was around when the little girl came home so she could hear her reading.

'I have three friends.' Jasmine said, offering their names proudly. 'But Penny's my best friend.'

'And you like this school better than being with the nuns?'

The child nodded solemnly. 'And I like sleeping here too in this house. It's nice being with you.'

Evie was touched as well as relieved. At least Douglas could have no grounds to complain.

On Thursday afternoon, Evie set off to Miss Helston's house with Jasmine. The teacher lived with her parents on the outskirts of George Town.

When Miss Helston answered the door, she seemed unduly pleased to see Evie. She ushered them inside. Turning to Jasmine, she said, 'Penny's already here. Go through to the garden. I've put some lemonade on a table out there and cake for you both to enjoy.'

Needing no further encouragement Jasmine scampered away into the garden to join her friend.

Mary Helston ushered Evie into a drawing room, with wide-open French windows giving on to the lawn. 'It's cooler in here under the fan and we can keep an eye on the girls. My parents aren't at home. They play bridge on a Thursday.' She paused a moment then said, 'I'm so glad you came. I was worried you might not.'

'Of course I came. Why did you think I wouldn't?'

Miss Helston shrugged. 'People are very cliquey here and I've never been one of the crowd. I thought one or other of them would have tried to poison you against me by now.'

'I prefer to make up my own mind.'

'Good. Because I'm hoping we'll get along.'

'I'm sure we will.'

They sat down to tea with home-baked scones and the conversation turned to Jasmine. Miss Helston confirmed that she had settled in to her new school and was already a popular member of the class. 'Jasmine's bright. A bit shy, but growing in confidence every day. She loves singing and is a fast learner. I'd be a happy woman if all my pupils were as delightful as she is.'

'I'm sure her father will be pleased to hear that.'

'I don't know Mr Barrington, but I did know his late wife slightly.'

'Really?' Perhaps now Evie would get a different perspective on her predecessor.

'I didn't know her well, but you seem different from her. Felicity was part of a set – most of them weren't my cup of tea at all. Talking of tea, can I top you up? Or offer you another scone?'

Evie declined. 'I heard Felicity was very popular.'

Miss Helston raised her eyebrows. 'Was she? I wouldn't know, as I wasn't part of that crowd. But I did hear she hated Penang. Terribly homesick for England. Some of the wives struggle to adapt here. Of course, it's easy for me to say that, having spent most of my life here.' She gave an apologetic smile. 'But it's hard to adjust if your heart is in another country. The climate can be trying for them – not just the heat and the humidity but the fact that it never changes. Always hot every day. Lots of the *mems* miss the seasons. And a few of them struggle to grasp even the few basic Malay phrases you need to get by here.'

It was hard for Evie not to feel daunted by that herself.

Noticing her expression, Miss Helston hurried to add, 'Most of them get used to it in the end. Wait here a moment.'

She hurried out of the room and returned with a book. 'Take this, I have no need of it. I learnt Malay as a toddler from my *amah*. It's a dictionary called *Malay for Mems*. Everything you'll need is in there. Try a few phrases at a time and you'll soon build up your vocabulary. Even the Chinese and Indians know how to speak Malay so it's essential for communicating with your servants. And we Europeans tend to pepper our sentences with Malay words.'

'I have picked up that the *tuan* is the boss and I know I prefer a *pahit* to a *stengah*.'

Miss Helston laughed. 'Nothing like getting your priorities right. You certainly won't get far in Malaya without knowing what your favourite tipple is.'

'Thank you so much, Miss Helston. That little book will be an absolute godsend.'

'And there are many compensations to living in Penang. The beaches are beautiful. And it's cooler up in the hills. People enjoy living standards that are much higher here than they'd have in England. And the flowers and plants are stunning.' She leaned forward. 'Have you been up to Penang Hill?'

Evie shook her head. 'I haven't really been anywhere yet. Just short walks around George Town. I'm finding the heat exhausting.'

'You'll soon acclimatise. And up on the Hill it's much cooler. Maybe we could go together. There's a little train to take you up. The views are stunning. You can see the whole island.'

They arranged to meet the following week. As Evie and a reluctant Jasmine were leaving, Miss Helston said, 'And please call me Mary.'

'I'm Evie.'

They shook hands and Mary's face beamed with pleasure. 'I'm so pleased to have met you, Evie.'

Mary Helston had not exaggerated about the panoramic views from Penang Hill, which turned out not to be a single hill but a whole series of them. When they got off the funicular railway, Evie saw George Town laid out below them. Beyond the town was the narrow stretch of water which separated them from the mainland, and a cluster of small islands. The view across the Straits to the Kedah Peak took Evie's breath away. The crystal waters of the Straits were speckled with fishing boats, and the mainland was draped with the pale silvery green of distant paddy fields. She gazed out across the panorama and decided she had never seen anything so beautiful. All around them they heard the ceaseless susurration of cicadas and the trilling of birds. Even the trees were explosions of colour. Tulip trees – the flames of the forest – framed the views with their vibrant orange flowers like upturned claws. Evie wished she were a painter.

Mary told her the area had been developed by the British colonial settlers, seeking a refuge from the blistering heat of George Town.

In the shade of the tall hardwood trees, they ate the little savouries and slices of cake that Aunty Mimi had prepared for them. Mary pointed out landmarks and told Evie how the funicular railway had only opened fifteen years earlier. Before that, if someone wanted to get up here they had to climb up – unless,

like the wealthy British and Chinese, they could afford to pay
for half a dozen coolies to bring them up in a sedan chair.

They chatted for a while, Evie fascinated to hear about the
history of the settlement. After some time, a lull in the conversation encouraged her to ask the question that had been on her
mind.

'Do you know the Leightons?' she asked, certain of the
answer. 'Veronica and Arthur.'

Mary's lips stretched tightly. 'Everyone knows them.'

A brief silence followed and Evie was thinking perhaps she
shouldn't have raised the subject, when Mary continued. 'May I
be frank?'

'I'd expect nothing less.'

'*He's* all right. In fact he's rather a good egg. But *she's* not
someone I like at all. In fact, I loathe Veronica Leighton with
every fibre of my being.' She brushed an insect off her skirt.

'Well, that's a relief. You're not alone in that. I can't bear her
either.'

Mary frowned. 'If I were you, I'd give her a very wide berth.
She's poisonous.'

'I must admit when I first met her, in London, I was awed
by her, but now, I've realised there's nothing admirable about
her. I've always made it a rule to look for the best in everyone
and I tried to find it in Veronica but I've failed. And I think she
despises me.' Evie gave a rueful sigh. 'But, you see, Arthur
Leighton is a close friend of my husband, so avoiding Veronica
is impossible. She turns up at the house without warning. She
bosses me about. Makes me feel stupid and inadequate.'

'No one can *make* you feel that way, Evie. Not unless you
choose to let them. Don't let her get under your skin.'

'Easy to say.' She looked up at the sky, a spread of blue,
unbroken by clouds. 'Veronica was best friends with Felicity
and takes every opportunity to tell me how fabulous Felicity
was and by implication how decidedly *un*fabulous I am.'

Mary made a little snorting sound. 'Best friends? Hardly. Veronica Leighton collects people then discards them. Felicity Barrington included. Everyone's terrified of Veronica so they all suck up to her. But I doubt anyone actually likes her. And that will have gone for Felicity too.'

Evie told her how she had overheard Veronica and her coterie talking about her in the ladies' powder room at the Penang Club, but omitted the details of what had been said. 'It was humiliating. So personal. Venomous.'

'I told you. She's poison. So what did you do?'

'I came out of the cubicle and made my presence known.'

Mary laughed. 'Good for you. I bet that shut them up and made them squirm.'

'I was shaking like a leaf, but I was jolly well determined not to skulk inside a lavatory cubicle while they performed a character assassination on me. But I wasn't going to stay there and be forced to socialise with any of them. So I went home.' Evie wasn't ready to confess that she'd left alone. It would be too humiliating and personal to admit, even to Mary, that her husband had abandoned her on their wedding day.

'Poor you. At least that got her out of your hair?'

'Not a bit of it. Veronica's far too brazen for that. She turned up at the house the following morning, bold as brass.'

Mary touched her lightly on the arm. 'I'm going to tell you something that I never speak of to anyone. It's very painful, but I want you to know the story so you'll understand just exactly what Veronica Leighton is capable of.'

'You can trust me.'

'I was engaged to be married. His name was Ralph Fletcher and he worked for one of the big rubber companies on an estate on the mainland near Ipoh. We met when he was playing in a cricket match here in Penang. I fell for him immediately – he was handsome, funny, athletic, popular. I was thrilled to bits when he made it clear he was attracted to me too.' Her voice wavered. 'We were going together for about six months when he asked me to marry him. I didn't hesitate.'

Evie listened in silence, conscious of Mary's evident pain.

'For me, the idea of marrying a planter was a dream come true. Ralph worked for one of the biggest rubber companies in the Straits and he was doing well. His job meant he had to move from time to time to a different estate, sometimes to cover for a chap on long leave, sometimes because he was promoted. Ralph was a rising star. He was in shared accommodation – so we agreed to wait until he became assistant manager somewhere and he'd get his own bungalow on an estate. There's always been an expectation by the rubber companies that their male European employees should be bachelors and stay that way for at least two or three years. There are relatively few single European women out here and so the men, when they get their long leave at home, tend to spend their time in Britain hunting for a prospective wife willing to come out here.'

Mary's words put Douglas's offer of marriage into context for Evie.

Mary continued, 'I hated the thought of a long engagement, but we didn't really have a choice. We both agreed he'd give the job priority while he learned everything about rubber and climbed up the ladder.' She touched the third finger of her left hand, evidently conscious of the absence of the ring which must once have been there.

'At the weekends, Ralph played cricket and rugby, so he was over here on the island for matches at least once a month or I'd go over to the mainland and watch him play if it was reasonably close and someone could give me a lift. And we both loved to swim.'

Evie began to wonder where all this was leading, but listened intently.

'Ralph got a big promotion and was moved to a plantation near Kuala Lumpur. We decided we could set the date for the wedding.' She closed her eyes and clenched her hands into tight fists.

'If Veronica Leighton hadn't stepped in and wrecked it all, I'd have been married. Perhaps we'd have started a family. Ralph always said he wanted children. Three or four of them.' Her voice broke. 'Sorry, Evie. Talking about this is still so painful even though it was years ago.'

'I can imagine.' She took Mary's hand and squeezed it gently.

'When Veronica Leighton wants something she has to have it, regardless of whether it belongs to someone else. That goes for men too. She decided she wanted Ralph. He didn't stand a chance. He must have known she had a terrible reputation. Affairs right, left and centre.'

'Does Arthur know about the affairs?'

'He must do. She doesn't exactly keep them secret. But she always goes back to him. Every man she picks up she drops in the end.'

'Is that what happened to Ralph?'

'More or less. Once she'd seduced him and got him eating out of her hand. She was only interested in the chase, then she was ready to move onto her next victim. Apparently, it all started at some "do" at the *istana* of the Sultan of Selangor. I was in blissful ignorance. Ralph's letters had become less frequent but I put it down to the pressure of work and the responsibilities of his new job. Then he came to see me. Completely out of the blue.'

Mary stared ahead into the distance, evidently reliving the scene. 'He turned up at our house. Led me out into the garden.' Her voice wobbled. 'I could see Mum and Dad watching at the window. Mum must have guessed what was coming from Ralph's face when she let him in.'

Mary took a big ragged breath. 'He didn't beat about the bush. He came straight out and told me he had fallen in love with Veronica Leighton, that she was leaving Arthur and once her divorce came through he was going to marry her.' Mary closed her eyes. 'I couldn't believe what I was hearing. It was so out of character for Ralph. He said he was sorry, that he didn't want to hurt me, but his mind was made up.'

Mary thumped her fist down on the bench. 'It was like a bad dream. I pleaded with him – at that point I thought we could find a way through the mess. I thought he'd eventually come to his senses. After all, Veronica was more than ten years older than him. I convinced myself it was just a flirtation that had gone too far. Until he told me that to all intents and purposes they were already man and wife, that they'd...' She gave a little sob. 'You see... he and I... we'd never... We'd decided to wait until we were married.'

Mary bit her lip. Evie put her arms around her.

Pulling away, Mary continued, staring ahead at of her and avoiding Evie's eyes. 'I was completely shattered. My whole world crashed in around me, my entire future destroyed. I couldn't believe that this was the man I had loved more than anyone or anything, sitting there in my garden telling me these horrible things. It still hurts when I think about that day. All these years later.'

'Oh, Mary. It must have been devastating.'

'You can guess what happened next.'

'She went back to Arthur?'

'She never actually left Arthur. As soon as Ralph told her he'd broken off our engagement, she dropped him. All she'd wanted was to take him away from me. To prove that she could. To destroy what we had. That's what she craves. Winning. Vanquishing anyone in her path.'

Mary leaned back against the tree, drawing her knees up close to her, continuing to keep her eyes fixed on the far horizon. 'I'm sure having affairs with good looking men is part of it. But the real pleasure for Veronica Leighton is in wrecking other people's relationships. She never goes near men who are unattached, no matter how good-looking. But, for some unfathomable reason, men never learn.' She let out a long sigh. 'They're so vain. They all think it will be different in their case. Veronica's very good at convincing them of that.'

'Did Ralph try to win you back?'

'He knew better than that. He knew I'd never trust him again.' She wiped her eyes again. 'I think he genuinely was in love with her. He must have been, because he gave it all up. A promising career. A good salary. A life he loved.'

'Did he go back to England?'

'No.'

'So he's still in Malaya?'

She took a gulp of air. 'He killed himself.'

Evie gasped. 'Oh my goodness. How terrible. Oh, Mary, that's dreadful.'

'He hanged himself.' At last, she looked at Evie. 'So now you know exactly why I loathe Veronica Leighton.'

'How on earth did you go on? You must have been crushed.' Evie shook her head, shocked to the core by her new friend's story.

'I thought of leaving Penang. But where would I go? I've never been to England. I suppose I could have gone somewhere else in the Straits Settlement but I'd hate to leave my parents – we've always been a close family and after what happened they were the only reason I kept going. They helped me through it all. No, I prefer to stay here – although there are some places that are too painful for me to go to anymore such as the Penang Swimming Club where Ralph and I spent so many happy times together.'

Mary stared into the middle distance, and Evie could see she was still on the verge of tears. 'It's inevitable that I come across Veronica Leighton sometimes, so when I do, I look straight at her, until she has to look away. It's a battle of wills I will never lose – I fix my eyes on her to remind her of the evil she has done. One day she'll burn in hell for that I hope.'

'Maybe one day you'll meet someone else. Someone worthy of you, Mary.'

'That won't happen. I'm fully reconciled to spinsterhood. I would never trust another man.' She pulled her shoulders back. 'It's not so terrible. I love teaching. I love the kids. There are much worse lives than mine.'

EIGHT

Evie had no idea how long Douglas had been sitting on the side of her bed, watching her. As she became aware of his presence, her first emotion was relief. He'd come back. He hadn't abandoned her. He was still her husband. These thoughts were rapidly followed by the realisation why he was there – that all he wanted of her was to give him a child. No doubt in a few minutes he would begin doing again the thing he'd done to her last time, causing her pain, while at the same time reinforcing her loneliness. There was no point getting upset – she'd signed up for this with her eyes open. Douglas hadn't lied to her; he'd always made it clear exactly where the cards fell. She could have walked away. She'd chosen not to do so.

'What's the time?' she asked.

'Just before eleven. I wasn't sure you were awake.'

'I am now.' She pushed her resentment away and added, 'Are you joining me?'

Douglas said nothing, but quickly removed his silk dressing gown, letting it fall in a heap on the floor. He was naked and she averted her eyes as he got into the bed beside her.

This time, although what he did to her was devoid of any

tenderness and gave her no pleasure, it was mercifully less painful. When he'd finished, he rolled off her and she realised he intended to go back to his bedroom, back to what she thought of as his shrine to Felicity. 'Don't go,' she said, grabbing his arm. 'Stay here with me tonight.'

He grunted, but didn't move from the bed. 'I thought you'd be more comfortable on your own. Cooler.'

'No. I'd like you to stay. Please.' She bit her lip. She ought to feel humiliated having to ask him like that, but she didn't. She felt defiant. Stronger.

They lay in the dark, side-by-side, divided by silence. Evie hated the way – even after what they'd just done, after the shocking intimacy of the act – he closed himself off from her, cloaking himself in a wordless concealment she couldn't penetrate. She swallowed. Her stomach felt hollow.

What did she have to lose? The worst he could do was ignore her. If she didn't try to get through to him now it would be too late. She'd end up in years to come with a husband who came to her bed every couple of weeks, ignoring her the rest of the time.

If she were able to give him the child he wanted, wouldn't that make a difference? But that might mean he wouldn't come to her at all. She'd be no different from Aunty Mimi – a servant – just the *amah* to his children. No. She had to keep trying to break through to him.

Her voice sounded over-loud, echoing hollowly in the darkness of the room. 'Jasmine seems happy at her new school. It's bringing her out of her shell. Her teacher is delighted with her progress.'

A grunt.

'Don't you care?'

'Of course I care.' The mattress shifted as he rolled onto his side. To her relief she realised it was to face her, not turn his back. 'I'm just tired. Do you have any idea how exhausting that

can be for a man? And I'm not as young as I was.' Even in the
darkness she sensed he was smiling.

'Oh,' she said, taken aback. 'I'm sorry.'

'Don't apologise. I'm glad Jasmine is settling in and that you
two are getting along.' He paused, adding in a softer tone. 'She
needs a mother.'

'I've become fond of her. And I hope she's getting used
to me.'

'Why do you do that?'

'Do what?'

'Run yourself down, make yourself smaller?'

'I don't know what you mean.'

'You admit you've become fond of her but only that she is
"getting used to you". Why not say you've become fond of each
other? I'm sure that's true. Aunty Mimi seems to think so.'

'Really?' Evie felt a rush of pleasure at his words.

'Yes. Really. But you haven't answered my question.'

She didn't know how to answer it. It had taken her by
surprise. 'I don't know.' Hesitating, she added, 'It's just a
manner of speaking.' She gave a little forced laugh. 'I suppose I
don't want to count my chickens and all that. Jasmine's just a
child and she might change her feelings... I mean...'

'Don't complicate things. She's fond of you. Leave it at that.'

Evie didn't know how to respond, so decided not to. She
was shocked at what he had said. It had shown a perceptiveness
she hadn't expected from him. He was actually paying attention. Maybe he was right, and she did run herself down. All the
years of her mother doing it for her had caused her to assume
the worst and do it to herself first. And more recently, Veronica
Leighton had worn away what was left of her self-respect like
sandpaper scraping on soft wood.

But at least Douglas was talking to her. Listening to her. They
had actually had a conversation. Eager not to lose the moment,
risk him falling asleep or returning to that other bedroom, Evie

asked him how the past two weeks had been for him. She wanted to ask why he had left without telling her, but decided to avoid saying anything he might perceive as confrontational.

'Just doing my work. You wouldn't be interested.'

'But I would. I'd love to know about what you do.'

'I just plant trees, wait for them to grow, collect the sap from them, turn it into rubber and sell it.'

'Tell me about it.'

'Look, Evie, they're just trees. Go to sleep.'

'No. I'm interested. Tell me what's involved.'

Douglas made a sound that she took to signify exasperation. 'Not a lot to tell. I tap the trees, collect the sap in cans, tip it through strainers and let it coagulate, then turn it into sheets, roll it and squeeze the water out, smoke it for ten days, grade it and sell it.' He rattled it off like someone reading a manual.

'You do all that yourself?'

He laughed. Genuine laughter. No note of irritation this time. 'There are thousands of trees, so no, I don't harvest them all myself. I employ hundreds of coolies to do that.'

'So what do *you* do? Just watch them?'

His tone was sarcastic more than annoyed. 'Yes, sometimes I just watch them working. Make sure they're doing it right.'

'You're laughing at me,' she said.

'I do a lot of other things too.'

'Like what?'

He gave a long sigh, which Evie took to signify resignation, and said, 'It's like the army. I inspect the troops, issue orders, ensure they have the right kit to get the job done, that morale is high, that discipline is maintained, that they're rewarded or punished as appropriate.'

'Were you in the war? I never asked you.'

'Yes. One of the lucky ones.'

She was about to ask him to elaborate, when he went on. 'Of

course I have assistants to do most of the day-to-day management. Like the armed forces, there's a hierarchy. Clear responsibilities. It's not just growing and harvesting – it's also building roads and bridges, filling in disused tin mine shafts – the country's full of them – and clearing the jungle.'

'Gosh. I'd no idea so much was involved. I didn't think there'd be a lot to do since they're just trees. I thought it would have been quite easy. Well easier than crops that you grow every year.'

'Easy?' He sniffed.

'I thought you just left them to grow and then cut them down to get the rubber out.'

He gave a snort of derision. 'Didn't you learn anything at school? Rubber's not like timber. We don't cut the trees down; we tap them.' Evie shifted slightly to edge closer to him. Above them she could make out the dark shape of the motionless ceiling fan.

'When I first came out east, I intended to sell the plantations to one of the big rubber companies, return to England and live on the proceeds. That was what I told my wife. That was why she never forgave me when I didn't.'

'Why did you change your mind?'

She could see the whites of his eyes, pale ghosts in the dark of the room.

'The Depression knocked the bottom out of the rubber market. Prices collapsed. Costs rose. It was like being sucked into quicksand. I thought I was going to lose everything. I couldn't have given the land away. But secondly, and more importantly, I'd fallen in love with rubber.'

'Seriously?' Evie suppressed the desire to laugh. 'That sounds a bit odd.'

'It gets under your skin. Everything about the business.'

Taking advantage of the way they were actually talking at

last, Evie suppressed her nervousness and said, 'I'd love to see the plantation. Will you take me? Show me around.'

She felt him stiffen in the bed beside her. 'The estate's not a place for you.'

'Why ever not?'

'It's called *work*, Evie. I can't just swan about showing you around as if it were a day out. I've far too much to do. Besides, most of the time I'm not even here on the island.' He thought for a moment. 'The manager at Bellavista, Reggie Hyde-Underwood, could show you around I suppose. Benny can drive you up there.'

'I'd prefer it were you.'

'Reggie's more than capable. I'm needed over at Butterworth.'

'Butterworth?'

'My estate on the mainland is near there.'

'I didn't know you had two estates. I thought it was just up in the hills here on the island.'

'I inherited Bellavista, here on Penang, but when a chance came up to buy land on the mainland I took it.'

'I could come over to Butterworth one day. It's only twenty minutes on the ferry to the mainland. Or I could come with you and stay in your bungalow for a while. Just for a few days.' She tried to keep the pleading out of her voice. If he agreed and she liked it there, maybe they could eventually live there together.

'Out of the question.'

'I just want to see the place. Isn't that where you and Felicity lived when you were first married? I might like it. I'm not the same person as her.'

'No, you're not.' He flung back the sheet and got out of the bed, gathered up his discarded dressing gown from the bedroom floor and putting it on, moved to the door.

Evie was open-mouthed at the sudden violence of his reaction.

'Goodnight,' he said and left the room, closing the door behind him.

Left alone in the bed, Evie began to shake, suddenly cold, despite the warmth of the night. She pulled the sheet back over herself and curled into a ball. How had that happened? More to the point, why had it happened? All she had done was express an interest in his life and his work. Just as she'd believed she was beginning to make some progress in getting to know Douglas, in penetrating his indifference. Why had she rushed it, pushed him into a corner? Why hadn't she shown more patience, bided her time until he was ready? Or raised the subject over dinner? But there had been something about the intimacy of being here in bed that had made her bolder. And it had been going well.

She rolled onto her other side and punched the pillow with her fist. It was unfathomable. He was so touchy. One minute he'd seemed amused, interested, relaxed, then he had snapped shut like a clam. It must have been the mention of Felicity. Four years on, he was still clearly grieving for his late wife. Evie cursed her own stupidity. They were back to square one. She'd handled it clumsily. How was she going to regain his trust? She could never replace the beautiful Felicity, but she had to find a way to make him comfortable in her presence, to get him to see her for herself and not as a poor substitute.

NINE

When Evie came down for breakfast the following morning she was surprised to find Douglas still at the table, reading the *Straits Times*. After their argument last night, she'd expected him to have risen early and already left, avoiding an embarrassing encounter.

He looked up as she came in. 'I've given Benny the day off once he's dropped Jasmine at school. We can drive up to the estate at Bellavista and collect her on our way back.'

Evie was astonished. Fearing he might change his mind again if she hesitated, she hurried through her breakfast, put on some sensible flat shoes and they set off.

The road to the rubber estate was rough and winding, slowly climbing up through the hills at the centre of the island. Instead of the sleek vehicle that she had been driven in by Benny, they travelled in a battered old truck, its interior full of clutter and smelling of diesel. They drove past traditional stilted houses, the scent of fruits and spices heavy in the air – lime, mango, coconuts, nutmeg – and chickens and goats wandering free by the roadside.

Despite his evident change of heart since the previous

night, Douglas had resorted to his usual silence. Evie was nervous about speaking up again and risking his anger once more. Eventually, unable to stand the silence any longer, she told herself that he was her husband and she had to focus on the fact that last night he had spoken more to her than ever before. Surely that was something to build upon?

'The island here's very steep,' she said, thinking she must sound fatuous.

'Bellavista's on an escarpment so it's terraced and that means a lot more maintenance and effort. That's why I bought the estate near Butterworth. There was jungle to be cleared there – still is – we've barely touched the reserves – but the land is lower and flatter and easier to work and there's more of it.' His voice sounded relaxed, friendly even.

'You expanded onto the mainland since coming to Penang?'

'Yes. The previous owner wanted to return to England and I believed I'd got it for a good price.' His voice lowered and the enthusiasm was suddenly absent. 'Then the price of rubber collapsed and soon hit rock bottom. The big producers started laying men off right, left and centre. I thought I was going to lose everything. I couldn't have got out even if I'd tried. But I didn't try. I was determined to hang in and make a go of it. I knew things would eventually get better.'

'And have they?'

'Things *are* better. But it's taken years. The reason it's improved is because of the likelihood of war. Every country wants rubber for aircraft and lorries. But we've got a damned quota system now. They're trying to keep the prices high by keeping supply low. It's like trying to run a business with your hands tied behind your back.'

'Who're "they"?'

'All the rubber producers.'

'Why do you have to take notice of them? Aren't they your competitors?'

He gave a dry laugh. 'That's just how it works. You have to join the industry body if you want to sell anything. You have to abide by the rules. And like most rules, they're dreamed up by a committee. If you want to trade, you have to go along with it. Simple as that. But you can't possibly be interested in any of this?'

'I am,' she said. 'I want to know all about it. You obviously work very hard.' She wasn't going to admit that her assumption had been that as plantation owner, all he did was stroll through the ranks of trees, nodding sagely, while once a year, at a mythical harvest time, the workers leapt into action to collect the rubber. On the other hand, if she were truly honest, she had to admit to herself that she hadn't actually thought about it at all.

Douglas had warmed to his subject. 'It's the hardest, but most rewarding work I've done in my life.' His voice was full of rare enthusiasm. 'Each day brings a new challenge. Problems among the coolies, cyclones destroying nursery crops, a tiger prowling around the lines, machinery failures. So many things. In the City, I had to wear a suit and be shut inside an office all day. Here, I'm out on the estate, walking the divisions, talking to the men, solving problems, taking decisions all the time.'

His voice was animated and Evie felt a rush of pleasure. The conversation was cut short when they pulled onto a track between two crumbling brick pillars, one carved with the name Bellavista.

The bungalow was surprisingly grand for such an isolated dwelling in the highlands. Built by Douglas's grandfather in the first half of the last century, it was constructed from brick and half-timbered so it had a Mock Tudor appearance that made it look more appropriate to Surrey than the Tropics. Back in England, Evie had understood the word bungalow to denote a single-storey dwelling, but here in Malaya it appeared to mean any white man's home. Surrounded by a wide veranda on three sides, the interior was cool and dark, the house being overshadowed by tall rubber trees. They went into a central wood-panelled hall, hung with incongruous oil paintings of stags and Scottish highland scenes, as well as an imposing portrait of what must have been Douglas's grandfather. Her own great-grandfather, she wondered? Or was it the other side of Douglas's family? She was about to ask, when a fair-haired, florid-faced man in his early thirties burst into the hallway and pumped Douglas's hand in greeting. 'Good to see you, sir. If I'd known you were coming and bringing a visitor we'd have rolled out the red carpet. Afraid you'll have to take pot luck today.' He glanced at Evie quizzically.

Douglas introduced him as Reggie Hyde-Underwood, the estate manager. When the manager found out Evie was the new Mrs Barrington, he pumped Doug's hand, shook Evie's more gently and called into the interior of the house. A few minutes later, a young woman appeared and was introduced as his wife, Susan. She was small, heavily pregnant and her face had a damp sheen of perspiration.

'So sorry, Mrs Barrington, I had no idea we were expecting company today.' She threw a look of irritation at her husband and wiped a hand over her brow.

'It was a last-minute thing,' said Douglas. 'My wife was keen to see a rubber estate.'

The couple exchanged glances, then Mrs Hyde-Underwood said, 'Well it's an unexpected pleasure.' She turned to Evie. 'I can't remember the last time Mr Barrington came up here.'

A look of annoyance flickered across Douglas's face. 'That's because I know the place is in good hands with Reggie here.'

Hyde-Underwood glanced at his wife again. They appeared to have a means of communicating without speech. He said, 'Why don't I give Mrs Barrington a tour of the estate while you find out what Cook can rustle up for us, darling. After tiffin you can show her round the house and garden while the *tuan* and I talk business.'

This plan appearing to suit all parties, Evie followed her husband and the estate manager. Once they were outside, she turned to Reggie. 'It looks like Mrs Hyde-Underwood is soon to have a baby.'

The man grinned from ear to ear. 'Our first. We're very excited.'

'Congratulations.' She couldn't help noticing a pained look cross her own husband's face.

Douglas let Hyde-Underwood do all the talking as he led them around the estate, pointing out the 'lines' where the coolies lived – long rows of corrugated-iron roofed single-storey dwellings. The roof slopes jutted forward beyond the buildings to provide a shelter and there were a few women, sitting on mats in the shade, preparing vegetables or tending to children.

'Bellavista is quite small,' said Hyde-Underwood. 'Less than a thousand acres. We have two hundred tappers working here. Mostly Tamils.' Beyond the lines was a large open area of bare flat ground. 'We do the muster here each morning at five-thirty,'.

'The muster?'

'Roll-call. If they're not present they don't get paid for that day. The muster's also the time we do any briefings, and allocate duties and work details.'

Evie glanced at Douglas. 'Five-thirty's awfully early.'

Reggie Hyde-Underwood answered. 'We have to tap the rubber in the coolest part of the day. The latex runs better then. It coagulates when the temperature gets too hot and seals up the cut. We break in the middle of the day for tiffin and a bit of a snooze and start again with other tasks in the afternoon until five. When I show you, you'll understand.'

He plunged into the ranks of rubber trees and they followed him. The trees were tall and straight and planted even distances

apart. The branches, instead of spreading outwards from the
trunk, grew upwards towards the light, the leaves small and glossy.
The mottled silvery bark was spotted with patches of lichen with
the areas of the trunks where tapping had taken place darker and
nobbled in texture. It was a gloomy place, the trees creating a dark
arched canopy over their heads, like the crypt of a cathedral.

Taking a hooked knife, Hyde-Underwood cut a diagonal slit
in the bark of a nearby tree. 'When it's cooler, the latex is more
liquid and runs down the slit into the collecting cup.' He
glanced at his watch. 'See here. It's already a bit too sticky and
it's sealing over where I made the cut. But if you do it before
dawn, the rubber runs freely.'

He led them through the groves of regimented trees.
Ignoring these and the little tin cups attached to their trunks, he
strode on until they reached a small group of workers, moving
along the rows, collecting the latex from the cups. The smell of
rubber caught the back of Evie's throat. It was everywhere. She
realised she had even smelled it in the Hyde-Underwoods'
bungalow.

Swinging sharply away, Reggie guided them towards a large
tin-roofed building. 'We process the rubber in here, ready to
send to the godowns in George Town and onwards to the
buyer.'

'Godowns?'

'Warehouses.'

Evie was beginning to get bored by all the explanations. She
wanted to show an interest in the business – particularly as it
was the one thing she had discovered so far that Douglas was
genuinely passionate about. But it was irritating that he was
leaving all the explaining to Hyde-Underwood. Evie would
have preferred it if Douglas had taken her on the tour himself.
After all he did own the estate – maybe he didn't want to put
his manager's nose out of joint. She told herself that was cred-

itable of him and tried to feign interest in what Hyde-Underwood was saying.

Inside the building was a series of large metal holding tanks.
'The latex from each division is weighed so we can monitor the
yield constantly. It's all about how much we can squeeze out of
every tree. Conditions were hard for several years. Some
planters have switched into spices or palm oil. But things are
looking up.' He stroked his chin. 'And talk of the possibility of
war in Europe is helping push the prices up further.'

Evie shuddered. 'I hope it doesn't come to that.'

'Of course.' Hyde-Underwood's already ruddy-cheeked
face grew redder. 'I mean it's the talk that pushes demand up.
Crikey! I don't want there to be an actual war. That's unthinkable. Not so soon after the last one.'

'There'll be no war. Don't alarm Mrs Barrington.' Douglas's
tone was hard, impatient.

'I'm sorry.' Hyde-Underwood looked abashed. He was
clearly nervous in Doug's presence – or perhaps it was the fact
that their unannounced visit had taken him by surprise.

'It's all right,' said Evie. 'I've just come out from England
and it's all anybody talks about back there.'

Hyde-Underwood went on to show her the holding tanks,
explaining how they measured and recorded the density. He
showed her the sheets of latex passing through rollers,
squeezing out the water, before being hung up to dry for days in
the adjacent smoke house. 'We grade each sheet into categories.
The boss here expects it all to be Grade One.' He winked at
Evie. 'Most of the rubber is sold in London by auction before it's
even processed. There'd be a terrific stink if the consignment
they've paid for turns out to be below par.' He paused, looking
again at Douglas, and Evie sensed he was constantly expecting
to be corrected, but Douglas remained impassive.

'During the Depression when the market slumped, many
estates, including this one, had to lay off a lot of crew. There was

quite an exodus of European planters from the Straits.' He looked again at Douglas. 'I was one of the lucky ones. But it was tough for all of us.'

'Enough of that.' Douglas spoke at last. 'The Depression's over.'

The blood rushed into Hyde-Underwood's cheeks again. He turned away and spoke rapidly in another language to one of the workers.

'Is that Malay he's speaking?' Evie asked Douglas.

'Tamil. He speaks both. And some Chinese.'

'Goodness. That's impressive. Do you?'

'Of course. It's one of the requirements of the job. All European planters need to pick up Tamil within eighteen months. And if they want to progress they learn Malay too.'

They walked on, Hyde-Underwood with them again.

'Were all these trees planted by your grandfather?' Evie asked Douglas, sweeping her hands towards the hillside which was covered with terraces of rubber trees as far as she could see.

Instead of answering, he jerked his head to Hyde-Underwood, who responded. 'The trees only last thirty years. Then we have to replant. It's a big part of the job – raising seedlings, cultivating, planting saplings.' He explained how the old trees were poisoned and cleared away to make room for new ones.

The last stop on the tour was to see workers chopping away undergrowth beneath a row of trees, clearing the ground and revealing the drainage ditch that ran down the space between the rows. The men were hacking through the vegetation with large curved-bladed knives which Hyde-Underwood told her were called *perangs*.

Hyde-Underwood suggested they head back to the bungalow for tiffin, when a cry went up from one of the men. '*Ular!*' The whole group began shouting '*Ular*'.

Hyde-Underwood moved forward but Douglas grabbed

Evie's arm and held her back as most of the men scattered. 'It's a snake,' he said.

Evie watched in horror as the largest snake she had ever seen emerged from the thicket and raced over the ground towards Hyde-Underwood. But one of the workers was ready for it, slashing at it with his *perang* in a frenzied attack.

Douglas shouted something in Tamil or Malay and the man stepped away leaving the snake in pieces on the ground.

'Probably dead with the first blow, but they like to hack them apart. Their idea of sport I suppose.'

Evie felt sick. She looked at her husband. 'Was it dangerous?'

'Not usually to humans. It's a python. Must be ten feet long.'

Her stomach churned, adrenaline coursing through her, but tinged with disgust at the savage nature of the worker's attack. 'A python? Don't they crush you to death?'

'They grab their victims in their coils then swallow them whole.'

Evie shuddered. 'What sort of victim?'

'Maybe a deer or a rat,' said Hyde-Underwood. 'They have no venom. It looks like this one had just had his tiffin.' He picked up a stick and poked at the side of the dead snake, rolling it over to reveal a large protuberance in the middle. 'A small deer I expect.'

Evie turned away. 'How horrible. Would the creature have been alive when it was swallowed?' She imagined the animal one minute prowling through the undergrowth and the next being swallowed into the dark interior of a python's belly.

'Doubt it would have known it was happening. They're fast, pythons. They attack by ambush and before the prey knows it, they've been wrapped in the coils and death's pretty instant. Heart failure, a zoologist chap once told me.' He shouted something to the men and they kicked the carcass away and turned back to the task of clearing.

'Why did they kill it then?'

'Provides a few minute's entertainment. Breaks up the day.' He shrugged. 'Better get back to the *Mem*. She'll not be happy if I return you late for tiffin.'

TEN

Back at the bungalow, the four ate lunch quickly. The Hyde-Underwoods gave no further hint of surprise at Douglas's sudden nuptials. Mrs Hyde-Underwood directed polite enquiries to Evie, who kept her responses minimal, wary of giving too much of herself away. In turn, Evie established that the Hyde-Underwoods were both from Yorkshire and Reggie had been in Malaya for eight years, with his wife joining him after three.

When the silent Malay servant had cleared the plates away, Douglas and Reggie left for the estate office to talk business and Mrs Hyde-Underwood led Evie outside.

'I'm preventing you having your nap.' Evie apologised.

'I rarely sleep in the afternoons these days.' The woman patted her stomach. 'This little creature makes sure of that. Always very boisterous in the afternoon. I usually sit in the shade on the veranda and try to read or sew. And it's nice to have company. We're very isolated up here and these days we don't often get into town.'

They walked to the rear of the bungalow, into a kitchen garden with vegetables growing in orderly rows.

'The *kebun* is glad my pregnancy is forcing me to take things easier. He's been less than happy to have the *mem* muscling in on his territory.'

Evie realised she was referring to the gardener and made a mental note to add the word *kebun* to her small but growing Malay vocabulary.

'I've always loved gardening and there's so little to occupy one up here, but all the bending over is a bit of a problem!' She flashed a smile at Evie. 'Do you enjoy gardening, Mrs Barrington?'

'I'm ashamed to say I've never actually tried it. I grew up in London in one of those big town houses in a square with only a communal garden and more recently...' Her voice trailed away. She didn't want to reveal her former employment was as a lady's companion. 'I lived in a house with a gardener who resented anyone helping. And I wouldn't have known where to start anyway.'

'Exactly. Just as I said. They're all the same these garden-ers.' Susan Hyde-Underwood wiped a hand across her brow, pushing her light brown hair away from her eyes. 'And I must admit gardening in the tropical heat isn't exactly fun.' She placed her hands on her stomach. 'In fact expecting a baby in this heat is also a bit of a trial.'

'But it's so much cooler up here than in George Town.'

Mrs Hyde-Underwood shuddered. 'I don't know how you stand it down there. We English roses wilt in all the humidity. Bad enough up here. The mozzies are terrible. Not to mention the stink bugs and flying ants. After a dry spell the floors are covered in their corpses. And you can end up with stink bugs floating about in your drinks. Revolting.' Her mouth twitched at the corners and Evie could tell she would have liked to be back in England.

Turning to look at Evie, she said, 'But I think you should

know I've told Reggie that if your husband should ever ask him to work over at Batu Lembah, I'm on the next ship home.'

'Batu Lembah?'

'The other Barrington estate. Near Butterworth. I presumed you would be living there.'

'No. At the moment I'm staying in the house in George Town. My husband joins us most weekends.' She swallowed, hoping the exaggeration wasn't evident.

'Right. Of course. I'd forgotten. The late Mrs Barrington didn't like Batu Lembah and preferred to be in town. I suppose all her friends were in George Town.' Susan Hyde-Underwood looked wistful. 'It can be very lonely being an estate manager's wife. All very well for the men. They have their work and the company that offers. But for us girls, most of the time you're the only white woman for miles, stuck on your own, day in, day out. If I didn't have my garden I'd probably have gone mad. But if Mr Barrington ever insisted we were to leave Bellavista and move over to the mainland, well, I'm sorry to say this to you, but we will definitely be heading straight back to England.'

'What makes you think he'd ask you to do that?'

'Nothing really. But this house was his family's home. And I suppose now I know about you... I have to admit, Mrs Barrington... I'm wondering whether he's brought you up here to look around with a view to you both moving here.'

'He hasn't said anything like that to me. Quite the contrary. I've been nagging him to show me around the estate – I was surprised this morning when he finally agreed. I suppose he thought it would be easier than bringing me over to Butterworth.' As she sought to reassure the woman, Evie admitted to herself that actually living up here might be preferable to George Town. At least it was cooler and far from the club and Veronica Leighton.

'I'm sorry. I just wanted to be straight with you. It's probably me being particularly anxious because of the baby being imminent.' She told Evie when it was due, adding, 'I've waited so long for a child. I'd begun to despair of it ever happening. I'd started to think it was the wretched climate here. And just as I'd given up hope, bingo! I realised it had happened at last. As you can imagine, we're both over the moon. Reggie's convinced it's a boy and a Malayan lady in one of the *kampungs* took one look at me and said I was having a boy. I'm increasingly sure of it myself, but I'll be happy either way.'

'And your husband?'

'Him too. He doesn't really mind.'

They had left the vegetable garden and reached a small lawn, surrounded by a profusion of flowering shrubs.

'I tried growing roses, but they didn't take well. Better to work with the plants that are indigenous. You must come and look at my orchids. My pride and joy.'

Beyond the lawn, they entered a maze of gravelled pathways weaving between the bending trunks and spiky fronds of palm trees and the big glossy leaves of bananas. The air was peaty, rich with the smell of soil and rotting vegetation. Above their heads, the area was draped with netting, presumably to keep the birds at bay. A collection of terracotta pots, containing smaller plants, hung from the branches of trees. In between the different shades of green were bright splashes of orchids, all shapes and colours – delicate peach, buttery yellows, vibrant cyclamen-like pinks and the softest mauves. In the background, Evie could hear the gentle tinkle of falling water and saw a small pond encircled with rocks.

'Your husband's grandfather apparently had a passion for orchids too. But things were rather neglected by Mr Barrington's uncle. I've a long way to go, but I'm working hard at restoring the area to its former glory and I'm building quite a collection.'

'They're exquisite,' said Evie. 'I can see why orchids have become a passion for you.'

Mrs Hyde-Underwood nodded. 'I just hope there'll be time for them once the baby's arrived.'

'I'm sure the... the kedan is it?'

'*Kebun*.'

'I'm sure the *kebun* will be only too happy to take over.'

The woman sniffed. 'I doubt it. Vegetables and mowing lawns are more his thing. But we'll see.'

Evie had the sense that behind her smiles, Mrs Hyde-Underwood was not as happy as she'd first appeared. Clearly devoted to her husband, there was nonetheless a sadness about her. Might living in Malaya mean Evie herself would eventually feel the same?

As if sensing Evie's thoughts, Mrs Hyde-Underwood assumed a cheery voice. 'Let's go and have a cold drink on the veranda. It's shady round the other side.' Without waiting for Evie to reply, she headed back towards the bungalow.

Sipping homemade lemonade, Evie suggested they move to first name terms, then asked her hostess if she had known Felicity.

'Not well. But we did meet once. Over at Batu Lembah. It was when I first came out here. Mr Barrington had just bought the estate there, and hired my husband from Dunlop's to take over at Bellavista as manager.'

'What was she like?' The question spilled out – but Susan Hyde-Underwood seemed to take it in her stride.

'Not very friendly, actually. She didn't have a lot to say and I was probably nervous myself and wanting to make a good impression meeting Reggie's boss's wife. That can't have helped.'

'I only met Felicity myself on one occasion – when I was fifteen. I do remember she was beautiful.'

Susan nodded. 'Frail and delicate. A bit like one of my

orchids. Fine for a flower but I'm not so sure it's such a great quality in a woman.'

Evie wanted to ask how Douglas had behaved towards Felicity, but that would be going too far.

But Susan evidently had no such compunctions herself. 'I couldn't understand how they'd come to be married, actually. She struck me as whiny and miserable. And a bit haughty too. As the wife of the *tuan,* one's expected to be a hostess and to put on a good show. She didn't strike me as being interested in any of that. She barely exchanged two words with me. It was frightfully strained. I couldn't wait to get away.' She beamed at Evie. 'Not like you at all.'

They sipped their lemonades. Evie liked the sour tang of it, the sharpness cutting through the initial sweetness. 'Did you make this yourself?'

'Heavens no.' Susan grimaced. 'I'm completely useless in the kitchen. We're lucky with Sulung. He's a terrific cook. How's your "cookie"?'

Evie rolled her eyes. 'He's very good. But the housekeeper, who I think is his wife, is a bit scary. She's a Chinese lady – Aunty Mimi. I've no idea whose aunty she is.'

'All the Chinese ladies seem to be called aunty.'

'But I've no complaints regarding her work.'

Susan arched her back and slipped her hands behind her. 'Don't mind me. It's getting harder to get comfortable, lugging all this bulk about.' She paused a moment. 'I must say, Evie, I think you're awfully brave.'

'What do you mean?' For a moment Evie thought she was talking about coping with Aunty Mimi.

'Coming out here to such a different life. And taking on someone else's child into the bargain.'

'Oh that.' Evie felt deflated. Was this yet another person who was secretly thinking she must have been desperate to have agreed to marry Douglas? 'Jasmine is a lovely girl. I'm already very fond of her.'

'But you can't have known Mr Barrington well. He hasn't left the Straits in years.'

Evie looked at the woman, expecting to see the contempt she had seen in the eyes of Veronica and the ladies gathered in the powder room at the Penang Club, but instead she saw only kind concern and interest.

'We had met a long time ago and more recently we... we corresponded.' She knew it was something of an exaggeration to describe two curt letters as corresponding, but she didn't want to admit the truth.

'How romantic!' Susan clasped her hands together. 'Mr Barrington is frightfully handsome, if you don't mind my saying. I do hope everything works out well for you both. He must have been dreadfully lonely. Of course he'd never admit that. Men never do.' She flapped a hand at a flying insect. 'I'm so fortunate with Reggie. We've been sweethearts since childhood. I knew we'd eventually marry. I suppose I also knew we'd end up out here – or somewhere in the colonies. All his school and university friends are planters or in the colonial service.'

The conversation was cut short when Hyde-Underwood and Douglas stepped onto the veranda.

'Time we were going,' said Douglas. Evie noticed he had a restless look about him, as if something was preying on his mind.

After saying their goodbyes, Evie sat in the front seat of the old Ford beside her husband. He let out the clutch and guided the car down the steep hill.

'Thank you for taking me up here. I enjoyed meeting the Hyde-Underwoods, and seeing how the estate worked was so interesting.' She was pleased she'd remembered to call it an estate and not a plantation.

Douglas said nothing. His face looked tense. She wanted to

ask him what the matter was but something made her hesitate. They drove in silence for several minutes, passing ranks of rubber trees on either side of the road and stretching up the hillside beyond. There was a palpable tension in the car. Doug suddenly jerked the steering wheel, and the car left the road and bounced along in between the trees on a rough track. She glanced at him, puzzled, but he remained silent, his jaw set hard and his expression inscrutable. Where were they going? Evie wanted to ask but her mouth wouldn't form the words.

After a few minutes, when the main road behind was no longer visible, they pulled into a small clearing. A single-storey wooden hut stood there, a collection of metal buckets and implements stacked neatly outside, under the overhanging roof.

Douglas halted the truck and jerked on the handbrake. Evie looked to him for an explanation but he was already out of the car and moving round to her side. Pulling the door open he reached in and grabbed her hand, drawing her out of the vehicle.

They went towards the hut, Douglas moving so quickly Evie had to scurry to keep up with him as he still had hold of her hand. He pushed the door open and they went inside. There was an unglazed window in the rear of the small room, but it was close to the rows of rubber trees which blocked most of the daylight so the room was dim and gloomy. Evie had no time to look around what seemed to be an empty space, before he was upon her, pushing her roughly against the wooden wall, pressing his body against hers, as one hand pinned her there and he fumbled at the front of his shorts with the other. She felt his mouth on hers. It was the first time he had kissed her, and she wasn't prepared for it, or for the hunger with which he did it. She found herself responding to him, excited, feeling her legs weaken under her as her mouth returned his kiss. He was gasping, pulling at her dress – pushing his hands up underneath the skirt.

'Wait,' she said, her own voice barely audible. She lifted her frock over her head and immediately felt his mouth on her neck as his hands moved behind her to release her brassiere. His mouth closed around her left nipple and she gave a little cry of pain then he pulled down her pants and entered her quickly. Evie cried out again. He wanted her. He desired her. There was nothing of husbandly duty about this. It was raw desire. She gave herself up to the moment, oblivious to the hard wood of the wall, rough against the bare skin of her back.

Douglas drew her downwards, and she found herself lying on the bare concrete floor as they moved in unprecedented harmony. She entwined her fingers with his. Instinctively, she wrapped her legs around his back, feeling the rough linen of his shorts – he was still fully clothed while she was completely naked. All Evie knew was that she didn't want him to stop. She drew him closer, deeper, wanting it to go on forever, to be doing what they were doing, to feel the sensation she was feeling, the ripples of pleasure running through her body. Looking up she sought his eyes.

Douglas drew back his head and looked down at her. 'Give me a son, Evie. I want a son.' With a cry he was done and rolled off her onto the floor. They lay side-by-side panting while Evie tried to gather her thoughts.

It was not what she'd hoped to hear. What happened next was not what she'd hoped would happen either. Douglas got up, adjusted the front of his shorts, ran his hand through his hair and moved to the doorway. 'You'd better get dressed. I'll wait in the car.'

Stunned, Evie lay on the concrete floor for several moments, staring at the closed door of the hut. She gathered up her clothes and put them on, trying to suppress the tears that were already rising. Whether they were tears of sorrow or anger she was unsure – probably a mixture of both. She bit her lip. Don't let him see you cry, Evie. Don't give him the satisfaction of knowing he's hurt you. She brushed the cobwebs off her dress and opened the door.

He started the engine as soon as she emerged from the hut. She climbed in beside him, trying to read his face, but he was staring straight ahead. Speaking in his usual clipped tone, he said, 'I apologise. That was wrong of me.'

Her heart lightened a little, waiting for him to explain why he'd left her lying on the floor in disarray.

'I don't know what came over me. I think it was Susan Hyde-Underwood so evidently pregnant. Seeing Reggie preening with pride that's he's soon to be a father. Hearing him say they're both certain it's going to be a boy. I kept thinking that could be you. My son inside you. I just had to act. It was a kind of madness. I'm sorry.'

'I liked it.' Her voice was barely a whisper. 'I liked what you did. I liked the way it was so sudden and unplanned.' She gave a little sob, her efforts at control failing her. 'For a moment I thought you might actually care for me.' She swallowed, fighting back the tears and realised she was shaking. 'But I was wrong about that, wasn't I? You weren't excited by *me*. You were excited by the thought of having a son. How do you imagine that makes me feel?' As she said the words, she wanted to retract them, wishing she hadn't told him how much he'd hurt her.

Beside her, Douglas continued to keep his eyes fixed on the road ahead, his jaw set in a hard line, his mouth tightly closed. He drove fast. Too fast, she thought, as they swung round the sharp bends, descending the mountain. Evie clung onto the door handle, trying to control her shaking, and struggling to hold back the incipient tears.

'I told you, this is a business relationship. I was very clear to you, Evie, my intentions towards you have never been romantic. I've apologised. It was the heat of the moment. It shouldn't have happened. It was inappropriate. Undignified. And it won't happen again. Not like that.'

He took one hand off the wheel and scrabbled in the glove compartment, producing a pack of cigarettes. Evie drew away when his hand accidentally brushed against her knees as he reached to close the catch before expertly lighting his cigarette. The rest of the journey passed in complete silence.

When they reached George Town he pulled up outside the house. 'I'll pick up Jasmine from school and drop her back here on my way to the ferry. Goodbye.'

Without waiting for an answer, he drove away, leaving her standing alone on the pavement.

ELEVEN

After Douglas had left, Evie stumbled through the rest of the day in a daze. Eating supper, seeing Jasmine to bed that night, sitting by her bedside listening to her reading, kissing the child goodnight – she did all this as if in a trance, her body acting automatically, while her brain was elsewhere. When Jasmine was asleep, Evie went downstairs. The house was silent and there was no sign of Benny. She went into the garden from where she could see Aunty Mimi silhouetted at the kitchen window washing the supper dishes.

The garden was dark, with a sea breeze stirring the leaves, helping cool her down and keeping the mosquitoes at bay. Evie breathed in the sweet heady scent of frangipani, and the soft, subtle pine smell of the casuarina trees. Moths circled in the light spilling from the drawing room onto the lawn.

From further down the street, cockerels were crowing, even though it was only late evening. She'd asked Mary why they did that – often breaking into full crowing in the middle of the night. Mary told her it was because the poor birds were kept in cramped bamboo cages, starved of food, in readiness for cock fighting. Evie shivered at the thought. So much about this place was alien to her, almost savage, far removed from everything and everyone she had ever known.

Utter loneliness swept over her, depressing her spirits, making her want to run upstairs, pack her suitcase and take the next ship back to Britain. She would never fit in. Never feel welcome or comfortable in this godforsaken country.

Evie's fragile self-confidence had been bolstered by her blossoming friendship with Mary Helston, and today she had enjoyed the company of Susan Hyde-Underwood. But Mary was occupied at the school each day and Susan, up in her highland eyrie, would soon be occupied herself with a small baby. That same self-confidence had been utterly shattered by the treatment Douglas had meted out to her.

She couldn't help running over and over what had taken place in that wooden hut amid the rubber trees, torturing herself with the way her husband had slipped from what had appeared to be a consuming passion into a cold distance and undisguised self-disgust. He had made his feelings clear. Evie was just a body to him. A vessel to carry his child. Douglas had no interest in her as a person, as a woman, as a wife. He saw her only as the means to an end.

It was an obsession, this need for a son, eating away at him. Evie felt sick to the pit of her stomach at the thought that the passion and excitement she'd believed she had engendered in him had originated with the swollen belly of Mrs Hyde-Underwood. Even standing here alone in the dark of the garden, her face burned with shame and embarrassment.

Hearing a footstep behind her, she spun round to find Arthur Leighton standing in the shadows, watching her.

'I'm sorry, Evie. Did I scare you, creeping up on you like that?'

Evie breathed in relief when she saw he was alone. Facing Veronica tonight would have been unbearable.

'Not at all. I'd fallen into a brown study, lost to the world.' Evie forced a smile to her face. 'Let me get you a drink, Arthur. It's delightful to see you. You've saved me from myself.'

'Feeling melancholic, eh?' He nodded. 'And yes, I'd love a drink. Seems you and I are both spouseless this evening. I'll have a *stengah*, please.'

They walked into the drawing room and she mixed his whisky and soda, and a gin and bitters for herself. 'Benny's off today,' she said. 'I hope I've got the proportions right.'

He took a sip. 'Perfect.'

Wandering back out to the lawn, they moved, without comment, to sit on the wooden garden chairs in the half-light from the drawing room.

'Where is your wife tonight?' She couldn't bring herself to say Veronica's name.

'Playing bridge. I was over in Butterworth and after a quick supper at the club I thought I'd drop by and see how you were getting along.'

Evie tried to inject some enthusiasm into her voice. 'I'm beginning to settle in.'

'Doug not around?'

'He left this afternoon for Batu Lembah. We went up to Bellavista today so he could show me how a rubber estate works.'

Even in the half-light she could tell Arthur was frowning. 'He doesn't plan for you to move to Batu Lembah with him?'

Again she tried to sound cheerful but her voice was hollow. 'With Jasmine at school here, it's more practical for us to be in George Town.'

'I see.'

'I was very taken with Bellavista though. So much cooler up there.'

'Maybe you should suggest moving up there. It is his family home after all.'

'I'm pretty sure the Hyde-Underwoods would never agree to switch to Batu Lembah. Susan Hyde-Underwood lost no time making that clear to me today. I think she finds the humidity a trial. Doug can't afford to lose her husband and it's pretty clear that's what would happen if he was asked to relocate. And apparently there are a lot of challenges at Batu Lembah that Doug wants to tackle himself. Lots of jungle to cut down and re-plant.'

'Is that what he told you?'

Evie felt herself reddening. 'Well not in so many words. The main reason is Jasmine.'

'I see.'

'Look, Arthur, is there something you're not telling me?'

'No! Not at all.' He spoke quickly. 'I was just wondering though, why he didn't leave Jasmine at the convent school in Butterworth as a day-girl. It's less than twenty miles from Batu Lembah. You could all have been under one roof.'

Evie didn't know what to say. Why was she feeling the need to defend her husband's inexplicable behaviour? She took a gulp of gin too quickly and began to cough.

Arthur leaned forward. 'Forgive me, Evie. I shouldn't be speculating. I'm sure Doug has his reasons – or rather you both do – it's none of my concern... Only...'

'Only what?'

His voice was low. 'It's just that I've become very fond of you and I can see you're unhappy and that pains me.'

'Unhappy? I can't imagine why you should say that.' She tried to sound indignant, but knew she just sounded lost.

Arthur leaned towards her again and this time took her hand. 'I wish I could help you. I wish...' He looked at her and she saw something different in his eyes.

She turned away, uncertain where this was leading and suddenly nervous.

Perhaps Arthur was similarly affected, as he dropped her hand, got up, and said, 'Remember, Evie, I'm always here for you. Any time you're in trouble I'll be here. Please, don't hesitate to call me.' Then he turned and went inside. On the threshold he looked back to say, 'Thanks for the scotch. I needed that.' A few moments later, she heard the front door close behind him.

Swigging down the remains of her gin, she got up, went inside and mixed herself another one. She craved oblivion tonight. A need to wash away the memory of Douglas and herself on the floor of that hut. A need to wipe out the knowledge that he didn't care a fig for her and she knew he never would.

It was only as she was climbing into bed, her head whirling from the copious amount of gin she had drunk, that Evie thought again of Arthur Leighton and remembered the surprise she had felt when he took her hand. The look in his eyes at that moment had scared her. It had been so intense. If she didn't know that Arthur was devoted to Veronica and if Douglas hadn't made her only too aware how unattractive she herself was, she would have sworn that he had looked at her with longing. Pushing the thought from her head as being preposterous and surely a product of her inebriation, Evie curled into a tight ball and fell immediately asleep.

It was just over three weeks before Evie saw Douglas again. She was glad of the long time, as it had dulled the pain a little.

Instead of arriving at the weekend he turned up mid-week and told her that the following evening they would be entertaining guests for dinner.

Evie's heart sank at the prospect. Would the party include any of those awful people she'd met at the club on her wedding day? She didn't think she could survive a whole evening with the likes of them. 'Who have you invited?' she asked, curtly.

'One of the inspectors for Guthrie's and Reggie Hyde-Underwood – his wife is in the hospital over in Butterworth. They've just had a boy.' His mouth twitched.

'That's wonderful news. What have they called him?'

Douglas looked away. 'You'll have to ask him that.'

This reminder of what had happened between them made Evie nervous. She didn't know how to behave around Douglas any more. Not that she ever had.

'Oh and the Leightons.'

She'd expected as much. 'The man from Guthrie's what's his name? And what *is* Guthrie's?'

'Rogers. Clifford Rogers. His wife will be with him. Don't know her name.'

'And Guthrie's?'

'One of the big rubber companies.'

'But I thought you said you own your estates directly.'

Douglas sighed pointedly. 'Don't ask so many damned questions, Evie. Everyone knows everyone here. As the chief inspector for all Guthries' estates throughout the Straits, Rogers knows the lie of the land. I want to talk to him. It's called doing business. I expect you to keep his wife happy while we do that.'

Evie swallowed, feeling battered. 'And the Leightons? Why will they be here?'

Douglas's eyes narrowed. 'Because Arthur is my friend.' The sub-text was that it was not her place to ask why. But as an evident afterthought, he added, 'And because I suspect Clifford Rogers will want to pick Arthur's brains about the political situation. As I said, it's called "Doing Business". Your part in that is merely to keep his wife entertained. Surely that's something even *you* can manage?'

It was like a slap in the face. She burned with suppressed

rage. What right did he have to treat her this way? As if he resented her for his own bad behaviour.

That night, after a silent supper, during which Evie felt too intimidated and angry to attempt conversation, she told Douglas she was going to bed early and went straight up to her bedroom. She sat in bed reading, finding it hard to concentrate on the words on the page as her head whirled with all the things she wished she'd said to him but had been too afraid to utter.

About five minutes after she'd turned off the light and turned over onto her side to sleep, she heard the bedroom door open and Douglas's footsteps crossing the wooden floor. Furious, Evie pulled the sheet up over her ears and called out. 'Go away! I don't want to be with you.'

She heard the sharp intake of breath. 'Damn it, Evie. You're my wife. We talked about all this. I ask little enough of you.'

He reached a hand out to pull back the sheet on his side of her bed.

'I meant what I said. I won't be treated this way.'

'What are you talking about?'

'The way you behaved to me on the way back from Bellavista. The way you talked to me this evening. I won't have it.' She could feel herself shaking.

'I told you I was sorry. I shouldn't have done what I did.'

'And I told you it wasn't what you did, but what you said afterwards. How do you imagine it made me feel? To be told that it was the sight of another woman's pregnancy that made you want to have relations with me. You made me feel like... I'm just a ... just ... a brood mare on a farm. I am *not* an animal. I am a human being.' Tears of rage ran down her cheeks and she hauled herself up into a sitting position.

Douglas said nothing. He turned away from her and walked out of the room closing the door quietly behind him.

When he was gone, Evie hugged her arms around her. She couldn't believe she'd just said all that. But it had to be said. If he decided to call a stop to their joke of a marriage, so be it. He could send her back to England. She'd be glad if he did. Anything would be better than feeling the way he made her feel. She thumped the pillow with her fist. How had she ever harboured the delusion that they could make this marriage work?

TWELVE

The following morning, Evie went to speak to Aunty Mimi about the menu for the dinner. It was immediately apparent that the Chinese woman already knew of Douglas's plans and had decided with the cook what the menu would be. Evie left the house, feeling superfluous.

As tonight could well prove to be her swan song in Penang and in her brief marriage, she was determined to look her best. There wasn't time to follow Veronica's advice about using her local Indian tailor, so she decided to go to a dress shop that Mary Helston had mentioned, which sold ready-made garments.

She took the road along the coast to get there – about a fifteen-minute walk. Evie loved seeing the marine traffic on the busy strait that divided the island from Butterworth. Sampans with strange pleated sails were dotted about on the azure blue water, interspersed with the curved straw roofs of junks. Beyond, plumes of smoke rose from steamer funnels – the ferry to Butterworth and an array of small tramp steamers carrying goods around the Straits Settlements and Sumatra and on towards Java, Ceylon and India.

Lines of palm trees alternated with telegraph poles and bright bursts of orange from the flame-of-the-forest trees along Marine Drive. Bicycles, rickshaws, motorcars and small vans wove between each other and occasional ox carts with their palm-leaf canopies protecting sugar cane, coconuts, or vegetables, stacked in precarious towering piles. In between the various vehicles, people hurried along, on foot and on bicycles or in rickshaws, many wearing wide straw coolie hats tied under their chins. Evie noticed a Malay woman standing beside a water pump, trying to scrub the dirt off her small wriggling children. A grassy sward separated the road from the beach, where the golden sands were lapped by the whispering waves of a calm blue sea.

As she walked, absorbing the chaotic yet beautiful scene, an image of the Hampshire village where she had lived with Mrs Shipley-Thomas formed in her mind, dull and tame in comparison to the East. But at least when she was back in England she'd be free of the humiliation that was her constant diet here in Penang.

She turned off the waterfront, into a wide street lined with stores and shop-houses. Colourful posters advertised Tiger Balm and Tiger Beer as well as cigarette brands, and there were numerous signs in Chinese characters. The dress shop was a large establishment with windows that gave onto the street. Evie peered through the glass and was reassured to see a wide selection of European day and evening dresses. She went inside.

Later that evening, as she sat in front of the looking glass adjusting her hair and applying a light touch of lipstick, Evie wondered if her new dress was suitable. It had been an extravagant purchase, but Douglas had been as good as his word and paid her a generous allowance. And soon he would have nothing more to pay for, once she was on a ship heading back to England.

Evie wasn't the type to want revenge, to try to get as generous a financial settlement as possible. She was used to making her own way in the world and had no wish to profit from this sad and sorry episode in her life. Better to move ahead. Find a new path. It wasn't as if she hadn't tried – she'd met Douglas more than halfway. But she wasn't going to lie down and let him trample over her like a doormat.

She was nervous about the evening ahead. Apart from dealing with her husband's quixotic behaviour, she was worried about seeing Arthur Leighton again, after their conversation in the garden. Had she imagined the look in his eyes? Suppressing the thought, she convinced herself it was her imagination. After the coldness of Douglas, it was only natural that she should seize upon any form of kindness in a man and misinterpret it. Besides, odd as it might seem, Arthur was a married man and had to be in love with Veronica. Why else would he forgive her marital infidelities – if, as Evie was sure, Mary Helston had told her the truth?

Standing up, Evie surveyed her image in the cheval mirror, smoothing the silk fabric over her hips. She liked what she saw. Maybe she wasn't a sylph, like Veronica Leighton – she was more statuesque – but she did look elegant. The bias-cut of the gown was flattering, hugging her body as it curved, before flaring softly below the hips, and the pale mauve shade perfectly complemented her green eyes. Not bad, she told herself. Not bad at all.

Feeling more confident, she went downstairs. Douglas was at the open French windows of the drawing room, a *stengah* in his hand. He glanced at her as she came in but said nothing.

Benny was on duty dispensing drinks and handed her a gin and bitters. Evie took the drink, feeling awkward again. How was it possible that in just thirty seconds her confidence could

plummet thanks to the moodiness of the man she'd married?
She sat down. If there was going to be a conversation, he could
damn well initiate it. Otherwise, she'd sit here in silence.

A moment later, Reggie Hyde-Underwood was shown in by
Aunty Mimi, full of delight about his new son, who, he told
Evie, was to be called Stanford after the child's maternal grandfather. Evie glanced sideways at Douglas, but he had turned
away and was adjusting his cuff links.

'And your wife?'

'Splendid, thank you, Mrs Barrington. The old girl came
through it all with flying colours. They say she and the baby
should be able to come home after a few more days' rest.'

Douglas had moved over to the sideboard to instruct Benny,
needlessly, on Reggie's drink. It was clear to Evie that his
manager's evident joy in fatherhood was riling him. To her
relief, the Leightons and the Rogers all arrived at the same time
and the party, served with their 'stiffeners', moved into the
garden, where scented torches were burning to stave off the
mosquitos. The ghostly glow lit up the flowering trees and gave
an ethereal magic to the scene. It had been raining earlier in the
evening and the air was full of the soft perfume of rain-
drenched flowers and the citron smell from the torches.

Evie's battered confidence returned when she saw the
admiring look in Arthur Leighton's eyes.

'Evie, you look stunning tonight,' he said, before being
called over by Douglas to join the group of men. She felt a small
thrill of pleasure at the compliment, starved as she was of any
appreciation by her husband.

'Nice frock.' Veronica looked Evie's gown up and down.
'Didn't I see it in the window of that shop just off Marine
Drive?' She shook her head and wagged a finger. 'You didn't
take my advice and go to see Mr Ramanathan?'

'I'm afraid I was pushed for time.'

'Silly girl! He could have run you up something in a couple

of hours. Then there'd be no risk of running into someone else wearing the same thing.' Her tone dripped disdain. 'You do know that shop is always at least a season behind? Mr Ramanathan could have made you a gown straight out of the latest issue of *Vogue* magazine. The man's a genius.' She raised an eyebrow. 'Aren't I right, Dorothy?' Mrs Rogers was slightly behind her. 'I'm telling our hostess about the skills of Mr Ramanathan.'

Ignoring Veronica, Dorothy Rogers moved forward to greet Evie and introduce herself. Mrs Rogers gave her a warm smile. Evie was determined not to let Veronica Leighton get under her skin any more. Her decision to leave Douglas and Penang bolstered her confidence. Yes, despite her nerves, she was going to enjoy herself this evening. It was a pity neither Susan Hyde-Underwood nor Mary Helston were here, but she would make sure to be as charming as possible to Dorothy Rogers, whom she sensed was less than enamoured of Veronica.

Mrs Rogers managed the unusual feat of appearing both approachable and formidable – the kind of woman who commanded respect, didn't suffer fools, but was perennially cheerful. In her late fifties, she had a matronly figure of the sort Evie's father used to describe as well-upholstered. Her eyes twinkled with what looked like wry amusement – probably at Veronica's expense. Evie liked her at once.

'Do you and Mr Rogers live here in George Town?'

'I wish we did. No, we're down in KL.'

'KL?'

Veronica's laugh trilled. 'Really, Evie! Kuala Lumpur.' She nudged Mrs Rogers conspiratorially. 'Evie's been here for weeks but you'd never know it.' As an afterthought, she added, 'Dear girl that she is,' and beamed at Evie like a proud parent. 'I've tried to take her under my wing, but she will insist on doing things her own way.'

Bristling, Evie tried not to let her feelings show. 'What's KL like, Mrs Rogers?'

'Do call me Dorothy.' The woman gave her a friendly smile. 'I love it. Not as nice as Penang though. I loved living here in George Town after the war years. Clifford worked his way up the ladder with Guthrie's and we brought up five children in Malaya. I'm glad all that constant moving from estate to estate is behind us. Our next move will be back to England when he retires.' She glanced towards her husband who was deep in conversation with Arthur Leighton. 'In the meantime, Clifford still does a lot of travelling including to London once a year to meet with the board and deliver his annual report.' She squeezed Evie's arm. 'And I go with him, which is such fun as three of our children are living back there. All married. I do love to see the grandchildren.'

Evidently bored by the turn the conversation had taken, Veronica moved to join the men who were gathered in a group. She linked arms with Douglas and Reggie Hyde-Underwood and in a teasing tone said, 'So, Dougie, when are you and Evie going to follow in Reggie's footsteps and pop out a son and heir to the Barrington fortune?'

Evie wanted to slap her. Douglas had a face like thunder and Reggie chuckled in embarrassment.

'Really, Veronica, you are a card. Have you no shame!' Dorothy Rogers tried to make light of the moment. 'Poor Doug doesn't want to be quizzed like that! They've only been married five minutes.'

Evie glanced at Arthur and saw he was frowning, cringing even. Veronica appeared unperturbed.

Past caring what Veronica thought of her, Evie said, 'I could ask the same of you and Arthur, Veronica.'

They were saved from hearing Veronica's response by the announcement from Aunty Mimi that dinner was served. The party moved into the dining room. Veronica threw Evie a look that would have frozen boiling water.

Evie had arranged the seating, placing herself between Arthur Leighton and Clifford Rogers, opposite Reggie, who was between the two other women. Douglas sat at the head of the table, with Clifford on one side of him and Veronica on the other. Evie hadn't consulted her husband about the seating plan but had assumed he would want to talk to the Guthrie's boss. Placing Veronica on his other side was a deliberate ploy. She knew Douglas would have preferred one of the other men, but it was now likely the conversation would be between Douglas, Reggie and Clifford, cutting Veronica off and leaving Evie free to talk to Arthur and Dorothy Rogers at the other end of the table. She felt slightly ashamed that she had been so calculating, but it was no more than Veronica deserved.

To her relief, the dinner passed without incident and Evie took quiet satisfaction in the sour expression on Veronica's face as her repeated attempts to steer the talk in another direction failed, against the constant discussion of rubber price movements, fluctuating market demand and the restrictive quotas imposed by the rubber industry association.

At the other end of the table, the conversation between herself, Dorothy, and Arthur was about music, books, and life in Penang. Dorothy Rogers urged Evie to visit the swimming club and the picture house and the beaches at nearby Batu Ferringhi.

Since the Rogers were travelling up to northern Kedah on the mainland the following morning, the party broke up early, and Evie stood beside Douglas on the doorstep as their guests left. Veronica took Arthur's arm and draped it around herself as if to signal ownership. She gave Evie a sour look, before replacing it with a joyless smile. 'Well *done*, darling!' she said to Evie in a voice that oozed insincerity, clearly not pleased at the way she'd been marooned at the other end of the table.

When they'd gone, Evie felt relieved that she'd got through this test without mishap. She'd not tripped or stumbled and had spilled no gravy – a triumph in itself! 'I think that went well. Don't you?'

Douglas grunted.

'I hope you got what you wanted from it.'

Another grunt.

'Well, I'm going to turn in.' She moved towards the staircase.

He reached for her wrist and drew her back. 'Let's have another drink first.'

Evie hesitated, before deciding there was no point in delaying the inevitable. Better to get on with the news that she was leaving him and going back to England. She followed Doug into the drawing room and watched while he poured a brandy for himself, shaking her head when he offered her a drink.

Perched on the edge of the sofa, she watched as he slugged down the brandy and poured himself another, then took off his jacket and flung it carelessly on a chair.

He stood, leaning against the wall, looking at her, but saying nothing. His tie was undone, his dark hair unruly, where he had pushed his hands through it. She felt an unexpected rush of desire for him, seeing him there like that, slightly dishevelled, his forehead damp with sweat. But it was no good. They couldn't go on like this, ricocheting back and forth while she had no idea what he was thinking or how he was going to behave. Never knowing whether he was angry with her. Even tonight, she had no idea whether she'd said or done something wrong during the evening. Was he about to tell her he wanted to end their marriage?

She decided she had to take the initiative. Taking a gulp of air, she said, 'This isn't working out. It's time we admitted it. I can see you're not happy about tonight. And I can't handle your swings of mood any more. I'm going to go back to England. If you'll pay for my trip home that will be the end of the matter. I don't want anything more from you.' She raised her palms towards him, wishing she'd accepted the offered drink. Convinced he wasn't even going to dignify her with a reply, she started to get up. She might as well go to bed and try to tackle him again in the morning. At least he'd be sober then.

But Douglas put his glass down and moved towards her, pulling her into his arms. Evie was stunned. Her head against him, she felt his chest rising and falling as he breathed. His hands went to her hair, his fingers threading through it as he tilted her head back and bent to kiss her.

Evie jerked away. 'What are you doing?'

'What do you think I'm doing?' His voice was slightly slurred as he reached for her again. 'Let's go upstairs.'

'Don't you listen at all?' She stepped backwards.

He moved towards her, drawing her into his arms again. His eyes locked on hers and she felt herself weakening.

'I couldn't wait for them to go. For us to be alone.' His hands were everywhere, running over the silk of her dress, following the curve of her hips. He made a little groaning noise, and kissed her. The kiss was hungry, as if he were intent on devouring her, consuming her.

Evie wanted to kiss him back, but a little voice inside told her not to. How many times would they go down this road? She had to be sure he wasn't playing games with her again. 'Stop!'

'Please, Evie.'

She pulled away from him and went to sit on the sofa, drawing her knees up in front of her protectively. 'I can't keep doing this. I feel like a tennis ball, batted and slammed around the court and never knowing which side of the net I'm on.'

Douglas crouched in front of her, his hands against the sides of her legs. His eyes fixed on her, his expression anguished. 'I'm sorry. I always seem to mess things up between us. Give me another chance, Evie.'

She breathed out a long deep sigh. 'I'm not sure I can. I don't think I can bear being treated like this anymore.'

'Treated like what?'

She looked at him in irritation. 'One minute you act as if you want me, then the next you can hardly bear to be in the same room. You never speak to me. You never tell me how you feel. You're abrupt to the point of rudeness. You disappear. You're cold. You've made it clear you feel no desire for me – only for the idea of having a child. I can't do it any longer.'

He went to sit beside her, his body slumped forward.

Evie wondered whether to get up and go up to bed, leaving him there. She tried to make herself feel contempt for him, but instead she felt only sadness.

Eventually he spoke. 'I know. I realise how hard you've tried. You were wonderful tonight. And you look wonderful too.' His fists were clenched on his knees, his knuckles white. 'Look, Evie, it's complicated. Please give me time. I know it will get better. *I'll* get better. Please don't leave me.'

His face was a picture of remorse, his breathing ragged. She hesitated, uncertain whether to believe him. He took her in his arms again and began to kiss her. This time it was slow, tentative, and she found herself responding. Drawing her up to her feet, he took her by the hand and led her up the stairs.

When Evie woke the next morning, to her surprise Douglas was still lying beside her. To her even greater surprise he was looking at her. She felt her cheeks redden, remembering what had happened the night before, what they had done, how she had felt.

'I was watching you sleeping,' he said, stroking a lock of hair away from her forehead. He bent his head and brushed her mouth with his. She felt the roughness of his unshaved chin against her skin. He was smiling. 'Thank you, for staying. Thank you for last night. For everything.'

A warm glow spread through her. Was this how it was going to be from now on? Had she at last broken through his coldness? Might he even be beginning to care for her? She was about to reach for his hand, to put her own hands on his body, to redis-cover the pleasures of the night before, when he swung his legs off the bed and bounced onto his feet.

'I have to go.'

She pulled herself up to a sitting position. 'Now? Can't you stay a while?'

'Duty calls. I'll see you in a couple of weeks.'

'Where are you going?' As he put on his dressing gown, Evie noticed the familiar look of irritation cross his face and she felt a hollowness in her stomach.

'I have a rubber estate to run.' His voice was cold. It was as if a switch had flipped inside him. Without a further glance towards her, he was gone.

THIRTEEN

Once Jasmine had left for school, Evie, determined not to dwell on what had happened between herself and Douglas, decided she needed to get away from the house. Remembering what Dorothy Rogers had said the previous evening about the pleasures of the Penang Swimming Club, she asked Benny to drive her there. An act of bravery, when inside all she wanted to do was climb back into bed and hide away from the world.

When they arrived at Tanjung Bungah, to the north of George Town on the coast, Evie was glad she'd come. Telling Benny to return for her in a few hours, she went into the rambling late-Victorian clubhouse to change into her swimsuit, delighted that the place was relatively quiet. Steering clear of a group of women occupying deckchairs on the lawn near the long blue pool, she went to the far end and slipped down the metal ladder into the salt water.

Evie had learned to swim on family holidays in Cornwall and the South of France. Her father, a strong swimmer, had taught her, and she had happy memories of those halcyon childhood days, before her mother embarked on her infidelities and her father had fallen prey to the pressures that led to him embezzling money and taking his own life.

Being in the water imbued Evie with energy. She powered up and down the pool, telling herself just one more length, but unable to stop. Eventually, exhausted but revitalised, she clambered out. Reluctant to face the heat, she sat at the pool-side in a shaded area, her feet dangling in the water. The pool ran parallel to the beach and the azure sea looked tempting. She could see the familiar outline of Kedah Peak from here.

The memory of the manner in which Douglas had left her that morning, his curtness after the tenderness of the night before, made her feel low again. But she was bigger than this. Bigger and stronger than those shallow people at the Penang Club, bigger and stronger than her volatile husband. Evie had a choice – either let Douglas wear her down and make her feel small and insignificant, or rise above his selfishness and find her own path. She wasn't going to let him drag her down; she wasn't going to let herself be a hapless victim.

Sitting here, legs dangling in the cool water, she made up her mind. It may not be the life she'd wanted, but it was so much better than her humdrum existence in Hampshire. Better even than being married to a man like Douglas back in Surrey, left at home while he commuted to the city. So what, if he was away from home for two weeks at a time? At least she wasn't standing in a suburban kitchen instructing the cook, bored out of her mind, watching the rain through steamed-up windows.

She breathed in the sea air, felt the heat of the sun on her arms, splashed her legs about and gazed at the beautiful view. Penang was a paradise island, known as The Pearl of the Orient. How could she complain or feel sorry for herself when she had all this to look at and enjoy? She was beginning to acclimatise to the heat. Her role as Jasmine's stepmother gave her purpose – the trust between her and the little girl was growing every day. She had a good friendship with Mary Helston, and in

Dorothy Rogers and Susan Hyde-Underwood she'd met two other women whose company she enjoyed.

And Douglas? Yes, he had reverted to type this morning when she'd asked where he was going, but last night and first thing this morning he had been everything she'd hoped for. But didn't that make it even harder? Having experienced another Douglas, it was so dispiriting to find the old one was still very much present.

Don't dwell on the bad, she told herself. Focus only on the good and it will grow. He had shown desire for her – maybe it was the idea of her as mother of his children – but nonetheless he had desired her. That was enough for now. She would do whatever she could to give him a son. She would never deny her bed to him again. And that meant she had to stop daydreaming about Arthur Leighton. He was a married man, out of bounds and she told herself not to confuse his kindness and interest in her with attraction.

Besides, it wouldn't be only Douglas who would be pleased by her having a child – the thought of a baby of her own, flesh of her flesh, a little part of her, seemed the most desirable thing in the world to Evie, as she sat here in the sunshine.

Moving away from the pool-side, she walked across to the retaining wall separating the pool from the sea. The swimming club was raised above a rocky outcrop and Evie clambered down to sit on a smooth rock, cooled by the spray from the sea as it hit the rocks. Behind her was a terrace, vibrant with flowers – scarlet salvias and orange and pink zinnias and below, beyond the rocks, a long sandy beach. The air here was fresher than in the city, cooled by the sea breezes. Gazing towards Kedah Peak, she felt as if she was inside an Impressionist painting.

Lost in her reverie, she didn't notice Arthur Leighton until he was scrambling over the rocks towards her. He was wearing swimming trunks and had evidently been in the sea. His hair was wet and his body tanned. Without his usual baggy clothing,

Arthur Leighton had a lean sun-tanned body and long muscular legs. Evie had expected him to be scrawny, unfit, but instead Arthur had an athletic build.

He bent down, crouching in front of her. A drip of water from his hair landed on her leg but the shiver that ran through her was less from this than from the unexpected pleasure of seeing him.

'I didn't expect to find you here, Evie. What a pleasant surprise.'

'After what Dorothy said last night, I decided I'd have to come and see if this place was as delightful as she said it was.'

'And?'

'It's magical. Truly beautiful. I had a delicious swim in the pool.'

'It's a good time to come. It's always quiet in the middle of the week. Most people turn up at weekends and in the late afternoon or early evening to cool off and enjoy a sundowner while watching the sunset.'

'Shouldn't you be at work?'

'Don't give me away, Evie. I often come to the beach when I get a quiet spell. It can be insufferable cooped up inside all day when I'm here in George Town. And I get no chance to swim when I'm on the road.'

He looked at her. That same intense look that made Evie feel exposed, slightly uncomfortable, as if he wanted something from her but couldn't bring himself to ask.

'Come with me. You need to swim in the sea.' He took hold of her hand and pulled her to her feet. Self-conscious in only a swimsuit, she draped her towel around herself like a sarong, and followed him over the hot sand.

They walked for a couple of hundred yards, keeping to the shade as the sand was burning hot in the full sun, following the curve of the coast, away from the Swimming Club. The shore was beautiful: the pale sand interspersed by smooth dark rocks like whales emerging from the deep. Palm trees, bent by the wind, leaned over and offered protective shade, as did casuarinas with their distinctive pine smell. In the distance she could see the brilliant primary colours of a small Chinese temple.

Arthur looked at her. 'You love it here, don't you? I can tell.'

'It would be impossible not to.'

'Malaya's a beautiful country, with kind and gentle people and the sun shining every day.'

'You must be very good at your job to have been sent here.'

'I was lucky. I put the time in. And maybe I got it because I didn't particularly want it. They're like that. Reluctant to give you something if you really want it. I actually would have preferred to stay in Nairobi.'

They sat down on the sand, close to the water's edge where the beach narrowed and the casuarina trees still cast some shade.

'Why? Is Africa as beautiful as this?'

'It's different. When I was there, the only way I could get to the beach was if I managed to grab a few days leave in Mombasa. East Africa's hot but it's a dry heat. None of the suffocating humidity we have here. Penang is beautiful but it's tame in comparison. There's nowhere like Africa – sometimes on the savannah you feel you've been transported to prehistoric times. All these strange wild animals moving across empty scorched plains – wildebeests, elephants, rhinos. It wouldn't be hard to imagine dinosaurs lumbering along among them. Miles and miles of grasslands. Acacia trees. Tribesmen and herders doing what they've been doing for thousands of years. Africa makes one feel small and insignificant, a tiny speck in the vastness of the continent. It has a savage beauty like nowhere else. Very different from all this.' He gestured with his hand.

'So why did you leave?'

'It was time to move on. It was impossible to refuse the job here.'

She wanted to ask him what Veronica had thought about it, whether she had instigated the move as it was hard to imagine her liking those vast primordial plains, but Evie didn't want to spoil the moment by allowing mention of Arthur's wife.

They said nothing for a while, until Arthur, staring ahead at the distant horizon, broke the silence. 'I was young, ambitious, but lacking connections. Just pond life lurking in the depths of the Foreign Service, watching while less capable men were promoted ahead of me just because they went to the right school.' He leaned back, resting on his elbows. 'I had to work harder, be cleverer than my colleagues, but no matter how much effort I put in, I always came up short. I became the indispensable right-hand man to a succession of very average, barely competent officers, all of whom patted me on the head like a dog, and then promoted the idiot in the next desk. There's something bred into public school boys – and the Etonians in particular – a deep-rooted sense of entitlement. I, on the other hand, had to sweat blood and scrabble for the leftovers.' He sighed. 'Sorry, Evie, I must sound cynical and bitter. Anyway, I kept my head down and tried to do the job so well that they wouldn't be able to ignore me. But it never worked. I was always that reliable and indispensable fellow who wasn't "one of us".'

'But you went to Oxford, didn't you?'

'Yes. But that merely gets you in the door of the Colonial Office – it's the old school tie that gets you advancement. Doug is "one of us". But the funny thing is, he never gave a damn. He's always accepted people for what they deliver not where they come from. That's probably why we get along.'

'But Doug wasn't in the Foreign Service.'

'Good lord, can you imagine? Doug and diplomacy are not a marriage made in heaven.'

Pushing away the thought that neither were Doug and Evie, she continued to listen, rapt.

'To cap it all, as a single man, I wasn't exactly first choice in the pile either. The foreign service like to get good value for money and see wives as unpaid employees. They even assess them and grade them, as well as their husbands.'

'Really? Why?'

'So much of the job revolves around entertaining people, and the wife is key to the success of that. The service want their men to choose wives who are perfect hostesses and conversationalists, as able to chat to an irascible Turk with poor English, as an African tribal chief or the Sultan of Selangor.'

'And Veronica can do all that?' Evie hoped her voice didn't give away her disbelief.

'Veronica is a consummate actress. For her, it's a role and she steps out onto the stage and plays it. She has a limitless supply of small talk, always knows the best places for visitors to go, the right people for them to meet. And she knows better than anyone how to flirt and flatter and is bloody good at organising things.'

Evie reflected that, apart from bossing her about and telling her where to buy her clothes, Veronica had never thought it necessary to do any of this in her case.

Stretching her legs out in front of her alongside Arthur's longer ones, Evie churned up the sand with her heels. 'If you don't mind my saying it, Arthur, you two seem an unlikely couple. But I suppose they say opposites attract.'

He gave a dry laugh. 'We're more alike than you think. At heart we're both selfish ambitious people.'

'*You* don't strike me that way at all. Not selfish. And there's nothing wrong with being ambitious.'

'Maybe there is when it causes you to do things you're ashamed of.'

She looked at him, puzzled, but he looked away, avoiding her eyes, jumped to his feet and reached out to pull her up. 'Enough talk. It's time we had that swim, then I must get back to the office.'

They ran together into the warm sea. Evie struck out, cutting her way through the blue water. Arthur was right. It was even nicer being in the sea than in the swimming pool. And there wasn't a soul around. He swam after her, catching her up. 'You're a strong swimmer,' he said. 'It's hard keeping up with you.'

Arthur was laughing, the sun lighting up his tanned, wet face. He looked different without his glasses. Less serious. Until today she'd never seen him as sporty, but now she was all too aware of his strong athletic build. Suddenly she didn't want him to go back to his office. She wanted him to stay here all afternoon with her, talking to her under the casuarina trees, telling her about Africa.

But what was she thinking? They were both married. The problems with Douglas were clouding her judgement. Evie started to swim back to the shore, but Arthur grabbed her arm and pulled her towards him. For one insane moment Evie thought he was going to kiss her. He pulled her closer. Their eyes met and she held her breath, but he moved away.

'Sorry,' he said, speaking too quickly. 'I thought there was a shoal of jellyfish. But it was only seaweed.'

She looked back at him, angry with herself for misreading the signs. Then, without knowing how it happened, she was in his arms and he was kissing her, as she had never been kissed before. They were almost out of their depth and Evie held tight to him, wrapping her legs around him to stay afloat as they kissed, frantically, passionately.

Arthur moved his head back and broke away. 'That was unforgivable of me. I'm so sorry, Evie. I promise you it won't happen again.'

She reached for him, holding onto his arms as they drifted further out of depth. 'It wasn't just you. It was me too. And I want it to happen again.'

He closed his eyes. 'You're my best friend's wife. I had no business starting what can never be finished.'

Evie was swamped by a wave and he took her hand and they struggled back out of the sea. Collapsed onto their towels, she was confused, no longer sure of herself. Sure only that no matter how wrong that kiss had been it had felt more right than anything she'd done since coming to Penang.

She had to break the silence, the terrible silence that was surrounding them and smothering them. As if to mirror that, a rogue cloud crossed in front of the sun, darkening the beach.

'Douglas doesn't love me,' she said. 'He only married me to have a child. I have threatened more than once to go back to England. Every time, he promises to change, but he never does. He's cold towards me. I sometimes think I disgust him.'

Arthur jerked his head round. 'That's impossible. How could you disgust him? You're the loveliest person I've ever met.' He put his head in his hands and bent forward. 'Oh, Evie. If only things could be different. In another life. I know I could make you happy.' He took a sharp intake of breath. 'I think I'm in love with you and have been since the ship. I think about you all the time. I'm going crazy.'

Evie stared at him, astonished, but at the same time her heart lifted inside her, her breath jerky and uneven as she took in what he was saying.

'But you have to know, I can never do anything about it. It would be wrong. I could never betray Doug. And I couldn't do it to Veronica.'

Evie felt a rush of anger and indignation. She had never expected to have been put in this position, to be sitting half-naked on a deserted beach, with her husband's best friend, after the most passionate kiss she had ever experienced. Adultery went against everything she believed in, but how could she possibly deny the reality of how she was now certain she felt about Arthur?

'You can't do it to *Veronica*? What about what she's done to you?'

Arthur stared at her, visibly shocked. 'You know? About her affairs? How?'

'I've become friends with Mary Helston.'

He squeezed his eyes shut and his lips formed a hard line. 'Look, Evie, I know how it looks. You probably think like wife, like husband. But I promise you, until today, I've never laid a hand on another woman. I was out of bounds. It won't happen again.'

A rush of bitterness hit her. She'd never had to grapple so closely with so many emotions and felt ill-equipped to do so.

'I feel a fool. A stupid fool. You won't tell Veronica, or Douglas?'

'Why would I do that?' He looked horrified.

'I have no idea.' She felt tears rising. 'I have absolutely no idea about anything anymore.'

'It's all my fault. I should never have let it happen. I could tell you were unhappy. It made me want you all the more. To show you how I feel, but I've made everything worse for you.' He took her hand in his. 'Evie, I am in love with you, but I can't ever leave Veronica. I had no right to behave in the caddish way I've done today. Please forgive me.'

'I don't understand. If you don't love her why did you marry her in the first place? Why are you so bound to Veronica?'

'Because she's an extremely vulnerable woman. And because I owe her my career.'

Misery wrapped around Evie like a thick fog. Any capacity for joy had been sucked out of her. 'What do you mean? I don't understand.'

Arthur sighed, reaching behind him for his trousers. He pulled out a cigarette from a crumpled packet and lit it. 'Veronica can't help herself where men are concerned. Dr Freud would have a field day with her.'

Evie nodded, feeling hollowed out. How had this magical time turned so quickly into abject misery?

'She's more vulnerable than she appears. Dark moods descend on her without warning, like a blanket, blotting everything else out. She suffers from a kind of existential despair.'

Evie felt scornful. Surely, he didn't expect her to believe that?

Arthur continued to avoid her gaze, his voice quiet. 'When she gets one of these black spells, she shuts herself away and will see no one.' He lifted his eyes to meet hers at last. 'That's what was wrong on the ship. She wasn't seasick at all. I'm sorry.' He gathered up a handful of sand and let it trickle through his fingers. 'Veronica's a complex woman. Far more than I realised when we first met. Yes, she's shallow, rude, snobbish, all those things that I know you see in her. I cringe myself at her behaviour. But the Veronica I first knew was very different.'

'How?' Evie stared at him, feeling angry.

'For a start, even though she acts as if she were to the manner born, she comes from a humble background.'

Evie's eyebrows shot upwards and she couldn't help a disbelieving snort.

'Her father was a Russian merchant seaman and her mother was a half-caste – the grandmother was a Kikuyu woman who was the common-law wife of an Irish settler. She was shunned by her tribe when she went with him. He died of drink in a Nairobi slum and Veronica's mother became a prostitute. So not exactly out of the top drawer. Veronica has always gone to great pains to keep her family tree a closely guarded secret.'

Evie was dumbfounded. 'No one knows?'

Arthur's lips stretched into a mirthless smile. 'Doug knows. He doesn't care a jot about such things. But no one else has a clue. No one in Malaya has ever guessed that she has a less than perfect pedigree.' He laughed drily. 'In fact, they probably think she married beneath her station with me.'

Evie said nothing. Everything she had understood to be truth was imploding.

'What I'm about to tell you no one else knows. Not even Doug. Can I trust you?'

She nodded, feeling miserable.

'One of her mother's clients...' Arthur turned his head away from her. 'One of them interfered with Veronica when she was only twelve. Look, Evie, I'm not going to beat about the bush – he raped her.'

Evie was shocked. It was hard to comprehend something so horrible happening to Veronica. 'That's horrible – she was a child!'

'She ran away and was found on the streets and brought up in an orphanage by missionaries. Despite what happened – or maybe because of it –Veronica has a core of steel. She worked hard and eventually talked her way into a job in the typing pool in the District Commissioner's Office.

'She was a good worker and already knew how to project herself in a positive light – she charmed the DC.' Arthur paused, brushing sand off his leg as he gazed out to sea. 'You have to understand something else about Veronica, what happened to her made her promiscuous. It's a compulsion with her, as though she believes her only value lies in her body and men's appreciation of it. She'll sleep with a man she despises, because knowing she's desired makes her feel better about herself.' He looked up at Evie. 'But the truth is she despises *herself.*'

'That's awful. But why did you marry her?' Evie could hear the resentment in her own voice.

He scratched the back of his palm, evidently nervous telling her all this.

'We were friendly. But no more so than with anyone else in the office. Then one evening, after everyone had gone home, I found her crying. She thought she was alone in the office.' He stopped, frowning. 'Or maybe she wanted me to think she'd thought she was alone.' He gave a dry laugh.

'It all came out. She'd been having an affair with the DC. A man in his fifties. Married with children of course. And she'd just found out she was pregnant.'

Evie gasped. 'Had she told her boss?'

'At that point, no. I urged her to tell him the next day.'

He got up and started pacing back and forth in front of Evie as he spoke. 'The next morning the DC summoned me into his office. Veronica was already in there. He was angry that Veronica had confided in me about what had happened. Otherwise he'd probably have dismissed her and hushed the whole affair up. He said if I ever told anyone what had actually happened between them my career would be over.'

Evie opened her mouth.

'But if I were willing to marry Veronica, he'd recommend me for promotion to a dream posting, as long as it was far away from Kenya.'

'He said all that? Just like that? What did Veronica say?'

'Nothing. She sat there in silence, looking at the floor.'

'So what did *you* say?'

'I told the DC I wanted to stay in Africa. I wanted to be promoted on my own merit.'

'And?'

'He told me if it was based on merit I'd have been promoted two years earlier and unless I married Veronica and got her out of his way I'd continue to be overlooked. Not an ounce of remorse. He bumbled on about how he'd been caught on a sticky wicket and that things had gone further than he'd intended. The fact that he was Veronica's boss and married with five children had no apparent bearing on the matter. The unspoken implication was that Veronica was a latter-day Jezebel.'

Evie bit her tongue – her saying that it was a pretty accurate description was unlikely to be well received.

'I was stunned. I asked Veronica what she wanted to do. She said she wanted to marry me. Begged me to agree. So I did.' He sighed. 'I'm not proud of it. I was young, foolish and in need of a wife. She was alone, pregnant and facing the certain loss of her job.'

'I don't know what to say.'

Arthur was still pacing up and down. 'We left Nairobi a few weeks later, as man and wife. Veronica set out to make my career advancement her personal mission. She became the perfect administrator's wife, playing the part so well she's forgotten where fiction and reality meet. I'm the only one who's ever seen the other side of her: the frightened little girl whose childhood was stolen by a drunk in a filthy Nairobi shanty. I'm the only one who ever witnesses her when the black cloud descends and she's filled with self-loathing to the point where she sometimes wants to take her own life.'

'She's tried to kill herself?'

'Threatened to.' He shook his head. 'But I've no doubt she'd do it if it came to it.'

'What about the pregnancy?'

His face clouded. 'Veronica lost the baby. And she can't have any more. She saw that as a punishment. Another reason to hate herself.'

Evie felt a twinge of guilt, remembering how she had put Veronica on the spot the night before about her and Arthur being childless.

Arthur reached for his towel. 'So that's why I can't leave her. Why I can't abandon her. It would be placing a sentence of death upon her.' He rubbed the towel through his hair. 'But it's not only that. We're both selfish and ambitious and, if I'm honest, I'm more so than she is. The truth is I recognised in Veronica something in myself – a burning desire to better herself. I don't love her. I never have. She doesn't love me either. We don't even sleep together. That's another thing. Despite her promiscuity, Veronica doesn't actually like that side of things. I live like a monk.'

He looked up above their heads into the dark interior of the casuarina tree, then dropped his gaze again to meet hers. 'You are the only person on earth I've told about all this, Evie. My marriage to Veronica is a form of mutualism – we have a symbiotic relationship. If I were to leave her it would also be the end of my career. They don't like divorced men in the civil service.'

He pulled his trousers on over his sun-dried trunks and said, 'I have to go. I'm already late. I'm sorry.' Giving her a tight-lipped smile, he turned and made his way along the beach towards the glint of metal through the trees which was his car.

Evie felt numb. Yet at the same time, relieved. She told herself that what had happened in the sea had been a flash of madness. They had both been caught up in the moment, and now she had to put it behind her.

Arthur Leighton had gone out of his way to try to make it hard for Evie to feel anything for him. He had tried to persuade her he was a selfish, ambitious man who had put his career before everything else. But she sensed his main rationale for taking on Veronica had been compassion. The idea of Arthur as a cold and ruthless careerist didn't square with everything else she knew about the man who had just held her in his arms and kissed her passionately.

There was something corrupting about Malaya. A sense of decay. Something that made even the most decent of people lose their moral code. Just thinking about the oddness of the Leightons' marriage made her feel queasy. She reminded herself that her own was no less odd and had also been born out of pragmatism not love.

FOURTEEN

A few days later, looking for distraction from her almost constant thoughts of Arthur Leighton, Evie collected Jasmine after school for a visit to the Waterfall Garden, the botanical garden on the outskirts of George Town. They wandered through the tropical paradise of winding footpaths, colourful flowers and waterfalls, with wild monkeys screaming as they swung through the trees. Jasmine had never visited the place before and was delighted to see the monkeys at close quarters.

They lost track of time and had to hurry back towards where Benny would be waiting for them in the motor car. Jasmine skipped along beside Evie and after a few minutes she reached up and took her hand.

'I'd like you to be my mummy, but I don't want you to die.'

Evie pulled up short, horrified. She bent down beside the little girl and scooped her into her arms. 'Of course I won't die, Jasmine. What on earth gave you that idea?'

'I'm the only girl in my class at school who doesn't have a mummy. Betty Foster says my mummy lost the will to live. She said her mummy told her.'

'What nonsense. Betty must be a very silly girl. Your mother got sick and that's why she died. It's terribly sad, but it does happen to people. Remember how I told you my daddy had died as well?'

'Did he get sick, too?'

Evie swallowed, hating to lie to Jasmine, but she couldn't possibly tell her what actually happened. Anyway he *was* sick – sick in the head to do something so stupid. She nodded. 'It was a long time ago.'

'Were you a little girl?'

'Not as young as you. But still a girl.'

Jasmine's arms went up around Evie's neck and clung to her tightly. 'I thought I didn't want a new mummy.' The big eyes narrowed and the rosebud mouth formed a pout. 'But I changed my mind. Will you be my new mummy, Evie?'

Tears sprung to Evie's eyes. 'I'd like that very much indeed.'

'And can I call you Mummy?'

'Nothing would make me happier.'

Satisfied, Jasmine dropped her arms and took her stepmother's hand. 'Come on, Mummy, before it gets dark.'

That afternoon proved to be another turning point in her relationship with Jasmine. Evie found herself looking forward to the child's homecoming from school each day and she relished the chance to spend time with the little girl. Jasmine was clearly desperate for affection but there was still a slight caution, as if she was nervous that Evie, like Felicity, might suddenly disappear from her life. Evie wondered what Jasmine had meant when she'd told her that Felicity had been mean to her. If only there were someone she could ask. She was afraid to bring it up with Douglas. The obvious person would have been Arthur, but after what had happened between them, he'd be going out of his way to avoid seeing her alone and it wasn't something she could ask him about in company.

.   .   .

Douglas returned to the house the following Sunday morning and told her he would be staying for one night and they would be spending the evening with the Leightons at the Eastern & Oriental hotel, where every Sunday evening the house orchestra performed a concert on the lawns. His manner was brusque, businesslike, as though he were addressing an employee, not the woman he had made love to with uncharacteristic tenderness only a week before.

'Will there be anyone else going?'

'No. Just the four of us. It's my birthday. September 3rd.'

'Oh my goodness. I'd no idea, Doug. I haven't got you a gift.'

His voice was a snarl. 'I don't want a gift. I'm not a schoolboy.'

'But if it's your birthday.'

'It doesn't mean I want a gift.'

It was another punch in the stomach. She didn't feel like a wife at all. The way he spoke to her was more suited to his assistants or his housekeeper. Curt. Snappy.

Arguing was pointless. 'How old are you?' she asked lamely.

He looked upwards and sighed. 'Forty-three. And before you ask, I don't want a cake with candles on it either.'

She took a sharp intake of breath. 'I wouldn't presume.'

'Good,' he said. 'I'm going to play a round of golf. Be ready for seven. We'll have dinner at the E&O before the concert.' He started to walk out of the room, then looked back at her and added, 'Wear that dress again. The one you wore for the dinner.'

Fuming, she sat down, her hands on her thighs to steady her shaking. Not a how-are-you?, not even a question about Jasmine – and certainly not a touch or a kiss. She was starting to think she was married to two different men.

Taking a deep breath, she told herself that at least he'd noticed the dress and must have liked her in it.

She went out into the garden to find Jasmine, who was busy telling stories to her dolls.

When they walked past the giant floral displays of birds of paradise and protea, into the elegant restaurant at the Eastern & Oriental, the Leightons were waiting at the table. Evie was nervous about being in their company for the first time since her afternoon on the beach with Arthur, hoping her face wouldn't give away her tangled emotions. The prospect of being near to Arthur filled her with both dread and exhilaration. No matter how many times she had replayed their kiss in her head it still seemed like a dream – but a dream that set her heart racing and filled her with a desperate longing to experience it again.

But all personal concerns soon fled. Arthur rose from the table to greet them, his face furrowed. Even Veronica looked pale and edgy.

'We declared war on Germany today.' Arthur's mouth was drawn into a tight line.

'When?' Douglas gave a little shake of the head. 'We knew it was coming.'

'Less than an hour ago. Eleven in the morning in London. The PM's speech was on the wireless but there was so much static it was barely comprehensible.' He reached into his jacket pocket and handed Douglas a sheet of paper. 'Here's the transcript.'

Douglas scanned it rapidly before handing it back to Arthur, who turned at once to Evie and offered it to her. The words 'no such undertaking has been received, and that conse-quently this country is at war with Germany' were stark. While it was true that the prospect of another war in Europe had seemed an inevitability for a long time, being far away in Malaya had made it feel remote and removed.

Arthur said, 'I have to go back to the office after dinner. I can't stay for the concert. Sorry.'

Evie was alarmed. 'Surely the war won't affect us out here, will it?'

Arthur's expression was grim. 'It affects the whole empire. Many people will want to go home to assist with the war effort. Plans have to be made. And...' He glanced at Douglas. 'The whole situation is volatile. The Japanese—'

'The Japanese are too busy with China,' Douglas interrupted. 'They'll never attack us here. They'd have to be insane. The jungle is our protection. Not to mention Fortress Singapore.'

Arthur shook his head. 'I don't want to argue with you, Doug. But I simply don't agree. We know they want Malaya. They want the tin and they want the rubber. They've had spies all over the Straits for years. And they could come at us from the north. From the Siamese – sorry I keep forgetting it's Thai now – border. The situation is extremely volatile.'

Doug sneered. 'From the north? No one would be mad enough to do that.'

Veronica interjected. 'I find all this talk of war very depressing, don't you, Evie? And I agree with Dougie. Hitler's too far away to worry about, and a bunch of Japs are never going to have the guts to invade. I have faith in our army and air force. Not to mention the strength of the Royal Navy. Britannia rules the waves.'

She leaned forward, her hands with their perfectly manicured nails, resting on the edge of the table. 'We seem to have forgotten today is Dougie's birthday and we have to celebrate. We can't let a rotten old war get in the way.' With a wave of her hand, she summoned the waiter, who arrived at the table with a bucket of champagne. As he poured the drinks, Veronica added, '*My* main concern is that with France at war too, the supplies of "shampers" may get rather low.' She rolled her eyes. 'So, let's drink and be merry, while we can.'

Arthur's face showed a flicker of irritation but he said nothing.

Veronica leaned forward again, glass raised to drink Doug's health. She pressed a small box into his hand. 'A little birthday gift from me and Artie. Hope you like them.'

'I told you, Veronica. No gifts.'

'Do shut up, Dougie, and open it, you old spoil-sport.'

The box contained a pair of monogrammed gold cuff links.

'The date's on them too, so it looks like you'll have a permanent reminder of the day war was declared.' Veronica sipped her champagne. Turning to Evie, she asked, 'And what did you give to your handsome husband?'

Evie felt her face burning, but was saved from having to answer by the arrival of a man at their table. He asked Arthur about the state of play with the war declaration. Once introductions were made – Bob Cameron was the local chief of one of the shipping lines and Evie realised he was the father of Jasmine's friend Penny – the waiter arrived to take their orders and Evie avoided having to admit that she hadn't known it was her husband's birthday.

After Cameron left, the conversation remained on the subject of war.

'Are many people likely to return to England to fight?' Evie asked Arthur.

He shrugged. 'A lot of chaps want to give Hitler a bloody nose, but to be honest, the war effort is best served by staying here producing rubber and tin. We'll be needing a lot more in the coming months.'

Evie glanced at Douglas, who said nothing.

'One thing that will be happening though, is stepping up the training of the volunteer forces. More TEWTs.'

'What's that?' Evie asked.

'Tactical Exercises Without Troops.'

'More like Trivial Exercises to Waste Time.' Douglas was clearly not in the best of moods.

'One of the problems is that many of my colleagues seem to fear Communism more than they fear the Japanese,' said Arthur, ignoring him. 'Worried that Communists are stirring up the workforce.'

'Not my workforce.' Douglas leaned back in his chair, arms folded.

'His Majesty's government persists in trying to keep on the right side of the Japanese.' Arthur shook his head. 'And that's in spite of the fact that we've known for years that this country is crawling with Japanese spies. There have been enough Japanese pearl-fishers to have mapped every cove and inlet of the entire peninsula. But we let them get away with it under our noses.'

Veronica groaned. 'Boring.'

Ignoring her, Arthur went on. 'The government's also standing back and letting the Japs buy up most of our iron ore, regardless of the fact they're turning it into armaments.'

'The government's stupid.' Doug put his palms together and rested his chin on his fingertips. 'They need to listen to us here on the ground. No one trusts the Nips – and the Chinks feel the same way we do about them. They're not to be trusted. You know where you are with Chinamen – they want to strike a hard deal, outwit you if they can. But the Japs hate us to the core and the brutality of what they've been doing in the war in China over the past couple of years is a damned disgrace. Sheer brutality.'

The conversation was interrupted by the waiter bringing their main course of roast pheasant. Evie looked around the large restaurant and noticed that everyone appeared to be subdued. The sound level was lower than one might expect and several people were already leaving to return home. It seemed

completely wrong to be sitting here drinking champagne –
something that only Veronica appeared to be doing, the rest of
them with untouched glasses.

Wanting to hear more about the political situation, Evie
addressed her husband. 'Why did you say you think the volunteer exercises are pointless?' she asked. 'They've been doing a
lot of that kind of thing back in England.'

'That's the trouble. They're only geared to train people in
war, European style. What the devil use will that be if it comes
to a war here, where we should be learning jungle warcraft?'

Arthur nodded. 'I can't argue with that, Doug.'

'Maybe you need to start drumming it into the heads of your
bosses.'

'I do my best. The fundamental problem is that my lot and
the military are at loggerheads. *We* understand the country.
They think they understand war.' Arthur pushed away his plate.
'They're so bloody over-confident. They think the peninsular's
impregnable and consider the Japanese inferior combatants. I
just hope they won't live to regret those massive assumptions.'

Veronica gave another groan. 'For pity's sake, will you two
stop droning on about politics. This is meant to be a birthday
party!'

As she spoke, the maître d' announced over the microphone
that the resident orchestra would not be performing as it was
judged inappropriate in the light of the events of the day. There
was not so much as a murmur of disapproval, apart from Veronica, who confined her protest to a rolling of the eyes, then said,
'It's ludicrous to be cancelling things when there's not yet been
a shot fired.'

Arthur spoke, his voice chilly. 'Hitler's invaded Poland. Isn't
that reason enough for you, Veronica?'

'That was actually a couple of days ago.' She had a petulant
expression on her face.

'Chamberlain had to wait for the French.' Arthur blotted

his mouth with his napkin, then laid it beside his plate. 'And I dare say he was doing everything possible to avoid war.'

'Appeasing the Hun more like.' Doug appeared to be still out of sorts.

'Please forgive me but I'm going to skip the pudding,' said Arthur. 'I have to get to the office before nine as there's a call coming in from Singapore. The Chief Minister has been meeting with the military chiefs. He's going to give us a debriefing.' He got up from the table. 'Sorry, old chap. Not a great end to your birthday. If I take the car, will you be able to drop Veronica off?' Then he was gone.

Evie felt a mixture of relief that Arthur had left, with a contradictory sense of loss. She glanced across at Veronica, who was occupied with the champagne, tipping her husband's untouched drink into her glass.

'Waste not want not!' Veronica declared. 'They'll soon be telling us we've all got to be thrifty, so I'd better do my bit for the cause.'

Douglas got up from the table. 'Excuse me, ladies. I'll be back in a few minutes. I need to talk to someone over there. I won't have a pudding either, so go ahead and order yours without me.' He moved away to the other side of the dining room to a table where two couples were drinking coffee and smoking. Evie saw him bending to talk to them and felt excluded and abandoned.

When she turned back, she realised Veronica was studying her.

'You're wearing that charming mauve frock again.'

Irritated, Evie said, 'Douglas likes it.'

Eyebrows raised in disbelief, Veronica didn't comment further. Instead she changed the subject. 'I hear you were at the swimming club the other day.'

Evie felt her face turning crimson. Had she and Arthur been seen? Were those women in deckchairs cronies of Veronica? Had they spotted her walking off down the beach with Arthur? Her stomach flipped. 'How did you know?'

'Arthur told me.'

A shiver ran over Evie's body, prickling her skin. What had he said? And why? It was a terrible betrayal.

'He says you're a strong swimmer.'

'I love swimming.'

'Yes. So does Arthur. I don't at all.' She gave a transparently fake smile to Evie. 'But now the war's here Arthur won't have any time for that.'

'Yes, I imagine he's going to be very busy.'

Veronica slugged the rest of her champagne down, reached over to take Douglas's flute and tipped that into hers, fixing Evie with a cold stare. 'And even if he isn't, he won't have any time for that.' She took another sip. 'Any time for *you*. Do I make myself clear?'

Evie gaped, astonished. Before she could muster a response, Veronica rose from the table and waved at a couple walking towards the door.

Turning back to Evie, she said, 'Tell Dougie I decided to get a lift with the Browns. They have to drive right past our house.' She swept away, leaving Evie shocked and alone at the table.

FIFTEEN

The following morning, after Douglas had left for the Batu Lembah estate, Evie picked up his unread copy of the *Straits Times*. Glancing at the editorial, she was drawn into reading it. Evidently Britain's declaration of war was to be interpreted as a cause for rejoicing. Remembering the conversation of the previous night about the complacency of the colonial government and the military, she read with disbelief:

'At this safe distance from the scene of battle, with our defences perfected and Japanese participation in the struggle on the side of Germany an extremely remote possibility, Malaya has little to fear.'

She folded the newspaper and set it aside. It was impossible to concentrate. The war seemed very remote from her here, whereas what had happened the night before still caused her stomach to churn.

She knew she had no business thinking the way she did about another woman's husband. Yet she couldn't help herself. Arthur had taken her in his arms when they were in the sea, leaving her in no doubt that he desired her. He had also made it crystal clear that he was tied irrevocably to Veronica. He'd also made the importance of his career clear. Then Veronica's revelation that she knew about the encounter on the beach, and her veiled threat, made Evie start to doubt her own reason.

It was hard not to conclude that the Leightons had some bizarre consensual 'arrangement'. Mary's revelation that Veronica had frequent extra-marital affairs and Arthur always accepted her back made Evie feel sickened. While she'd accepted his explanation about Veronica's depressive behaviour and his obligation to her, the fact that he had told Veronica about their meeting at the beach made it hard not to construe that he had been using Evie in a retaliatory gesture to make his wife jealous.

Whatever the truth, Evie was completely out of her depth. She had never known anyone behave in the odd ways the Leightons and Douglas did. Perhaps it was the pressure of living for so long far away from one's roots? Even her own mother, when she had committed adultery, had waited until her husband's death before running off with her lover. But that wasn't strictly true, was it? Evie had to acknowledge that it could well have been her mother's intention to leave that had triggered her father's crime and subsequent suicide.

So here she was, caught between an uncommunicative and often cold husband, and a man to whom she was strongly attracted but who had made it clear he would never act upon it. As the thought formed, she felt a frisson of guilt – surely *she* would never act on it either? But the memory of that embrace in the sea wouldn't leave her, and her thoughts kept returning to it and reliving it. Yet Arthur had betrayed her by telling Veronica. Somehow she couldn't believe that to be the case. Veronica had to be lying. Surely? Was the woman playing mind games with her?

Even though Veronica's words, if they were true, were

evidence of Arthur's perfidy, Evie couldn't – wouldn't – believe it. Just thinking about him made her breath shorten, her skin tingle and her heart race. A shiver of pleasure ran through her whole body from merely being in the same room as him. It was as if there was an unbreakable thread running between them, anchoring her, tethering her to him so that she couldn't break away – didn't want to. The mere thought of being close to him, across the same table filled her with a crazy joy. Crazy because there was no logic to it at all. Joy because her whole being sang. She and Arthur were meant to be together. Deep inside she felt an unshakeable certainty about that. But it was pointless. Futile. What cruel fate had determined they should be married to other people?

Over the weeks that followed, Evie went out of her way to avoid seeing the Leightons whenever possible and ensured she was never alone with Arthur. On the rare occasions when they did meet, his manner towards her was courteous but distant – yet often when she looked up suddenly, she caught him watching her, only for him to look away again immediately. Meanwhile her relationship with Doug continued in its odd seesawing fashion. Most of the time he was away at the estate and on the weekends when he was in George Town he was frequently involved in what he continued to maintain were pointless exercises with the Volunteers. Conversation between them was limited and driven entirely by Evie. But he continued to come to her bed. There, communication didn't involve words. Evie was grateful it didn't.

As the days and weeks after the declaration of war turned into months, the initial shock experienced by the expatriate Europeans that their countries were at war with Germany, turned into an atmosphere of 'business as usual'. In fact, it seemed rather than that, it was 'business is booming', as the

Straits Settlements enjoyed an unprecedented surge in demand for rubber, tin, iron ore and other minerals. The only cloud in the life of many of the expatriates was the shock of the sinking, in late November, of the former P&O liner, *Rawalpindi*, which had been well known to the numerous old India hands. The loss of the ship off Iceland, while on convoy escort duty, had brought the realities of the war closer.

As December arrived, Evie wondered what her first tropical Christmas would be like. She'd disliked the festive season since her father's death. All it did was reinforce her own isolation and loneliness, especially in the knowledge that so many families were happy and rejoicing in each other's company.

Mrs Shipley-Thomas had always spent Christmas at the home of a friend in Haslemere, leaving Evie to her own devices. Once Evie had got past feeling sorry for herself she'd at least enjoyed having the freedom of the house, able to please herself until her employer returned the day after Boxing Day.

But here in Penang, Evie had a husband and a child to spend the holiday with. She had extracted a promise from Douglas that he would be at the house in George Town for four days over the holiday season, and Jasmine was already showing growing excitement. For Evie it seemed bizarre to be talking to the little girl about the forthcoming arrival of Father Christmas, when the absence of winter, not to mention chimneys for Santa to climb down, made it a greater stretch of the imagination than would usually be required. In the end, she told Jasmine that the sleigh would land on the roof and Father Christmas would skim down the drainpipe and enter the house via the drawing room windows.

'Isn't the kid a bit old for all that?' Douglas shrugged when she explained her strategy.

'She's only seven, Doug! Not exactly an adult yet.'

He rolled his eyes. 'I suppose I'd better give you some extra money to buy her presents.'

'What should we give her?'

Douglas shrugged again. 'Your department. Don't ask me.' He reached in his pocket and pulled out his wallet. 'Better get something nice for yourself too. Jewellery or something.'

Evie was about to protest. It summed up his attitude to her – unwilling to spare the time to get her something personal for Christmas. She felt her annoyance rising but bit her lip and looked away. She didn't want him to see that she was hurt. It was almost five months since she'd arrived in Penang and in all that time he had shown not a sign of affection. That he had made it clear she wasn't to expect it, when they had struck their bargain, didn't alleviate the pain.

Once Douglas had gone, Evie decided to put on a brave face and enjoy spending his money to make Jasmine's Christmas a special one. As to buying a piece of jewellery for herself, she would have none of it. She wasn't going to give him the satisfaction. Should anyone enquire as to what her husband had given her as a Christmas gift, she'd tell them he hadn't. In fact it was hard not to relish the thought of shaming him that way. And she wasn't going to buy anything for him either.

Returning in the car with Benny, the seat beside her laden with gifts for Jasmine, Evie softened a little. The festive atmosphere had got through to her. She wasn't going to use Douglas's money to buy him a gift, but there was nothing to stop her making him one. It would be more personal. It would be a demonstration that while he might be uncaring of her, she was still trying her best to make the marriage work.

'Pull over, please, Benny.' They came to a stop outside a large Indian fabric store. 'I won't be long.'

Inside, it was an Aladdin's cave of fabric. A vast array of saris, woven and embroidered silks, bright colourful cotton

sarongs, bolts of linen, voiles and muslin, as well as khaki cotton
for the shorts that all the European men wore.

She selected some plain white Egyptian cotton and a small
piece of black silk, delicately embroidered with Chinese dragons. Adding a couple of skeins of embroidery thread and some
silk cord, she went to the counter to have the fabric measured
and cut, then paid for her purchases. She would work on her
gifts in the evenings after Jasmine had gone to bed.

A few days later, Evie made a trip to the doctor's. She had
missed her period two or three times and it eventually dawned
on her that she might be pregnant. Terrified that it might prove
to be a false hope, she was a bag of nerves as she sat in the
waiting room.

She'd never needed to visit a doctor before and was self-
conscious about being examined by a strange man, but told
herself if the news was good it would be worth it.

The news was good. Dr Oates, a jovial character with a
shock of white hair and a broad smile, asked her a few questions,
made a quick examination of her breasts and pronounced that
she was indeed expecting a baby.

'I'd say baby should be ready to greet the world in June or
July next year.'

'What happens now? Do I have to have plenty of rest?'

'Only as much as you feel you need. I'm a great believer in
the benefits of regular exercise – even for expectant mothers.
Pregnancy is not an illness.'

Walking home – she had not wanted Benny to know about
the visit to the doctor – Evie was euphoric. At last she could tell
Douglas what he wanted to hear. For once he would have to
acknowledge she had done something right.

She wanted to choose the right moment to tell him the
news. Of course, that depended on him being in George Town.

· · ·

In the run-up to Christmas, Penang was an endless whirl of parties, concerts and dinners. Evie was grateful that she could use the excuse of Doug's absence to avoid most of them. Perhaps it was her condition, but she had lost any inclination for alcohol – not that she'd been a great drinker before. The festivities included several organised by Jasmine's school – but these Evie had no wish to duck. Her telephone calls failed to persuade Douglas to come across from the mainland to watch all or any of the school concert, a recital by the choir in which Jasmine performed a solo, sports' day and the obligatory nativity play, in which his daughter was to play an angel. Evie knew if she told him about the baby he would probably come, but this was about Jasmine and she was irritated that he considered it too much trouble to witness his daughter's performances.

Evie sat alone, applauding enthusiastically and trying to put on as bright a face as possible for the little girl, who was inevitably disappointed at her father's absence.

In the school hall, looking round the room as the choir sang, Evie noticed there was a reasonable turnout of fathers. Attendance had been almost universal when it came to the sports day, with her husband one of the few absentees.

Douglas was never unkind towards Jasmine. It was more a case of benign neglect, paying her less attention than he paid to his dog, Badger. Occasionally Evie caught him looking at the child as if she were a curiosity. Maybe he was looking for similarities with her mother? Evie never dared ask. Most of the time though, he ignored the little girl, tolerating her chatter but rarely engaging with it.

There was one seasonal event that Douglas didn't shirk. On Christmas Eve, a mixed doubles tournament took place each year at the tennis club. Evie discovered that the tradition was for husbands to partner their wives. She remembered that in

order to duck out of a social engagement she had lied to
Veronica that tennis wasn't her game. Yes, she hadn't played in
years, but she had once been a formidable force on the court.

'Do we have to play?' she asked Douglas. It didn't seem
right that he was able to make time for this but not for any activ-
ities at Jasmine's school.

'It's expected.' He gave an audible sigh. 'Don't you play
tennis?'

'Yes. I can play. I just hate those clubby things.'

'You can go home when we're knocked out. I'll have to stay
for the prize-giving. My grandfather donated the trophy.'

'Can't *you* play?'

He looked at her as though she were a fly he'd like to swat
away. 'Of course I can play. What do you mean?'

'You said "when we get knocked out".'

'There are one or two good players. The rest don't take it
very seriously. Look, Evie, all we have to do is put in an appearance. I have very little time to play these days.'

'Were you ever any good?'

'Penang Tennis Club mens' singles champion for five years.'

'Oh, crumbs.'

'Felicity couldn't bear to play in the heat. She only played
once and we were knocked out in straight sets. So you don't
need to worry that you've a lot to live up to.'

'I'll do my best. I haven't played much since school.'

Jasmine was to accompany them, as the Christmas Eve tournament was evidently a family occasion, with a children's tea
laid on and a visit from Father Christmas. The child
thrilled to be included in the excursion, which many of her
classmates would be attending too.

As soon as they arrived at the tennis club, Jasmine ran off to
join her friends. It was the first time Evie had been in a large
gathering with her husband since their awful post-wedding
party at the Penang Club. She looked around and saw several

faces she remembered from that day. Douglas had timed their arrival so that they wouldn't have to wait around for long before the matches began and they went straight to the club house where the draw was being made.

An elderly woman, whom Evie remembered was the widow of a former government official, was making the draw. Evidently she was a benefactor of the tennis club and an active committee member. Doug's and Evie's names were drawn after a few minutes. As the portly woman reached into the box to pull out the slip of paper which would determine who they were to play first, Evie could have sworn she exchanged a glance with Veronica Leighton, who was standing on the other side of the room. To Evie's horror, the woman unfolded the paper and read out 'Mr and Mrs Arthur Leighton'.

Douglas muttered, 'It'll be a short match.'

Evie swivelled to face him. 'Why do you say that?'

'Veronica plays several times a week and Arthur's one of the few players here who can beat me. And I haven't picked up a racquet in months.'

'Pessimist!' she said.

It took Evie a while to get into the rhythm of the match and adjust her play to Douglas's. They lost the first three games to love. It was impossible to mistake the smug triumph on Veronica's face. Arthur was an excellent player, hitting deep strokes from the baseline, while Veronica was agile and graceful moving around the court.

As Evie gradually settled down, telling herself to relax and enjoy the sensation of playing again, she began to enjoy it.

They held Douglas's service, then Veronica served for the second time. Evie was ready for her, returning her opponent's first service with confidence and winning the point. A series of crisp volleys saw Evie and Doug winning the game. Evie was relishing the feel of a racquet in her hands again. Why had she ever stopped playing? It was exhilarating and a great way to release all her tensions and frustrations. Veronica, struggling to get to the net from the baseline, was confounded when Evie delivered a succession of short lobs. Veronica grunted in exasperation. The more angry and frustrated she became, the more she fluffed her shots.

The match progressed with Veronica growing increasingly irate at her failure to counter Evie's service. After a number of unforced errors by Veronica, the Leightons lost the first set six–four.

Evie saw the look of surprise – and what she realised was respect – in her husband's eyes. Good – it was about time he gave her credit for something. She was secretly thrilled that she hadn't confessed to winning the tennis singles cup at her school, ten years earlier.

A crowd of spectators had gathered to watch the progress of the match and the unexpected trouncing the Leightons were getting. So far, Arthur hadn't lost a service game and rarely conceded a point, which was making Veronica's failings more evident. Douglas too held his own service games so the match came down to the tussle between Evie and Veronica.

Changing ends after another held service by Evie, Arthur, said, 'Well played, Evie. You're certainly giving us a run for our money.'

'A damn good thrashing I'd say,' said Douglas. Evie felt a glow of pride. Her satisfaction was underscored by the fact that Veronica Leighton's face was transfigured by anger. The slight woman was unable to match the strength and power of Evie's groundstrokes and her frustration was increasingly apparent. As Evie smashed another return across the net, the ball bouncing too high for her opponent to reach, she said to herself, 'That one's for Mary.'

Veronica began to argue with virtually every line call by the umpire, a retired army officer, who was distinctly unamused.

This behaviour earned her a quiet reprimand from her husband and loud murmurings from the crowd.

Then it was over. The second set went to the Barringtons, six–two.

Veronica picked up a stray ball, hitting it broadside straight into Evie's ribcage, causing her to double over in pain. 'Frightfully sorry. Didn't notice you were standing there.'

To Evie's astonishment, Arthur grabbed Veronica by the arm, jerked her towards him and told her to get her things as he was taking her home.

'I'm not going home. I'm having a drink. Don't be a bad sport, Arthur. We have to drink the health of the victorious couple. Surely you're not going to be a sore loser?' Her words were spoken with venom.

But Arthur was in no mood to argue and the Leightons left the court.

Evie and Douglas won their next two matches but were knocked out in the final by a young army officer and his former gym instructor wife. There was no sign of the Leightons.

Evie basked in the admiration of Jasmine who insisted on holding onto the runners-up shield on the short car ride home. She secured her parents' permission to display it in her bedroom, alongside the ribboned medal she herself had won the same day in the egg and spoon race.

SIXTEEN

That night, when Douglas came to her bed, Evie told him she had been to see the doctor. 'I wanted to be sure before I told you, but it looks like we're going to have a baby. Apparently, it will be in about six months.'

Douglas's face was transfigured for a moment by amazement and joy, but to Evie's horror his expression quickly changed to anger.

'You're pregnant and thought it was a good idea to fling yourself around a tennis court all day? What the hell do you think you're doing! You're putting my child at risk.'

Evie gaped at him, taken aback. 'But I asked the doctor and he said exercise was a good thing. He says it's a lot of old-fashioned stuff and nonsense that pregnant women should go into a kind of purdah.'

'Going for a gentle walk, he means. Maybe a couple of lengths of the swimming pool. He certainly didn't mean pounding around a tennis court for the best part of a day.'

'It wasn't all day.'

'It was several hours all told.'

'But I feel fine. Better than I've felt in ages. I enjoyed the exercise. I thought you enjoyed it too.'

'You mean you enjoyed giving Veronica Leighton a thrashing.' His face was full of anger. 'I can't believe how irresponsible you've been, Evelyn.' He flung back the sheet, got out of bed, and left her room.

Evie stared at the closed door, misery swamping her. Never mind two steps forward, one step back, with Doug it was one forward and three back. No matter how hard she tried, she always came up short as far as her husband was concerned. And the one special card, the last ace in her pack had been played, and the game was lost.

She asked herself, was he right? Had she taken an undue risk? She hadn't fallen, hadn't overtired herself. And the doctor had said exercise was not only harmless but beneficial. She remembered the vicious retaliatory shot Veronica had sent her way, smashing the ball into her ribcage. It could just as easily have struck a little lower and put her unborn child at risk. Her hands moved protectively over her belly. There was no sign yet of her pregnancy, no swelling evident. She lifted her nightdress and looked down at her ribs where already a purplish tinge was spreading. What an idiot she had been. Just a few inches lower and she might well have lost the child. Anger at herself – and at Veronica Leighton bubbled up inside her to mix with a growing sense of remorse.

She got out of bed, put on her dressing gown and went across the room to the door. Moonlight flooded the landing as she crept along it towards the master bedroom. She eased the door open only to find it was deserted, the bed untouched. A cold fear clenched her stomach. Had he gone? Returned to Batu Lembah? Abandoned them at Christmas. Tears rose involuntarily and she cursed her own stupidity. She should have waited to tell him until the memory of the tennis match had faded – or had the good sense not to play in the first place. It was her own fault. She had been playing fast and free with her marriage and the life of their unborn child. An overwhelming desire to wind back the clock, to relive and reorder the past day, swept through her, only to be replaced by a heavy oppressive sadness. She had messed things up badly. And how would she break the news to Jasmine that her father wouldn't be with them at Christmas?

About to return to her bed, although certain she couldn't sleep, she heard a sound downstairs, a chinking of glass. Was he still here? She tiptoed down the staircase and across the hall. Her husband was standing framed in the open French window, looking out onto the moonlit lawn, a whisky in his hand. Relief washed over Evie.

Scarcely daring to breathe, she moved across the room and went to stand beside him. 'I'm sorry,' she said, her voice barely a whisper. '*Really* sorry. I'll go and see the doctor again straight after Christmas and make sure everything's all right.'

He continued to stare across the garden but said nothing. The cicadas were emitting their endless high-pitched vibrations. Avoiding her eyes, he started to speak at last. 'It's just that...'

She touched his arm. 'I know. I understand how much having this child means to you. I was wrong to take a risk like that.'

She saw Douglas was still angry.

'You don't want the baby, do you? That's why you did it.'

Evie was aghast. 'Not want the baby? I want nothing more. What on earth makes you say that?'

'The tennis. Provoking Veronica.'

'I was trying to win the match. I thought you were too!' She started to feel indignant.

'That ball she slammed at you. You wanted her to do it. Why don't you admit it, Evelyn?'

'Call me Evie! And that's absolute poppycock. That ball got me right in the ribs and hurt like hell but it wasn't anywhere near the baby. I certainly didn't want it to happen. I'm desperate to have this baby. I thought you'd be as pleased as I am.' The anger bubbled up. Anger and frustration that they appeared to be completely incapable of communicating with each other. No matter how hard she tried, he slapped her down. Well, she'd had enough.

To her astonishment, Douglas made a strange choking sound and she realised he was struggling to control his emotions. Instinctively, she reached for his arm and guided him to the sofa. He sat beside her, his head in his hands. Evie waited, saying nothing, conscious of the sound of his breathing, mingling with the chorus of cicadas. Trying to argue or reason with him was pointless and would drive him further away from her. There was clearly something damaged at the core of the man. It must be to do with his loss of Felicity and her own apparent shortcomings in comparison. How could she possibly compete with a dead woman, one whom he had clearly sanctified, one who could no longer afford him any opportunity for criticism – if indeed she ever had? Evie felt bleak. Lost and lonely. Unsure what to do or say, she remained beside him, silent, waiting.

Eventually he stirred, glancing at his wristwatch. 'It's gone midnight,' he said at last. 'Happy Christmas, Evie.' He reached for her hand and raised it to brush it lightly with his lips. 'I'm sorry. I was unfair to you. I am happy about this baby. More than you can imagine.'

Relief and happiness rushed into her. She gave him a broad smile. 'Me too. I made you a present for Christmas. Would you like to open it now?'

'You made me something?' He looked astonished.

She went over to the cabinet in the corner of the room and took out two gift-wrapped parcels. 'They're only small things, but they're all my own work.' She gave a little laugh, embarrassed.

He unwrapped the first gift, revealing a pile of half-a-dozen white linen handkerchiefs, each hand-embroidered with a monogram, DB. 'You made these yourself?'

She nodded, happy that he seemed pleased with them. 'I like to sew. Go on. Open the other.'

He did as she asked, drawing from the wrapping paper a black silk pouch with a woven cord clasp. 'What is it? It's beautiful.' He ran a finger over the Chinese dragons.

'It's a pouch for your tobacco.'

He shook his head and she saw his eyes were misted. 'No one, no one, has ever gone to the trouble to make something for me. It must have taken you ages.'

'I did it in the evenings when Jasmine was in bed. I wanted to give you something personal.'

'Thank you, Evie. It means a lot to me.' He looked sheepish. 'Did you get something for yourself?'

She shook her head. 'I don't need anything.'

'I have something for you. It's an heirloom I want you to have. Wait here.'

He disappeared into the study and she could hear him unlocking the door to the desk. He returned with a small leather box, slightly faded and worn around the edges. 'It belonged to my mother and my grandmother before her. I'd like you to have it.'

Evie flipped the box open to reveal a gold ring with a pearl surrounded by tiny diamonds. She swallowed. 'Did this belong to Felicity before me?'

Douglas looked aghast. 'No, of course not. No one's worn it since my mother. She died when I was ten.'

'It's beautiful.' She put it on her finger and held out her hand. 'So delicate and it fits perfectly. Thank you, Doug.'

Later that night as she lay awake in bed with a sleeping Douglas beside her, she remembered how he had looked horrified at the idea of Felicity owning the ring. She didn't think he'd been appalled at her suggestion that he'd been insensitive enough to have given her something that had once belonged to his late wife. No, it was the idea of giving Felicity the ring in the first place that was abhorrent. Maybe things weren't quite as she'd thought.

SEVENTEEN

Jasmine was overcome with excitement on Christmas morning. It was Evie's first Christmas in the presence of a child, and she found the little girl's pleasure infectious. Jasmine cried out with delight when she opened a box to find a grinning Shirley Temple doll inside. Even Douglas managed to crack a smile, and was willingly drawn, once the Christmas dinner had been consumed, into assisting his daughter in the construction of a *Bayko* suburban house, with its own garage made of bakelite bricks held together by steel rods.

From time to time, Evie glanced at her finger where the ring Douglas had given her sparkled. She watched her husband playing with their daughter, and contentment suffused her. It had been a long and difficult road but she believed that at last she had arrived. She was home. Douglas may not love her, and she no longer thought she loved him either since her feelings for Arthur had surfaced. But they had reached an accommodation with each other. She was growing used to his unpredictability and volatility and he was beginning to show her some respect that might one day evolve into something more – especially once the baby arrived. Evie sent up a silent prayer that it would be a boy. But if it wasn't, they would keep trying until he had the son and heir he longed for.

Douglas looked up from where he and Jasmine were lying on the floor, the plastic pieces spread out in front of them. His eyes and mouth twitched slightly in an approximation of a smile.

Jasmine, intercepting the glance, called over to Evie. 'Come and help us, Mummy. There's so many pieces. Please!'

Reluctant to break into such a rare father and daughter communion, Evie hesitated, but Douglas reached a hand up and drew her down to join them on the floor. 'You're not getting off so easily. We'll be here all night otherwise.' He rolled his eyes in mock frustration.

'Nonsense. You're loving it! Every man's dream is to build things.' But inside, a wave of triumph and happiness swept over her – she was part of a family again. Less than a year ago, back in Hampshire, she wouldn't have dreamed it could be possible. She hitched her skirt up and knelt beside Douglas and Jasmine and was soon as absorbed in the task as they were.

The family construction project was interrupted when the door opened and Veronica and Arthur came into the room.

'Merry Christmas, one and all!' Veronica called loftily, no sign of the previous day's anger in her demeanour. Heart sinking, Evie scrambled to her feet.

'What a touching little scene!' Veronica's tone was heavy with sarcasm. 'You're playing happy families!'

To Evie's amazement, it was Douglas who replied, 'Not *playing*, Veronica.'

A look of annoyance flickered over Veronica's face, but she recovered, plastered on a fake smile and said to Jasmine, 'We've brought your Christmas gift.' She thrust an elaborately wrapped parcel into the child's hands.

Jasmine opened it to reveal a doll's tea set and immediately expressed her thanks.

Waving a hand airily, Veronica said, 'Now surely it's your bedtime, little girl? Time for the grown-ups to play.'

Evie suppressed her rising fury. In response, Arthur squatted down on the floor beside Jasmine and the model house and said, 'I've always wanted to have a go at one of these. When I was a boy I'd spend hours making things with my Meccano set.'

Veronica gave an exaggerated sigh and what was obviously a forced and false laugh. 'Boys will be boys.' Her voice was patronising. Addressing Evie, she said 'What does a girl have to do to get a gin sling around here?'

As if summoned by magic, Aunty Mimi appeared with a tray of canapés, followed by Benny, who set about mixing the drinks. The men accepted their usual *stengahs,* Veronica, a gin sling, and Benny was about to mix a gin and bitters for Evie.

'No gin for me, thank you, Benny. I'll have a lime and soda.'

'What on earth's wrong with you, darling? It's Christmas Day for goodness sake.' Veronica turned to Benny. 'Stick a large gin in there.' She indicated Evie's glass.

'No!' Evie jumped up and stayed Benny's hand. 'No gin for me thank you, Benny.' Addressing Veronica she apologised, 'I just don't fancy alcohol much lately.'

Veronica looked her up and down then glanced towards Douglas who was still occupied with constructing his little piece of suburbia with Arthur and Jasmine, before fixing her gaze on Evie. 'Surely you're not in the Pudding Club?'

Jasmine looked up. 'What's the Pudding Club?'

Quickly, Evie said, 'It's for people who eat too much Christmas pudding.' She was damned if Jasmine was going to find out about her condition from Veronica Leighton. She'd tell her herself in her own good time.

Arthur looked mortified. He threw an apologetic glance at Evie and said, 'That's enough, Veronica.'

Jasmine, oblivious, said, 'Mummy's not in it as she hardly had any pudding at all.'

'*Mummy?*' Veronica's eyebrows shot up. 'I say!'

'Veronica!' Arthur's voice was low but the anger in his tone unmistakeable.

Douglas, evidently bored with the Bayko kit, got up and flung himself into a chair. 'Mrs Leighton's right, Jasmine. It's time for bed.'

Jasmine picked up Shirley Temple and asked Evie, 'Will you come up and read me a story, Mummy?'

Relieved to escape, Evie took her step-daughter's hand, asked the guests to excuse her, and left the room with Jasmine.

As she went up the stairs she could hear Veronica begin her inquisition of Douglas and she hoped he would tell her nothing. She didn't want news of her pregnancy to be spread around George Town by the malicious Veronica.

Half an hour later, after Jasmine was asleep, Evie ventured back downstairs, full of trepidation. The drawing room was deserted and she could hear the murmur of voices coming from the garden. She picked up the scattered pieces of Bayko from the floor and put them back in the box, moving the half-finished house onto a side table, ready for Jasmine to finish tomorrow. Her back was turned to the garden when she felt a hand on her arm. Spinning round, she came face-to-face with Arthur. Her heart thumped inside her ribcage.

'I'm really sorry,' he said. 'About everything. Her behaviour yesterday at the tennis club and just now. She promised me that if I agreed to come tonight she would apologise to you, but she hasn't and instead she's made matters worse.' He glanced behind him. 'Is she right? Are you having a baby?' His face looked stricken.

She nodded. 'Please don't tell her.'

His mouth was a tight line. 'She'll have wormed it out of Doug by now.'

'No, she won't.' She said it with certainty.

Arthur frowned.

'I think we should go outside and join them.' She realised her voice sounded clipped, abrupt.

'Evie?' Arthur looked at her pleadingly. 'I haven't been able to stop thinking about you. Why have you been avoiding me? I—'

She cut him short. 'Look, Arthur, I don't want to hear it. You went straight home and told Veronica about what happened at the beach. I thought I could trust you. Did you both have a good laugh at my expense?' The suppressed anger rose up inside her.

He looked aghast. 'I don't know what you're talking about. I said nothing to her. Why, in God's name, would I tell her?'

'She warned me to keep away from you. It made me feel cheap and tawdry. And now I'm ashamed of myself for trusting you in the first place.'

'Evie, I promise you. I don't know what the heck you're talking about. Is that why you've been avoiding us? Is that why you haven't been near the pool or the beach? When did she say all this? What exactly did she say?' He seemed to be avoiding using his wife's name.

'It was on Doug's birthday. At the E&O. After you'd left. Douglas went off to speak to someone on another table and she pounced on me. Told me you'd told her about our swimming together at the beach and made it crystal clear that I was to keep away from you. I felt utterly ashamed. Mortified.' She hesitated. 'Is that what you two do? Come home and share your extra-marital shenanigans with each other? Is that what your marriage feeds off?'

Arthur went white. 'How could you think that of me, Evie?'

'What else am I supposed to think?'

Arthur shook his head quickly and repeatedly, then he touched her arm again. 'I promise you, on my honour, Evie. I knew nothing of this. Someone else must have seen us together at the beach. She's never breathed a word of this to me. And I feel sick that you could imagine I would have gone home and told her about you and me.'

'There is no you and me.' Evie brushed him aside and went out into the garden. She wasn't going to offer Veronica Leighton any further reason to suspect her and try to humiliate her.

The Leightons didn't linger long. Veronica was clearly annoyed at the way Douglas and Evie were getting along and frustrated at her failure to prise out any information about whether or not Evie was pregnant. Arthur was preoccupied, silent and as tense as a taut spring. Evie heaved a sigh of relief when they left, leaving only the scent of Veronica's *Shalimar* in their wake.

Later that night, as Evie lay beside Douglas in bed, she was starting to drift off to sleep when she heard his voice, barely above a whisper.

'Thank you, Evie. That was the best Christmas I've spent since I was a child before my mother died.'

Evie felt a rush of pleasure.

The dark, silent room and the fact that they couldn't see each other appeared to have made Douglas uncharacteristically garrulous. 'After my mother was gone, my father had no time for me. I was packed off to prep school then Eton.'

'Was it awful? Being sent away from home so young?'

'Not awful. It would have happened anyway. But I missed my mother dreadfully. She was ill for a long time and they wouldn't let me see her.'

'What was the matter with her?'

'I'm not sure. No one told me what was wrong. I suspect it was a tumour of some kind. They tried to keep her illness from me and when I had to know, my father said she was too ill to be troubled and wouldn't let me go near her room.'

'Oh Doug, that's terrible. And you were only ten.'

'According to my father, not too young to develop a stiff upper lip. I made the mistake of shedding tears when I heard Mama had died. My father struck me and told me to show some backbone. After that, I spent all the holidays at school. Even Christmas. He couldn't bear the sight of me.'

Evie reached for his hand, but he drew it away and rolled onto his side. 'Goodnight.'

After a few minutes he was asleep, but she could find no such solace herself.

EIGHTEEN

One Sunday in early January, Mary Helston offered to take Evie, with Jasmine and her school friend Penny, to swim in the Jungle Pools at Taiping on the mainland. It was Evie's first trip across on the ferry since arriving in Penang. Mary had borrowed her father's motor-car and Evie was glad to escape from George Town and to do so without the company of Benny. Evie felt constantly under a microscope worried that the servants compared her with Felicity and found her wanting. And while the Malayan was always courteous and correct, Evie had never managed to accustom herself to being driven about in a large car by a servant. She felt out of place and uncomfortable, remembering her own years as a paid companion. Today would be a relaxing change, and she approached the trip with excitement and a sense of liberation.

It took almost two hours to get to the Taiping Jungle Pools. The place was in a magical setting in the hills, in the midst of thick rain forest. It was a marvel of Victorian construction – a series of three pools built into the hillside, connected by concrete steps and walkways and fed by a natural waterfall. The colonial administration had created it to keep civil servants, planters and other Europeans entertained and able to relax, away from the suffocating heat of the coastal plain. Up here, the water was cool, in contrast to other swimming pools where it was always tepid at best – although at times it could appear a little murky.

There was a water chute that older children took great delight in sliding down, diving boards and a third smaller, shallow pool for children where the two little girls could play more safely. Sunlight filtered through the canopy of trees, dappling the lush ferns and glinting off the surface of the water. The joyous whoops of frolicking children and the chatter of adults mingled with birdsong, the trilling of insects and the sound of water rushing over the falls.

After a leisurely swim, Evie and Mary sat down on their towels on the wood-topped concrete parapet that ran alongside the children's pool, watching the two girls splashing about. Evie was glad to be in her friend's company. Mary had never again mentioned the loss of her fiancé. While her eyes sometimes betrayed that her sadness was still close to the surface, she had found a way of keeping it concealed.

'How are you settling in? It must be around six months you've been here now,' asked Mary.

'Five. To be honest, at first I thought I'd never settle. It's been incredibly hard to adjust. I think I underestimated how much. But now... well, I've never been happier.' She gave Mary a broad smile.

'That's super news. I'm so pleased for you.'

'It wasn't just acclimatising, although that's been hard enough, but getting used to my new circumstances.' Evie pulled off her swimming cap and ran her fingers through her hair. 'I'd forgotten what it was like to be part of a family. Years of living and working as a paid companion to a kind but crotchety old lady had narrowed my horizons – not to mention living in a tiny village in Hampshire where nothing ever happened. And now

I've been catapulted into a whole new world, as well as learning to be a wife and a mother.'

'You and Jasmine seem to get along famously.'

Evie turned her gaze to watch her step-daughter as she jumped, knees bent under her, into the water, emulating the dive-bombing of the boys in the pool. The eight-year-old emerged, coughing and spluttering and rubbing her eyes. But before Evie had a chance to check that she was all right, Jasmine was clambering out of the pool and getting ready to repeat the manoeuvre. 'Just look at her! She's in her element. And I have you and the school to thank for that.'

'No. You have to credit yourself. You've given Jasmine the love and care she'd obviously been craving since her mother died.'

Evie hesitated, before deciding if she couldn't confide in Mary she had no one to confide in at all. 'I sometimes wonder if she was craving it even while her mother was alive.'

'What makes you think that?'

'Just something Jasmine once said to me. She told me her mother was mean.'

'*Mean*? In what way?'

'I don't know. It was clearly upsetting her so I didn't press her.'

'Can't you ask your husband?'

Evie gave a little involuntary snort. 'In a word, no.' Seeing the dismay on Mary's face, she decided to show the same trust in her friend as Mary had shown to her when she'd recounted the story of her fiancé. 'What I mean is – that's been part of the difficulty of adjusting. Doug and I were virtual strangers when we married. We'd met only once. Years ago. He asked me to marry him by letter, completely out of the blue. And it was a very short letter at that.' She looked down, embarrassed, and kicked her legs back and forth lightly against the parapet. 'Things are good between us now... I think... but at first... it was jolly hard. I assumed he found it hard to accept me after the loss of his wife and... well... he's not the kind of man who talks a lot.'

Mary laughed. 'Your typical Englishman. You don't need to tell me. I've seen enough of them here. The English public school system has a lot to answer for.'

Evie nodded. 'He was educated at Eton. They don't exactly go out of their way to help boys express their feelings. And I've only just discovered that his mother died when he was ten and his father would have nothing to do with him and packed him off to school.'

'That's a familiar story here. Not necessarily that parents don't want to have their children around them, but that they send them off to boarding schools back in Britain and only get to see them for a few weeks every year. As a result, most of the men out here have never grown up properly – they behave as if they're still at boarding school and they haven't a clue how to talk to women. We're an alien species!' Mary cocked her head in the direction of the big pool where a group of young men were horsing around, whooping and yelling while carrying each other on their shoulders and ducking one another under the water. 'They leave the tender embrace of their mothers and *amah*s for a regime of 'six of the best', tightly reined-in emotions, and playing pranks.'

'Douglas isn't the prank-playing type.' Evie laughed lightly. 'He's quite the opposite. Rather serious. Apart from business, he has little time for socialising at all. His only real friend is Arthur Leighton and I think they get on because they're so different.' She felt an illicit thrill to be mentioning Arthur's name. 'Probably because Arthur didn't go to public school.'

'He's done extremely well for himself.'

'He's a clever man.' Evie told herself she had to stop this urge to speak about Arthur. She didn't want to give away her still-present feelings for him. Forcing herself back to the topic of Douglas and Jasmine, where the conversation had begun, she said, 'Anyway, what I was saying, is that it's often been quite tricky for my husband and I to understand each other, but things are so much better. Christmas was really special.'

Mary Helston looked wistful. 'I find Christmas hard. It reminds me of how much I've lost.' She leaned back, setting her mouth in a firm line. 'Better not to dwell on all that.'

Evie had been about to tell Mary that she was expecting a child but decided now was not the best moment. Mary would have to know eventually, and Evie wanted her to be the first outside the immediate family.

Jasmine and Penny rushed up, full of excitement, bursting with energy and spraying water everywhere as they approached. Evie wrapped a towel around Jasmine and rubbed her dry as Mary did the same for Penny. The two little girls giggled and jostled each other.

'She is!' whispered Penny. 'Ask her, if you don't believe me.'

'She isn't,' said Jasmine.

Penny jerked a shoulder against her friend. 'I bet she is. My mummy's always right.'

'Right about what?' Mary Helston asked, provoking another fit of giggles from the two girls.

Jasmine struggled free from the towel and put her hands on her hips. 'All right.' She faced Evie. 'Penny says you're going to have a baby.'

'What?' Evie could feel her face turning the colour of a beetroot.

'I heard Mummy telling Daddy. She said Mrs Leighton told her that Mr Barrington's new wife was expecting a baby. Then Daddy said, "That was quick work" and said that Mr Barrington didn't waste any time. Jasmine says it isn't true but Mummy told Daddy that Mrs Leighton had it from the horse's mouth. But that's silly as babies don't come from horse's mouths, they come from ladies' tummies.'

'No, they don't.' Jasmine pouted. 'That's just daft. The nuns told me the stork flies down from heaven and leaves them under a gooseberry bush.'

Scarlet-faced, Evie looked at Mary, unsure what to say or do.

Mary Helston took charge. 'Penny Cameron, how many times have I told you not to spread tittle tattle? If Mrs Barrington is expecting a baby it's up to her to tell whoever she chooses *when* she thinks fit. Nothing good comes to people who tell tales and talk behind other people's backs. If and when Mrs Barrington is going to have a baby she'll tell Jasmine herself. I don't want to have to mention this again. What do you say to Mrs Barrington?'

Penny looked sheepish. 'Sorry, Mrs Barrington.'

Jasmine rolled her eyes as if to say I told you so. The two girls took each other's hand and ran off into the sunshine to join the other children.

'Thank you,' said Evie. 'I didn't know what to say. I was taken aback.'

'Is it true?'

'Yes. But I didn't tell Veronica Leighton. She waltzed in on Christmas evening and tried to force copious amounts of gin on me. Maybe it's because of being pregnant but the very thought of drinking makes me feel sick these days, so I refused, and she jumped to conclusions. I neither confirmed nor denied, and I'm pretty sure Douglas wouldn't have done either.' Then Evie remembered she'd told Arthur. Had he broken his promise and told Veronica after all? If so, that probably meant he had also lied about not telling his wife about their meeting on the beach. But before she could dwell on this, she felt Mary's arms enveloping her.

'Oh, Evie, that's marvellous news! I'm so happy for you. When did you find out?'

'I saw the doctor just before Christmas and I only told Douglas on Christmas Eve.'

'He must be thrilled.'

'Yes, he is. I was going to tell you next. And Jasmine. But as you say, it's finding the right moment. And it's still quite early. Less than twelve weeks, the doctor says.'

Mary glanced at her friend's stomach. 'Certainly no sign of it yet.'

'Looks like I'm going to have to get ready for a conversation with Jasmine about the birds and the bees.'

'Not the horse's mouth!'

'No, not the horse's mouth. Gosh, don't children grow up quickly these days?'

'They feed off each other's curiosity. But it's probably best to tell them as little as possible. Preserve their innocence as long as we can.'

'So, what do you think I should do?'

'Nothing. Jasmine will probably have forgotten soon. Maybe when it starts to look obvious you can tell her the baby's in there. But she's far too young to be told how it got there.'

Evie laughed. 'Oh goodness me! I certainly wouldn't go that far – she's only recently turned eight!'

Dragging Jasmine and Penny away from the pools was quite a challenge, but Mary was keen to get most of the drive back to the ferry done before it fell dark. The little girls chattered away in the back seat and to Evie's relief, there was no further mention of babies.

After about an hour in the car, Jasmine announced that she needed to go to the lavatory.

'I told you to go while we were in the changing rooms. There's nowhere around here. You'll just have to hold on, darling,' said Evie.

'I didn't need to go then but I'm desperate now.'

'You drank too much pop.'

'Please Mummy! I don't want to wet myself.'

They were passing through a *kampong* and there were many Malays about.

'Once we're out of the village I'll try and find a place to stop and you can go behind a tree.' Mary glanced over her shoulder at the little girl.

Just then, Evie saw a sign at the roadside. *Batu Lembah. Barrington Rubber.* 'Turn off here, Mary. It's my husband's estate. We can call in and Jasmine can use the bathroom. Better than having to go by the roadside.'

Mary swung the car onto the gravel track. 'Looks like the bungalow and offices are over there,' she said. 'It's good we don't have to go far.'

A few hundred yards ahead, the rubber trees gave way to a *padang* that Evie guessed was where the musters were held. A line of wooden dwellings ran along each side of the open grassy area, and just beyond was a small building raised above the ground in the traditional Malay style, with a veranda running around it and stairs leading up to the open front door. It had a shabby air of neglect.

Mary parked the car at the side of the house and Evie and Jasmine jumped out. 'We'll only be a few moments. I won't hold us up,' said Evie. Thinking better of it, she added, 'Tell you what. Why don't I get the housekeeper to make us some tea before I go? You can meet my husband.'

Mary flicked the ignition off and she and Penny followed them out of the car.

Jasmine was already running up the steps, excited at the unexpected chance to see her father. Evie followed close behind her.

Douglas didn't notice them at first. He was sitting at the table, his head turned towards the woman standing behind him. Bare to the waist and shoeless, he was wearing a sarong and the woman was massaging his neck and shoulders.

Evie froze on the threshold as Jasmine cannoned across the room, bouncing up and down. 'Daddy, Daddy, I need the bathroom. I'm bursting and I'm going to wet myself.'

Doug's head whipped round and his face signalled shock at seeing his wife and daughter.

Behind Evie, Mary reached the top of the steps and, taking in the significance of the scene immediately, she grabbed Penny's hand and led her back to the car, hissing to the girl to be quiet, as she started to protest.

Doug flicked his head sideways to the Malayan woman and spoke to her rapidly in her own language. The only words Evie recognised were *bilk mandi*, which she remembered meant bathroom. The woman was slight, with delicate features, waist-length hair and of an indeterminate age, although Evie guessed she was older than she appeared. Feeling her knees buckle and her throat dry up, Evie watched, mute, as the woman took Jasmine's hand and led her out of the room.

Evie's eyes swept around the room. It was spartan – barely furnished apart from the table, on which were the unwashed dishes from an interrupted meal. Behind her husband, she glimpsed an unmade bed through an open doorway. She felt the bile rise in her throat. Her hands flew to her mouth as her body began to shake. Leaning back against the door frame, she tried to gather her thoughts. How was this happening? How could he? Like a punch in the stomach, her world and everything she believed in crashed around her. No! Oh God, no!

Douglas said nothing, staring at her in shocked silence.

She hissed at him, 'I don't want that woman near our daughter.' She stumbled along the corridor where she found the woman waiting outside the closed bathroom door. Pushing her out of the way, Evie opened the door and found Jasmine inside pulling up her knickers. She waited, numb and in shock as the little girl dipped the dipper into the large Shanghai jar, poured it into the ceramic wash bowl and washed her hands.

'Come on, darling. Do hurry up.' She tried to keep the emotion out of her voice but realised she was almost croaking.

'Miss Helston always says we must wash our hands when we go to the lavatory.' Then, 'Why are you crying, Mummy? What's the matter?'

Her step-daughter's lip was trembling so Evie forced herself to breathe deeply and gather her composure. 'I'm not crying, darling. I've just got something in my eye. We need to go right away as Miss Helston doesn't like driving in the dark and we don't want to miss the ferry.'

Expecting Jasmine to argue, Evie was relieved that, as if sensing something bad had happened, the girl complied and followed her out of the bathroom. There was no sign of the Malayan woman when they emerged.

Back in the main room – there was no way that Evie would dignify the scruffy space with the word drawing room – Douglas was pacing up and down.

'Go to the car, Jasmine,' she said. 'Tell Miss Helston I'll be out in just a moment. I need to speak to your father first.'

Jasmine went outside to join the others without protest.

Evie looked at Douglas, still struggling to believe what she had witnessed. 'How could you? Knowing that I'm carrying our baby. How could you?' Her voice trembled but she willed herself not to cry.

Douglas looked down, but said nothing. Apart from the instructions to the woman, he hadn't spoken a word since they'd arrived.

'Who is she?'

'My housekeeper.'

'Your *housekeeper*?' She could hear the contempt in her own voice. 'I have to get those girls home. But you need to know that you have crushed me. Broken me.' She felt her emotions start to spin out of control. 'I can't talk about it now.' She moved towards the door as he called out her name.

Standing on the threshold, she looked back at him. 'How long has this been going on?'

'Look, Evie—'

'No. On second thoughts, I don't want to know. You disgust me.'

She rushed down the steps and into the waiting car. 'Drive! For goodness sake, drive please, Mary,' she said, her voice barely a whisper.

NINETEEN

The last half-hour to the ferry port at Butterworth passed in silence, apart from the rhythmic squeak of the windscreen wipers as they drove through a sudden tropical deluge. In the back of the car, the girls had fallen asleep, Penny's head on Jasmine's shoulder. Mary Helston drove with her eyes fixed on the road ahead. When Evie had got into the car her friend had squeezed her hand, but said nothing. Evie was grateful for the silence. The thought of speaking about what had just taken place filled her with horror. She preferred to wallow alone in her misery and anger.

Her thoughts were in turmoil. Douglas's betrayal was devastating, especially after the Christmas holidays they had spent as a family, the close approximation to affection that he had been beginning to show her, and his pleasure at the child they were going to have together. Yet all that time he had been tucked up in his sordid love nest with his native whore. No wonder he spent most of his time at Batu Lembah. No wonder he had refused to bring Evie there. She had been taken for a fool.

Over and over again, her mind replayed the scene in the bungalow. The woman's hands gently kneading his naked back.

The tumbled sheets on the unmade bed. Had they just finished love-making? Had they merely stopped to have some food? Is this what happened every time he was away from George Town? Every night? How long had it been going on? With a chill that froze her to the marrow in spite of the sultry heat of the evening, she wondered who else had known about this. The Leightons? She found it hard to imagine that Veronica wouldn't have found a way to let her know, to take pleasure in the telling. But Arthur? As Doug's best friend he must surely have known. And she remembered the knowing looks the Hyde-Underwoods had exchanged when Douglas had brought her to Bellavista; their surprise that he had married.

Evie felt nauseous but it had nothing to do with the baby. She had so far experienced none of the morning sickness that the doctor had warned might blight the early weeks of her pregnancy. She prayed for the drive to be over and longed to be alone.

During the twenty-minute ferry crossing, Mary spoke to her at last. 'Evie, I want to remind you that you can always count on me. I know you won't feel like talking at the moment, but when you do, I will be waiting. I can't make it any better, but at least I understand how you must be feeling.' She drew her lips into a tight, rueful line and pulled Evie into her arms and gave her a hug. 'And if you want me to take Jasmine off your hands while you talk to your husband, just tell me. Since Penny lives next door to me they can play together and I can give them both their tea.'

'Thank you. But I don't want to talk to him ever again.' Evie's voice was a whisper. She gripped Mary's arm. 'Does everyone in George Town know? Have they all been laughing at me behind my back?'

'No. I'm certain they don't know. George Town's like a village. I'd have heard if there were rumours flying round. And, as you will have gathered this afternoon, Rowena Cameron,

Penny's mum, is one of the biggest gossips on the island. I've not heard a squeak.'

Two days later, Evie woke in the middle of the night, needing to go to the lavatory. To her horror she found she had lost some blood.

Panic gripped her. Was she losing the baby?

Staggering to the staircase she went downstairs, through the house, into the garden and hammered on the door of the single-storey building where Aunty Mimi and the other servants slept.

Benny appeared at one of the far windows, then Cookie opened the door. Aunty Mimi, her hair down, stood behind him.

'Aunty Mimi, please come. The baby...' She clutched her stomach.

Saying something rapidly in Chinese to Cookie, Aunty Mimi left the lodge and followed Evie back across the lawn and into the house. After questioning Evie, she led her back to bed and told her she would bring tea as soon as she'd summoned the doctor.

Evie sipped the tea, fear and anxiety weighing heavy upon her. She had already lost her husband and now it seemed fate was about to steal her unborn child. More than ever now she was desperate to have this baby.

By the time the doctor arrived, Evie was in tears, convinced she was miscarrying – although there had been no further bleeding.

It was a duty doctor, a younger man, who examined her, told her the baby's heartbeat was good and that minor bleeding did not always mean a miscarriage. Telling her to take it easy and come into the surgery to see Dr Oates as soon as she felt well enough, he said, 'He'll want to keep an eye on you, but I'm sure it's nothing you should be worried about, Mrs Barrington.'

. . .

The following morning, with still no word from Douglas, Arthur Leighton arrived at the house. Evie had got into the habit of rising to join Jasmine for breakfast, before returning to her bed, unable to face the world. That morning, she was still sitting in the dining room, clad in her dressing gown, her hair uncombed, breakfast untouched, when Arthur was shown in by a frowning Aunty Mimi.

Evie looked up and saw his face was drawn and his eyes full of concern. She stood up. He moved across to her and she realised he intended to embrace her. Backing away, she said, 'Did he send you here?'

Arthur nodded.

'Too cowardly to do his own dirty work. He's spineless.'

'He wants to talk to you.'

'I don't want to talk to him.' She slumped back into her chair, and pushed her teacup out of the way. 'Did you know? Oh, God, why am I even asking that? Of course you knew. You're his best friend.'

Arthur shook his head, his face stricken. 'I didn't know, Evie. I promise you I'd no idea. Doug is a very closed person. He tells me very little and certainly didn't tell me that. He found it hard enough to tell me when he turned up at my office last night.'

'Why don't I believe you, Arthur? Why can't I believe anything you or anyone else in this godforsaken country tell me?'

He pulled out the chair next to hers and sat down. 'Because I care about you, Evie. I know that's probably the last thing you want to hear right now. But I hate to think of the pain you must be going through.' He paused. 'Because I love you.'

Evie snorted. 'Stop! I *don't* want to hear that. My husband is disporting himself with a Malayan whore while I'm carrying his child. No, Arthur, your declarations of love are the last thing I want to hear.'

'I didn't mean it that way, Evie. We both know you and I can never have what I'd like us to have, but that doesn't mean you don't matter to me more than anyone or anything in this world.'

Slumping forward, she rested her head on her hands. 'Go away, Arthur. I can't even cry any more. I have no tears left. Everything is ruined. I was trying so hard to make a life with him. I thought at last we were a family. And he's destroyed it all.'

Arthur said nothing but placed a hand on her arm. She found the contact strangely comforting and began to cry.

'I may be going to lose the baby,' she said.

'What?'

'Last night I lost some blood. Aunty Mimi called out the doctor.'

'What did he say?' He frowned with concern.

'Bed rest. Wait and see. He said bleeding doesn't always mean the worst. If I can get through the next few days I'll be past the first twelve weeks and that's meant to be the most dangerous time for miscarrying.' She lifted her eyes to look at him. 'Part of me *wants* to lose the baby. To punish Doug. It's all he cares about. I'm just a vessel to carry his child, like a hermit crab. I'm not a proper person in my own right.' She rubbed at her eyes.

Arthur handed her an unused napkin.

Through her tears she said, 'Why am I saying this? I don't really want to lose the baby! I don't. Even if it has to grow up without a father. I couldn't bear to lose it. I just don't want *him* near it. He's an unfit father. A lying, cheating, faithless man.'

'Look, Evie, it's because of the baby and Jasmine that you must let him talk to you. He wants to explain. He's a mess. Distraught. Please, give him a chance. Just listen to him. I'm saying all this because I care about you. Because I want the best for you. And the best thing is that you and he manage to patch things up and look for a way forward.'

'You mean him, me and his Malayan whore?'

'She's gone.'

'Gone? Where? Back to her *kampung* down the road where he can visit her when he pleases? I don't want to know about his sordid arrangements. I don't want to hear his feeble excuses. He's a liar.' She dragged the napkin over her eyes then flung it down on the table. 'Why the hell didn't he marry that girl in the first place and have lots of little half-breed children instead of dragging me across the world?' Turning to look at Arthur, she added, 'No, don't bother to answer that. It's not the done thing, is it? All right for the Dutch or the French to marry local girls but the British frown on it, don't they? What's the expression? *Infra dig*, that's it, isn't it? No, they wouldn't like it at the Penang Club, would they? They wouldn't approve of that at all.'

Arthur said nothing, but put his hand back on her arm.

'I wish to God I'd never agreed to marry him. If I'd stayed in Hampshire I'd have had a quiet uneventful life, but at least it wouldn't have been one of utter misery. I've put everything into this fragile chance of happiness. I've worked hard trying to make this miserable marriage work.'

She glanced at him quickly, before looking away. 'Even though, ever since that day at the beach, I knew I couldn't love him, because of loving you. But I put you out of my thoughts and I tried so hard, so incredibly hard, to be the best possible wife to Douglas. I refused to let his moods get me down. I put a brave face on when he used my body but showed me not an ounce of affection. I took an interest in his damned rubber business. I cared for his daughter. Not once did I complain about his absences. I tried every minute of every day to love him and hoped and prayed that he might come to love me.'

Arthur waited patiently, his face anguished, saying nothing, until eventually Evie spoke again.

'Where is he?'

'Waiting outside in his car.'

She slumped forward. After a few moments she sat upright. 'Very well. Let's get it over with.'

Arthur left, and shortly after, Douglas came into the dining room. He moved around the table and sat on the other side facing Evie. He looked haggard. There was a couple of days worth of stubble on his face, his hair was unkempt and there were dark rings under his eyes. He seemed to have lost weight and his face was gaunt and pallid despite his sun-tanned skin. Evie waited for him to speak.

'I'm sorry,' he said. 'You shouldn't have had to walk in on... that.'

'So if I hadn't *seen* you, it would be fine? As long as I didn't know about your dirty little love nest? As long as I hadn't interrupted what you were up to? If I had sent you a telegram to warn you that I was coming to visit you could have hidden her away and it would have been all right, would it?'

'When you walked in I'd just told her she couldn't stay any longer. That we were finished.'

Evie snorted. 'Yes, it looked like it. A perfectly normal way to end a relationship – make love all day long then, while she's giving you a massage, tell her to pack her bags.'

'It wasn't a relationship. She was my housekeeper. And we hadn't been making love.'

'Shut up, Doug. I don't want to hear any more. You disgust me.'

'But that's it. It was just sex. It didn't mean anything. And when you walked in I'd already told her it was over. It was only a massage. It didn't mean a thing. None of it meant anything.'

Evie snorted in derision, got up from the table and was about to move towards the door.

He leaned across and gripped her arm, holding her back. 'Please hear me out, Evie. I beg you.'

She shook her arm free of his hold. 'I don't understand you at all. I feel polluted just listening to this.'

'It started after Felicity and I parted.'

For a moment Evie thought she'd misheard. 'Parted?'

'My marriage to Felicity was the biggest mistake of my life.' He shook his head rapidly and added, 'No the second biggest. The biggest was what has just happened.'

His words shocked Evie. 'Go on,' she said, curious to hear about Felicity – even though she knew it would make no difference to the final outcome.

'I was besotted with Felicity. She was the most beautiful creature I'd ever seen and I believed I was in love with her. But once we were married I soon discovered she was mean-spirited, always finding fault in everything and everyone. Joyless. From the early days of our marriage she denied me her bed whenever she could. It felt like a miracle to me when we found out she was expecting Jasmine. I'd hoped that Penang would have been a new start for us but it was Felicity's idea of hell. She hated the place and hated being pregnant. The birth was difficult and she showed no affection towards the baby and wanted little or nothing do with her. She made no secret of her contempt for me.'

'Yet you loved her.'

'I *loathed* her.' He looked at Evie and she knew he was telling the truth.

'Why do you keep a shrine to her upstairs?' She jerked her head upwards to the ceiling. 'In your bedroom.'

'That's not my bedroom. I never go near it. When I'm in this house and haven't spent the night with you, I sleep in the small room next door.'

'But all her clothes are still in the main bedroom. All her personal things. Jewellery. Everything.'

'Are they? You can get rid of them. I told Aunty Mimi to do that after Felicity died. I don't know why she didn't.'

Evie was stunned. Things were turning out to be the opposite of what they had seemed.

'When I bought Batu Lembah I hoped things might change. Felicity didn't like Bella Vista. But from the moment we crossed the threshold of Batu Lembah she made it clear that she didn't want to be there. It used to look better in those days. More furniture, pictures, home comforts. But she never liked it. She was angry all the time. One evening I came home to the bungalow to be greeted by screaming from Jasmine. My wife was beating her with the handle of her hairbrush. Jasmine was only three. That's when I sent Jasmine to the convent. For her own protection. I took on the house in George Town and Felicity moved back there. I'd come into town just for meetings, tennis, functions at the club and so on, just to keep up the facade that our marriage was functioning.'

He stopped and ran his hands through his hair. His expression was grim. He was evidently finding telling her all this painful.

Breathing out loudly, he said, 'Felicity couldn't bear the physical side of marriage. After Jasmine was born she wouldn't even entertain the idea of letting me near her at all.' He put his head in his hands. Looking up at her, a picture of misery, he said, 'I'm only human. A man has needs. I'm not proud of what I did, but that's how it started with Nayla.'

'Don't say her name. I don't want to know. And that might be how it started but it doesn't explain why it went on. It doesn't explain why you married me and kept on having relations with her. Kept on living with her as man and wife.'

He winced. 'It was never as man and wife. I told you it was only sex. I feel nothing for her. I never have. She was obliging, undemanding, uncomplicated–'

'Stop. I don't want to listen to her many virtues.'

Douglas sighed. 'I'm trying to explain, Evie. After Felicity, who shuddered every time I came near her, Nayla... I mean the Malayan woman... was easy and relaxed. It meant as little to her as it did to me. Just physical pleasure.' He looked away. 'God, Evie, it's bloody hard telling you all this.'

'Swearing won't make it any easier. And if it's hard telling it, I can promise you it's much harder having to listen to it.'

'I'm sorry. Anyway, after Felicity died, I knew I needed a wife. One I could be seen with in company. A mother for my children. I thought marrying you was an arrangement that would suit us both – and I was very straight with you from the start. You have to give me that much.'

'Oh yes. You were certainly straight. Brutally so.'

He looked ashamed. 'But gradually I realised I was beginning to feel for you. I didn't know how to deal with that. I hadn't expected it. I was afraid. Scared of my own emotions. I didn't know what to do.'

'You didn't know what to do? How about telling me? How about showing me?'

Doug's voice was choked. 'I nearly did. I tried. That night you told me about the baby. I didn't know how to tell you I cared for you. The only other person I've loved was my mother. After she died, my feelings died with her. I don't know why I couldn't say those words to you.' He stopped, looking at her hands. 'You aren't wearing the ring I gave you.'

'I have no intention of wearing it again. Give it to your whore.'

'Oh God, Evie. Please, don't. I *do* care for you. Please believe that. Even if it's too late. But please don't say it's too late.' He gave a strangled sob.

'You're only saying all this because of the baby.' She stared at him, waiting for his reaction to what she was about to tell him. 'Well, you may not have to worry about that much longer as there's a chance I might be losing it.'

His face crumpled, then he jumped up and moved across to her and pulled her into his arms, holding her against him. Evie was too stunned to speak.

'What makes you think you're losing it? What's happened? Are you all right? You don't look well. It's all my fault. I've done this to you. I've hurt you. Is that why you think you might be losing our baby?'

'I've lost some blood. It's a possibility.'

Douglas eased her away from him slightly so he could look into her eyes. 'The thing I care about most is *you*. I don't want anything to happen to you. I couldn't live with myself.' He drew her tight against his chest again, cradling her head in his hand. 'I won't be able to live with myself anyway if you can't forgive me. If you won't give me another chance.'

Evie jerked away from him. 'I'm going upstairs to lie down. The doctor says I need bed rest. Leave me alone, please.'

'Will you think about it, Evie? Please. Will you give me a second chance? I promise you that woman has gone forever. I've hired a houseboy. He's the cook's younger brother. It's an all-male household now.'

Evie shook her head. 'I don't know, Doug. I just don't know anything anymore.'

TWENTY

She hadn't lost the baby. There was no repetition of the blood loss, the doctor made encouraging noises and Evie began to breathe again. She also started eating again – determined not to do anything else to put her unborn child at risk.

Three days after Douglas had come to see her, she summoned Aunty Mimi to the drawing room and gave her instructions to clear Felicity's things out of her former bedroom.

'I don't care what you do with them. Burn them if you like. Give them away. Sell them. But I don't want them in this house any more.'

Aunty Mimi's face contorted into a look of defiance. She started to speak but Evie lifted her hand for her to stop.

'The *tuan* has told me he had instructed you to clear out that bedroom, yet you didn't, so you'd better do it right away. And I don't want to hear any argument.'

'But Missy Leighton say no touch any-sing. It *Mem*'s, not yours, Missy Leighton say.'

'Do you work for Mrs Leighton? Does Mrs Leighton pay your wages?'

The old woman shook her head.

'Then you will do as Mr Barrington and I tell you. *I* am the *mem* in this house now.'

Aunty Mimi was affronted, and said, 'Missy Leighton say you no stay Penang. You go home England soon.'

'Aunty Mimi, I am going to tell you this now and I don't want to hear any more from you.' Pointing towards the bottom of the garden where the servants lived in a series of rooms in a single-storey structure, Evie said, 'If you prefer to take your orders from Mrs Leighton you had better go out to your room, pack your bags and ask Mrs Leighton to give you a job, as you will no longer have one here.' Evie grew taller as she spoke, taking confidence from the sound of her own voice. 'I have absolutely no intention of going back to England. You need to empty the contents of that bedroom immediately as I will be using it. I want you to move my clothing in there as soon the items in the wardrobes and dressing table have been cleared out. Everything! The small bedroom which is Mr Barrington's room will eventually be the baby's bedroom.' She paused for breath. 'Is that absolutely clear? You can put anything belonging to Mr Barrington in the room I have been using.'

'Yes, *Mem*.' There was the ghost of a smile playing across the Chinese woman's face. 'Velly good.'

As Aunty Mimi left, Evie exhaled slowly, relief flooding through her. She'd had enough of creeping around, afraid of her own shadow. Things were going to be different from now on. Doug's words had taken her by surprise. She wasn't ready to forgive him. Not yet. But there was a possibility that eventually she might.

In the meantime, *she* would be making the rules. The first one was that he return to George Town every single weekend. She intended him to sleep apart from her. It was too soon to contemplate taking him back into her bed. He had first to prove that he was ready to play the part of father to Jasmine, if he was to be permitted to do the same for their child. If he wanted a family, he could damn well act like a husband and father. If he wanted her to believe that he cared about her, he had to show it.

Evie decided to absent herself while Aunty Mimi, aided by The Boy, set about the task of moving the contents of the bedrooms. Telling Benny she would be back in time to accompany him to collect Jasmine from school, Evie set off from the house on foot.

She had always enjoyed her solitary rambles around George Town, loving the hubbub, the mixture of people, the buzz of commerce. After so long resting in bed, confined to the house, it was a relief to be outside. Early that morning it had rained heavily, and the air was clearer, with a light sea breeze tempering the growing heat of the day.

After strolling past the bastion of Fort Cornwallis with its thick brick walls, Evie turned off and plunged into the nearby streets. Eventually finding herself in a square with a collection of stalls and kiosks, her nose and throat were assaulted by an overpowering, sweet smell of incense. Across the square was a small temple, with the characteristic Chinese swooping curved roof, adorned along the ridge with dragon statues. There were shrines and stone statues outside, where people gathered to thrust bunches of smouldering joss sticks into jars filled with sand, before bending or squatting in prayer and devotion. Looking around, she could see no other Europeans, but no one seemed bothered by her presence so she walked freely around the space. There was a covered well, where people were collecting water, and piles of stacked wooden cages each containing a small bird. The square was a peculiar mixture of sincere devotion and casual commerce.

Hesitantly, Evie went up to the entrance of the temple building and was glad to find it quiet and almost empty inside, although the scent of the burning incense was more intense than in the square.

The light was dim, provided only by the faint glow of candles and the daylight from the narrow open doorway she had entered through. She squinted to see. In front of her was a small gold-painted shrine. Evie moved towards it and stood for a while in silence, drinking in the calm and quiet of the place after the chaotic scene outside. Her eyes adjusted to the gloom and she saw the shrine was crowded with a collection of painted figures, the male ones dressed like emperors in ornate robes with long drooping moustaches, one or two goddesses, other figures resembling evil-looking ogres, and among them gold-painted animals such as horned deer or sea creatures. Oranges and other fruits were stacked in neat piles with what she assumed to be votive messages written in Chinese on little cards. The smell of the burning joss sticks was intensified by the perfume from flowers, stacked around the shrine in tall vases. Curved metal lanterns and red streamers hung from the ceiling.

Evie was transfixed by the scene and felt a strange calm enveloping her after all the trauma, fear and bitterness of the past days. Without thinking why, she stood with her head bowed and closed her eyes.

She took stock of her situation, letting her mind run free. She realised that she had only ever seen Douglas with her eyes and not with her mind or her heart. Never managing to get past his dark good looks, hers had been a shallow love – no love at all – based on aesthetic appreciation not true feelings. How could she love someone she couldn't communicate with? They shared no interests. Had nothing in common. She and Douglas spoke different languages and inhabited different worlds. Perhaps what had happened was a rude awakening, a message that she should give up trying to make their marriage work.

Her feelings were entirely different with Arthur. She was certain that in him she had found – but could never have – her soulmate. No, she mustn't think about Arthur.

When Evie opened her eyes again there was a diminutive

man in grey robes standing in front of her. A monk or priest, she assumed. Mumbling her apologies for intruding in this place of devotion, she was about to leave but he called out to her. His voice was soothing, gentle. He spoke to her in English.

'No need run away, daughter. Temple of Harmony welcome everyone who show respect. As you have done.'

'Thank you. I only stepped inside for a few moments but I'm glad I did. It's so peaceful and calm here. Being here has already made me feel much better.'

He nodded his head slowly. 'You feel better? Why you feel bad before?'

She looked at his face and saw only kindness in his eyes. But before she could answer, he asked, 'You want drink some tea?'

Evie nodded.

He led her to a doorway at the side of the shrine. 'In here quiet place.'

Never thinking to question why she should follow this stranger, she went with him into an ante-room, presumably leading to the monks' quarters.

They sat on cushions on the floor and the monk poured her tea in a fine bone china cup, delicately patterned with entwined leaves. Evie sipped the hot liquid and felt her new sense of calm grow. Without knowing how or why, she found herself telling the stranger about her fears for her marriage and for her baby.

He looked at her over the top of his cup. 'Baby is good. Baby safe. Baby inside you, so you must be kind to self. You must first love self to love baby.'

'Myself? You think I need to be kind to myself?' She looked at him in surprise. 'What a funny thing to say.'

'Not funny. Everything begin with self. Only when you love self can you make room in heart for love this baby and for love husband. You first be kind to self. Not angry.'

'And you think I'm not kind to myself? You think I'm angry?'

'Are you? You tell me, daughter.'

Evie thought for a moment. It was such an odd thing to say. The very idea of loving herself seemed peculiar. Vain. Unworthy. 'In my religion we are taught to love God and love others. Not ourselves.'

He shook his head. 'Only when love self can find space to love gods and love others. When we love self we can begin to make space in soul to show mercy and kindness to others without judge them.'

'But my husband has betrayed me with another woman. You think I must forgive him? I mustn't judge him?'

'You not listen. First you must forgive self. Be kind to self.'

Evie remembered the brief conversation she had had months ago with Douglas when he had told her she was too hard on herself. Perhaps there was something in what this man was telling her now.

'Only when love self can spirit make space for other soul,' he repeated. 'Space for husband soul to lie in your heart. When you do not love self you cannot love other.'

'Gosh.'

'Compassion come first. Love self. Then show mercy to other. Forgive. But must forgive self first before can forgive other. This is nature. This is how we live in nature at peace with all gods and all world.'

Evie put down her cup. It was such a lot to take in – and yet if she had understood correctly, so simple. 'You have certainly given me much to think about.'

'For husband and wife to live well together they must be Yin and Yang. Must accept and understand differences. Must live and let live.' He got to his feet, bent forward in a bow to her. 'Time you go. Remember, to make space in spirit for other soul must start with self.'

'May I come again? I'd like to understand more.'

'I am always here. But if you listen well, you no need. Listen to heart. Gods are everywhere and will speak to you.'

Outside, Evie blinked in the brightness of the day after the dark interior of the temple. She glanced at her watch and saw it was almost time for Benny to leave for the school, so she hurried all the way back to the house.

Her unexpected meeting with the Taoist monk had raised her spirits. His reassurance about her baby's safety had oddly made a greater impression on her than had the doctor's. He had sounded so sure, so certain. And his strange pronouncements about self-love made sense the more she thought about them. Meeting him had come at exactly the right moment and his words repeated themselves in her head as she walked along. Maybe she did need to forgive herself – for doubting herself, for belittling herself. For believing herself unworthy of being loved. She remembered the way Douglas had accused her of running herself down and making herself smaller. Yet perhaps today, in standing up for herself with Aunty Mimi, she was already beginning to learn that lesson. The words of the monk had both excited her and yet also made her rather afraid.

It was ironic that just as Douglas had admitted that he cared for her, Evie had no longer been sure she could ever feel anything for him again. The damage was too deep, the hurt too severe. And she didn't want to admit it, but she knew that despite there being no possibility of ever being with Arthur Leighton, it was proving extremely difficult to stop herself wanting him and loving him. But stop she must. Douglas, Jasmine and the unborn baby were her life. She had to gather up the broken pieces of marriage and family and stitch them back together again. And if that meant stitching her self-respect back together that's where she'd start.

TWENTY-ONE

The only person Evie told about her strange encounter with the Taoist monk was Mary Helston.

'There's a lot of wisdom among the Chinese,' Mary said, 'if only we listened to it. We British are all too quick to assume that we have all the answers and that other races and cultures are decidedly second-best with nothing to offer us.'

'Are you religious, Mary?'

Mary thought for a moment. 'I go to church. I believe in God. But I received little comfort from the vicar when Ralph died. I suppose I go more out of duty, and because it's expected. But I feel closer to God when I enter a church outside of the services and just sit down and pray in silence. Or even don't pray at all.' She smiled. 'To tell the truth, Evie, I find being somewhere like Penang Hill or walking along the beach I can just as easily talk to God. He doesn't discriminate where He goes.'

'That's exactly what my monk said. He told me the gods are everywhere and you need to listen for them. I felt close to God talking to that monk. He was so quiet and gentle and ... well, *good* I suppose. He seemed to think that we don't need special buildings to find God. Better to look inside one's heart and in nature.'

Mary tilted her head to one side, considering Evie's words, then said, 'I find those temples too fancy with their painted statues and choking incense. And if they genuinely believe God is present in the natural world why go to the trouble of building all those gaudy temples?'

Evie felt rebuffed, afraid that Mary must think her silly. 'Well, you could say the same about building churches.'

'I do.' But her friend squeezed her hand. 'Anyway I'm glad this monk has revived your spirits and made you feel more positive.'

'Do you think he's right about needing to show forgiveness and understanding to Doug? You were there at Batu Lembah. You saw that woman.'

Mary stretched her legs out in front of her. They were sitting on a fallen log on the shore, under the casuarina trees. Further along the beach Jasmine and her friend Penny were racing each other between two rocks. Mary tilted her head in the direction of the girls. 'I know nothing about marriage, but I'm going to ask you a question. Why do you think Penny spends so much time with me?'

Evie felt a rush of guilt. It had never occurred to her to ask. She had been grateful never to have had to have anything to do with Penny's mother, Rowena, one of the members of Veronica's 'witches' coven'. 'I suppose I imagined her mother was always busy,' she said, lamely.

'If you call being passed out in bed drunk or dosed-up with pills busy, then yes, she's often busy.'

'Gosh. That's dreadful. Poor Penny.'

'And when she's not out cold, Rowena's at it hammer and tongs with her husband. We can hear them through the walls, screaming at each other night after night.'

Evie put her hands up to her mouth, shocked. 'Why?'

Mary shrugged. 'They just don't get along. In fact they can't stand the sight of each other. Not helped by the fact that Rowena found out Bertie had been having an affair with one of the taxi girls at the Eastern & Oriental Hotel.'

'Taxi girls?'

'Professional dance hostesses. Men pay the E&O for a ticket to dance with them and the girls get half the proceeds. While most of them are perfectly respectable, some of them are rather too willing to do more than dance.'

'And he got caught out?'

'He did indeed. Red-handed. Rowena plays bridge most afternoons. Bertie Cameron is the director of one of the shipping companies, so, as the *tuan,* he can come and go from his office as he pleases. One afternoon, Rowena was feeling unwell during her bridge game. So she ducked out after a couple of rubbers and went home to lie down. She walked in on them in bed.'

'How horrible!'

'Yes. Rowena's been exacting her revenge ever since. The atmosphere between them is poisonous. That poor child is caught in the middle.' Mary sighed. 'Don't be like Rowena, Evie. Try and find a way to forgive and forget, for Jasmine's sake and your baby's.' She studied Evie's face, her eyes anxious. 'I hope you don't think I'm a terrible gossip? Only, since Rowena would win all the prizes for that herself, I feel somewhat justified.'

'You see their problems as Rowena's making?'

'No. Definitely not. They're both as bad as each other. He's not shown an ounce of remorse. In fact it's as if he resents her for finding him out. I suppose he thinks she should have been a dutiful little *mem* and pretended she'd seen nothing. No, I can't blame her for raising the roof. But I blame them both for doing nothing to heal the wounds afterwards and making that poor child suffer as a consequence.'

Mary gave another sigh, an anguished expression on her face. 'Look Evie, I've been agonising about whether to tell you this but I've decided I'm going to. I overheard Penny talking to Jasmine. She seems to think that her parents are so caught up in bickering with each other and have no time for her, and that's proof that they don't love her.' Mary paused. 'Jasmine told her that she thinks you and her father are going to be like that too. I hate to let you know this, but Jasmine believes it's her fault that you and Mr Barrington have fallen out. She traces it back to her having to use the toilet on the way back from Taiping. I know it's wrong but it's her childish logic. When I heard her I didn't think it would be right for me to intervene. Maybe you need to find a way to straighten her out. It's not up to me. But if you follow that monk's advice and start building bridges with your husband she won't need to be straightened out, will she?'

Evie stared at her, stricken. 'Jasmine blames herself?'

'Children often get the wrong end of the stick.' Mary looked at her sadly. 'I'm going to pass on one piece of advice. My Granny once told me that the secret to a happy marriage was to think of love as a verb and not as a noun. It's something you do and you show; not a state you're in.'

'I think your Granny would have got on well with my monk!'

'Very probably.' Mary got to her feet. 'If I could change one thing in my life it would be to have buried my pride and tried to forgive Ralph. Once he was dead, pride and indignation and hurt feelings meant nothing. Come on, we'd better get those girls back for their tea. Mum has been baking queen cakes.'

That night, after Jasmine was in bed, Evie put on the pearl ring her husband had given her at Christmas. Downstairs, she sat down at the ornate lacquered desk in the study, took a sheet of paper and wrote a brief letter to her husband, telling him he could come home at the weekend. She decided against stating the terms for his return and the change in the allocation of bedrooms. That could be left until he was here and she could deal with it face-to-face.

The following morning, she was about to tell Jasmine that her daddy would be coming home for the weekend, but decided not to chance it. If Doug failed to turn up, the little girl would be devastated.

But he did turn up. Not only that, he arrived that evening instead of waiting until Saturday as she had expected and as was his usual custom. He had made more of an effort with his appearance than his previous visit. No sign of the unkempt hair. No stubble on his shaved chin. He was wearing an open-necked, well-pressed shirt, a pair of pale linen trousers in place of his habitual shorts, and his hair was neat and looked freshly washed. But there was a look of unease around his eyes and he appeared nervous.

'You got my letter? I didn't expect you until tomorrow.'

Douglas looked surprised. 'What letter?'

'I wrote to say you could come home this weekend.'

He moved across the room, relief washing over his features. 'You did? The post is often slow at Batu Lembah. Thank you, Evie. Thank you.' He went towards the drinks cabinet. 'This calls for a celebration.'

Something inside told her not to make things too easy for him. Forgiving him didn't absolve him from the original crime.

'Sit down first. You can listen to me before you have a drink in your hand.'

Douglas looked abashed, but complied, taking a seat opposite her.

Evie spoke first. 'I've been doing a lot of thinking since we talked. And for the sake of the baby and for Jasmine, I've come to the conclusion that we have to try and repair the damage.'

He started to speak but she lifted a hand to stay him. 'Look, Doug, you've had your chance to talk. Now it's time you hear me.'

He nodded, leaning back in the chair, his eyes fixed on her.

'Damage is the right word,' she said. 'You need to acknowledge that you have damaged me and cut me to the quick. But not only me. You need to accept responsibility for what your daughter saw that afternoon. Jasmine believes that my tears and my sadness are her fault. She's blaming herself for causing us to go to the estate that afternoon. I don't think she understood what was happening but she knew there was something wrong. I've tried to hide my feelings from her but she senses when things aren't right. Her confidence and security have been shattered so you and I have to make things right for her.' She placed one hand over the other, covering the pearl ring on her finger.

Douglas was frowning, his mouth drawn into a tight line. He leaned forward and put his head in his hands.

Resisting the urge to comfort him, Evie went on. 'Her best friend Penny is the Camerons' daughter so she knows what having warring parents means. That's the reason why I'm agreeing to take you back and to do what I can to repair our marriage.'

Doug moved off the chair and came to sit beside her, reaching for her hands. 'I've made a hash of things, Evie. I wish I could wind the clock back, but I promise you, it will be different from now on. You won't regret it.'

She drew her hands away from him. It would be all too easy to let things ride but it was important she seized the moment and didn't completely capitulate. 'If you think I will fall gratefully into your arms and forget everything that's happened, you're wrong. Yes, I want to forget. I want to be a wife to you again. I want us to be a family. But you have come so close to destroying everything and I'm going to need time for the wounds to heal. If I'm to forget the past we have to start to create a future, and I need you to help make that happen.'

'I promise you, Evie. I'll do whatever it takes.'

He reached for her hands again. She was about to move them away but she remembered the words of the monk and this time let him take them.

'I've moved your things out of the small bedroom. We'll need that for the baby once it's old enough to sleep in there. Your things are in the room next door.'

His face lit up.

'*I* won't be.'

His face fell.

'Aunty Mimi has cleared out the main bedroom and I've moved into it. The cradle can go in there with me for the baby's first few months. Until it's old enough to sleep in a cot in its own room.'

'You're all right? And the baby's all right?'

'Yes. At least, according to the doctor.'

'Thank God!'

'But I will be sleeping alone. At least for the moment.'

'I see.'

'Do you? I'm not sure you do.' Evie got up and opened the shuttered French door to the garden, letting the clamour of the cicadas and the cockerels, as well as the softest of breezes, into the room. She turned back to look at him. 'You destroyed my trust. I promise you I will work hard to find a way to forgive you for that. But please don't expect that it's going to happen overnight.'

He looked at her with an expression that mingled sorrow with what might even have been admiration. 'You're wearing the ring again. Thank you.'

'I'm going to turn in, Doug. Good night. I'll see you tomorrow.'

As she left the room, Evie thought she'd handled the situation well. Yes, Evie, she told herself, the road to loving him must start with loving yourself. And that means taking pride in your own strength and tenacity. She made her way slowly up the staircase.

TWENTY-TWO

As her pregnancy progressed, Evie realised exactly what Susan Hyde-Underwood had meant about the discomforts of expecting a baby in the heat and humidity of Malaya. Growing in bulk she felt lopsided, the increasing heaviness of the baby cumbersome and awkward in front and causing backache. Perspiration gathered between and under her enlarged breasts and chafed at her skin. She longed for the child to be delivered so that she could reclaim her body.

The only relief was in swimming – a blessed opportunity to cool down, the weight of her belly supported by the buoyancy of the water. According to the doctor, swimming would also help strengthen her back. Going regularly to the Penang Swimming Club in the mornings, she was unlikely to run into Arthur Leighton at that time of day, when he would be occupied in his office or out travelling. Evie was still careful to avoid finding herself alone with him.

It would have been over-generous to claim that things were harmonious between her and Douglas. He did seem to be making a greater effort, but there were still times when his impatience flared. In line with their agreement, he returned to George Town every Friday evening and remained until the early hours of Monday morning. Much of the time though, he was closeted in his study, working on papers at his desk. He had also begun to play tennis again regularly – mostly with Arthur.

At Evie's urging, Doug was starting to spend more time with Jasmine, occasionally coaching her at tennis, and joining them both on Sunday afternoon trips to the Penang Swimming Club. He had also helped his daughter to finish their joint construction project and the completed Bayko house had a permanent place in Jasmine's bedroom.

Jasmine was thriving. She and Penny had joined the Brownies and were happily involved in the weekly meetings, as well as working towards their activity badges. Since one of these was basic first aid, both Evie and Douglas were frequently subjected to their arms being bandaged-up in slings and having imaginary wounds treated.

So, on the surface, all was well in the Barrington household, but Evie had to constantly remind herself of what the monk had said, particularly about Yin and Yang. Douglas and she definitely embodied marked differences in temperament and interests, so it was a continual struggle for her to attempt to understand him and embrace those differences. Trying to become close to a man who was intensely private, afraid to express his emotions, and whose greatest passion in life was growing rubber, was proving a challenge. Evie was all too aware that her husband was often impatient with her, irritated by her questions and her desire for conversation. She kept telling herself it was impossible to expect that a man of few words would be capable of changing into one who shared her interests and was ready to talk about them.

On the long silent evenings when, after Jasmine was tucked up in bed, Evie sat in the drawing room with her husband, she mostly read a book, while he rustled his way through the *Straits Times,* smoked his pipe and drank whisky. It was at times like these, alone with Douglas in a silence broken only by the sound of a ticking clock, that Evie couldn't help her thoughts straying to Arthur Leighton, imagining how different it would be if it were him sitting opposite her. With Arthur the time flew by, without her noticing. They never lacked topics for conversation, each interested in what the other had to say. Arthur didn't have the repressed emotions of Doug – in fact Evie suspected Arthur had a constant battle to keep a lid on them. She forced her attention back to the room, to her husband, to the father of her unborn child. Instead of wasting time on what might have been, she must focus all her energy on building a future with Doug.

They rarely went out. Neither of them enjoyed the mindless pursuit of pleasure by the Europeans in Penang. It jarred with Evie that while, back in England, people were coping with the blackout and rationing, here there were plentiful supplies of food and drink and a constant round of parties. It seemed sybaritic and selfish when there was a war on.

Occasionally they entertained at home, Douglas needing to talk business with dealers, inspectors and other estate owners, more conducive over a good dinner. Once or twice, when one of their guests was a single man or visiting Penang without his wife, she invited Mary Helston to make up the numbers. But it was apparent that Mary came because she didn't like to refuse, and clearly felt uncomfortable if there was any possibility the man might see her as fair game, or if she suspected Evie of trying to matchmake. Evie was sad that Mary was alone, but her friend assured her that she was perfectly happy with her unmarried state, living with her parents.

Evie managed to avoid inviting the Leightons to these dinners unless Doug absolutely insisted on their presence. The hostilities between her and Veronica had not abated. But she couldn't keep putting her husband off when he enjoyed Arthur's company. And were she wholly honest with herself, she did too. With Arthur at the table, she was guaranteed an interesting evening, although whenever he left, Evie felt deflated, bereft, and wishing that it were he who shared her life.

She and Douglas began to share a bed again after a couple of months had passed. He was nervous, tentative around her, afraid that making love might harm the baby, even though she reassured him that the doctor said it would be fine. There had been no further blood spotting and the doctor had said, as long as they were careful there was no reason not to continue having sexual relations until about six weeks before the birth. Yet there was no excitement in their lovemaking. If anything, it had returned to the mechanical motions of the early days of their marriage and became less frequent as time went on and her pregnancy advanced. Evie suspected that he found her inflated body and swollen belly unappealing. For her part, his presence in bed was tiresome – the heat was bad enough without his body beside hers making it worse.

By April, Evie was seven months pregnant and feeling increasingly tired, when an invitation arrived from Rowena and Bertie Cameron for the three Barringtons to attend a party at the Penang Club. The occasion was the couple's tenth wedding anniversary. Remembering what Mary had told her about Bertie's affair, Rowena's drinking and the constant fighting, Evie was surprised that they'd decided to mark the occasion.

'Do we have to go to this, Doug?' she asked. 'I barely know them.'

'Of course, we do,' he snapped. 'Bertie Cameron is the *tuan* of the biggest shipping company in the Straits. I need to stay on the right side of him. It's good for business.'

That was always Douglas's retort if she raised an objection to anything. Evie suspected that he used business as an excuse for retiring to his study and avoiding any pressure to converse. Yin and Yang she reminded herself. Respect the differences. Besides, how could she possibly deprive Jasmine of going to the party when Penny was her best friend?

Surely she could put on a brave face, grit her teeth and get through one afternoon there. And it was only the afternoon, with the assumption that people would go on elsewhere in the evening. While the grownups were drinking cocktails and eating canapés, there was to be a tea party for the children, complete with a conjuror. As soon as Douglas mentioned this to Jasmine, the little girl began bouncing up and down on her chair in excitement.

By the time the day of the party arrived, Evie felt like a whale on legs. Walking was akin to waddling, and her confidence – never high when in the vicinity of the club – was at rock bottom. Her pale yellow frock pinched under the arms and flattened her over-large breasts uncomfortably, but she had nothing else she could squeeze into that was suitable for a formal party during the day. Looking at herself in the mirror, she frowned at what she saw. Weren't women supposed to bloom in pregnancy? She felt like a wilting flower. The primrose yellow of the dress made her appear jaundiced and washed out. A frump. That's what she looked like. She told herself she didn't care. Those shallow people could sneer if they wished.

The gathering was huge. Everyone who was anyone in Penang was there and the party had already spilled out onto the club lawns, when the Barringtons arrived. No expense had been spared. There were huge silver tureens filled with ripe juicy strawberries that someone told Evie had been specially flown in from Australia. Champagne flowed and flunkies moved between the guests ensuring their glasses were always full. Evie wished she could join the children instead – they were all sitting cross-legged on the side lawn, drinking orangeade and eating Eskimo Pies while the conjuror entertained them. A glass of iced water, a choc ice and somewhere to sit would be preferable to champagne and strawberries and milling around making polite conversation with people she barely knew.

Amidst the throng, she spotted Mary Helston. It was unusual to see Mary at the club but, of course, as the Camerons' next door neighbour she had felt obliged to accept their invitation. Mary was deep in conversation with a man in airforce uniform. Evie had never seen him before. Perhaps this might be the beginning of a romance for her friend.

Setting her champagne flute down, she asked one of the waiters if she might have some water or a glass of fruit juice. Douglas had melted into the crowd and she could see the top of his head as he talked with Bertie Cameron and Reggie Hyde-Underwood. She looked around to see if she could spot Susan Hyde-Underwood but there was no sign of her. No doubt the fortunate woman had been able to use her young baby as a reason for not attending.

Edging to the side of the crowd, Evie thought she'd slip inside the club building and try to find somewhere to sit underneath a cooling fan. A hand tapped her on the arm and she turned. It was Dorothy Rogers.

'Evie, how delightful to see you here.' The woman looked her up and down. 'And don't you look well. Positively blooming! When are you due?'

'Late June. Possibly early July.'

'Ooh, not long! Well, congratulations, my dear. You look frightfully well on it. I'm delighted for you and Doug.'

'Is Clifford here?'

Dorothy nodded her head in the direction where Doug was. 'He's just spotted your husband so he shot off to put the world to rights with him. No doubt he'll be complaining about the lack of preparation for the possibility of war here. It's all Clifford ever talks about these days. Is Doug the same?'

'Not really. He's very much of the school of thought that

Malaya's impossible to invade. Although he doesn't seem to have a lot of faith in the armed forces if it does happen.'

Dorothy shook her head in silent acknowledgement of the last point.

'Arthur Leighton says Sir Shenton Thomas is a decent chap,' said Evie, of the Governor. 'But none of them seem to take the threat to the Settlements seriously. I do hope they're right.'

'Men always seem more interested in scoring points off each other.' Dorothy nudged Evie's arm. 'It'd be a different story if we girls were running things! I always say, if you want to get a job done, ask a woman!'

'There are so many people here,' said Evie, changing the subject. 'Do you know the Camerons well?'

'Unfortunately, yes.' Dorothy gave her a wink.

'I've only met them a couple of times but Jasmine plays with their daughter, Penny.'

'I suppose you know Rowena and Bertie are daggers drawn?'

'I had heard something on those lines.'

'God knows why they're throwing a party to celebrate their marriage. They'd be better off holding a wake.' Dorothy rolled her eyes. 'I shouldn't gossip but some of these people deserve all they get.' She looked at Evie with concern. 'But you must be exhausted standing around like that, Evie, when you're carrying a baby. Let's go inside and find somewhere quiet to sit down and have a natter.'

'Dorothy, you're a mind reader. And it had better be some-where near the ladies' room. I have to go rather frequently.'

'You don't need to remind me. I had five of the little blighters. I spent my life running for the lavatory. But you'll soon see it was all worth it.'

They started to move towards the building, passing a few

yards away from Mary Helston, who was still in deep conversation with the uniformed man. Evie waved at her friend but didn't interrupt, pleased that she was evidently having a pleasant time and enjoying the company of the stranger.

Inside, she and Dorothy found a spot with some chairs, secluded behind a line of tall potted ferns, where there was a through draught from the lawns to the open front doors. An enormous ceiling fan was whirling and added to the cooling effect. Seated, they carried on chatting. A waiter brought them drinks – an orange juice for Evie.

Evie thanked Dorothy for recommending the swimming club. 'It's my special treat. I try to swim most days.'

'Lucky girl. When I had my first two we were in the middle of nowhere with no swimming pool within driving distance. I used to fill the bathtub with cold water and sit in it for ages.' She laughed. 'Fortunately, when I was expecting my third we were in Singapore and the swimming club there was a godsend.'

'Here you are! I wondered where you were heading off to.' Mary Helston emerged from behind the ferns. 'A nice quiet spot. Away from the throng. Very wise.' She glanced towards the RAF man who was still accompanying her. 'May I introduce Frank Hyde-Underwood. You must know his brother Reggie, who works for Mr Barrington. Frank, this is my dear friend, Evie Barrington.'

Evie shook the man's hand and introduced him and Mary to Dorothy Rogers.

Frank Hyde-Underwood looked nothing like his brother. Older, he didn't share the florid complexion and tendency to chubbiness of Reggie. Tall, of slim build, with a small moustache, he was a good-looking man. He told Evie he was stationed at the airfield at Butterworth.

Frank and Mary sat on the sofa opposite the two women and the four chatted. Frank was clearly enchanted by Mary –

although Mary's own expression gave nothing away. Evie mentally crossed her fingers that perhaps he might penetrate the teacher's self-protective armour. Mary Helston deserved to have someone to make a fuss of her.

The ferns parted and Veronica Leighton's head peered though. 'Hiding in the corner are you, Evie?' she said. Her voice was slurred, indicating she'd already had too much to drink. 'Not that I blame you, in your state. You must be terribly hot having to drag all that bulk around. Are you sure it isn't twins? You look like a ship in full sail.' She gave a supercilious laugh.

Frank Hyde-Underwood raised his eyebrows. 'I think Mrs Barrington looks very elegant.'

'And who are *you*?' Veronica's voice was arch and flirtatious. 'How could I have possibly missed such a handsome man? Are you new to Penang? I do so love a man in uniform.'

Before anyone could respond, Veronica had moved around the clump of ferns. When the RAF man rose politely, she slipped onto the sofa between him and Mary Helston. She sat twisted sideways, with her knees touching the airman's, her back turned on Mary.

Anger rose in Evie. How could Veronica do that? And to Mary of all people. Before she could say anything, Mary was on her feet and, muttering that she had forgotten something, rushed away. Evie hauled herself up to follow her, and saw that Frank was about to do the same, but Veronica had a restraining hold of his arm. As Evie passed her, her foot caught Veronica's and she slipped, sending the contents of her glass of orange juice over Veronica's white silk dress.

Evie gasped, 'Awfully sorry, Veronica, I don't know how that happened.'

Veronica let out a wail. 'You clumsy great lump! It's ruined. My frock is absolutely ruined.'

Dorothy Rogers fished in her handbag and produced a linen handkerchief. 'Here you are, Veronica. Why don't we go to the powder room and get some cold water on that. I'm sure we can get most of it off.'

The wailing continued as Dorothy took hold of Veronica's elbow and marched her away.

Evie turned to Frank. 'I think I need to make myself scarce. I'd better go and confess what's happened to Veronica's husband and maybe you will want to find Mary.'

The man looked grateful. They walked together towards the open French doors. 'I think I owe you a debt of gratitude for rescuing me, Mrs Barrington.' He winked at her. 'What a dreadful woman.'

Arthur was in conversation with a man Evie didn't know. Uncomfortable about interrupting him, she tried to catch his eye. He looked across and she lifted her hand and beckoned him, hoping that he would be able to extricate himself. A few moments later he was at her side.

'Are you all right, Evie? What's the matter?'

'I'm afraid I had a bit of an accident. I tripped and managed to spill orange juice all over Veronica's dress. I don't think she's too happy and will probably want to go home and change.'

Arthur raised his eyebrows and sighed. 'I can imagine. Thanks for telling me, Evie. Where is she?'

'With Dorothy Rogers in the ladies' room. I'd go and tell her you're waiting, only I think I'm the last person she'll want to see.'

'No problem. I'll find someone else to fish her out.' He was about to move off when he asked, 'Are you all right yourself, Evie? I haven't seen you for ages.' His expression was sad.

Evie felt her stomach flip. Why did he always have this effect on her?

'I'm fine. I didn't spill the drink deliberately. I caught her foot and tripped.'

'You mean she put her foot out and tripped you.'

'Surely not! No. I can't believe she did that.' She hesitated.

'I didn't intend to spill my drink all over her, but I can't say I'm unhappy that it happened. Veronica was about to do it again. To Mary Helston. Mary was with an RAF officer and they seemed awfully happy talking to each other. Then Veronica came along and... well... you can imagine.'

He closed his eyes for a moment. 'Yes. You can spare me the details.' He gave her one of his sad-eyed smiles. 'Thank you, Evie.' He touched her arm and a shiver of electricity ran through her.

'I'd better see if Mary's RAF officer has found her again.'

'Maybe I'll see you later?' Then he was gone.

Evie was relieved to see Frank and Mary standing together in the shade of a tree talking intently. There was no mistaking it, the officer was keen on her and, as far as Evie could tell, Mary seemed to like his company too. Rather than butt in on their conversation, she went to join Douglas.

As she was walking across the lawn, a commotion began behind her. Evie looked round and saw Veronica running over the grass towards her, pushing people out of her way as she went. Indignant voices and spilled drinks marked her rapid progress over the club grounds. When she was in front of Evie, she pulled up, pointing her finger.

'You did it on purpose. You poured a drink over me. You're jealous because you're like a great big whale and your husband can't stand the sight of you.' She stood right in front of Evie, her face contorted, her eyes bloodshot, with dirty smudges of mascara underneath them. 'You're trying to steal my husband. Well, you can't have him. So get lost. Go back to England. No one wants you here. Not even your husband. Once you've popped that baby out he'll be going straight back to his little housekeeper.' Angry tears rolled down Veronica's face.

Evie stared at her in abject horror. How did she know about Doug's affair with his housekeeper? Had she been wrong to trust Arthur?

Doug appeared at Evie's side. This provoked more anger from Veronica.

She spun round to face him. 'Yes. I know all about your sordid little affair. I stopped by Arthur's office and overheard you telling him. So don't even try to deny it, Doug.'

All around them, people were watching in silent disbelief. This kind of display never happened at the august Penang Club. If the crowd had expected an upset that afternoon it would have been from the Camerons, but the two of them, like everyone else were staring in astonishment at Veronica, Doug and Evie.

Arthur Leighton pushed through the crowd and took his wife's arm and drew her away. 'Show's over, people. Veronica isn't feeling well,' he said, and led her away to their car.

For a moment there was a horrified silence, before the band, which had been playing quiet waltzes, struck up a lively dance tune and people drifted back into their groupings.

Douglas looked at Evie. 'I think it's time we went home too. I'll go and fetch Jasmine.'

'She isn't going to be pleased. She's watching the conjuror.' Evie looked in the direction of the large group of children.

'That's too bad, because we're going.' He turned on his heel and went off to collect his daughter.

Evie waited, uncertain what to do next. Mrs Rogers appeared at her elbow. 'That woman's got a screw loose. I've always thought so. I don't know how her husband puts up with her. She's a walking nightmare.'

Evie looked at her. 'Honestly, Dorothy, I didn't do it deliberately. I tripped and my hand slipped.'

'Well, you jolly well should have done it deliberately. She got what she was asking for, the trollop. I'm sure it must have been the hand of God guiding you.' Addressing the nearest people in a loud voice, she said, 'I saw exactly what happened and I'm afraid Mrs Leighton doesn't emerge from this well.' Her voice was full of authority and a few people smiled at Evie in sympathy.

'I'm afraid I've probably upset Doug now,' Evie said quietly to Mrs Rogers.

'Not if he has any sense. Everyone knows the woman has had it coming to her for a long time.'

TWENTY-THREE

They drove home in silence, Doug's face set hard. Evie knew it was because of what Veronica had said about her trying to steal Arthur, rather than the references to his own infidelity. She decided to say nothing. Why should she? She had nothing to explain as it wasn't true.

The following morning, Evie was sitting in the garden, thumbing through the *Straits Times* after Douglas had set off for Batu Lembah. An uncharacteristically sulky Jasmine had gone to school, still full of resentment at their early departure from the party. Doug had also been in ill sorts and had chosen to spend the night in the guest room. There had been no discussion of what had happened at the Penang Club and Evie decided it was best to let matters lie until they had each had a few days to let it pass.

Evie looked up as Arthur Leighton came towards her across the terrace.

'You've missed Doug, I'm afraid,' she said. Trying to keep the acidity from her voice she added, 'How's Veronica?'

'It's you I came to see, not Doug. I want to apologise for what happened yesterday.'

'It's not up to you to apologise. It wasn't your fault.'

'I'm afraid it was.'

'What on earth do you mean?'

He pulled up a chair and sat, his head in his hands. 'I can't go on like this, Evie.'

'Like what?'

'Staying with her, when every day that goes by, I loathe her more. No worse than that. I loathe myself for getting into this situation. I'm ashamed of myself. Ashamed that I put my career before everything else when I agreed to marry her. Because she helped my career along I stood by while she spun increasingly out of control.' He looked up at Evie, his face a picture of misery. 'I should have stood up for myself and refused to marry her.'

'You had little choice about that. And you were helping her. If she'd had her baby, things might have been different.'

'If she'd had the baby, things could well have been worse. Can you imagine Veronica as a mother?' He let out a long sigh. 'But the truth is she feels less of a woman because she hasn't had a child. And that's what was getting under her skin with you yesterday.'

'I don't understand at all, Arthur. Plenty of other women have babies. This can't be the first time she's come across an expectant mother at the Penang Club.'

'She doesn't care about the other women. They're all in thrall to her – or scared of her. She queens it over them. Her problem is with you because from the very first time she met you, you refused to be cowed by her.'

'What?'

'That time you met her in London. She was spitting tacks when she got back to the hotel. She wanted to boss you around, have you hanging on her every word, doing as she told you. Just like everyone else.'

'Oh, for heaven's sake, Arthur, I was absolutely terrified of her.'

He looked up and smiled. 'Maybe. But you didn't let her see that. You didn't give way to her. You've always known your own mind, Evie, and Veronica can't bear that. She wants to play cat and mouse and you refuse to be mouse.'

'But that doesn't excuse what she did yesterday to Mary Helston.'

'She knows Mary's your friend. It's all a game to her. A game that's completely out of control.' He brushed a hand through his hair. 'But most of all, she's angry because she knows how I feel about you.'

Evie was horror stricken. 'You told her?'

'I don't need to. Veronica's not stupid. She can tell. I never looked at another woman until I met you. I can't hide it. She knows me too well. Even on the ship she realised I was falling in love with you. That's why she's always been so beastly to you.' He put his head in his hands again and gave a sigh as if he were carrying all the troubles of the world. 'I can't disguise how I feel. It's obvious that I worship the ground you walk on, Evie. And I can't sleep at night for thinking about you. For wanting you.'

'Stop, Arthur, please! This isn't right.'

'That's the trouble. It's the only thing that *is* right. You and me.'

'You've said it yourself before.' Her voice was low. 'We can't ever be together. We're married to other people. That's the sad and sorry truth of it and there's nothing we can do to change that. We're not the kind of people who walk out on our marriages, Arthur.'

'I know. And I know I've said that myself. So many times. But I've come to a decision. I can't go on this way. I'm here to beg you to come away with me.'

Evie felt as if a tidal wave was sweeping over her, carrying her off, helpless and out of control. Gripping the wooden arm of her chair, she said, 'Arthur, you're not serious. You can't possibly mean that.' Her breath was jerky. She closed her eyes.

He reached for her hands, holding them in his. She felt that same bolt of electricity she had experienced before at the touch of his skin against hers. Dizzy, disorientated, she struggled to reply, wanting to give in, to abdicate all responsibility to him. His look was intense, determined, certain.

He bent his head, turned her hands over and touched her palms with his lips. He looked up at her again and said, 'I love you, Evie. Body and soul. That's all that matters.'

At that moment her unborn baby turned over inside her and kicked her soundly. She pulled her hands away from Arthur and placed them over her swollen belly. 'It's not just you and me any more. I have the baby to think of. *Doug*'s baby.' She felt tears begin to well in her eyes. 'I love you, Arthur. Desperately, totally, crazily. But it's too late. That day at the beach it might have been different. But not now. I can't do it.'

'I'll take care of you and the baby.'

She touched the top of his head with her hand, running her fingers through his hair. 'Oh my dearest darling. You can't. We can't. This is Doug's child and you know as well as I do how much it means to him. And in his peculiar fashion I think he does love me and you are his only friend. It would be such a terrible betrayal I think it would kill him. How can I possibly do that to him? How can you?'

'You can do it because it's no more than he deserves. He's treated you appallingly. To do what he did with that woman. He's forfeited all right to your loyalty.'

Evie shook her head slowly. 'How can you say that? You of all people. You who came here after that dreadful day and asked me to talk to him. You who said it was the best thing for me.'

His face crumpled. 'You've no idea what that cost me. How I've cursed myself ever since. It's the bloody awful wish to try and do the right thing. The decent thing. But the right thing is the wrong thing. The only thing that's right is that you and I belong together.'

'Arthur, my love, I won't argue with you. How can I possibly disagree when I feel the way I do, but it's too late. I can't possibly leave Doug now.'

He leaned back and pulled out a rare cigarette, lit it and took a deep draw. 'I'm leaving Penang, Evie. With or without you. I want you with me. But if you won't come I have to leave anyway. I can't go on like this, being so close to you and unable to be with you. I've tried. Oh God, I've tried, but I can't do it any more. And I can't go on watching Veronica spiral ever downwards, knowing that I'm the cause of it.'

'You're leaving? Where?' Evie felt as though the ground was coming up to meet her.

'Singapore. I've been offered a position there, reporting directly to Sir Shenton Thomas. I accepted it this morning. I'm leaving straight away.' He looked up at her, his eyes full of love and Evie almost weakened. 'Please, Evie, come with me.'

She kept her hands across her belly, to feel the presence of her unborn child, willing it to give her strength to hold her course, when every nerve in her body was screaming at her to give way, to say yes to Arthur. And it wasn't only the baby, there was Jasmine too. Her family. How could she abandon the little girl who had lost her own mother and placed all her trust and love in Evie? 'No,' she said, trying to control the quaver in her voice. 'I can't do that, Arthur.' She took a big gulp of air. 'I won't do that.'

'That's your final decision?'

She nodded, mutely. 'And you need to get help for Veronica. Maybe moving to Singapore will be the best thing for her too. A new start for you both.'

'Last night when we got back from the club she threw another fit and tried to stab me with a carving knife.'

'What? She tried to kill you?'

He ran his hands through his hair again. 'Look, Evie, you've seen how she's spiralled out of control.' He put his head back, staring up at the cloud-covered sky. 'I just can't do it any more. It's not just because of how I feel about you and me. I can't cope with her any more. The drinking. The drugs. The aggression. The infidelities.' He heaved a deep sigh. 'No one else knows this, but she's started picking men up and bringing them home with her. I don't know how long it's been going on, but last week I got back after a late meeting to find her with a man. In our home.'

'Oh God. That's horrible.'

'A young assistant manager for Guthrie's. Off the boat a few months ago.'

'I'm sorry, Arthur.'

'I'm not sorry. It's made me realise I was caught in a trap. I don't care about the consequences any more. I've spent years trying to do the right thing by Veronica, feeling sorry for her, for what happened to her, for her problems. I'm done. I've nothing left to give.'

'You have so much to give.' She fixed her eyes on him. 'Things were better between you both before I arrived. Weren't they? You can make them better again.' She screwed a handful of her cotton skirt into a ball, squeezing it tightly as she forced herself to say these things that she didn't want to say. 'Think of your career.'

'Sod my career!' He squeezed his eyes closed. 'Sorry, Evie. I didn't mean to swear at you.' He shook his head. 'But that's all I've ever thought of until now. But it isn't enough. Nothing is enough without you.' He slumped forwards, his head in his hands.

Evie didn't know what to say. The thought of no longer seeing Arthur, of no longer having him in her life, was unbearable – even if his presence had never been in the way she really wanted. But if either of them were to make something from this mess they had to put each other out of their minds and find a way to make their marriages work. The only way was to be brutal. Swallowing, she forced herself to say, 'I will never leave Doug. The vows I took when I married him I took seriously. If I'd known I'd fall in love with you I'd never have made them, but I did, and I intend to stand by them. I'm going to do my utmost to make things work and I think you need to do the same with Veronica. She needs medical help, but most of all she needs you, Arthur. You've been her anchor and she must feel cut adrift.'

His face contorted as he absorbed the impact of her words. 'You're telling me to stay with her? In spite of everything?'

'You have to do what's right for you. But one of the reasons I fell in love with you is that you are a good man. God knows there's no love lost between me and Veronica but I do feel sorry for her. Her behaviour is a cry for help. To you. The question is, are you ready to listen to it?'

He sat beside her saying nothing. The crowing of the captive cockerels down the street mingled with the clatter of dishes from the servants' quarters at the end of the garden.

If only they could stay here in this garden, in this moment, away from everyone and everything that placed demands upon them. Held inside a bubble, frozen in time.

Eventually Arthur spoke, staring ahead of him into the middle distance. 'You're right of course. You're so much wiser and stronger than me. If we can't be together, we must each make the best of what we have been allotted.'

A wave of relief was mixed with a stab of pain at the prospect of him going away and no longer being part of her life. Pain that was also – she had to acknowledge it – resentment of Veronica for what she would see as a personal victory. The pain was all the sharper knowing that Veronica didn't want Arthur for himself, only for what he represented, like a game trophy on a white man's bungalow wall.

'You'll take her with you to Singapore?'

'I'll try and persuade her to see a specialist. Someone who might be able to help her.'

'I expect getting her away from here will be a big step on the road to recovery.' As she said the words they sounded false, insincere to her. If she were to speak the truth it would be that Veronica Leighton could go to hell or be locked away in an asylum for all she cared. Instead she said, 'You're doing the right thing, Arthur.'

He grunted. 'Good old Arthur. Always reliable. Always ready to do the right thing.' His eyes were anguished. 'When all I want to do is the wrong thing. All I want to do is hold you in my arms again and never let you go.'

'Please. Don't talk that way. You're making it worse for us both. After today we must never again speak of this. We need to pretend we've never said what we've said. Never felt the way we feel.'

'What's said can't be unsaid and what's felt can't be unfelt.'

'But we can make sure we say no more.'

He got up and began to pace up and down.

'When will you leave?'

'Within the next few days.'

Her heart lurched. 'Why so fast?'

'There's a lot to do. I'm going to be involved in a new joint liaison committee. They're planning to up the military presence in the Straits. Don't know how much or when, but there's talk of a new man coming out later this year to coordinate the Allied forces. We need someone to make it clear to London that Malaya needs more defences.' Arthur shook his head again, frowning. 'It's impossible to get decisions out of them at the moment. Now that Churchill's taken over and things have hotted up in Europe, no one in Whitehall wants to think about Malaya.'

Evie didn't want to talk about the war. She didn't want to

talk about anything. All she wanted was to be held by Arthur, but her duty was to Douglas, Jasmine and her unborn baby. She bit her lip to force herself not to give in to tears.

Arthur moved to her and drew her to her feet. He stood, holding her against him. She could feel his chest rise and fall as he breathed, could hear the beating of his heart. Her eyes filled with tears but she swallowed them and eased herself away from his hold. 'You'd better go.' Looking over his shoulder, she saw Aunty Mimi at the kitchen window watching them. How much had she witnessed?

Arthur went to take her in his arms again.

'No! Aunty Mimi can see us. Please just go, Arthur. Go.'

He looked into her eyes, his reflecting his visible pain.

'Goodbye, my darling. I love you. I'll always love you.'

Evie turned her head as he walked away, then went down the garden, away from the kitchen windows, so that prying eyes wouldn't see that her heart was breaking.

TWENTY-FOUR

As Evie's pregnancy advanced, so too did the war in Europe. With the invasion of France, the surrender of Belgium, the retreat of the British Expeditionary Force to Dunkirk and their subsequent dramatic evacuation, all the news from England seemed to be bad news.

Sitting in the King's Theatre, watching newsreels of German Panzer tanks rolling through the streets of Paris, Evie felt numb, hollowed out. She remembered a few glorious days she had spent in the French capital with her parents *en route* to the Cote d'Azur for a holiday. Seeing giant swastikas hanging from the Arc de Triomphe and jackbooted troops parading in triumph along the tree-lined boulevards, was chilling. Placing her hands over her swollen belly she asked herself what kind of world she was bringing her child into. What kind of future might he or she expect when it looked a foregone conclusion that Hitler's next target would be across the channel? And were he to succeed, there would be no need for any Japanese invasion of Malaya, as the spoils of the British Empire would all fall straight into Hitler's hands.

In the darkened theatre, a tide of loneliness and hopelessness washed over her. The hole that Arthur Leighton had left in her life was vast. She may not have seen him often but knowing that he was in the same town, that she might bump into him any day in the street or at a function, had made a greater difference than she had realised, until he was gone. Yet every time she allowed herself to think this, she was consumed by guilt. She had to focus on her family. Arthur had no part in that. Despite his past infidelity, her husband was her future and dreaming of another man was disloyal.

These last weeks, as her delivery approached, all she wanted was to free herself of the cumbersome burden of carrying the baby. She wanted her body back, to be free of the weight, the discomfort, the constant need to go to the lavatory and the crushing backache. Yet here in the darkened picture house, watching what was happening in the world, Evie wanted to keep her baby safe inside her. Bringing it into such a terrible terrifying world felt too heavy a responsibility.

The baby was in no hurry to be born anyway. It was into July when Evie finally went into labour – what turned out to be just a few days before the start of the Battle of Britain. The only battle Evie cared about now was the one in her own body as she struggled with the pain of delivering her child.

To her great relief she produced a healthy boy. Douglas arrived at the hospital in Butterworth, grinning broadly, behind an enormous bouquet of flowers. He bent over the bed and kissed her lightly on the brow. 'Thank you, Evie,' was all he said, but his delight was evident.

Sitting stiffly in a chair at her bedside, he gazed, rapt, at the tiny red-faced, wrinkled bundle as Evie cradled her son in her arms. A frown creased Doug's face and he looked at her, anxiety in his eyes. 'I don't know how to be a good father to him.' He stretched his lips into a tight line. 'I don't know what to do, how to be all the things my own father wasn't.'

Evie was about to laugh. Such an odd thing to say, but she

could see his nervousness was genuine. She wanted to say, just love him, but that seemed a step too far for a man like Douglas. He'd think it soppy and sentimental. Love was not a thing for fathers to admit feeling for their sons. So, she said, 'Just be here for him. That's all you need to do.'

Douglas frowned. 'But he's so small, so helpless.'

'He won't be for long.' She tried to convey reassurance. She was about to add that Douglas should just be himself, then told herself that if 'being himself' meant constantly changing moods, frequent absences and impatience, it was hardly a recipe for good parenting. 'Look, Doug, your father wasn't around for you. All you need to do is make time for this little chap, talk to him, spend time with him.'

Her husband nodded, his face grave. 'It seems such a weighty responsibility now that it's happened. He'll inherit the business. I have to make sure he's prepared.'

Evie shook her head, smiling. 'There's plenty of time for that.' She stroked the baby's cheek lightly with a finger, marvelling at the perfection of his tiny, perfectly-formed, rosebud mouth. 'We'll have to choose a name for him.'

'That's already decided. He'll be named Hubert.'

'What? Don't I get any say?' She was indignant. Her little boy was not going to be a Hubert. Far too serious and stuffy. Not to mention old-fashioned.

'In this instance, no. The firstborn Barrington son is always named Hubert. My father was and his father and so on for generations back.'

'*You* weren't!'

'That's because I wasn't the firstborn son.'

Evie stared at Douglas, shocked. 'You have a *brother*?'

'I did. He died.'

'When? How? Was it in the war?'

Douglas tensed. 'I don't want to talk about it.'

'For goodness sake, Doug. I'm your wife! Don't I deserve an

answer to that? You can't just announce you're calling our son after your late brother without so much as telling me a thing about him. Until now, I wasn't even aware he existed.'

Douglas stared at the backs of his hands where they lay flattened on his thighs. 'It happened when I was nine. Not long before my mother died. Hubert – or Bertie as Mother and I called him, was eleven.'

Evie felt a swell of emotion, and instinctively held her new son closer to her. 'How awful that must have been for you. I'm so sorry, Doug.'

He turned his head away and stared into the middle distance. 'It was my fault.'

Evie could barely breathe. 'Your fault? How could it be? You were only a child. Not much older than Jasmine.'

'We were playing hide and seek. At our family home in Lincolnshire. I climbed out of one of the attic windows onto the roof. We weren't supposed to go into the attic and certainly not out onto the roof, so I thought Bertie would never find me. I was going to wait up there until the time ran out so I'd be the winner. But he spotted me from the terrace and came rushing upstairs to tag me.' Douglas squeezed his eyes shut and took a few short breaths. 'I heard him come into the attic and so I hid behind a chimney stack. When he climbed out onto the roof I crept up on him and said boo. He jumped out of his skin with fright, lost his footing and fell from the roof, screaming.'

Evie's free hand shot to her mouth and clamped over it. Sensing her distress, the baby began to cry. Evie stroked his head and the child calmed at once.

'I climbed back down into the attic and ran downstairs. When I got outside, the gardener was already there on the terrace. He yelled at me to go back into the house. He didn't want me to see what had happened to Hubert.' He looked up at Evie. 'But I did see. And I've never been able to un-see what I saw that day. Or un-hear his scream as he fell to the ground.'

'Oh, Doug.' She reached her hand out to take his but he got up and moved away to stand by the window.

'I never owned up to what happened. I didn't tell them I was up on the roof too. That makes me a moral coward.'

'No. You were a frightened little boy who was probably in shock.'

'Bertie was my father's favourite. After he was killed, Father couldn't bear to look at me. It was as if he was always thinking the wrong son had died. When my mother got ill and died too there was no one left to object when he sent me away.'

He turned back to look at her. 'So you know my terrible secret, Evie. Do you see why I have to call my son Hubert?'

She looked at the little bundle in her arms. 'Hubert it is.' She shivered. It was neither the name nor the legacy she wanted for her child. Bending over she kissed her son's plump cheek.

He can be christened Hubert she told herself, but we'll call him Hugh.

While the war raged on in Europe, and the Blitz began in England, life in Penang continued much as before – but with some token efforts by the expatriates to 'do their bit'. Douglas was increasingly involved in exercises with the defence volunteers. He remained scathing about the value and relevance of what they were doing, claiming that no war on the peninsula would ever be fought that way, if indeed it were to be fought at all. Like many of the planters, he suggested that his local knowledge and familiarity with the language might prove useful in assisting the regular army with planning and liaison, but all such offers were rejected as impractical or unnecessary. Objections to the traditional warcraft they were drilling in were always brushed aside by the regular army, with the assertion that they may well be required at some point to return to help defend Britain or assist in a counter attack on the continent of Europe. No one appeared to take seriously the threat of an invasion of Malaya itself – including Douglas. Eventually he resigned himself to participating anyway, and acknowledged that the small-arms training was useful and brought back his days in the officer training corps at school.

Evie, like most of the women, was pressed into service in sewing parties, knitting balaclavas and socks for the troops and for Red Cross parcels destined for Prisoners of War.

The Barringtons steered clear of the many fund-raising parties organised on behalf of war charities by the Patriotic Fund. With a small baby, Evie had no desire to venture out and Douglas was scathing about the wasteful nature of such efforts, with more money spent on alcohol and petrol by the attendees than could possibly have been generated in donations or ticket sales. Evie mentioned this to Mary, who told her that the Chinese were far more effective in raising money for the war effort and did so without recourse to partying.

Mary Helston rarely spoke about her friendship with Frank Hyde-Underwood and Evie knew better than to press her on it, taking satisfaction from the fact that it was evidently flourishing. The RAF officer was not often on the island however, being frequently required to be in Singapore for exercises, and his flying duties involved reconnaissance flights all over the peninsula.

Motherhood was proving an unexpected joy to Evie. The baby was placid and a good sleeper. Comparing notes with Susan Hyde-Underwood, when the latter dropped in to see her, bringing baby Stanford, made Evie realise she had been blessed with an exceptionally tranquil child. Susan's son was anything but, and judging by the heavy lids and dark circles around her eyes, she was suffering from lack of sleep as a consequence.

Jasmine had taken to her baby brother and, without a trace of sibling jealousy, mothered Hugh and lavished affection upon

him. It was a close contest between Jasmine and Aunty Mimi as
to who would make a greater fuss over the baby. The little
Chinese housekeeper took it upon herself to act as Hugh's *amah*
and informed Evie that it had once been her role with Jasmine,
making it clear that she would tolerate no one new being taken
into the household to undertake such duties. As Evie had had
no such intention she was more than willing to accept this
extension to the housekeeper's duties.

All in all, it was a happy time for Evie, yet deep inside her
there was still a hollow ache at the absence of Arthur Leighton
in her life. She knew what she felt for him was both wrong and
pointless but it didn't stop her feeling it. If anything, his absence
made her feel more strongly about him. She would castigate
herself for disloyalty. Why were her husband and two children
not enough? Guilt gnawed away at her insides, though she had
no reason to feel guilty since, apart from that kiss in the sea,
nothing had happened between them. She almost wished she
had something more to feel guilty about – at least she'd have a
memory to treasure and relive. Then she blamed herself for
thinking that too.

Douglas, for his part, once Evie had forgiven his affair,
behaved as if it had never happened at all. There was no repetition of his declaration of his need for her and love for her. He
remained taciturn and often morose and showed no romance
and little affection. She wondered whether he saw love-making
as just another sport – something to be enjoyed like any other
physical activity. Eventually, Evie accepted that this was how
he was and nothing would change that. He was one of a genera-
tion of men who believed that overt displays of affection were
sentimental and unmanly. He had told her once that he cared
for her. For him that was enough – he evidently believed that,
once said, there was no need to keep repeating it.

In mid January 1941, when Hugh was around six months
old and she had begun to wean him, Evie decided she needed

some distraction, and suggested to Douglas that they host a small dinner party the following Friday evening.

'If you must,' he said, ungraciously.

'I'm thinking of you too.'

This elicited only a grunt.

'Who shall I ask?'

He shrugged. 'Whoever you please. It's all the same to me.'

'I was thinking of the Rogers, but I understand they're in Batavia.'

Another shrug.

'For heaven's sake, Doug. Try and show a bit of interest.'

'It's your department. Whoever you invite is fine by me.'

Controlling her irritation, she said, 'In that case, I'll ask Mary and the Hyde-Underwoods and I'll tell them to bring Reggie's brother. He seems to have taken quite a shine to Mary.'

'Good.'

'I mean you get on well with Reggie, and Frank seems a very affable fellow—'

'Look, Evie, I've told you, it's fine by me. I'll be home in plenty of time.' Softening, he added, 'I suppose it does give me an opportunity to discuss Reggie's proposal for a new rolling machine. Saves me a trip up to Bellavista.'

'I'll tell Susan to bring Stanford with them – he can be put in the cot in Hugh's nursery.'

She asked herself why Douglas always had to be so grumpy but at least he had accepted the plan without further objection. He got on well with Reggie and although he had only met Frank briefly, he appeared to find him tolerable. So, it was a surprise to Evie when on the appointed evening, their guests had already assembled and Doug had yet to put in an appearance. He had promised to be in George Town by six and now at seven he was still missing.

Trying to hide her irritation, Evie escorted the guests onto the terrace outside the drawing room, where Benny was waiting to serve them with drinks. If Hugh were to wake and she had to attend to him, there would be nobody to entertain their guests. She had tried several times to telephone the bungalow at Batu Lembah but there was no reply, so Douglas was presumably on his way. She glanced at her wristwatch, telling herself that it was only a small gathering – and of friends who knew Doug's quirks and so would understand. It was unlikely they'd be offended.

The conversation began, as usual, with discussion of the distant war. Tonight they were talking about the situation in North Africa where the British and Australians were tackling the Italian army and *Regia Aeronautica*.

Changing the subject, Evie turned her attention to Frank. 'How are you finding life in Malaya?' Not so long ago, that question had been frequently asked of her.

'I feel bad that I'm sitting the war out over here while most of the RAF are giving the Luftwaffe a good thumping. It's tough finding out how many of the chaps I learned to fly with went for a Burton during the Battle of Britain.' He glanced at Mary. 'But there are definite compensations to being here in Malaya.' It was clear that the young officer was besotted.

'Well, I can't imagine why you'd want to be back there.' Susan Hyde-Underwood shivered visibly. 'Those poor young men sacrificing their lives.' She shook her head, her eyes grave. 'But we must be thankful that the Germans have lost more pilots than our boys.'

'Yes, the lads put up a terrific fight.' Frank lit a cigarette. 'Can't help feeling guilty when all I do is fly around in my Brewster Buffalo looking down on endless empty jungle.' He frowned. 'Present company excepted, but I get very cheesed off when I see so many people out here acting as though there's no war. The bombs are dropping back home and here they sit in the sun, sipping scotch all day and playing bridge.'

'Not all of us.' His brother looked affronted.

'I did say present company excepted. People like you, Reg, and Mr Barrington are doing work that's absolutely essential to the war effort. But not everyone is.' He looked at Mary again. 'Remember that dreadful woman we met at the Penang Club? The drunkard you rescued me from.'

Mary looked uncomfortable.

'I saw her again the other day. A few of us were having dinner in Raffles in Singapore and she came into the restaurant. Sloshed again. Slurring her words. She managed to knock over one of those enormous flower arrangements. She screamed abuse at the maître d' when he tried to steer her out of the dining room. No sign of her husband – I wouldn't blame him if he'd buggered off and left her. She's an absolute disgrace.'

'I don't think we want to talk about Veronica Leighton, Frank.' Mary's tone was quiet but firm.

They were interrupted by the ringing of the telephone inside the house.

Evie sighed. 'That will be Doug to say he's been delayed.' She hoped she didn't sound as annoyed as she felt.

She started to get up but Benny came out onto the terrace and addressed Reggie. '*Tuan,* you must come to the telephone.'

Reggie went into the house.

His wife, looking pale, said, 'I dread to think what that might be. Reggie's assistant at Bellavista is a first rate fellow who would never dream of calling unless it was an emergency he absolutely couldn't handle himself.'

Mary and Evie made reassuring remarks until Reggie returned, his face ashen.

'There's been an accident.'

Susan gasped. 'What? Who?'

'That was Batu Lembah.' His expression was grave. 'It's Doug. He's had a fall.'

'A fall? How? What's happened? Is he hurt?' Evie was on her feet.

'I don't know the details. Just that he fell into the shaft of a disused tin mine. He's still down there. Frank, can you come with me? I need to get over there to help organise a rescue party to get him out.' Looking at Evie, he said, 'I'm sure he'll be fine.'

Evie's heart lurched in her chest and she struggled to breathe. 'I'm coming with you.'

Mary moved to her and put an arm around her shoulders. 'Evie, you'd be better staying here. The baby needs you.'

'I need to be there for Doug when they get him out. He may be badly injured.'

'I don't think that's a good idea, Evie.' Susan looked at her husband for confirmation.

'I don't care whether it's a good idea or not. I'm going with you, Reggie. Are you going to stand here all night arguing or are we going to go?' To Susan she said, 'Can you look after Hugh? Aunty Mimi will make up some formula if he wakes in the night. Otherwise he's doing well on solids already.'

Mary, sensing that Evie was immoveable, said, 'I'll stay with Susan. I want to be here for Jasmine in case you're not back before she wakes up.'

Evie hugged her friend. 'Thank you. The guest room is made up and there's a day bed in the nursery. Aunty Mimi will get you anything you need.'

She rushed upstairs to kiss her sleeping baby, then followed the two men out to the car.

TWENTY-FIVE

All the way to Batu Lembah, Evie tortured herself with fears as to what her husband must be going through. Despite the brevity of the telephone call and the lack of information, she kept quizzing Reggie for details.

'But how badly hurt is he? Why haven't they got him out? How long has he been down there?'

Reggie kept repeating that he knew no more than he had already said. 'The Assistant Manager just said Doug was over-seeing jungle clearance in a remote part of the estate with a small gang of coolies and had fallen down a mine shaft. I've no idea if anyone saw it happen. The jungle's littered with disused tin workings and most of them are unmapped. We have to hope it's not too deep but we can't tell until we get there and can assess the situation properly.'

It was after nine when they arrived at the estate. Mike Overton, the Assistant Manager, was waiting on the steps of the bungalow to meet them. Evie shivered, remembering the last and only time she had been here at Batu Lembah. She decided it must be a truly cursed place.

The small group gathered inside the bungalow where the

house boy made Evie a cup of tea, which she drank gratefully, the warmth and sweetness helping allay the shock.

'No one saw what happened,' Overton began. 'The *tuan* was doing his usual inspection rounds. He'd gone out to the north-east quadrant where we were clearing virgin jungle.'

'Was he alone?' Reggie interrupted.

'Yes. But there were fifty coolies working out there. That's why he went over there, to see how they were getting on. They claim they never saw him.'

'So how did you find him?' Evie asked. 'How did you even know he was missing?'

'His dog, Badger. He was barking and going berserk. But there was no sign of Doug. The men stopped what they were doing and went after the dog. It took them some time to find him as some of the forest there is impassable. Then they raised the alarm.'

'So where is he?' Evie was growing in impatience.

'At the bottom of a shaft to a tin mine. The countryside is pitted with them. There was a virtual Gold Rush here for tin in the last century. They dug shafts all over the place. If they didn't find any tin they just abandoned the workings and moved on. The jungle in some areas is like Swiss cheese. We lost a coolie a few months back. Fell down a shaft and no one noticed. When he was missing from roll call the alarm went up. It was nearly two days before we found the body. What was left of it.' Overton gave a little shrug and Evie took an instant dislike to the man and wanted to thump him.

Oblivious to Evie's distress, Overton ploughed on. 'Mind you, that coolie might not have fallen. You never know with some of the Tamils. There might have been a fight and one of them could have killed him and dumped the body down a shaft.'

Reggie stepped in. 'That's enough of that, Overton. The *mem* doesn't want to hear all this. We need to talk about Doug.'

The Assistant Manager had the grace to look embarrassed. 'Sorry, Mrs Barrington. I didn't mean to cause offence.'

'Can we get to him now?' Reggie asked.

'I can take you there but it's doubtful we can accomplish much until daylight. Not unless we want to have someone else at the bottom of a shaft.'

'Take us there now. I want to see the way the land lies and be ready to get him out as soon as the conditions allow. All right with you too, Frank?' Reggie placed a hand on his brother's shoulder.

'I'm in.'

'I'll come with you.' Evie moved towards the door,.

Reggie stepped in front of her, palms towards her. 'No, Evie. I must insist. You'll do more harm than good. You've no idea of the conditions out there. You don't know the jungle. We don't want you at the bottom of another shaft. It would be better for you to stay here and raise the doctor on the phone. Telephone the Wellington estate, tell Freddie Reynolds there what's happened and ask him to rustle up a rescue party and get over here as soon as he can. We'll also need bandages and clean water, antiseptic. The houseboy will do what you ask.' Turning to Overton, he instructed, 'Right. Torches, rope, stretcher, blankets. Let's go.'

When they had gone, Evie set the house boy to work to gather the medical supplies and went into the sparsely furnished room that evidently served as her husband's office. At the desk she picked up the telephone, called the exchange and asked to be connected to the Wellington estate. The *tuan*, Freddie Reynolds agreed to alert the local doctor and promised to be at Batu Lembah himself within an hour.

The rest of the night passed in a blur for Evie as she paced up and down, waiting for the rescue party to return from the forest. The house boy, Ahmad, was a willing helper. He stayed

on hand and before Evie needed to ask, he was ready with a
fresh pot of tea.

In an effort to distract herself, she picked up the copy of the
Straits Times that Doug must have been reading earlier in the
day. It was full of news of the British and Australian defeat of
the Italians at Tobruk in North Africa. Evie pushed the paper
away, unable to read it. Doug must have been sitting here at this
table reading this paper, blissfully unaware that he was about to
have an accident. For the umpteenth time, Evie prayed that he
would prove to be unharmed. Perhaps a sprain, cuts and
bruises, a broken limb even. But, please God, let it be nothing
more serious, like a broken neck or a spinal injury.

As the dawn broke, she grew even more restless. Frustrated
not to be waiting at the top of the shaft when they brought her
husband up, she paced back and forth in a stew of anxiety.

It was almost noon when the rescue party returned,
carrying Doug on a stretcher. Evie rushed down the steps of the
bungalow and ran to meet them.

'Is he all right? How badly hurt is he?'

Frank Hyde-Underwood took her by the arm and tried to
steer her back towards the bungalow. Evie jerked away from
him and leaned over the stretcher. Doug, unconscious, was
covered by a cotton sheet, soaked with blood where his legs
were. His face was bathed in sweat and streaked with blood.
His sun-baked skin was as pale as the sheet that covered him
and his hair was matted.

Frank put an arm around Evie to hold her back. 'They need
plenty of room, Mrs Barrington. The doc wants to move your
husband straight to the hospital in Butterworth. His leg's badly
damaged.'

'Why is he unconscious? Is he going to die?' A wave of fear
crashed into her.

Frank's expression was stern. 'He's in a great deal of pain.
Getting him out of that shaft wasn't easy for him. Your

husband's an extremely brave man. Once we got him out the doc gave him a shot of morphine to knock him out for a while until he can be treated.'

'So it's his leg? Nothing else?'

'The doc doesn't think so. Just cuts and bruises.'

Evie watched as the stretcher bearers walked slowly with their burden towards Doug's truck. They laid him, still on the stretcher, onto the open truck-bed and the doctor climbed up beside him, along with one of the Tamil workers. Reggie Hyde-Underwood jumped into the cab and started the engine.

'I'll drive us there, Mrs Barrington,' said Frank, indicating Reggie's car.

'No! I'm going on the truck with him.'

She clambered onto the truck-bed opposite the doctor, and asked, 'His leg's broken?'

'I'm afraid so. He was lucky not to have broken his neck as well. It looks like he smashed into an overhanging rock on the way down, took a hammering from that and carried on falling, landing badly, feet first. His left leg seems to have taken the full impact and his whole body weight so it's a very serious break. But I'm just the local quack. Simple fractures, cuts and bruises and mild doses of malaria are about my limit. We'll need to see what they say at the hospital.'

'But all the blood?'

'Extensive lacerations where he hit the rock. But none seem to be very deep. But we won't know until they examine him in Butterworth. The light was poor and I couldn't get a proper look. The priority is to get him to hospital.'

The doctor wouldn't be drawn any further, so Evie could do no more than hold her unconscious husband's hand as they bumped along the road to Butterworth.

An anxious time followed as she waited with the Hyde-Underwood brothers in the corridor of the hospital while the doctors examined Doug. Evie tortured herself with wondering what was happening behind the closed doors to the trauma unit.

After more than an hour, a white-coated doctor approached her and introduced himself as Dr Van Den Bergh. His expression was grim and Evie's heart skipped a beat, fearing that he was about to tell her that Doug was dead.

'Your husband has sustained multiple fractures to his left leg, Mrs Barrington. He's fortunate not to have broken his neck or damaged his spine as well.'

Evie felt a rush of relief. It was only a broken leg. People broke arms and legs all the time. Doug was clearly in a lot of pain but it could have been so much worse. She saw the doctor's face was radiating discomfort.

'What else?' She was frightened. 'There's something else.'

The doctor sucked his teeth and said, 'It's one of the worst injuries I've ever seen. The entire tibial plateau is shattered – that's the area under the knee cap, and his upper and lower leg bones and ankles are smashed into several pieces. The bones have pierced the skin in several places. The lacerations, the nature of the break and the fact that he has been lying with open wounds in the midst of the jungle means infection is inevitable. I'm afraid we're going to have to amputate or he will likely die of blood poisoning.'

Her vision blurred and she felt her legs weaken. The doctor indicated a chair and drew another over and positioned it in front so he could face her as he spoke. Frank and Reggie stood behind Evie, listening.

'What exactly do you mean? Why can't you put his leg in plaster?'

'The breaks are too numerous and too severe for that to be possible. And even if it were, there's still the probability of infection from the lacerations and the exposed bones. He's been lying for hours with open wounds in the jungle. There's a strong possibility of osteomyelitis setting in – an infection in the bone itself. In fact, I'd go so far as to say infection is a certainty. That's why we have to remove the affected area before the poison can spread and take over his entire body, which would mean certain death.' He looked her straight in the eye. 'I'm sorry to be so blunt, but you need to understand the gravity of the situation.'

Evie gasped, bile rising in her throat. It was as if she had been flayed, her body unprotected by skin, her nerves jangling and raw. 'Does he know? Have you told him?'

The doctor nodded. 'Yes. And that's the problem. He's refused permission for us to perform the amputation.'

Evie wanted to howl. 'If his leg is removed, couldn't he have an artificial limb fitted?'

'Yes. I've told him that. Given time, he should be able to walk again with a prosthetic limb.' He paused to draw breath. 'I understand you have a young family, so Mr Barrington has much to live for.'

'Let me be sure I've understood this properly. You're saying if he doesn't permit you to remove his crushed leg, he will die?'

The doctor nodded slowly. 'Almost certainly. I'm sorry.'

'And even though you've explained that, he's told you he doesn't want you to do it?'

The doctor looked down. 'Yes.' He raised his eyes to meet hers. 'I need you to try to convince him to let us go ahead.'

'You're positive it's the only way to save his life?'

'Absolutely certain.'

'Then you must do it. Whether he likes it or not.'

'I can't. Not if he withholds his consent. We can't force a man of sound mind to undergo the amputation of a limb against his will.'

'But in war they must do it all the time. Look at the last war. There were so many amputees.'

'In the heat of the battlefield and possibly if a man was unconscious and unable to give consent and it was a matter of urgency, but your husband is conscious and has had a full explanation of the gravity of his situation. I have shown him the X-rays and he is adamant he doesn't want his leg removed.' He gave a little sigh. 'To tell you the truth, if anything, I was more explicit about the consequences with him than I have been with you. Our only hope is that you can prevail upon him.'

Evie jumped up and ran into the side room. She bent over the big metal sink, retching. The loss of his leg was doubtless a terrible blow for a man like Douglas but the prospect of him dying was unthinkable. She was carrying an unbearable weight of responsibility. It was like being trapped under water.

Evie took big gulps of air and told herself to hold together for Doug's sake. Later there would be time for tears. Right now she had to be stronger than she knew how.

'May I go in?' she asked the waiting Dr Van Den Bergh, hearing the tremor in her own voice.

'Yes, but not for long. We'll need to give him more morphine soon to deal with the pain.' The doctor stood up, his face showing his exhaustion.

In an odd detachment from the reality of Doug's condition, she wondered whether the doctor had been on duty throughout the night and how often he had to break news like this to relatives.

'I'm sorry to place all this on you, Mrs Barrington. But time is critical.'

'How long do we have?'

The doctor's voice was steady. 'Once septicaemia sets in he'll be unlikely to last more than forty-eight hours.'

Numb and barely able to think straight, Evie nodded and followed the doctor into the room. 'Five or ten minutes,' he said before leaving her alone to face her husband.

Doug was lying on his back, eyes closed, his brow furrowed with pain, his face ashen. Evie stood beside the bed for a moment, uncertain what to do or say. She reached for his hand.

'Evie,' he said, opening his eyes.

She bent over him and dropped a kiss on his brow. It was ice cold but clammy with sweat. With her handkerchief she wiped his forehead. His skin felt as though death was imminent.

'I'm sorry,' he said. 'I've made an utter hash of things. I went crashing through the jungle without paying attention to what was under my feet. I should have known better.' He closed his eyes for a moment and winced with pain. 'I'm a damned fool.

She stroked his brow. 'Never mind all that. The doctor has told me he needs your permission to perform an operation.'

'Damned quack. Wants to cut my leg off. I told him to bugger off.'

She tried to keep the fear out of her voice. 'But Doug, the doctor knows what he's doing. He says if he doesn't amputate, your life is in grave danger. Worse than that. He says you will almost certainly die.'

'My life's over anyway.' He turned his head away on the pillow. 'Whether he chops it off or not I'll never be whole again.' He turned back to look at her again. 'I'd be a cripple for the rest of my life. I can't live like that.'

Evie could hold back the tears no longer. The dam had broken. She grabbed his hand, squeezing it tightly in her own. 'Please, Doug. Don't do this. You have so much to live for. Little Hugh. And Jasmine. And me. We need you.'

He sighed. 'They're not taking my leg. I'll go to my grave with it. I intend to stay whole. How can I run the estates from a wheelchair?'

'The surgeon says you can be fitted with an artificial leg. You can learn to walk again.'

He snorted derisively. 'He's no idea what's involved in running a rubber estate. I'm an active man. That's my life. You know that, Evie. I won't be carved up like a piece of meat. I'd rather be dead.'

He looked away from her. 'Anyway it's right that I should

be punished for what I did to my brother. My death isn't going to be as quick as Bertie's, but it will be soon.'

Her tears were driven by anger as well as sorrow. 'Don't speak like that. You were not to blame for your brother's death. You were a little boy. You meant your brother no ill.'

'I'm too tired to argue. Please go, my darling, so they can give me another shot.' His face contorted with pain and he clutched her hand. 'I'm grateful to have a chance to say goodbye to you. Seeing you again was the only thing that stopped me using my gun to shoot myself when I was in that hole. Now go.'

She started to protest, but recognising that his pain was clearly intolerable, she bent over him and kissed him again. 'I'll be back when you've had some rest.'

He reached for her hand. 'Please respect my wishes, Evie. If you care at all for me, let me go the way I want to go.'

The door opened and a nurse entered. 'You'll have to leave, Mrs Barrington. Your husband needs to sleep. You can come back tomorrow morning.'

Tears streaming down her face, Evie moved towards the door.

His voice was faint as she touched the handle. 'And thank you, Evie. Thank you for putting up with me. For giving me my son. I know you'll bring him up to be a better man than me.'

Her heart breaking, she pushed the door open and left him to the nurse and the comfort of a hypodermic needle.

Dr Van den Bergh was waiting in the corridor. He looked at her anxiously and she shook her head. 'I'll try again when he wakes up,' she said.

The doctor frowned. He didn't need to say anything. She could read in his eyes that he was thinking it may already be too late.

'Isn't there anything else you can do to stop infection?'

'We're doing all we can. We're giving him sulpha drugs – the strongest anti-microbials we have. But his natural resistance is low because of the loss of blood and the stress of the pain. He was lying injured for several hours before he was brought to the surface. Time is the enemy here, Mrs Barrington. We'll give him morphine to reduce his pain and help him sleep while we let the drugs try to do their work. You should go home and get some sleep yourself. You need to think of your baby. And Mr Barrington tells me you have a little girl. She needs you too. Come back tomorrow morning.' He placed a hand on her arm. 'Say your prayers that after a night's sleep, he may change his mind.'

Evie allowed herself to be ushered out of the hospital to return to George Town with Frank and Reggie.

She wanted to be alone, to fold her baby in her arms and never let him go. What kind of a world had she brought him into? A world where God would allow a man like Doug, so strong, fit and healthy, to be cut down in his prime.

To her relief, the brothers left her on the doorstep and didn't offer to come inside. It was already eight in the evening. Incredible to believe that only the previous evening she'd been sitting in the garden here with her guests, unaware of Doug's plight. In that brief time her entire world had been changed irrevocably.

Aunty Mimi opened the door, eyes brimming with tears. 'Solly for *Tuan*. I light many candles in temple today for him.' She looked away. 'For you too, *Mem*,' she said, before disappearing into the kitchen.

Mary Helston was waiting in the drawing room. She opened her arms and wrapped Evie in an embrace.

'My poor darling. Frank called me from the hospital and told me what's happened.' Her eyes filled with tears. 'How is Doug?'

'He wants to die. He's decided to die. I need a stiff gin.' She moved towards the sideboard but Benny appeared and did the honours, while proffering his good wishes for the *tuan*. Evie collapsed into a chair.

'It's food not alcohol you need, Evie. When did you last eat?' Mary face was full of concern.

Evie waved her hand dismissively. 'Where's Jasmine?'

'Upstairs helping Susan bath the babies. She's anxious to see you, but I asked if I could have a few moments with you first.'

'What does she know?'

'Just that her daddy has had an accident and is in the hospital.'

Evie put her head in her hands. 'How the hell I am I going to tell an eight-year-old her father's going to die.'

Mary closed her eyes. 'Oh, Lord, Evie. Surely it won't come to that?'

'Short of a miracle it will. Even if I manage to change his mind in the morning it may still be too late to prevent blood-poisoning.' She ran her fingers through her tangled hair. 'He's made up his mind to die. Doug is an obstinate man and he refuses to contemplate losing a leg. He thinks death is preferable.'

'You have to tell her the truth. If you dress it up she's going to be even more shocked when she finds out. Tell her he's had a terrible accident and prepare her that he may not make it. Children are more resilient than we give them credit for.'

Evie began to cry softly. 'I don't think I'm strong enough to get through this.'

'Yes, you are. You are the strongest person I know.' Mary gave her another hug. 'And tomorrow, once he's got over the shock, he may look at things differently.'

'Tomorrow may already be too late. I need to talk to Jasmine.'

TWENTY-SIX

Telling Jasmine what was happening to her father was the hardest thing Evie had ever had to do, but the child made it easier. The little girl listened solemnly, then said, 'I'll be like you. We'll both have no daddy.' Lip trembling, she was clearly struggling not to cry, and Evie's heart lurched as she gathered her step-daughter into her arms.

'We'll have to be strong for each other and for Hughie,' Evie said, stroking the little girl's hair. 'Sometimes I'll be very sad and I'll need you to cheer me up and sometimes you'll be sad and I'll try to cheer you up.'

'What happens if we're both sad at the same time?'

'Oh, my darling!' She squeezed the child tight against her breast. 'We'll have to hope that Hugh can cheer us both up.'

Jasmine nodded, her face grave. 'Hughie's always good at making me smile. He's a very happy baby. He makes me happy too.'

Unable to sleep all night, Evie was up and dressed at dawn and asked Benny to drive her to the car ferry and on to the hospital in Butterworth. When she arrived, she found Arthur Leighton sitting in the corridor outside Doug's room. Seeing Evie, he rushed towards her and wrapped her in his arms.

Evie stood rigid as a pole. To give in to her emotions, break down and be comforted by Arthur, would feel like an act of disloyalty to Doug. To be embraced, however innocently, as her husband lay dying a few feet away, was not something she could allow, no matter how much she longed to.

'Have you seen him?' she asked, pulling away.

Arthur shook his head. 'The doctors are in with him now.'

'How did you know? When did you get here? I thought you were in Singapore.'

'The bush telegraph travels fast. As soon as I heard what had happened, I drove up. I was in Klang so it wasn't so far. I drove through the night. I got here about ten minutes ago. No one's told me anything yet. Is he all right?'

'No. He's not all right,' she snapped, nerves frayed. 'If they don't amputate his leg he's going to die. He's refused to let them. And it may already be too late.' She crumpled into a chair and Arthur sat down beside her. He took her hand but she jerked it away. Seeing him there, his long legs whole inside their light flannel trousers, his skin tanned and healthy, made Evie want to scream.

'Have you talked to him?' Arthur asked.

'Yes, but he won't listen. Seems to think it's better to die than to be without a leg. Never mind his children. Never mind me.' She gave a groan of exasperation.

'Would you like me to have a go? Maybe I can talk some sense into him.'

Evie was irritated. Why did he think he would have more influence than she had, when she was Doug's wife? But anything had to be worth trying. And arguing with Arthur, who was, after all, Doug's only friend, was not going to solve anything. She nodded, helpless and angry with the world.

The door opened and Dr Van Den Bergh emerged with another doctor. Evie jumped to her feet.

'Mrs Barrington, can we have a word? This is my colleague Dr Fabian. He's our expert in tropical medicine and infectious diseases.' Seeing Evie hesitate, he added, 'It won't take long and afterwards you can see Mr Barrington.'

'Would you like me to come with you?' Arthur's voice was tender and concerned.

She shook her head and followed the two medical men down the corridor and into an office.

It was Dr Fabian who spoke. 'You need to prepare for the worst, Mrs Barrington. Your husband has deteriorated during the night. While we can't confirm septicaemia until we have time for the blood cultures to show it, he has the symptoms. His breathing is rapid, he has a high fever and his blood pressure is dangerously low. He's passing no water and there are signs that organ failure is beginning. It's also possible that his kidneys were crushed in the impact of the fall and that is contributing to their failure.'

Evie gasped. It was too late. She looked at Dr Van den Bergh, who shook his head. 'I'm sorry. There's nothing we can do now except make him as comfortable as possible.'

The room was spinning around her and she tried to make her mind focus. 'But the drugs? Are you saying they didn't work?'

'The conditions he was lying in at the bottom of that mine shaft and the high temperatures made his open wounds a breeding ground for bacteria,' said Dr Fabian. 'Sulpha drugs are the most effective we have at combatting bacteria, but to be honest your husband was probably already beyond our help by the time they got him out of the mine. He was down there for more than fifteen hours. My opinion is that, even had we removed the limb last night, it would have been too late to halt the progress of the disease. It was already almost twenty-four hours after he sustained the injuries before we received him here.'

She was trembling. 'How long does he have?'

'It's hard to say. He has a strong constitution but he has been through a lot and his resistance is extremely low. I'd say it's a matter of hours. I very much doubt he'll survive another forty-eight, and it may be less. I'm sorry.'

Evie couldn't take it in. It was too fast. Time was running out. She was utterly helpless. 'Is he conscious?'

'Barely. He's drifting in and out. We're giving him a lot of pain relief and that makes him very drowsy. As his body gradually loses function he will drift into a coma. I suggest you go in and say your goodbyes, Mrs Barrington.'

Walking back down the corridor, Evie was unsteady on her feet. She took large gulps of air and forced herself not to give way to tears. She had to be strong for the children. She had to find a way to be strong for herself. Douglas was the father of her child, the man she had tried so hard to love and who had, in his awkward way, claimed to love her.

Arthur was waiting where she'd left him. She quickly told him the prognosis and he closed his eyes and his mouth set hard. 'I'm so awfully sorry, Evie. For Doug and for you and the children.' His eyes were welling but his voice was steady.

She avoided his gaze. 'I'm going in to see him. I'd like some time alone then you can see him.' Heart hammering against her ribs, and skin prickling, she went into the room.

Doug lay surrounded by tubes, one from an oxygen cylinder into his nose, another attached to a rubber bag, presumably a catheter, a drip attached to his arm, his eyes shut, his breathing jagged. Evie approached the bedside, shocked at the deterioration in his appearance. A nurse was shaking a thermometer and frowned as she noted the reading down on a chart that hung on the end of the bed. Only six months ago, Evie had lain in a similar bed in the same hospital holding their new baby, with

Doug as her visitor. How was it possible that here they were, the same people in the same place, yet in such horribly different circumstances?

'Is he unconscious?' she asked the nurse.

'He's semi-conscious. But he may not be able to speak.'

Evie wanted to scream.

'So I'm too late?'

'No. Talk to him. He might respond, and if he doesn't, he'll hear you. The last sense to leave is hearing. I'll give you some privacy. I'll be just down the corridor if you need me.'

When she was gone, Evie sat at the bedside. She was afraid. This stranger wasn't Doug. This couldn't possibly be her strong and athletic husband: the man with a powerful tennis serve, the *tuan besar* who walked for hours around his rubber estates giving orders, his dog at his side, the man who had fathered two children and loved to drink whisky, the man of changing and unpredictable moods, and of few words, the husband who struggled to express his feelings and who had sometimes caused her to doubt he had any. The man lying in front of her was grey-faced and wizened, his breath barely discernible, his body broken, his strength gone.

Her over-riding emotions were pity and sadness. How had it come to this? How was it possible that a split second's inattention had led to this shocking transformation and imminent death?

Swallowing her fear, she wrapped her warm fingers around his cold ones. There was no response. It took an act of will for her to speak to him, as if she were already addressing a corpse.

'Doug, my darling, can you hear me? It's Evie. I'm here. The nurse says even if you seem to be asleep you can probably hear me.'

No response.

'I have a letter for you from Jasmine. I'm going to read it out to you.' She reached for her handbag and took out the folded note paper. 'Here's what she says: *"Dear Daddy, I'm sad that you have had a bad accident and are very poorly. Miss Helston is going to ask our class to say prayers for you. I am saying extra special ones. Just for you. Baby Hughie sends his love. Even though he can't speak I know he loves you as much as Mummy and I do."'* Evie struggled to steady her voice as she read the words. Gulping, she continued. *"'I got a new proficiency badge at Brownies. It's for swimming and has a frog on it. Mummy's going to sew it on my uniform. Got to go now. Lots and lots of love from Jasmine."* She's added about a hundred kisses and she's drawn a picture of you—' Evie had been about to say that the picture was of Doug playing tennis but stopped herself just in time.

She took another slow deep breath. She had to keep it together. Be strong. She mustn't make it harder for him.

Brushing a lock of hair away from his brow with her free hand, she noticed his normally thick lustrous dark brown hair was limp and thin under her fingers. God – even his hair was dying.

'Evie...' His voice was so faint she wasn't sure whether she'd imagined it. But he persisted. 'Want you... be happy... some-one... love you... you deserve.'

'Don't say that. Please, Doug. I can't bear it.'

'You made me happy... good wife... now you... loves you...'

'Oh, Doug. What are you saying?'

'Badger... Reggie.'

'You want Reggie to take care of Badger?'

He nodded. 'Arth...'

'Arthur's here. You want to see him? He's outside.'

She felt a faint squeeze to her hand. Afraid she was going to break down, she said, 'I'll tell him to come in.'

She rushed out into the corridor, afraid that she was about to collapse completely. 'Go in,' she said to Arthur. 'He's asking for you. I'm getting myself a glass of water. I'll be back in a few minutes.' She half ran down the passageway through the main door and into the garden, where she flung herself down on a wooden seat and gave in to tears.

By the time she returned, ten minutes later, Doug was sleeping. Arthur looked up from the bedside and stretched his lips into a wistful smile. She sat down on the other side of the bed and held her husband's grave-cold hand. The room was silent for several minutes, apart from the tick-tock of a wall clock. Ticking down Douglas's remaining time on earth.

At last Arthur spoke. 'He asked me to tell you he loves you and he's sorry for what's happened.'

Evie bristled, exposed, vulnerable, sat here with the two men she had cared most for, with the man she loved, relaying the dying declarations of the one she had married. It was absurd. Horrible. And it was wrong to be talking about Doug across his dying body. She choked back her need to cry out to rail against the horror of it all.

A nurse came into the room and took Doug's temperature. She studied her fob watch as she took his pulse, giving a sympathetic smile to Evie, then mouthed, 'Not long.'

After the nurse had gone, Arthur spoke again. 'I'd like to stay here with you both, if you don't mind me being here.'

'Don't you need to head back to Singapore?'

'I telephoned and left a message for Sir Shenton. I'm staying in Penang as long as I can be of help. Doug asked me to stay.' He looked down. 'Apparently I'm his executor.' His voice was low.

'I didn't know that. Thank you.' Far from angry at Arthur, she was grateful for his quiet presence.

The day passed. They kept a silent vigil at Doug's bedside, leaving only for Evie to telephone home to check on the children.

The nurse approached her as she finished the call. 'Why don't you go home and get some sleep, Mrs Barrington?'

'I'm not leaving him.'

The nurse nodded, her face sad. 'You and the gentleman need to go and eat something. I have to change the dressings. You need to leave the room for about twenty minutes. The canteen's open for another half hour.'

'Come on,' said Arthur, steering her along the corridor.

In the canteen, Arthur ignored her protestation that she couldn't eat, and ordered a plate of fruit and some sandwiches. As soon as they were in front of her, Evie realised she hadn't eaten in almost two days. She devoured a sandwich.

'I can't help feeling guilty, sitting here eating while he's lying there dying,' she said at last.

Arthur said nothing, but he nodded agreement.

'I still can't believe it's happening.'

'Neither can I,' he said. He sucked in his lips. 'It's so wrong. So unfair. Seeing a man like Doug laid so low.'

Evie put down the piece of mango she'd been eating and began to cry. Arthur leaned over the table and took her hand.

'I may not have loved him in the way I should have done...' She left unsaid the obvious reason for that. 'But I do love him, you know.'

'I know you do.'

'Even though he's often cold and finds it hard to express his feelings... but maybe that's why I care for him. Because I know how hard things are for him.' She paused. 'Did he tell you about his brother?'

'He has a brother?'

'Had. He died when they were children. See – he couldn't even bring himself to tell you, his best friend that.' She explained the story of Bertie's death and how Hugh was named after him.

'That explains a lot.'

'If he dies... when he dies... I don't think I'll ever get over it, Arthur. I'll always wonder if I could have done more for him.

Made him happier. Been better at reaching him. He was so closed off. I tried but maybe not enough.'

Arthur smiled sadly. 'You couldn't have done more, Evie. And you did reach him. He told me this morning that you were the best thing that happened to him. You were everything to him, Evie. You have nothing to regret.'

'He said that?'

Arthur nodded. 'He really loved you. He's still full of shame about what he did with that woman. I told him you had forgiven him.'

'I have.' She voiced it with certainty. She *had* forgiven him. 'I know he was remorseful. He just struggled to articulate it. He hurt me, but I believe if he'd known the consequences he'd never have done it.' She squeezed her hands into tight fists. 'Or am I being too generous? Just because he's dying?'

'We both know Doug's a complex character – that's why we both love him.' Arthur gave her a thoughtful look.

Uncomfortable, Evie changed the subject. 'How are things with Veronica?'

He looked down and sighed. 'She's in a place in Singapore. They're trying to sort her out. She'd gone haywire. Drinking.' He put his palms together and intertwined his fingers. 'The doctors there are confident they can help her.'

'And you? What do you think?'

'She's admitted she needs help. They say that's half the battle.'

'Good.' Evie pushed away her plate and got up. 'It must be twenty minutes now.'

Back in Doug's room, Evie and Arthur drowsed, drifting in and out of half-sleep, unable to settle, unwilling to leave, sentinels either side of Doug's bed.

At one point during the night, she awoke to see Doug had

opened his eyes and was looking at her. She bent forward and took his hand. 'I love you, darling,' she whispered. Unable to reply, an oxygen mask clamped over his face, his mouth quivered into an approximation of a smile and his eyes sent back a silent message of love and sadness. He closed his eyes and there was no sound other than the slow rasp of his breathing.

She looked up to see if Arthur was awake, but he was dozing in his chair. She turned her gaze back to her husband. His face was grey, lined, haggard, the toll of the past days etched there. He was unrecognisable, helpless. She had already lost him. The man lying here was a shell, the remnants of what Doug Barrington had once been. A silent tear rolled down her cheek.

The hours passed. A nurse came in from time to time to monitor his vital signs, and night turned into early morning. Around the edges of the ill-fitting hospital curtains the pitch dark was softening into a grey dawn. In the distance she could hear voices, footsteps and the clatter of metal. The world was waking up. She yawned.

Something else had changed. She sat bolt upright and saw Arthur do the same. They exchanged a wordless look that indicated they both knew Doug was no longer there. No death rattle. No last gasp. Just a soft fading away. Arthur got up and went to fetch the nurse who confirmed Douglas Barrington was gone and offered her sympathies. Evie bent over her husband's body, stroked the stray lock of hair back from his brow and dropped a kiss onto his cold lips.

It had happened so quickly. The previous morning, she had arrived at the hospital determined to convince Douglas of the need for amputation, and here she was, just a short time later, looking at the empty shell of his broken body.

She was a widow with an infant son and a little girl who had now become an orphan. How had it come to this?

. . .

Arthur Leighton took care of everything. He informed everyone who needed to know of Doug's death, arranged the funeral, ensured the bank would release funds for wages to be paid at Batu Lembah, asked Mike Overton to act as estate manager until Evie could make a decision on the future of the estates. He even collected Badger from Batu Lembah and transported him into Reggie Hyde-Underwood's care at Bellavista. Evie was particularly relieved about this last matter. Badger would have been a constant reminder of his master's absence.

Veronica did not attend the funeral, presumably because of her treatment. Evie was grateful that she didn't have to contend with her.

Afterwards, there was a small gathering back at the house. Evie could barely take in what was happening, sitting listlessly as a stream of people offered their condolences. She had cause to be grateful to Mary. Her friend ensured that Evie's guests were all watered and fed and moved among them, acting as the hostess that Evie lacked the strength to be.

TWENTY-SEVEN

Jasmine was at school and Evie was sitting in the garden, staring into space. Now that Douglas had been laid to rest, the shock of his death and its manner was receding, to be replaced by a numbness and a feeling of being cast adrift. Even though Douglas had rarely been present at the George Town house, the knowledge that he would never return made her feel as if she no longer had any right to be there.

Before the funeral, Arthur had assured her that there was plenty of money in the bank, and the income from the two rubber estates, and from an inheritance from Douglas's late mother, meant that she and the children would be well-provided for. Money was the last thing she needed to worry about.

Hugh was sleeping in a bassinet beside her, in a shaded part of the garden. She gazed at his perfectly formed face and wondered how she was going to manage to raise the child in a way that Doug would have approved. How was he to grow up without the guidance and support of a father? How was she going to make the right choices for her son – the choices that Douglas would have made?

And she missed Douglas. Yes, he had often been cold and distant, but he had cared for her in his own clumsy way. Her week no longer had a focus now he would no longer be returning to George Town for the weekends. In the big bed, she felt lonely and lost and longed to have him beside her. She missed the intimacy of making love, the feel of his body against hers, the physical pleasure they had enjoyed.

She examined her little boy's face, trying to identify any feature of Douglas. He had inherited his father's dark hair, and his eyes were the same blue, but it was impossible to detect anything more. Evie told herself that something would become apparent as the baby grew up. Besides, there was no discernible evidence of her in the baby either. She hoped Hugh would grow up to look exactly like Douglas – those dark good looks would stand him in good stead – but not that he would inherit his father's melancholia or his inability to express his feelings. No, she had to make sure of that.

The heat was oppressive, with no breeze. Evie had a sudden overwhelming need to get away from the house, to escape the tragic air that Aunty Mimi and Benny were projecting, to escape the constant reminder that Doug would never again stand on the veranda outside the drawing room with a *stengah* in his hand. She picked up the bassinet and went inside where she transferred Hugh into his pram, and told Aunty Mimi she was going out for a while.

As she went to open the front door, there was a knock. It was Arthur Leighton.

'You're going out?' he said. 'I came to say goodbye. I'm driving back to Singapore today.'

'I was going for a walk. I can put it off.'

'No, don't. May I walk with you? Where are you heading?'

'There's a little Taoist temple I like to visit.' Until the words came out she hadn't realised that was where she intended to go.

They began walking.

'Is that the one near the Fort? The Temple of Harmony? I know it well. Outside is chaos and inside it's an oasis of tranquility.'

'That's it exactly. A very peaceful place. There's a monk there who once gave me some advice. I was hoping he might be able to give me some today.'

'What did he advise you about?'

She hesitated then decided to tell him. There was something about Arthur that made it impossible to hold anything back from him. 'It was after I found Doug with that Malay woman. The monk helped me find a way to forgive him, to give our marriage another chance.'

Arthur said nothing.

'I was thinking he might have some words of wisdom for me about how to cope with being a widow while still in my twenties.'

Arthur's lips tightened and a nerve twitched at the edge of his mouth. He turned to face her. 'Evie, I wish I could make everything different. I wish I could be here with you all the time, to support you.'

'Thank you. You've been a rock for me. I couldn't have got through the funeral without you. And those last hours at the hospital.' A tear ran down her cheek. How was she going to cope, without Douglas and now without Arthur too?

They walked along a quiet, tree-lined street, Evie pushing the pram with Hugh still fast asleep inside. Abruptly, Arthur stopped and pulled her into his arms. He crushed her against him and she could feel the beating of his heart through his white cotton shirt. 'I love you, Evie, more than life itself. I've tried to make it otherwise but I can't. And now, seeing how lost and lonely you must be feeling, all I want is to be with you. To make things better for you.'

'Don't,' she said, a surge of anger running through her. 'Your best friend is barely in his grave and you're saying things like that.'

'I'm saying them because I have to say them. Because of Doug dying like that. So unexpectedly. So quickly. It's made me realise how fleeting life is and how important it is to grasp hold of the possibility of happiness.' He drew her closer. 'I love you, Evie, and you know as well as I do that we're meant to be together.'

She pushed him away. 'Stop it. I don't want to hear any more.'

He put his hands on her shoulders. 'Evie, listen to me. I love you. Desperately. Totally. Completely. With every fibre of my being. I realise while I'm still married to Veronica I have no right to say this to you, but I want you to know that I am going to find a way to free myself. Being in that rest-home is helping her. I just need to give her some more time. I know I can convince her she'll be better off without me—'

'Stop it! I told you. I don't want to hear this, Arthur. What kind of woman do you think I am? My husband has just died. You're still married. And I don't want to hear any more about your bloody wife.' She took hold of the pram again. 'Now go. Now!' And without waiting for an answer she moved away, walking at speed from him, without looking back.

To her relief he didn't attempt to follow her. She felt herself shaking as she pushed the pram. The baby began to wail, perhaps sensing his mother's distress. Her legs were like jelly, so she stopped and sat down on a bench, taking her baby into her arms to comfort him.

Why was life so damn hard? What would Douglas feel? His best friend declaring his love to his widow, just a day after he was buried.

The truth was her anger was with herself even though it was directed at Arthur. She was consumed with guilt. Yes, she missed Douglas. Yes, she grieved his death. She wanted him to be here for his children. She wished he hadn't died. Yet what Arthur had said was true. She loved him body and soul and yes, yes, yes, she knew they were meant to be together.

The rain began. A typical Malayan shower, arriving without warning and often ending just as quickly. It started with light drops that refreshed the oppressive air, before rapidly turning into a torrent, splashing up and soaking her legs as she sat on the bench. She put Hugh back in the pram, pulling the canopy up to protect him, then set off walking rapidly towards the temple. Evie always enjoyed tropical rain. It was so different from the rain in England. It was steamy and often the sun arrived before the shower finished, evaporating the water so any cooling effect was short-lived. But as she hurried along, the sky was dark and the rain unrelenting. Evie looked upwards, letting the water cascade down her face, washing away her tears. Upwards to heaven. Was Doug there? Watching her? She felt an overpowering need to talk to the monk.

The rain stopped just as she entered the square of the Temple of Harmony. Leaving the pram outside, she picked up Hugh and went into the building. It took a while for her eyes to adjust to the gloom. At first she thought the space was empty, jumping when she heard the soft voice behind her.

'You have brought your child. A beautiful baby. I am very happy for you.'

'Thank you,' she said to the monk. 'He's seven months old and I've been meaning to bring him here to meet you for some time. His name is Hugh.'

The monk studied her face. 'You have great fortune and yet I see you are still unhappy. Would you like to talk?'

Evie nodded, intensely grateful for the man's perception. Just being in his presence had a calming effect upon her. She followed him into the anteroom where they had taken tea before.

'So. Are things still difficult between you and your husband?'

'My husband is dead.'

The monk nodded, unfazed. 'He was sick?'

'An accident. He had a bad fall and got blood poisoning and died in less than forty-eight hours.'

'I see you are very sad.'

'Yes. I did everything you said. I tried so hard. I forgave him. We were reconciled.' She looked at the sleeping child in her arms. 'He was so happy about the baby. Life together wasn't perfect, but we had found a way to make it work. I can't believe he's gone.'

The monk said nothing, but looked at her expectantly, so Evie stumbled on to fill the silence. 'It's so unfair. Unjust. What kind of god strikes a man down at only forty-three? And when he's recently become a father. What a cruel god to punish us like that.'

The anger welled up inside her. She lowered her eyes. 'I think it's a punishment. My husband believed he was being punished for causing the death of his brother when they were children, but he was wrong. God wouldn't punish him for something that happened accidentally when he was a child – God was actually punishing *me*.'

'Why would God punish you?'

She looked up and met his eyes.

'For loving another man.' There, it's out, she thought, squeezing her eyes tightly shut. If she expected a thunderbolt to strike her down, it didn't happen.

'You betray your husband with this other man?' The monk's gaze was steady.

'Only in my thoughts. I tried so hard to be a good wife. To put aside my feelings for the other man. I worked hard to make my husband happy.'

'And you did. You tell me he happy about beautiful baby. Yes?'

'Yes. He was. He wanted a son desperately.'

'So why you say God punish you for that? You plan leave your husband for this other man?'

'No!'

'I ask again why you think God punish you?'

She looked down, twisting her fingers round each other. 'I don't know.'

'Death is part of life.' He looked up at her, his eyes kind and his voice calm and reassuring. 'Without death, is no life. Flowers bloom then die and dying make new growth possible. Watch your son grow. See how he see magic in new things. In things you no more see. He see magic in things you think dull. Look your children. They are future. Husband return to nature. He now part of world around you. He part of your children. You will see husband in son as boy grows. In him, husband lives on in new life. This is the way of the world.'

She stared at the monk. 'So, I shouldn't feel guilty?'

'You learn nothing? Remember what I say you before. To find love you must first learn to love self. Forgive self. Not blame self.'

Evie felt a weight lift off her shoulders.

'Remember you made husband happy. You good wife. Now you be good mother.'

'Thank you. I will do my best.' She was about to take her leave but then blurted, 'But the other man. He has been good to me and he arranged the funeral. I've treated him badly even though he has been a rock to me. Just now he told me loves me and I was angry. I shouted at him.' She twisted her hands again.

'Remember to love self. Love self and trust your god. God will help you find peace. Goodbye, daughter.' He rose to his feet and disappeared behind the curtain.

Evie stared after him, uncertain if she was any the wiser, but feeling a sense of calm that she had lacked when she'd walked into the temple. She planted a kiss on Hugh's forehead and left the building.

TWENTY-EIGHT

The world changed again for Evie in December 1941, with the news of the bombing of Pearl Harbour by the Japanese. Nerves among the expatriate community had been taut since the summer, when the Americans had initiated an embargo of Japanese oil and implemented sanctions and, thanks to Vichy France, the Japanese now had air bases in Indo-China, so the threat had moved dangerously close to Malaya. But with Pearl Harbour and the simultaneous amphibious landings at Kota Bharu on the north east Malay coast near the Thai border, all pretence that the Japanese were not to be taken seriously disappeared. Both the USA and Britain were at war with Japan.

Earlier in the war, the British had been clear that, in theory, the priority for defence after Britain itself, was Malaya with its mineral and rubber wealth and the strategic harbours of Penang and Singapore. Yet Churchill and the War Cabinet had overturned this assumption and dropped Malaya below the Middle East and Russia in the pecking order. Only Singapore had any serious defensive presence – but with insufficient and obsolete aircraft, below par divisions, no tanks or anti-tank guns. On top of this, there was serious dissent between the military and government authorities. The Commander-in-Chief of the combined military forces complained of alarmist press reporting and seemed more intent on discrediting his colleagues than facing the prospect of the enemy.

In Penang too, there was internal bickering, a refusal to allocate sufficient funds to civic defence and a neglect of air defences, rendering the island vulnerable to attack. The authorities were guilty of bungling – trenches had been dug, only to be filled in again, and there was a general refusal to face the possibility of invasion.

Life for Evie had, until now, been completely focused on her two children. No thought of leaving Malaya had entered her head. Penang was their home. It was her husband's final resting place and she and Jasmine tended his grave regularly. Besides, where would she go? To return to Britain was unthinkable. Not only was there danger there, the voyage itself was long and beset with risks. Her family's livelihood depended on the income from the rubber estates and since Douglas had always intended his son to inherit and manage these eventually, Evie wanted to stay true to his intentions. That meant staying put.

But on the morning after the attack on Pearl Harbour, Evie was woken at seven, not by the crying of Hugh, but by the scream of sirens. Was the unthinkable happening? Penang under attack. Pulling on her dressing gown, she picked up her son, who miraculously had remained asleep throughout the air raid warning, but now began grizzling. Soothing him, she went across the landing to Jasmine's bedroom. The little girl, already dressed, was standing at the window, looking up at the sky.

'What's happening, Mummy? What was that noise?'

Evie hated to frighten the child but if the war had come to them it would be impossible to shelter Jasmine from its realities. 'It's an air-raid warning. It's to make sure we are ready to take shelter if the Japanese attack.'

'Will they attack us, Mummy? Are we going to die like

Daddy? Karen Morrison in my class said her granny got killed by a bomb in England. Will they drop bombs on us here?'

Evie's throat constricted. 'No!' She tried to inject confidence into her voice but in truth she was absolutely terrified. She had been a child herself in the last war but that happened over the Channel in another country.

'It's probably just a test – to make sure everyone has time to take shelter if we need to.' As she said the words, she realised how hollow they sounded. If George Town was attacked there were no civilian shelters. 'Let's go downstairs and have some breakfast.'

'Am I going to school today?'

Evie hadn't even thought of that question. But in an instant she decided. 'No, darling, you can stay at home with Mummy and Hugh today.' Until she knew exactly what was going on she wasn't going to be separated from her children.

When they came downstairs, Aunty Mimi, Cookie and Benny were standing in the hallway, talking animatedly.

'Do you know what's happening?' Evie asked.

'I count eight planes in sky. Fly to south of island.' Benny looked angry. 'Japanese attack airfield at Bayan Lepas. Very bad.'

'Aunty Mimi, can you give the children their breakfast. I'm going to use the telephone.'

Evie went into the study and sat down at the desk. She felt lost without Douglas. Who to call? She wished she hadn't pushed Arthur Leighton away. She didn't even know how to reach him in Singapore. He must surely know what was happening. After all he worked for the governor. Maybe if she rang the exchange and asked for Sir Shenton Thomas's office they'd put her through. She told herself not to be foolish – even if she were able to reach Arthur he would be far too preoccupied with the Japanese invasion attempts to tell her what a single precautionary sounding of the air raid siren meant. And

Benny was probably right. They were headed to the airfield in the south of the island. They'd be safe here in George Town. Better to call Reggie Hyde-Underwood who was in the Volunteers and would surely know what was going on. As she about to pick it up, the telephone rang.

'Evie, we're closing the school today,' Mary Helston said. 'Don't send Jasmine in.'

'What's happening, Mary? What were the sirens for?'

'I don't know. I can't talk now. I have to call all the other parents. I'll come over as soon as I've finished.' Her voice was strained, anxious.

Little more than an hour later, Mary was at the door. The two women embraced.

'God, Evie, I'm worried sick. They've attacked the airfield at Butterworth as well as Bayan Lepas. It took an absolute pummelling. I could see fires burning across the Strait as I drove over here. Frank...'

Evie held her friend tightly. 'Frank's there, not in Singapore?'

'He's in Butterworth. He got back from training in Singapore two days ago.' Mary began to cry. Silent tears that ran down her cheeks. She didn't attempt to brush them away. 'He told me they'd be sitting ducks if the Japanese were to attack. Those Buffalo things they fly are out of the ark. They have no chance against the Japanese Mitsubishis.' She gave a strangled sob and Evie led her to a seat and sat down beside her, putting an arm around her friend.

Mary was shaking. 'The Japanese planes smashed the American fleet to bits, so what chance do Frank and the other chaps have in their bloody useless, clapped-out excuses for planes?'

'Do you really think they've attacked the airfield?'

'I know they have. Apart from my seeing the fires, Dad is plugged into all the latest information. He says even though they attacked the airport here on the island, most of their efforts were directed at Butterworth. Giving it a pounding. There were only about half a dozen of our boys there to mount a defence. One of them is Frank.' She gave a wracking sob. 'Evie, I agreed to marry him. When he got back from Singapore we had dinner at the E&O... I ...' She held her hand out and Evie saw she was wearing an engagement ring.

'Oh, Mary,' she said. 'I don't know what to say.'

Later that day the bad news was confirmed. The air attack on the aerodrome at Butterworth was intense with the entire RAF and Australian airforce presence wiped out. The enemy had been careful to use only anti-personnel bombs on the runways, presumably to preserve them for their own eventual use.

Mary told Evie she didn't know whether Frank Hyde-Underwood had been one of the few airmen who had managed to scramble but had been shot down by the superior Japanese aircraft, or whether he had been one of the victims of the annihilation on the Allied presence on the ground at RAF Butterworth. Either way, he had almost certainly lost his life and with it, Mary Helston had lost her second chance of happiness.

Over the following days, as well as bombing the two airfields, the Japanese attack included a less successful attempt to sink all the ships in the port at George Town. The city was completely unprepared. Within three days of the Pearl Harbour attack, the Japanese had total supremacy of the skies above Penang and soon after that, the last of the Brewster Buffalos, sent up from Singapore after the first attack as reinforcements, limped away from Butterworth.

The civilians of Penang were now alone, and on the 11th December the Japanese began to bomb George Town. There was incredulity among the population that this was happening to them.

Evie and the children had taken shelter in the relative safety of Bellavista, up in the hills above the city. She stood beside Susan and Reggie Hyde-Underwood on the lawns where she had once walked with Susan to admire the orchid garden on her first visit to the estate, looking up at the sky.

Reggie had taken the inevitable, but still unconfirmed, death of his brother stoically but Evie could see that he and Susan were badly shaken.

Clutching Hugh tightly in her arms, Evie stared up at the regimented planes, flying like geese in a perfect V-formation across the pale empty canvas of the sky. They couldn't see the bombing from Bellavista, but they could hear it. It lasted for two long hours and left the Chinese quarter a burning ruin. Later Evie discovered the planes had not only dive-bombed the buildings, including the Temple of Harmony, but had machine-gunned the streets, killing many unsuspecting citizens who had been standing outside to watch what would happen. Among them, Evie would soon discover, was Aunty Mimi's husband, Cookie, who had been on his way back from the market. She never discovered the fate of her friend the monk.

Two days later, the news spread through George Town and throughout the island that the order had been given to evacuate the entire European population from Penang.

An uncharacteristically pale Reggie walked into the drawing room, where Evie and Susan were drinking tea. 'Arthur Leighton is on the telephone. He wants to speak to you, Evie.'

Picking up the receiver, she felt a rush of emotion as she heard the familiar but long-absent sound of Arthur's voice.

'Evie, are you all right? The children?'

'Yes, we're all well. Reggie and Susan have been wonderful. We're safe up here away from the city.'

'For now, but not for long. You know we're evacuating you all?'

Evie bit her lip, torn between a wish to say that they'd be fine up here in the hills and a very real fear that more danger was imminent.

'It's only a matter of time before they invade. Who knows what they'll do once they've taken the island. Sir Shenton's already taken the decision to get you all out, because the Chiefs of Staff are withdrawing the troops from Penang. It's going to be a complete capitulation. The island is being abandoned. The Japanese imperial flag will be flying there within days.'

Evie gasped.

'Percival wants to withdraw and abandon so he can focus the troops on the mainland rather than splitting his resources. George Town is about to become an open city.'

'Dear God, how has it come to this?'

'I could write the book, but right now my job is to manage the evacuation. I'm in Butterworth. The first train has already left. You need to get here as fast as you can.'

Evie's heart lurched. He was here.

Arthur's voice was urgent. 'Look I don't have long so I want to make sure you do exactly as I tell you. Reggie knows the drill. You all need to get down to George Town. We're getting everyone onto the ferries and then on trains to Singapore.'

'Singapore? But—'

'No buts. Just do it. No time to spare. We have to get you to safety. The clock's ticking.'

Evie was numb. 'I need to let Aunty Mimi and Benny know. They're still in the house in George Town.'

'Europeans only.' Arthur's voice was clipped, and she could detect the anger underneath it.

'I can't leave them! Aunty Mimi's husband, our cook, has been killed. It happened in the street. The Japanese were machine-gunning people from the planes. I can't abandon my servants here with the enemy coming.'

'Orders. I have no say. The decision has been taken that it's Europeans only. It's come from the top. From Duff Cooper himself. The local population will have to fend for themselves. It stinks but I can't do anything about it. I have to go, Evie. Hurry up. I'll keep a look out for you. But don't waste time looking for me at the port. Just get the hell out of here. Do as the officials tell you. You'll all be safe in Singapore.'

By the time they got to the quayside that night the queues for the ferries were long. Amidst the crowds, Evie caught sight of Benny and called out to him. He was heading away from the port. 'Where are you going, Benny? Where's Aunty Mimi?'

'I go back to house. They say can evacuate me because in Volunteers but can't bring wife and children. Also Aunty Mimi and Boy. So I must stay. Can't leave them behind. Only Europeans go.'

Evie felt a rush of anger. It was appalling. 'That's a disgrace!'

'Volunteers can leave but no wives and children. So no one go. Can't leave families behind.' He shook his head, his face lined with anger.

It was unjust. Disloyal. Not only had men like Benny joined the defence volunteers in good faith but they had served the European population dutifully for decades. Now they were to be abandoned, left behind to the mercy of the Japanese.

Before she could say any more, Evie was swept up in the crowd around her and moved forward in the crush as the next ferry docked. She looked back as the mass of white humanity pushed her forward, and saw Benny walking away from the quayside. What would Doug have said? He had employed Benny since he came to Penang – and his uncle before him. Aunty Mimi too. They were part of the fabric of the Barrington household and because of the sweep of a pen in Singapore, they and others like them were to be left to their fate.

When the ferry landed in Butterworth, she spotted Mary with her mother and father in the crowd. Before she could push her way through to them, Arthur Leighton appeared at her side.

'I've saved you seats on the train. Women, children, elderly and disabled. Men will follow later, once we've got you all away. Most of us will drive. We don't want to leave any usable vehicles here for the Japanese. Veronica will be waiting for you at the station in Singapore.'

'Veronica?'

'Things are better with her. She's stopped drinking. Thrown herself into the war effort. But there's no time to talk. I need to get you on that train.'

Arthur steered her across the concrete, signalling the Hyde-Underwoods to follow. To her relief, Mary Helston and her parents had seen them and worked their way over to join them.

Arthur broke the news that Mr Helston and Reggie would have to travel by road, reassuring them that they would all be reunited in Singapore.

Mary's face was gaunt and her eyes cold. Evie had never seen her usually smiling friend looking so angry.

Arthur helped the women and children into the carriage. Evie hung back.

'What about you?' Evie asked him.

'Never mind about me – you and the children need to get to Singapore.'

'What happens then?'

'Veronica will explain. We're getting you on a ship out.'

'But I thought Singapore was safe?' Evie was alarmed.

'For now. Can we talk a moment?' He looked over his shoulder. 'In private?'

Evie handed the baby to Mary and got down from the train.

Arthur was waiting behind a baggage cart piled high with suitcases, waiting to be stowed on the train.

'Three days ago the *Repulse* and the *Prince of Wales* were sunk. Our best warships, crucial to defence.' He looked into her eyes. 'We've well and truly messed this up, Evie.' Glancing around him to make sure they weren't overheard he added, 'I think Singapore will fall too. Intelligence reports say the enemy are already moving down the peninsular. We've all assumed they'll attack by sea but I think they'll come by land.'

'But how? They'll never get through the jungle and the roads aren't big enough to handle mass troop movements.'

'That's what everyone has been saying. But everyone's wrong.' His lips stretched tightly. 'They're using bicycles. Tens of thousands of bicycles.'

Evie gasped. 'Whereabouts are they?'

'A day or two away – at most.' Taking advantage of the confusion of people, he pulled her into his arms and drew her head against his chest. She heard the steady beat of his heart. 'We've lost Malaya, Evie. The game's practically over. Our airforce is destroyed, the army's clogging the roads up as they race back to Singapore. There's no attempt to try and keep the Japs at bay. I have never been so ashamed in all my life. Look at what's happening.' He swept a hand out to indicate the crowds of Europeans pushing their way onto the train. 'Complete capitulation. Abandonment of the locals. Every white man for himself. And my job is to help make this sorry shameful mess happen.'

'Will everyone leave Singapore too?'

'That's not the plan.'

She looked up at his face and read in his eyes that while it might not be the plan it was the likely reality. The unthinkable was happening. Malaya, part of the crown jewels of the British Empire, would soon be a Japanese territory.

'I have to go, my darling. I don't know when I'll see you

again. But whatever happens, I want you to know that everything I said before is still true. I love you utterly and completely. If we make it through this war I promise you, my dearest love, I will find a way to be with you, to marry you.'

Evie swallowed. A shiver ran through her body. 'I'm sorry how I behaved the last time we met.' She met his eyes. 'And you need to know, I love you too. I always have, even when I tried to pretend I didn't.'

He held her face between his hands and looked into her eyes. Evie felt as if the world had stopped. Fearful of what lay ahead, she asked, 'But why won't I see you in Singapore? Where are you going?'

'I'm staying behind. I've been training in jungle warfare at the Singapore 101 Special Training school. Too little too late, but we'll do the best we can.'

Evie thought she was going to stop breathing. 'What are you talking about, Arthur?'

'It was set up in July. They've been training military and civilians – policemen and planters, locals too. We're going to be in small teams, working behind the Japanese lines. But we've left it too late for an effective plan. We just have to do the best we can.'

He looked away. But Evie didn't need to hear the words to know what the implications were. Douglas was dead, Aunty Mimi's husband and Frank were and it was probable Arthur would be killed too.

A tear rolled down her cheek. Arthur took his thumb and wiped it away. Bending towards her, he kissed her softly on the mouth. 'Stay safe, Evie. I love you.' He left without a backward glance, melting into the throng of people.

TWENTY-NINE

The train journey to Singapore passed in a blur. The carriages were packed, people sitting or standing in the corridors, and Evie sent up a silent prayer of thanks that Arthur had been able to secure seats for them. As well as Mary Helston and her mother, Susan Hyde-Underwood and Stanford, four other women and two schoolboys shared the cramped space.

Evie forbade herself from feeling any discontent, knowing that she and all the other passengers had walked out on the servants, shopkeepers, policemen, gardeners, estate workers, teachers and students that made up the non-European population. These people loathed and feared the Japanese as much as the whites did. Aunty Mimi had witnessed her husband being gunned down in the street. The old lady had loved and cared for Jasmine and her baby brother. Years of faithful service, of trust and loyalty, betrayed. Evie felt an acute sense of shame. She looked over at Mary, who was sitting in silence gazing into the darkness beyond the window. Most of Mary's teaching colleagues were Malays. How must she feel, knowing that they had been let down? And Benny, who had served with the Volunteers, recruited by Douglas and an enthusiastic member, assiduous in attending drills and exercises. Benny had a wife and four small children. What would become of them?

Lurching along in the darkness, the sticky tropical heat of the Malayan night bathed Evie in sweat. It was hard keeping Jasmine and the two schoolboys entertained, not to mention the baby and Stanford, who was now a toddler, when there wasn't even anything to see through the window. Hugh, at eighteen months old, was a substantial weight to hold in her arms for a train journey of more than ten hours. Staring blankly into the blackness of the jungle, broken only by the lights of kampongs, she saw occasional fires burning in the distance – a token belated effort towards the failed scorched earth policy of the British.

Her thoughts returned to Arthur. She tried to picture him, hiding in dense undergrowth, boot polish applied to his face, as he moved secretly behind enemy lines. Her imagination kept failing her. Where were those enemy lines and where and how would Arthur and other white-skinned men hope to hide from detection? While Arthur, and no doubt his colleagues, spoke Malay, it was impossible he could pass as a native. As well as the risk of being caught by the advancing Japanese, there was the risk of being seen and betrayed by frightened local villagers. Their abandonment by their former white masters surely made their support for any stay-behind British unlikely. And no doubt, if the Malays didn't turn them in to the Japanese, and the British guerrillas were subsequently discovered, the repercussions would be fatal for the Malays, so who could blame them?

She squeezed her eyes tightly shut. It was all too horrible to think about. If Arthur was operating undercover, he would lack the protection afforded by a military uniform. Not that Evie had a lot of confidence that the Japanese would respect the Geneva Conventions anyway. She'd heard enough about the terrible massacres that had taken place in China in the Sino-Japanese war to make her feel sick to the stomach.

Hugh, as if sensing that tonight was no night for misbehaving, had gone off to sleep quickly, lulled by the movement of the train as it hurried along between the dark shapes of palm oil and rubber trees and virgin jungle. Evie let her thoughts drift back to Arthur's final words to her, his promise that if they both got through this war alive, they would one day be together.

It was almost a year since Douglas's death. The passing of time had helped her to accept what had happened, but she still missed her husband. She hadn't loved him the way she loved Arthur. They had never been soul mates, but she had cared for him deeply despite his shortcomings as a husband and a companion. Now that she'd had time to reflect on her marriage and Doug's character, Evie believed she had come closer to understanding him since his death than she ever had while he was alive.

Douglas had been damaged as a child and that damage had persisted into the character of the adult man. It had stunted him, crippled him emotionally just as the fall into the tin mine had crippled him physically. But Evie was beginning to feel able to follow the words of the Taoist monk and forgive herself for her inability to love Douglas as much as she would have liked to or thought she ought to. And at last, she could forgive herself, because with his death she had completely forgiven him.

Looking past her reflection in the train window into the inky blackness beyond, Evie allowed herself to think of Arthur again in a way she'd forbidden herself from doing over the months since Doug's accident. That soft brush of his lips against hers tonight had reignited a fire inside Evie that hadn't burned since the afternoon on the beach in the weeks before war was declared. How long ago that seemed. Another era.

When she and Arthur had sat side-by-side under the casuarina trees, the idea of the British abandoning Malaya had been inconceivable. Now it was happening. By the same token, the once inconceivable possibility of her having a future with Arthur Leighton now seemed tangible. But they both had to get out of Malaya alive first – and the Axis Powers must be defeated before any future was possible. That felt like a faint hope. But hope was all she had left. Hope, and her two children.

Jasmine, sitting beside her, was sleeping, her head resting against Evie. Less than three years ago, Evie hadn't even known this little girl existed. Now she loved her as completely as if she were her own child. That was another thing to be tackled in the future. She must formally adopt Jasmine. There must be no ambiguity about their relationship, no conditions attached to her love.

As the train reached its destination, officials entered the carriages and handed typewritten notices to every adult refugee. Evie read the printed words with growing alarm. The orders were stark. Childless women were to get off the train and remain in Singapore. Women with children, who were ungenerously described in civil service officialese as "ineffective", were to remain on board. They were to be delivered straight to the waterfront and transferred onto a vessel bound for Australia.

This was too soon, too sudden. Evie couldn't face the thought of being bundled with her children, as well as Susan and Stanford, onto a ship and sent off to a place she didn't know at all. And most of all, she didn't want to leave Mary. Not when her friend was grieving the loss of her fiancé. Mary needed all the love and support she could get. Evie didn't want to be separated.

But it was no good. Mary and her mother were ushered off the train with all the other adult women without dependent children. Evie was angry yet powerless. She tried to get off too, but was ordered to remain on the train.

Arthur had been right. Veronica Leighton was indeed waiting on the platform. Wearing an uncharacteristically simple cotton frock, she exuded a business-like manner and clearly relished being in charge. Her fingernails were devoid of their signature red polish, her hair looked as though she'd dragged a comb through it and there was no trace of her usual immaculately applied makeup. She pushed her way through the crowds of passengers leaving the train and came to stand beneath the window where Evie was leaning out.

'Veronica, they won't let us off the train. Apparently we're to be taken straight to a ship and packed off to Australia. Can you speak to someone? Susan here doesn't want to leave without Reggie. He's driving down from Penang. And I want to stay with my friends.' She gestured towards the platform where Mary had seated her mother on a bench while she tried to locate their suitcases.

'There are to be no exemptions from the evacuation order, Evie,' Veronica said briskly. 'I'd even managed to get you a hotel room which was a bloody miracle, but they're adamant you can't get off the train. Frightfully sorry. You're going to Batavia first where you'll be put on a ship for Perth. It's all arranged.'

Evie saw Susan was in tears beside her. Behind them Stanford had started wailing. She leaned out of the window to speak to Veronica again. 'Can't you pull some strings? Not for me. Just for Susan. Her husband will be here in a day or so. She doesn't want to be separated.'

'No strings left to pull, darling.' Veronica lowered her voice to make sure only Evie could hear her. 'And when her husband gets here he'll be expected to stay and fight. We may have lost Penang but they aren't going to give up Singapore. For some reason, the army hasn't even attempted to defend the Perak River. Arthur said the plan was to dig in there and hold the positions but I heard just now from a chap I know in Percival's office that they've just upped sticks and headed south.'

Evie stared at her. Abandoning Penang had been inconceivable but it had just happened. It seemed Britain was walking out on the entire country. She looked back into the carriage where Jasmine was sitting patiently with Hugh in her arms. The children had to come first. She had to get them out. Slipping an arm around Susan she said, 'We have to do as they say and get the children to safety.'

In her anxiety about being held on the train, Evie had forgotten about the Helstons. She looked over Veronica's head to the crowds of refugees moving through the station but Mary and her mother had disappeared.

'What's happening to everyone else?' she asked Veronica. 'My friend Mary and her mother were travelling with us.'

'I don't know yet. But there's plenty of work to be done. Once the mothers and children are gone, they'll probably ship anyone else out who wants to go, but most people will be staying on here I imagine. We need men to fight and women to help in the hospitals and so on.'

'What will you do?'

Veronica shrugged. 'I'm rather enjoying myself actually. Life had got frightfully dull lately. Nothing like a bit of war to spice things up and keep one busy.' Her voice was chirpy. It was as if she had long been waiting for a chance to play this role and was enjoying it immensely.

Evie stared at her. Where was the woman who had rolled her eyes and groaned at the thought of supplies of French champagne drying up? The woman who claimed war and politics were such a bore. She remembered Arthur telling her that Veronica was a consummate actress and knew how to play the part of the colonial administrator's wife to perfection. She was clearly doing that now.

Veronica soon disabused her of any notion that this change

was more fundamental, when she added, 'Singapore's terrific fun at the moment. Uniforms everywhere. Parties at the club every night.' She gave a little laugh. 'And I do so like a man in uniform.'

Noticing the anxious look on Susan Hyde-Underwood's face, she quickly added, 'Don't worry, Suze, losing Singapore would be unthinkable. Our boys will stop the Japs before they get anywhere near. Righto, I must go.' She looked back at Evie. 'I'll try and find your friend Mary. She can have that hotel room.' Then she walked away, her right hand raised and twirling in the air in a gesture of farewell as she vanished into the crowds.

THIRTY

Australia felt like exile to Evie. She was relieved to have brought the children to safety but was desperate for news of her friends. She devoured the newspapers and discovered that Europeans from the entire Malay peninsula had crowded into the small island of Singapore. Officers as well as the rank and file of the retreating British army, engineers, planters, tin miners, civil servants, and their wives and children, all racing for safety to the impregnable fortress that Singapore was claimed to be.

The men were drafted into service to lay barbed wire on the northern shore, which had been left undefended in the misguided assumption that the only conceivable attack by the Japanese would come by sea from the south.

But on the 15th February, the island that had been the strategic pivot of the British Empire in the east, the gateway and presumed defence to the dominion of Australia, was toppled in what would later be described by the Australia Prime Minister as 'an inexcusable betrayal' by the British. The Japanese had achieved the unthinkable and Singapore and the Malayan peninsula now flew the imperial flag.

Of Mary Helston, Evie heard nothing. There was nowhere to make enquiries regarding the whereabouts of unrelated individuals and the assumption was that, unless she and her parents had escaped before the fall of the city, Mary would now be in a civilian internment camp.

The women were placed in cramped accommodation via the Red Cross – Perth and the surrounding areas were awash with refugees, not only from Malaya but also from Darwin and Hong Kong. After delays during which they were granted government loans of around three pounds a week, both women were able to access their own funds via the Australian banks. They managed to rent a bungalow together, pooling the childcare and supplementing their income by taking in paying guests.

After several months in Australia, Susan was notified by the Malayan Agent for Tokyo Cables that Reggie was interned in the civilian camp in Changi, Singapore. This came first as a relief, then a source of anxiety to Susan.

Time dragged for Evie. It was not that she disliked Western Australia – the climate was pleasant after the mugginess of Penang and the beaches a welcome playground for the children – but she felt displaced, rootless. Neither she nor Susan wanted to risk the long sea voyage to Britain, knowing the perils of U-boats and airborne attacks. After their experiences in Penang they were grateful to be away from the main theatres of war.

Three months after the nuclear bomb attacks on Hiroshima and Nagasaki, and the subsequent Japanese surrender, Evie returned to Malaya. Susan had left for England as soon as Victory was declared in Europe in May 1945.

Meeting Mary Helston again shocked Evie to the core. Approaching the bungalow in George Town where the teacher had lived with her parents, Evie was anxious and unsure whether she would find anyone there. The closed shutters and neglected garden reinforced these doubts. The figure who opened the door caused her to gasp.

Mary Helston was emaciated. Her arms and her legs were scarred and discoloured and her skin hung from her bones with barely any flesh. Dark rings circled her hollowed eyes and her cotton dress billowed about her, many sizes too large for her stick-like frame. Mary's previously thick lush hair was thin as a baby's, cropped short and choppy.

'Evie.' The voice was flat. She gave a hollow laugh. 'I know. I look hideous. Would you believe I've already put on almost a stone. You should have seen me the day we were liberated. Come in.'

She led Evie into the drawing room at the back of the modest house. It was cool in there, the shutters and French doors shut against the light. Evie couldn't help remembering how they used to be always open so that the garden seemed part of the house.

'Every day I get a little better. They say it will take time. It took more than three years to get into this state so I can't expect to get well in just a few months.'

'Your parents?'

'Dead.'

'Oh Mary, I'm so sorry.' Evie felt tears welling up inside her.

'We left it too late to get away from Singapore. Mum and I volunteered at the hospital. We didn't want to leave without Dad. He was determined to do his bit. And we never thought Singapore would fall. When we finally got on a ship, the Japs intercepted us in the Straits of Malacca and we were arrested. They took Dad to Changi from where he was sent on to a forced labour camp and died there. Mum and I were kept together but she died just six months before liberation. Dad had been due to retire this year. He was fit and healthy and could have had a long life, but they killed him with hard labour, starvation and disease. Mum was only fifty-eight.'

Evie didn't know what to say. How could any words of comfort be adequate in the circumstances? In the end she asked, 'Frank?'

'Yes. I found out while we were in Singapore. They told me he was killed in that first air attack on Butterworth and the island. He was shot down in flames over the Straits. Wouldn't have stood a chance.'

They lapsed into silence. Mary looked up at Evie. Her eyes were so empty it was disconcerting, as though she wasn't really seeing. 'Enough about me. How was Australia? You got there safely?'

Evie nodded, feeling guilty. 'To Perth. It was fine. Susan Hyde-Underwood was there too, and lots of other women from here. We all looked out for each other. Some of us volunteered at a hospital. Caring for injured troops.'

'The children? How's Jasmine?'

'She's nearly fourteen. Quite the young lady. She's been marvellous. Such a support to me. And Hugh has turned five.'

'Where are they?' Mary's voice was flat.

'Here in George Town. At home, with Aunty Mimi. Jasmine wants to see you.'

'I don't think that's a good idea. Please, Evie. I don't want anyone to see me this way.' Mary shook her head violently.

Evie shivered. This wraith in front of her didn't seem like her old friend. 'I'm going back to live in England. I think you should come back with us.'

'Come *back*? It wouldn't feel like that to me. I left there when I was a small child. The place means nothing to me.'

'But it would be a fresh start. A new beginning after the war. Put it all behind you.'

'Why do I want a new beginning? I'd rather stay here with what's left of the old world. With everything I love. All the little things. Things of beauty after so much hate. After all the brutality.'

Mary's eyes looked into space, appearing to be seeing something beyond the gloom of this shuttered room. 'How could I leave everything I love about this island? The moths at nighttime on Penang Hill. The golden orioles and the kingfishers. The sound of the breeze in the casuarina trees. Heavy rain hammering on the rooftops. How could I give up all that? What for? My memories of England are vague but they're all cold and gloomy. And I've seen the newsreels. No, thank you. *This* is my home and always will be.'

She gave a little shake of her head. 'I'd never fit in in England, Evie. I'd be odd and angry and out of place. And how can I possibly leave here when everyone I've loved died in Malaya. Mum and Dad, Frank, and before him Ralph. Surely you can understand that, Evie? This country is my country and always will be.'

'But everything will change. I've heard the war has bankrupted Britain and it no longer has the resources to hang onto the Empire.'

Mary shrugged. 'I welcome that change. We British betrayed Malaya. Let them down. We have no right anymore to try to determine the country's destiny. The British empire is dead. It's just a matter of letting go in an orderly manner. Maybe it will take years but I want to be a part of a new Malaya. As soon as I'm fit, I'll be going back to teaching.'

She wove her bone-thin fingers between each other, and Evie saw that her fingernails were discoloured and ridged. Whatever Mary had been through during the Japanese occupation had left its mark, physically as well as emotionally. Evie lent forward and placed her hand over her friend's.

Mary looked up at her. 'I'll never tell you what happened to me in that camp. I'll never speak of it to anyone. But there's one thing I do want to tell you. It will probably surprise you.'

Evie waited.

'I owe my life to one person. She kept me alive when I was ready to give up. She forced me to go on. And in the end, she sacrificed her own life for me and for another woman – barely more than a girl really. We both lived because Veronica Leighton protected us and ultimately sacrificed her life for us.'

'Veronica?' Evie was shocked. 'How? What did she do?'

Mary's eyes were dull, void of expression. 'In the camp Mum got dengue fever and was weak from starvation. Mum only lasted as long as she did because Veronica stole some medicine. The Japs kept all the medications from the Red Cross parcels. We had nothing. Veronica was clever. I don't know how she did it, but she got medication for Mum. But in the end it wasn't enough. Mum was too weak. When she died I had to dig her grave. Veronica and some of the other women helped me make a wooden crate as a coffin and helped me carry it across the camp to where the grave was.'

'Oh, Mary that's horrible. To have dig your mother's grave. I'm so sorry.'

'That was the least of it. Everything that happened to us in that camp will go to the grave with me. But every day for the rest of my life I will be grateful to Veronica Leighton for what she did for me. She may have been a bitch for most of her life but when faced with what we faced, she chose to do the bravest thing I have ever known. When they caught her they executed her. We had to watch. That's all I'm going to say. Please don't ask me anything more.'

An icy chill spread through Evie's veins. No matter how much she had loathed Veronica Leighton, that she had been murdered in cold blood by the Japanese was too brutal to contemplate.

After a few moments silence, Evie asked, 'Do you have any idea what happened to Veronica's husband, Arthur?'

Mary shrugged. 'No idea. He's probably dead too. He wasn't in Singapore. I do know that.'

'That night we left Penang, he told me he had trained to stay behind. To hide in the jungle and try to perform sabotage. Behind their lines.'

'Well, he's almost certainly dead.'

Unable to control her emotions, Evie began to sob.

Mary looked up in surprise. 'My God! You have feelings for him, Evie? For Arthur Leighton. I'm terribly sorry. I was tactless. I wouldn't have been so blunt if I'd realised.'

Taking her handkerchief from her handbag, Evie wiped her eyes. 'Don't apologise. I only asked you in the hope that you might know something. I've been making extensive enquiries, but no one seems to have a clue what happened to him. I can't find any official records in Singapore or KL. That's why I've decided to go back to England. I'm hoping the Foreign Office might be able to give me some information about what happened to him.'

Mary stretched her lips into a tight line. 'Look, Evie, it's extremely unlikely he would have survived as a white man behind enemy lines. If he was lucky, he was killed in a skirmish. If he wasn't, and was captured, he would almost certainly have been executed.'

Evie shuddered. But something inside was telling her that if Arthur was dead, she'd know it. She'd be able to sense it, and she didn't.

Mary broke the silence. 'What will you do when you're back in England?'

'Get the children into schools. Buy a home for us. I've been making enquiries and it appears I can sell Batu Lembah to one of the big companies. I never want to set foot in that place again. It's cursed for me. I'm renting the house in George Town. Thank God, Aunty Mimi and Benny both came through the war. They want to stay on there to look after whoever rents the place. And I've given them each a little nest egg. It was the least I could do after the government abandoned them.'

'And the other estate? The one the Hyde-Underwoods managed?'

'I'll keep Bellavista if Reggie wants to continue to manage it or sell to him if he wants to buy – Douglas wanted Hugh to take over from him eventually. I always intended to stay close to Doug's wishes. But I can't live my whole life based on what he wanted. And it's not right for Hugh to be forced to follow in the steps of a father he never knew. He has to make his own choices.'

'And you? What about you, Evie?'

'I'll keep looking for Arthur. That's all I want to do.'

THIRTY-ONE

At a coveted window table in the Lyons' Corner House in Coventry Street, near Piccadilly Circus, Evie was sitting with Jasmine and Hugh, surrounded by carrier bags full of school uniform. She was exhausted. Remembering Mary Helston's assertion that England was always cold and gloomy, Evie had to admit her friend was right. Today had been draining, trailing from shop to shop, an increasingly tetchy Hugh dragging his feet, while Jasmine tried not to show her boredom with the whole business. London was grim, foggy, and still bearing the scars of the Blitz, gaps in rows of buildings like missing teeth, bomb sites everywhere. Getting the school uniforms had been a trial – to get each child kitted out had necessitated visits to several different stores as rationing meant stocks were desperately low.

During their time in Australia, Hugh and Stanford Hyde-Underwood had formed a solid friendship, so that it was unthinkable that they should be separated in England. Reggie had returned to Bellavista and Evie had agreed a plan for him to continue to manage the estate with an option to buy eventually. She herself had no wish to go back to live in Penang.

Susan felt the same, refusing to return with her husband. The couple had talked of holidays and Reggie coming to England each year, but Evie sensed their marriage would never recover from the war. Reggie had survived internment in a camp in Borneo but, like Mary Helston, was unwilling to talk about his experiences, which had driven a wedge between the couple.

Susan was living with her elderly parents in the north of England and Stanford was to attend Reggie's old boarding school. Hugh had kept up a constant barrage of requests to be allowed to join Stanford but, at only five years old, Evie told him it was out of the question. How could she send her little boy to a distant place where the discipline was probably tough and where he would grow up too quickly and too far from her? The thought of Hugh becoming as emotionally stunted as his father had been was intolerable.

Usually Hugh could prevail on his mother to get his own way, but in this one decision Evie was determined not to budge. In a war of attrition, Hugh had won the concession that, if he still wished to board once he turned eight, he could join his friend. She hoped and prayed that, by then, time and distance would have caused Hugh and Stanford to grow apart and each of them to form new attachments. Meanwhile she would make the most of keeping her son at home with her and Jasmine, who was to attend the local girl's grammar school.

The café windows were steamed over, and the place was crowded with shoppers and theatre-goers, all divesting themselves of coats and hats and drinking cups of tea served to them by the Lyons' nippies in their neat black uniforms and starched white caps and aprons. Evie took a sip of her tea and, under the table, gratefully slipped off her shoes, seizing the chance to take the weight off her feet before they had to set off for Waterloo and the journey home to Surrey.

'In the war, Lyons used to make bombs,' announced Hugh.

He was always a gatherer of facts and information and was developing an encyclopaedic brain.

'Don't be daft,' said Jasmine. 'It's a restaurant. Maybe they made food in the war but not bombs.'

'They did too. They had a great big factory.'

A passing nippy looked over her shoulder and said, 'Your little brother's right. Lyons was in charge of running a bomb factory. I know 'cause I worked in it. My sister too.' She winked at Hugh and went off to whisk another table clear of crockery.

Jasmine rolled her eyes then pulled one of her woollen gloves from her coat pocket and rubbed the steamy window so she could look out. Crowds of people were trudging by, collars turned up against the chill air. None of them appeared to be enjoying the experience. Red double-decker buses and motor cars splashed puddles of water up from the road. It all felt depressing to Evie and she found herself feeling nostalgic for the sunlight of Penang, for the colours and noise and the bustle of Marine Drive.

Yet when she had paid her brief visit back to George Town en route to England from Australia, she had felt dispirited there too. The island had taken a hammering – not only from the Japanese when they invaded, but more significantly from the Allies in 1945. Evie had intended to visit the Temple of Harmony, but it had been badly damaged in the first round of bombing. Of the monk there was no sign. She'd stood outside the ruined remains of the colourful building and said a silent prayer that he hadn't been harmed.

Penang with no Arthur, Douglas, Susan, and with a changed Mary, determined to cut herself off from everything while she regained her strength, made Evie feel sad. Just as Mary believed she had no place anywhere else, Evie wondered where she herself belonged. It wasn't Penang, nor London. For her children's sake she had to make some kind of life in England, but it felt like a chore, not a positive choice. Perhaps she belonged nowhere – one of the many people made rootless and displaced by war.

She told herself to buck up. Her role was to make things as right as possible for Jasmine and Hugh, to give them stability, security and love, and to support them in whatever choices they made as they grew up. She stretched out a hand and pushed a stray lock of hair away from her son's forehead. He looked so like Douglas – the same thick brown hair and intense blue eyes. Sometimes there would be an echo of Doug in a small mannerism, an inclination of the head or an intonation of voice. But there was none of Doug's dark brooding or abrupt mood changes in Hugh. The little boy had a sunny disposition and Evie was increasingly sure if it had not been for the loss of his mother and brother and the cruelty of his unloving father, Doug might have been a different man.

Jasmine was looking out of the window, still watching the passers-by.

Evie glanced at her wristwatch. They needed to think about heading for Waterloo soon. Reluctantly, she pushed her feet back into her shoes.

Jasmine gave a little cry. 'Look Mummy! I'm sure that was him.'

Evie looked up. 'What did you say?'

'Maybe it wasn't. I don't know... Hard to tell as he's on the other side of the street.' Jasmine peered through the window.

'Who? What are you talking about, darling?'

'Uncle Arthur. He used to come to see us when Daddy was alive. You—'

Before Jasmine could finish speaking, Evie was on her feet. 'Stay here. Don't move. I'll be back.' She rushed out of the café, bursting through the door and onto the crowded street.

Dodging behind a bus and weaving between taxicabs, she reached the other side of the street, looking about her, frantically. If Arthur had indeed been there, how could she possibly spot him among all these people? Which direction had he gone in? She ran one way, stopped, and ran back the other way, panic mounting inside her. Why hadn't she been looking out of the windows herself? How could she have come so close, only to lose him in the crowds? It wasn't fair. It wasn't just. Tears of frustration pressed at her eyes and she stood on the pavement, coatless but oblivious to the cold of the day. If Arthur had been here, he had gone now. And maybe Jasmine had been wrong. After all, it was five years since she'd seen Arthur Leighton. Evie moved towards the kerb to return to Lyons'. A bolt of recognition shot through her and she froze, then spun round.

He was bent over, tying a shoelace. As he stood up, he saw Evie and his face contorted in shock. His skin was pale, his features gaunt, his eyes haunted. But it was Arthur. They stood facing each other on the edge of the pavement as people moved past them.

'Evie. Is it really you? I thought you'd died in the bombing. In Singapore.'

She stared at him, still trying to absorb this was actually Arthur. 'I wasn't in Singapore. I never got off the train. They wouldn't let us. They took us straight to the port. I left Malaya the day after I said goodbye to you in Butterworth.' The two feet of pavement between them felt like a widening chasm. 'And you? Everyone said you must have been killed. I asked everywhere. The Colonial Office. I went back to Penang. But no matter what they said, I knew if you were dead I would have known. I'd have sensed it.'

He winced and she felt unsure of herself. The cold of the advancing January afternoon made her shiver, standing there in just a skirt and jumper.

'You'll freeze to death. Where's your coat?' He undid his own and draped it around her shoulders.

Evie was shocked at the thinness of him. Arthur had had an athletic figure, tall, muscular, strong, even if he was often a sloucher. But his shoulders were stooped and he had the same gnarled and bony hands she had seen in Mary. He seemed to be avoiding her gaze.

'Where did you come from?' he asked.

'Over there.' She gestured across the road. 'Lyons Corner House. Jasmine saw you through the window. Come,' she said. 'Come and see the children.'

He guided her across the street. The noise of horns and the rattle of the trams preventing him from replying until they reached the other pavement.

'I can't stop, Evie. I have a meeting. Where are you staying?' He was still avoiding her eyes.

'I've rented a house. In Surrey. Near Reigate.'

There was a distance between them which Evie found inexplicable. As if they barely knew each other. Polite. Awkward. Strained.

'Look. I can't talk now. I have to go to the Colonial Office. I've given my notice and the Permanent Secretary wants to talk to me. I'm going to be late.'

'You're leaving the Foreign Service?'

'I've accepted a position at Oxford. Teaching and research. Colonial History.'

'I see.' She didn't at all. She didn't understand anything. Why he was so cold. So distant. As if they were mere acquaintances. Barely even that.

'How can I get in touch?' His voice was quiet. No enthusiasm. Evie realised he hadn't smiled once.

She pulled a scrap of paper from her jacket pocket. 'Do you have a pencil?' He handed her his fountain pen and she scribbled her address down and passed it to him.

'Thanks. We'll talk.' He put the paper in his pocket and, nodding, walked away.

Evie was crushed. Deflated. Didn't he care for her any more? He had behaved like a stranger. Her heart was breaking.

The journey home passed in a daze. After explaining to Jasmine that yes, it had indeed been Uncle Arthur, but he'd had to rush off for a meeting, she gathered their things together and ushered the children out of the restaurant.

On the train, Evie left Jasmine to respond to Hugh's chatter, and stared unseeing through the grimy train window, remembering that other train taking them through the Malayan night, away from Arthur and into an unknown future. She remembered the way he had held her on that station platform five years ago, when he'd promised they would one day be together. The feel of his lips as they brushed lightly against hers, amid the chaos of the platform at Butterworth. The way his eyes had looked into hers as though he were looking into her soul. Yet, the same man, the man she loved beyond reason, had stood in front of her, unsmiling, avoiding her eyes, before leaving her without even so much as a touch of his hand.

THIRTY-TWO

Not for the first time, Evie had cause to be grateful for the kindness and perception of her daughter. Jasmine sensed that all was not well with her mother. When they arrived home, Jasmine offered to cook the supper. When Evie sat listlessly at the table without eating, Jasmine saw Hugh to bed, telling Evie she herself would be having an early night and suggested Evie do the same.

The last thing Evie wanted was to go to bed. It would be a sleepless night. Better to delay the inevitable. She poured herself a rare gin and sat down to think through what had happened that afternoon.

Arthur had treated her like a stranger. How was it possible? Evie began to doubt everything. Had he been playing a game with her all along? But that was inconceivable. She knew as clearly as she knew her own mind, that there had been no dissembling in Arthur's declarations of love.

She asked herself if Veronica's presence had enabled him to love Evie at a protected distance and now that Veronica was dead, he was no longer interested, wanting only what he couldn't have?

None of it made any sense. Over and over and round and round she went, trying to imagine what had wrought such a change in Arthur.

She remembered how Mary had been. How she had said she'd feel awkward and out of place in Britain. Perhaps that was more a result of what had happened to her at the hands of the Japanese than a case of her not knowing England. Was it his wartime experiences that had made Arthur so closed and cold towards her?

She got up and poured herself another drink. She rarely drank at all these days and never alone, but she needed something to blot out all these confused feelings and the loss and grief that had hit her like a train. For it was indeed grief. She was mourning the loss of a dream. Of a man that perhaps no longer existed or maybe had only existed inside her head.

Sipping the gin, feeling the warmth of the spirit in her throat, she started to cry. Big silent tears. She let them flow. After tonight, she wouldn't allow herself that indulgence again. But now, in the moment, there was no point in trying to stop the tears. Forget Arthur. Forget Penang. Forget everything except those beautiful children sleeping upstairs, she told herself.

The gin must have made her drowsy, as she woke with a start, curled up on the sofa, at the sound of the doorbell. Evie got to her feet and went to the door. No one called in the evenings. And she knew so few people. Scarcely able to breathe, she opened the door, knowing with absolute certainty that Arthur would be standing there.

As soon as she saw him she knew her love for him was as strong as ever.

He looked wretched. 'I'm sorry, Evie.' He drew her into his arms and they stood there for a couple of moments on the doorstep, her face buried in the rough tweed of his coat.

'May I come in? I need to explain.'

Evie stepped backwards and took his hand, leading him into

the drawing room. 'Would you like a drink?' she said. 'I have no whisky but you're welcome to have a gin.'

He shook his head. 'A cup of tea would be nice.'

Still nervous, and unsure where things stood between them, she went into the kitchen and busied herself making the tea, her hands shaking. When she got back, he was pacing up and down in front of the fireplace. She handed him the tea but he put it aside on the mantlepiece.

'I wasn't completely straight with you before. I knew you hadn't died in Singapore and had got to Australia. I'd been a party to the evacuation plans. All the records were destroyed in the war but I found out the ship you would have left on got safely to Australia.'

'Why didn't you contact me?' She looked at him helplessly, as he continued to pace up and down. She sank into a chair.

'I didn't think you'd want to see me. To have anything to do with me.'

'Why ever not?'

'Because so much time had passed. You must have built a new life.' He hesitated. 'And because of what happened to me. Because of what I've become.'

'You're speaking in riddles, Arthur.' Evie felt bewildered. 'Nothing you've done can make any difference to how I feel about you. I love you and I always believed you loved me too.'

He went towards her, bending down to kneel on the floor in front of her chair. He took her hands in his. 'I do love you. It was only the thought of you, of seeing you again, that got me through those dreadful years. My first thought each morning and my last thought at night was of you. I'll love you, Evie, till the day I die. Nothing will ever change that. But *I've* changed. I've seen such things, done such things. I'll never be able to wash the stain of that away from me.' He leaned back on his heels. 'And look at me, Evie. See what's become of me. What they did to me. Under these clothes, my body is covered in welts. My back will never heal. I'll carry the marks the Japanese guards made on me for the rest of my life. I'm a broken man, Evie. A collection of scars and bones. How can I expect you to love me? If you could see me you'd feel only disgust.'

Evie's heart swelled and she slipped off the chair to join him kneeling on the floor. Bending forward, she kissed him, softly, feeling the warmth of his lips against hers. 'I can never feel anything but complete love for you, Arthur. You are the love of my life and I thank God for sending you back to me.'

She kissed him again, tentatively at first, then as he responded, their kiss deepened and his arms went around her, holding her as if he wanted never to let her go.

Evie let her lips explore his face. His thin lined face. The dark sunken area around his eyes. 'Come to bed,' she said at last. 'Show me those scars and I'll show you how much I love you.'

Arthur gave a deep, shuddering sigh. 'You need to know. I'm going away, Evie. The Permanent Secretary offered me a new posting this afternoon. I've accepted. I'm going to turn down the Oxford job. I'm leaving England.'

'Where? When?'

'In a couple of weeks. Kenya.'

Fear closed her throat and she felt her mouth dry. He had come to say goodbye. She felt a conviction that, come what may, she belonged with this man. She stroked a hand over his face. 'Where you always wanted to return. You've finally got what you wanted and deserved. Back to those primeval plains – that savage beauty you love so much.'

'You remembered?'

'I have remembered everything you ever said to me, Arthur. It's what's kept me going all these years.'

'Will you come with me?' His voice was quiet, disbelieving.

Her heart leapt inside her ribcage. 'Of course, I will. I'd follow you to the ends of the earth, Arthur Leighton.'

'Really? You'd leave everything here and come to Africa with me? A broken wreck of a man?'

'Try and stop me.'

'What about the children?'

'We come as a package. That's the only condition. As long as they want to come too. And knowing how Hugh feels about lions and elephants I think it's a foregone conclusion. I'd like Jasmine to want it too – but I have a feeling she will. But what about you, will you have us all?'

'Nothing would make me happier.' Arthur gave a rueful smile. 'He knew, you know.'

'Who knew? And knew what? You're speaking in riddles again.'

'Doug. He asked me to take care of you and the children. He said he knew you loved me.'

Evie was distraught. 'He knew?'

'He told me was glad. That we would have each other.'

'But you were married to Veronica.'

'Doug never liked poor Veronica. And maybe he knew what would happen. A dying man's vision. You heard Veronica died in a camp?'

Evie nodded. 'Mary Helston was interned with her. Mary told me Veronica saved her life. She said Veronica was the only reason Mary and several others survived. Veronica was incredibly brave and stole food and medicines. But the Japanese caught her in the end.'

Arthur's mouth twitched and a look of sadness darkened his face. 'Is that how she died? They executed her? Do you know how?'

Evie shook her head. 'Mary wouldn't tell me anything else. She can't bear to talk about her experiences under the Japanese but she wanted me to know what Veronica did for them all.'

'So, the poor girl finally found a way to redeem herself.

There was always a well of goodness deep inside Veronica. I'm glad it found a way to reach the surface.'

He kissed her again, slowly, lovingly.

'So, will you marry me, Arthur?'

'You're proposing to me?' His face broke into a broad grin and he drew her close to him again. Then he grew serious. 'You might want to change your mind when you see what they did to me. I'll understand if you do.'

'I promise you, Arthur Leighton. There is *nothing* that will ever make me change my mind where you're concerned – well, unless you decided you don't want my children too.'

'My dearest darling, Jasmine and Hugh will be loved and cared for by me as if they were my own. Doug was my friend. And I'm Jasmine's godfather.' He frowned. 'But that's the other thing you need to know. After what I went through, it's possible I may not be able to father a child of my own.' As soon as he'd said it, he added, 'I may be firing blanks. But as I can attest right now, I don't think there'll be any problems in getting the guns to fire.' He grinned at her.

Evie needed no more encouragement. She jumped to her feet and took his hand. 'Come on. We have a lot of time to make up, my darling.'

A LETTER FROM THE AUTHOR

Huge thanks for reading *The Pearl of Penang*, I hope you were hooked on Evie's journey – both personally and geographically! If you want to join other readers in hearing about my Storm Publishing new releases and bonus content, you can sign up for Storm's mailing list here!

www.stormpublishing.co/clare-flynn

If you enjoyed this book and could spare a few moments to leave a review that would be hugely appreciated. Even a short review can make all the difference in encouraging a reader to discover my books for the first time. Thank you so much!

If you'd like to sign up to my personal mailing list for updates and extra content, you can sign up here!

www.subscribepage.com/r4w1u5

My own visit to Penang was, alas, a brief one. I was on a round-the-world cruise and had been hoping to write my next book during the voyage. Unfortunately, I couldn't. It was almost as though I had a sensory overload from all those different places and none of them screamed a story at me. Then I arrived in Penang for a quick tour of the island. I can't put my finger on a place, a view, a moment, but as soon as we sailed away I knew I wanted to write a book set there. Little did I know that my short visit would spark not one but four books (and who knows

– there may be more in the future!). The Penang I visited is in many ways dramatically different from the one Evie experienced. Instead of the ferry to Butterworth there is a sweeping Chinese-built road bridge and George Town is full of high-rise apartments. But there are still elements that are unchanged from the time of Evie. I would love to go back and rediscover them – perhaps this time spending more than a day there!

Thanks again for being part of this amazing journey with me and I hope you'll stay in touch – I have so many more stories and ideas to entertain you with!

Clare

clareflynn.co.uk

ACKNOWLEDGMENTS

Thanks to Vicky, Alex and all the team at Storm as well as to Debi Alper who did the original edit, and to my fellow authors here in Eastbourne whose input was invaluable – Margaret Kaine, Merryn Allingham, Joanna Warrington and "jay" Dixon.

Thanks also to Sue Sewell and Debbie Marmor who read a late draft and gave me helpful feedback.

Special thanks to my fellow author and friend, Dr Carol Cooper who put me on the straight and narrow on sepsis (known at the time when the book is set as septicaemia). Any medical errors are my own.

I am indebted to the following works which provided essential background research on life in the Malayan peninsula and life on a rubber estate.

- *Out in the Midday Sun* by Margaret Shennan – full of gems on ex-pat life in Malaya pre-Independence.
- *Malayan Spymaster* by Boris Hembry – essential reading on rubber planters and the build-up to the Japanese invasion.
- *Castles in the Air* by Alison Ripley-Cubitt and Molly Ripley for more insights into ex-pat life and sea voyages in the 30s and 40s.

Printed in Great Britain
by Amazon

34066607R00192